Cognac *for* Breakfast

ALAN WOLFORD

D1404228

To Susan,
God bless!
2020

A man lives not only his personal life as an individual, but also, consciously or unconsciously, the life of his epoch and his contemporaries.

-THOMAS MANN
The Magic Mountain

PART I

No more may gulls cry at their ears
Or waves break loud on the seashores;
Where blew a flower may a flower no more
Lift its head to the blows of the rain;
Though they be mad and dead as nails,
Heads of the characters hammer through daisies;
Break in the sun till the sun breaks down,
And death shall have no dominion.

-DYLAN THOMAS
And Death Shall Have No Dominion

ONE

On a sunny morning in late January, Delta Flight 3427 from Atlanta was in a slow glide as it began its approach to Cyril E. King Airport on the western end of St. Thomas. Traveling incognito in caps, cargo shorts and deck shoes, forty-four-year-old acclaimed journalist Mark McAllister and his alluring wife Stella chatted quietly about their itinerary as the Boeing 737 descended.

Like a sea of diamonds, the Caribbean rose up to greet them, bringing to mind the many sunny days they recently shared on the pink-sand beaches of Bora Bora. Diving for black pearls, dodging sharks and falling coconuts, and exploring the underwater wrecks in the clear aqua waters surrounding their twenty-room bed and breakfast were favorite pastimes for the past two years.

They'd missed their Florida friends and oceanfront home at Villa Riomar in Vero Beach and looked forward to returning to their "Mayberry-By-The-Sea." A true diamond-in-the-rough, with its oak-canopied streets, nature conservation efforts and rich cultural history, Vero and its surrounding communities epitomized their vision of a perfect beach-side town.

Smiling to herself, Stella thought about their plans, eager to climb back aboard *Dream Girl* and delighted with the idea of being free once again to sail the blue Caribbean au naturel and become one with the sea.

Delving into her Louie Vuitton travel bag, Stella pushed aside the digital tablet containing her latest graphic designs and retrieved her pocket-size binoculars and Nikon camera. From her window seat, she handed the camera to Mark and focused the binoculars out the window, scanning a half-mile to the west for a glimpse of their recently-refitted yacht docked at the American Yacht Harbor. It never failed to make her smile whenever she heard her husband refer to the yacht as "the second love of his life."

This would be their first opportunity to capture aerial photos of the sixty-four-foot Baltic. Her colors were striking, with deep blue AWL-grip hull, light teak deck, white AWL-Grip aluminum spars and mast, and deep blue sail covers designed to match her hull. For a blue-water sailboat, she presented a unique blend of seaworthiness and opulence on the high seas. She was their time machine, their spaceship, their ticket to far away galaxies.

So far, it had been a relatively uneventful flight from their origin in Tahiti the day before, except for an unsettling period of turbulence over Hawaii last night. It had taken Mark two cognacs and Stella two double martinis to calm their nerves during the violent storm. Now, the couple were just beginning to feel a sense of relief as the third leg of an arduous journey halfway around the world was coming to an end, with an outcome that was yet uncertain.

Their photo op was interrupted by a commotion behind them. From the tail of the plane, a lanky, intoxicated man with a crazy look in his eyes jaunted past them gripping a stainless-steel canister. Frightened passengers turned in their seats to watch the drama unfold as the disturbed man ran down the aisle clutching the canister. In close pursuit were two female flight attendants, followed by a heavy-set man in a sport coat gripping a pair of handcuffs and an air marshal's badge.

"We're going down!" yelled the inebriated man as he vaulted past Mark and Stella toward the rear of the plane.

"Not to worry, folks, we'll be landing shortly," declared the air marshal, following closely and flashing his badge. Discretely, Mark slid his valise further under the seat with his foot to keep his new manuscript and four hundred thousand in Credit Suisse bank notes safe as he put a reassuring arm around his wife.

Turning to Stella, "Just when you thought it was safe to fly again."

Still tipsy from her two double martinis earlier, she caught his eye and winked. "Hi. I'm Claire Voyant, and I'm predicting we *don't* crash."

A concerned well-dressed woman seated behind them leaned forward to share what she knew about the intoxicated man. "He was complaining about his wife's divorce attorney earlier. I just hope that's not some kind of…ah…*explosive device* he's holding." Shaking her head as she looked over her shoulder, "Where do these head cases come from?"

"Just get us on the ground in one piece," pleaded another, pressing his hands together in mock prayer.

"I think they got his number," added a woman across the aisle.

"Yeah, six-six-six, wasn't it?" was the repartee from a passenger in a floral Tommy Bahama shirt.

A charter yacht captain in years past, Mark reflected on the many times he'd prevented drunks from falling overboard and sometimes felt like he'd been put on God's green Earth solely for the privilege of studying the effects of alcohol on otherwise intelligent people.

The commotion in the tail grew louder, and passengers were worried the man would attempt something really nuts as they turned in their seats to watch the crew subdue him. The troubled man's behavior brought to mind a similar episode on a flight to Rome a year earlier when the McAllisters were nearly hijacked by a psycho hell-bent on diverting the flight to Tehran after putting a knife to the pilot's throat. Crossing himself as he recalled the episode, Mark knew how lucky they were to have landed in one piece.

Many of the passengers were recording the scene on cell phones, perhaps intent on adding to the day's You Tube content. Like a surreal play gone amuck, they watched the deranged man knock one of the flight attendants to the floor as he tussled with passengers and crew for control of the stainless steel canister. With several hands groping for it, the canister fell to the floor, rolling forward down the aisle until it came to rest next to an elderly woman's foot. Watching it hit her foot scared her out of her wits as she squealed and kicked it away in fear.

"Stop filming me!" protested the intoxicated man. "I'm a paying passenger! Where the hell's the air marshal?"

"Right here, sir," pressing the man into his seat with one arm as he reached under his coat, "...and if you don't calm down, I'm going to have to..." With one of the attendants holding down his arm, the man tried to stand again and took an inadvisable swing at the marshal.

"*You* can't tase me! I'll bring this plane down!"

Left with few choices, the marshal yanked a stun gun from under his jacket and applied 80,000 volts to the man's chest. There was a chorus of gasps from passengers as the man screamed in pain before going limp. With the help of the flight attendants, the air marshal cuffed the unconscious drunk to the seat and checked for a pulse.

"He'll come around in a while," he assured everyone as he stood to a chorus of approval. "It's okay, folks," waving to passengers fore and aft like a politician garnering votes, "...everything's under control here."

The air marshal lowered his voice, and to the flight attendants he said, "Let's find that canister and prepare for landing. I'll inform the captain so they can take him into custody when we land."

All one-hundred-twenty-nine passengers breathed a collective sigh of relief as the crew stood to straighten their uniforms and collect themselves while they searched the cabin for the canister. The exception was one man in the front row who managed to sleep through the entire drama while watching *Santa Claus Conquers the Martians* on his tablet.

With the intoxicated man still unconscious and handcuffed to his seat, the 737 continued its descent as Mark equalized the pressure in his ears. He surveyed the cabin and noticed most of the passengers were still in animated conversations and obsessing with uploading photos to social media sites. The plane tilted to starboard, and he felt something roll into the side of his Sperry Topsider. Reaching down, he retrieved the stainless steel canister.

Alarmed, Stella asked, "What are you gonna do with *that*?"

With a straight face, "No worries, honey. It's not ticking." The Keurig canister smelled of scotch whiskey, and Mark shook it, then popped the top off for a look inside. Stella gave him an incredulous look as he tilted the canister and took a sip.

"Tastes like a single malt," he declared, wiping his lips.

"Are you nuts?"

"Probably, but I do love a good single malt," recapping it and tucking it deep into the seat pocket in front. "I would like to know how he got it on the plane past security, though."

The bald gentleman with glasses seated behind Stella leaned forward and extended his hand for a handshake. "You are one brave soul, there, fella. Can I buy you and your wife a drink after we land?"

Mark reached over his shoulder and shook the man's hand. "Thank you...very kind, but I'm not sure we'll have time. We've got a boat to catch," he explained. Turning to Stella, "So...shall we throw a party at Villa Riomar and invite our fellow passengers?" he joked. "They could all come over and stare at their cell phones."

Finding his idea amusing, "You're a nut." She aimed the binoculars toward the yachts in the harbor just in time to catch the colorful pennants flying from *Dream Girl*'s forestay. "Thar she blows, matey," in a girlie pirate's voice as she tapped on the window, "...third dock from the left, two slips in from the T-dock. See her?"

"Oui, mademoiselle. Tu l'aimes?" he asked, teasing her to see if she would respond with a twinge of jealousy.

"Oui, je l'aime bien tres beaucoup," she answered in her sing-song voice. Happy that the steel canister had proved to be little more than cheap entertainment, she gave him a flirty look, relieved there were no more nut cases vaulting through the plane as it swooped in for landing.

Their interlude was interrupted by the captain's voice on the intercom, requesting again that all seatbelts be fastened as the plane banked for final approach. One-hundred-twenty-nine passengers felt the plane shudder as the 737's air brakes deployed, triggering the sound of safety belts clicking all around.

The plane's descent steepened sharply. From past visits to St. Thomas, Mark remembered that the approach to the airport on the windward side of the island was a bit tricky and hoped they had an experienced pilot at the controls. Hearts beat faster as the vibrations from the landing gear and the sound of rushing wind over the fuselage increased. At sea, he was fearless, but strapped into a seat and not at the controls of an aircraft careening toward the ground at hundreds of miles an hour made him feel vulnerable.

The jet lined up for the runway, the wings leveling as Stella grasped his hand. She looked nervous, so he reached down and playfully squeezed her bare knee. Squealing in delight, his teasing managed to take her mind off the earlier incident as the hidden stainless canister rode safely in the seat pocket in front of them.

She mused about her immediate itinerary and the return voyage to Pelican Yacht Club in Ft. Pierce. Sailing nude in the sun with her hunky husband was one of her favorite pastimes, and her head was swimming with the idea of recreating the fantasies that he wrote about in his novels. For the next few days, she would have him all to herself.

At least, that was her plan.

TWO

After twenty hours in the air, they found themselves back aboard *Dream Girl* for the first time since her refit, safely delivered from deranged drunks and severe turbulence, but still undecided about which was worse.

The extraordinary marine craftsmanship produced by the Baltic boatyard in Bosund, Finland was something Mark had always cherished, and running his hand over the fine teak joiner work was like caressing a lover's bare skin. Listening to the hum, he stood beside the aft air conditioner and turned his attention back to his checklist before making final preparations to get underway. Since a near disaster ten years ago, the inspection of through-hull fittings had become a key part of his maintenance routine.

Aiming his pocket flashlight inside the teak housing, with a rag he wiped away the condensation from the brass fitting to check for leaks. Though an expensive refit, it looked as though the American Yacht Harbor mechanics had done a masterful job. With his ear against the teak cabinet, he listened to the whirring of the pumps and patted the bulkhead reassuringly as if she were his favorite mare.

He shouted up to Stella who was inspecting the rigging topside. "Good news, honey! The through-hulls are all nice and tight."

Squatting at the half-open porthole, she pulled her strawberry-blonde hair back and grinned at her husband. "That's great, honey, 'cause I know how much you admire quality workmanship."

The two mechanics stood on the dock and pretended to admire the yacht's graceful lines, but it was actually Stella's graceful lines that had caught their attention. "Screw me sideways on a pogo stick," muttered the scruffy mechanic wearing a Hard Rock Café T-shirt. "Who the hell is that in the black bikini?"

"Way above your pay grade, Bobby," replied the older mechanic.

Noticing the men on the dock ogling his wife, Mark chuckled to himself. "And *you,* always with an audience," he said through the porthole. Knowing how cumbersome the 50-amp power cables could be, he added, "Honey, see if you can get them to put some of that testosterone to work helping you gather the cables and fenders so we can get the hell out of here sometime today."

"Roger that, *mon capitaine,*" saluting playfully and looking forward to her favorite game as a submissive girlie pirate. She had a fleeting thought of asking for a professional opinion of their pirate games from Dr. Tremelle, but the names would have to be changed to protect the kinky. For her dockside fan club, she stopped for a moment and adjusted the fit of her bikini to make sure she had their full attention. "You guys wanna help me with the shore cables and fenders?"

"Whatever you need, ma'am," replied the muscular one wearing the black CAT cap, stumbling over the stanchions in his eagerness. Tipping his cap, "Sorry to see you leave, ma'am," as he stowed the shore cables onboard. Stella smiled at him politely and continued to tighten the receptacle caps until they were watertight.

With all five ship's batteries charged and the tanks filled with diesel and fresh water, *Dream Girl* had been fully provisioned by the marina's staff earlier that morning. Mark licked his lips, already tasting the salt spray as he anticipated the joy of putting his mistress through her paces.

Next stop would be Turks and Caicos, then on to Nassau, hopefully with prevailing southeasterly winds at their backs for the long northwestern leg to Florida.

Forty minutes later, they were making good headway, cruising northwest and running with a steady southeasterly. In open water, *Dream Girl* was surrounded by nothing but blue skies and the vast Caribbean Sea. Jib, main and staysail in perfect trim, the carefree investigative journalist regaled the sight as he sat at the helm and steered with his bare feet.

The sound of the wind in the sails and waves passing over the hull lulled him into a deeper state of mind, but his reverie came to a halt when his scantily-clad first mate emerged from the companionway hatch. "Hey, sailor. You look awfully serious. Captain like some company?" Watching her smooth the moisturizer over her arms and legs, she knew exactly how to get the captain thinking about her game.

Playing along in a pirate's voice, "We're beyond ye three-mile limit, so unbutton ye breeches, me heartie and tell yer captain what ye have in mind," his lips curling slowly into an inviting smile.

Finished smoothing the moisturizer on her shapely thighs, she disappeared below only to reappear moments later on the companionway steps stark naked, wearing only a sailor's cap. With her hips swaying invitingly, she sauntered to the deck and turned to him.

"*Mon capitaine*, First Mate Amber reporting for punitive duty as ordered, *sir*!" She stood at attention, saluting him with a mischievous smile.

He enjoyed her role playing. Pausing to admire her emerald green eyes, a gentle breeze tousled her strawberry-blonde hair as his eyes swept over her slender, taut arms and legs, and everywhere she was shaved to perfection.

"Reporting for duty as ordered, *sir!*" she repeated, waiting for his orders.

Trying to control his excitement, Mark reached to engage the autopilot so that he could join her on deck. "All righty then, matey." Rubbing his chin, he pretended to ponder an appropriate punishment. "Ye ready to polish the stanchions?"

"Yes, *sir!*" Stella went below, reappearing on deck with a bottle of polish and a cloth. On her hands and knees, she began to sensuously polish the port-side stanchions while wagging her derriere in a most provocative way. After a few minutes of her teasing, she looked up submissively to her captain for approval.

"And don't spill any or I'll have to spank ye bottom with me bare hand, matey."

"Yes, *sir!*" she responded, promptly spilling the bottle of polish onto the deck. Suspecting it was an intentional act of disobedience, he stiffened and prepared to deliver her punishment.

Crawling over the deck to his feet, she rose to her knees and threw her arms around the captain's legs to beg forgiveness. "Please*, mon capitaine*, don't spank me," she pleaded coyly, burying her face in his crotch for mercy, her cap falling off.

"And *now*, matey, you're out of uniform!" he barked.

She looked up into his eyes in mock regret. "Oh, *mon capitaine*, then will you have to give me more punishment?"

"You bet yer sweet ass, thar matey!" Dutifully, the captain checked their heading and sail trim before beginning her punishment. The jib was luffing slightly, but he didn't care, recalling what a buddy had said about God giving him a brain and a penis, but only enough blood to run one at a time. He delivered a dozen firm slaps to her upturned derriere, and with each one she squirmed and wriggled in secret delight while begging him to stop in a mock tone.

For the far more serious infraction of being out of uniform, to her delight, Mark ordered Stella to perform a list of menial tasks as she twisted and turned her body in the morning sun. In a bid for leniency, she poured him a tankard of Goslings Black Seal rum, and the more he drank, the more aroused he became.

"Avast, ye matey! Lower the yardarms!" hoisting his tankard, sloshing some Gosling's onto his chest. Drawn to the rum running down her captain's abdomen, Stella grabbed his hips and began lapping up the spilled rum. Mark was amazed at how much she enjoyed playing the sensual pirate slave in her own fantasy version of eighteenth century British naval lore. She was a submissive cat of a different color on the high seas, but at home, he couldn't get her to clean the crumbs out of the toaster oven.

After a few more minutes of "severe punishment", he decided her bottom was pink enough and yielded to her yearning. Rolling her onto the cockpit cushions, the captain gave her what she'd been longing for, only very slowly at first, since it was now his turn to tease.

She was insatiable. Their passions out-of-control, they made ravenous love on the cushions like the last man and woman on Earth, hungry to touch and taste, as if the future of mankind depended on their primal act of procreation. He had released a hunger in her that seemed to consume them like the afterglow of an exploded star.

Under the blue Caribbean sky, they flowed together like two rivers, 'til Mark couldn't tell her from him.

THREE

The next morning they were back under full sail, cruising gracefully and heading northwest on a light breeze. From under the shade of his tan "Bora Bora" cap with the manta ray logo, Mark watched the wind sculpt white fluffy cumulous clouds into gargantuan cartoon characters, or so he imagined as he pulled the shapes one by one from his box of animal crackers to match up those in the sky.

Stella was nestled next to him on her laptop, and studying her, he could tell something heavy was on her mind. Though he'd gotten used to her occasional sullenness, this seemed like something different.

"How 'bout an animal cracker?" he asked, holding one that looked like Porky Pig.

She looked up from her laptop and studied the cracker. "Honey, you know I don't eat pork."

"You're hilarious."

She gave him a brief smile and turned back to her computer. "I'm deleting my Face Book account. And Twitter. And Instagram."

"Why? I thought you enjoyed hooking up with your friends online."

She seemed resolute, continuing to thoughtfully tap away on the keyboard. "Why is it that we are so fascinated with sharing our most banal events with three billion people on the internet? I mean, c'mon," searching for a random entry on Facebook to read him. "Eric stopped for a Coke Zero and stepped on some chewing gum? Really?" He braced himself for more, and she obliged without looking up. "How has our most private information become so accessible, all in real time for the whole world to know? We're experiencing info overload."

Sometimes her rants confused him. "Will you get to the point before the next Ice Age?"

"Kiss my derriere," she whispered without looking up.

"That's a nice offer, honey. Maybe later."

Suppressing a smile, she continued. "What I'm saying is, our personal information isn't safe," scrutinizing her progress like it was a work of art. "We have no privacy anymore. Look at the Cambridge Analytica Face Book scandal. They collect all our personal information, sell it to advertisers for billions, and then say they can't control it and pay a huge fine. Three hacks and two hundred million accounts exposed just in the last six months. After all that, they want you to buy into their crypto currency. Did I tell you my new theory?"

"About?"

"Zuckerberg." Giving him a smirk, "I think he's really a robot."

He thought about it. "You could be on to something."

"And now we have Alexa, our new home cyborg, sharing our private conversations with strangers." Adjusting the fit of her "Dallas Gun Club" cap, she was about to summarize her rant as she looked up to see if he was getting it.

"You don't seem worried."

"About robots? Would it help if I was?" he asked. Enjoying his Zen perspective, she continued entering commands on her PC.

"Where is this all coming from?" he wanted to know. Still, she didn't look up. "Stella, talk to me. What's going on?"

As their eyes met, she shared the full weight of her concern. "Have you forgotten? *He* gets out this week."

"Who?" he asked, adjusting course with his feet to catch a wind shift as a whale breached on the far horizon.

"Hirt." Stella looked incredulous, in disbelief over how unimportant it all seemed to him. "I don't want him cyberstalking me. He gets out of Raiford this week." Mark looked unfazed. "Honey, don't you get it? Internet technology is rendering personal privacy obsolete. Everything that's connected is vulnerable to tracking," she explained, getting emotional. He gave her a sympathetic look as he tightened the jib sheet a notch.

She continued to lay out her strategy. "So, I'm introducing an algorithm that breaks up all my personal data into fractions of a second to make it impossible to track me online. Even the FBI won't be able to find me." Stella had always been lightyears ahead of him in her understanding of technology, and now she was losing him.

"And that's a *good thing?*" It was a reference to their friends at the Behavior Analysis Unit in Quantico, the group who helped them in their narrow escape from a murderous Mexican drug lord two years earlier. It was a violent affair, and they were lucky to have lived through it.

He realized she was becoming obsessed with being virtually invisible. Taking a lighter tone, "Honey…you've got *me* now. No worries. You know I'll protect you." She looked nonplused, so he added, "Or, you could just use an alias."

Her brow furrowed. "You seem very glib about this."

"What do you want me to do?" Her expression unchanged, he tried harder. "Sometimes the only truth I know is the look in your eyes."

Usually a sucker for his puppy-dog approach, "Don't give me that crap. Why should I exist online as someone else? I'd rather not exist at all. In a virtual world, I mean."

He was having a hard time wrapping his head around her new direction, hoping she'd leave him a few more breadcrumbs so he could follow along and figure it out. Always spiritual and kind-hearted, she could be complicated, though it wasn't in her nature to be mysterious.

"When you said let's get away from civilization for a while, you were right. We disappeared to Bora Bora and counted coconuts and black pearls, swam with the dolphins and the sharks for two years. Now, we're back. Right?"

She nodded. *"Oui, je suis d'accord.* But now, I want to be anonymous. So…my new policy is DFE!"

"DFE?" he asked.

"Delete Friggin' Everything!"

Late the next morning, the couple found themselves two-hundred-eighty miles northwest of St. Thomas, sailing in a light rain. At the helm, Mark checked the sail trim as his eyes searched the billowing grey-blue clouds ahead for signs of clearing weather.

The skies had darkened ominously, and today they traded in their *au naturel* outfits for some high-vis foul weather gear. Clinging to his arm, Stella huddled with him at the helm with their coffee and cognac. Knowing the weather was weighing on her mood, he pointed at a break in the clouds on the horizon. "Better weather coming, baby doll. New days ahead."

She scanned the clouds and sighed. "Let me know when the skies are blue again," giving him a peck on the cheek. "I'll be down below working on some designs for your new book cover."

Another hour passed, and the sixty-four-foot Baltic continued to cruise in a steady breeze as the sun began to peek out from behind a cloud. Ready to lay his head back, Mark considered setting the autopilot and taking a short nap at the helm when he heard the VHF radio suddenly crackle to life at the nav/com station below deck.

A male voice was alerting all vessels northwest of St. Thomas about pirates in the area, so he switched on the remote VHF feed at the helm to take in the details. The warning prompted a visceral response as he recalled the dangerous encounter with Somali pirates on his circumnavigation four years earlier, and his stomach tightened.

"Dream Girl, Dream Girl, this is *Cabaret."* It was the sailboat on the same course fifteen miles ahead that he'd traded weather forecasts earlier. The VHF chatter woke Stella from her nap in the main salon and now the conversation had her full attention.

Mark snatched the mike from its hook. *"Cabaret,* this is *Dream Girl."*

"Hey, just wanted you guys to know we were visited by some dodgy guys in a twin diesel trawler ten minutes ago. Uh…you should know they were dressed in some tattered blue uniforms and wore sidearms."

"Sidearms, huh? What did they want?"

"They asked for some food and water, so we tossed them some bags of canned tuna and bottled water. Seemed like they wanted more before they finally left. You guys are on a…more expensive boat so they may assume you have some cash aboard." Mark could hear some animated conversation in the background. "I would steer away from them. If you look like some rich yachties, they may be angling for more than just collecting another toll on the Caribbean highway."

"Copy that, skipper," pushing the matted hair under his cap. "What's their direction and speed?"

"Heading in your direction at about ten knots. Looked like a crew of four." Now very alert, he stood up and met Stella's eyes. With the new threat, Mark forgot all about the bad weather forecasted earlier.

"Are they equipped with radar?" he asked. Concerned, Stella slid back the hatch cover and emerged from the navigation cabin.

"Afraid so, skipper. I think that's how they found us. Don't want to alarm you, but I got the impression they're looking for a bigger prize than our little 30-foot Pearson." Mark wiped the rain from his binoculars and scanned the horizon, spotting a tiny speck on the horizon north of their position.

What's on your mind, guys?

After gathering more information, Mark thanked him for the heads-up and the two skippers signed off. The light rain wasn't letting up as he raised his binoculars for another peek at the horizon. The faraway speck was beginning to slowly take a darker form. Making a decision to douse the jib for a better view ahead, he released the jib sheet and coiled the furling line around the winch. Stella stood at the companionway stairway, wondering how this would play out as she thought of questions and possible scenarios. The couple were painfully familiar with stories of murdered yachtsmen thrown overboard by pirates who violently commandeered boats for drug runs. Trying to keep a positive outlook, Mark wracked his brain for ideas on how to counter the threat, and a strategy began to take shape. He spun the wheel forty degrees to port.

"We can't change the wind, but we can damn sure adjust our course." Stella stood at the hatch, waiting to hear more about his strategy.

"Honey, got an idea. Take the wheel while I go below and check the radar. Our new course is two-seventy, due west. Maybe we can dodge 'em." She nodded and stood up straight, zipping up her foul weather gear before taking the wheel and a seat at the helm. She studied the binnacle compass until the pointer indicated due west and eased the sheets. Outrunning the vessel was unlikely, but she understood their new direction would clarify the trawler's intentions.

"And if they change course to intercept us?" she asked as he stepped toward the main hatch.

"There is no way I'm gonna let anything happen to you, Stella," looking deep into her eyes. "We're both excellent marksmen and well-armed, and we've dealt with things far worse." She nodded in agreement. "Remember, everything we want is on the other side of fear. We dealt with Rosa, we can deal with this." Taking comfort in what he had to say, she'd never once regretted marrying this man.

"Bring me my nine millimeter, dear," she said resolutely. "And the duty belt with the extra clips." With a new confidence, she leaned across him to trim the staysail and main sheets, pleased to see that he had already furled the jib.

"Coming right up." Giving her a wry smile, "We needed to brush up on our target shooting anyway." Though they'd never heard of pirates operating this close to the Virgins, it was always good to hope for the best but be prepared for the worst. Mark disappeared down the main hatch to retrieve his M-16 and Stella's nine millimeter, along with a few white thirty-gallon garbage bags.

At the nav/com station aft of the helm, he switched on the radar and checked the chart plotter to map out their distance to the closest landfall. Having sailed to a point equidistant from Puerto Rico, the Dominican Republic and St. Thomas, he knew he couldn't count on any help from authorities in time to make a difference. As he feared, the radar showed that the unknown vessel had altered course further south to intercept them and was now about four miles north by northwest. At the rate the two boats were closing, he figured he had less than fifteen minutes to put his plan in motion.

In a calm voice, Mark tried raising the trawler's skipper on the VHF. After four attempts to hail the unknown vessel with no response, he switched frequencies to a secondary channel and made three more attempts to raise the vessel's skipper. His appeals were met only by the sound of background static and the pitter-patter of light rain on the deck.

With only one target on his twelve-mile radar screen, his instincts were telling him it was about to get dicey. More disturbing to him, the approaching vessel displayed no identification on the Automatic Identification System transceiver, and the AIS confirmed the unknown vessel had altered course due south and was closing at ten knots on an intercept course. A captain who shut off their ship's transponder was up to no good.

Stella yelled down to him from the helm. "Mark, that trawler is dead ahead." He could hear the alarm in her voice. "They're coming straight at us."

Below deck, Mark caught a glimpse through the lexan hatch. "I see it. Stay on a two-seventy heading. I'll be right up with a big surprise for our guests." He snagged his keys, and from the secret teak cabinet in the navigation cabin, he removed his M-16 along with four forty-round banana clips with hollow points. Reaching for Stella's Model 659 nine millimeter and extra eighteen-round clips, he stuffed the ammo in his cargo shorts and headed toward the galley.

On his way back to the cockpit, he grabbed four white plastic trash bags from under the galley sink in preparation for the showdown. His head full of dark thoughts, he hoped the trawler had a fiberglass or aluminum hull. Anything but steel.

Joining Stella at the helm in the light rain, he handed her the holstered nine millimeter and raised the binoculars for another look. Arming herself, Stella wrapped the automatic's black duty belt around her waist, cinched the Velcro fasteners and stuffed the extra clips into the belt's empty pockets.

"Yeah," muttered Mark as he adjusted the focus on his binoculars, "...kinda sinister-looking stinkpot, aren't ya?" His mouth felt dry. "No one on deck", he reported. "These guys are in for a rough ride if they get too close. They've ignored all my attempts to hail them and they've switched their transponder off." He lowered the binoculars and glanced at his mate. "And *none* of that looks very friendly." She looked anxious, so he gave her something to do.

"Here..." handing her the extra binoculars, then two plastic trash bags, "...inflate these, honey. Tie them off with these tie wraps and drop them over the side about ten yards apart. I'll do the other two. For our uninvited guests, I will demonstrate what an M-16 with hollow points can do from two hundred yards." Soon, they had four inflated white trash bags trailing in their wake, each one separated by a boat length.

Staring at the approaching trawler through her binoculars, Stella recalled her years as a competitive yacht racer when she was in her twenties, reminiscing about the ease with which she could put distance between herself and another boat. She wished it could be that easy now. Scanning the sky as a wind shift caused the sails to flutter, she reached past him to trim the sheets.

"It'll be dark in an hour," curling her strawberry-blonde hair around her ear. "Just in case they catch us after dark, what's Plan B, *mon capitaine*?"

Pondering her question, he regarded his wife's appearance. Even in the face of pirates on the high seas, here she was in foul weather gear, looking good and dressed to kill.

"Here, put your hood up," covering her head with it. "No one is coming aboard," he assured her. "I'll be on the bow sighting in the scope. I'm sure these bozos are watching us right now, so I'll give them something to think about." With a tissue, he wiped the moisture from the M-16's scope and checked the binnacle compass one last time.

"Just keep us steady on two-seventy and get ready for some noise," jamming a forty-round banana clip into the rifle. Slinging it over his shoulder, he grabbed the binoculars and headed toward the bow like a pit bull on crack. These were his two dream girls, and he was determined to prevent some pirate trash from taking them away.

Ducking around the staysail, he pushed off from the shrouds, stubbing his toe on a cleat and letting loose with a string of profanities. Ignoring the pain, he crouched at the bow and surveyed the situation again through his binoculars. The trawler continued to come straight at them. Aiming his glasses aft, he could see the row of white Glad bags drifting about two hundred yards astern as he positioned himself in the crook of the bow rail in a seated position.

Brandishing the assault rifle in the air, he wanted them to have a good look before resting the weapon in the crook of his arm. He took his time to sight in the trailing bag as he adjusted the windage and elevation. With the garbage bag in his crosshairs two hundred yards out, he readied to fire. Taking a deep breath, he let it out slowly and squeezed the trigger. Firing once, there was an ear-splitting *BANG!*

Hearing his first shot, Stella's heart skipped a beat as she stole a look astern with her binoculars to watch the first bag explode in a huge plume of water before retraining her glasses on the trawler dead ahead. Looking for a reaction, she could see two men on deck with binoculars. As it continued to close on their position, they could hear the groan of the diesels and see the peeling blue paint revealing a white hull underneath.

But there was no change in course or speed.

Through his binoculars, he noticed the absence of any flag of nationality flying from either her mast or stern. In further violation of maritime law, the vessel failed to display any identifying name or number anywhere on the hull. Taking his time, another minute ticked by as Mark prepared to fire again. Another very loud *BANG!* Then another, followed by a fourth shot.

Stella trained her binoculars astern and swept the sea for any trace of the white bags. None were visible, and her heart beat faster.

Refocusing on the trawler, now less than three hundred yards away, she saw one of the men lower his binoculars and enter the bridge. Another minute passed as Mark repositioned his body, this time facing forward. He'd given them enough warnings. Slowly and reluctantly, he took aim at the approaching trawler's waterline. Holding his fire, the sweat mixed with the rain and dripped from his brow as he hoped they would change course.

Heart racing from the adrenaline, his finger on the trigger, he took a deep breath and slowly exhaled. Just as he was about to squeeze the trigger and empty the remaining thirty-six rounds into her hull, the trawler veered sharply to port, continuing to turn until it was heading east in the opposite direction. A flood of relief swept over him, and for now, he was grateful for the lack of bloodshed. *Good move, buddy.*

Stella grabbed the bullhorn sitting next to her. "Nice shootin', Tex!" she called out to her marksman.

He cupped his hands around his mouth and yelled back, "Keep an eye on him, Stella! See if he doubles back around!"

Suddenly, the helm VHF squawked loudly with a string of static as they were hailed by an unidentified vessel. Stella turned the volume all the way up so Mark could hear from the bow.

The deep male voice with the island accent was unmistakable. "We sorry, mon. We tink you someone else. Put ting de guns away now." Then silence, followed by more static. Resting his neck backward into the curve of the bow pulpit, Mark looked back at Stella standing at the helm with her hands on the big stainless steel wheel. Ready to spot any course reversals, he continued to scrutinize the trawler until it was beyond the limit of binocular range. Another fifteen minutes ticked by before it disappeared over the horizon.

Making his way to the helm, Mark hugged his wife and could feel her heart pounding from the excitement. Reaching to unfurl the jib, in a pirate's voice, "Let's put some distance between that thar pirate ship and our lassie here! Full speed ahead, matey!" The two felt as if the weight of a thousand ships had been lifted from their shoulders.

Mark headed below to watch the vessel on the Faruno long-range radar. Winking at Stella, "Keep a wary eye, matey."

He had to be sure.

As the sun set, Stella watched the sky turn a beautiful cascade of red and dark orange hues before the twilight gave way to nightfall. Later, the stars began to twinkle with the promise of better days ahead. Entranced by the symphony of the wind in the sails, she leaned back to search the sky for her favorite constellations,

In the navigation cabin below deck, Mark continued to watch the trawler on the radar and AIS screens for another twenty minutes before deciding to by-pass the electronic wizardry. As the pirate vessel disappeared from his screens, he made a decision to switch off the AIS and running lights, but kept the radar on, gambling that passing the night in stealth mode and accepting the risk of a collision in open water posed less of a threat than being plundered by armed brigands. Like wolves, he knew pirates were pack hunters, and he would stay on the alert for further attempts to hijack the two loves of his life.

With the trawler out of radar range, he went topside to lower the radar reflector and reeled it down on the halyard. Tucking it under his arm to stow it below, he stopped at the helm to check on Stella and dim the binnacle light. Not worried, she'd seen him do this a few times before.

"We going incognito, skipper?" she asked softly. She looked tired in the dim lighting, her mascara smudged from the harrowing events earlier.

He smiled. "Sometimes going incognito is a good thing." She nodded as he gently wiped her smudged mascara away. In his pirate voice, he added, "I'll be back with a surprise fer ye, matey."

She heard him rummage around the galley before he reappeared with a split of cold Dom Perignon and two plastic champagne flutes. Popping the cork, he filled the glasses and offered her a toast under the star-filled night sky. It wasn't at all what she expected to hear.

Raising his glass, he proclaimed,

"I give the fight up; let there be an end,
a privacy, an obscure nook for me.
I want to be forgotten, even by God."

Her eyes seemed to light up in recognition of the verse. The perfect mantra for her new attitude toward social media, she raised her glass to his. "Beautiful verse." She rolled her eyes, searching her memory for the author's name. "An English Romanticist, wasn't it?"

"Robert Browning. 1835, I think," giving her a slight bow. "Benefits of a classical education." Touching glasses again, "To being invisible."

"To being invisible," she repeated before downing half the glass.

After they polished off the champagne, Mark took the first watch while Stella went below. Inhaling the sweet aroma of the salty ocean air, he sat back on the cockpit cushions and thought about what else he may have overlooked to ensure their safe passage. The VHF stayed silent, the weather ahead seemed more pleasant, and they had heard nothing more from the trawler.

An hour later, the lighting array of an ocean-going tug towing a large fuel barge appeared on the dark horizon. He guessed it was on its way to the Virgins with a load of petrol and changed course ten degrees south to pass astern of it. Still under sail in stealth mode, he was wary of being the subject of any idle VHF chatter that might draw them more unwanted attention, so he steered clear of all surface vessels.

With only the sound of the sea passing over the hull and the whisper of wind in the sails, he spent most of the night listening, watching and scanning the horizon for lights as Stella slept in the main salon.

Still, he didn't feel safe.

The tense encounter with the pirates had him wondering about another threat; what had become of the man who tried to kill his wife two years ago? Recalling the concern she'd expressed, he made a mental note to do some internet recon and check on Hirt's release from prison.

Looking east, he gazed at the moon in *Dream Girl*'s wake as it rose over the sea and ascended to join the procession of constellations in the night sky.

He found himself praying that the days ahead could all be as peaceful as this moment, but his crystal ball was telling him otherwise.

FOUR

On a cool evening in late January, Dr. Katherine Tremelle stood on the third floor terrace of the Vero Beach Resort and Spa watching the well-dressed guests drive up on the promenade deck below. The valets were eager to assist the Credit Suisse conference attendees as psychiatrists and research analysts stepped from their limos, pressing palms with twenty-dollar bills in their designer suits and gowns. The well-heeled guests continued inside to the auditorium for what would presumably be one of the most anticipated biopharmaceutical presentations of the year.

Staring off into the western sky, Dr. Tremelle took a deep drag on her Marlboro, anticipating a rush of nicotine to calm her nerves. She told herself she only indulged in the habit when she was nervous. Or when she drank. Or, before a major presentation. What she really needed right now was a double dirty vodka martini.

As tonight's keynote speaker, she was scheduled to introduce the latest human clinical trial results for Oconix Pharmaceutical's new Alzheimer's treatment. With billions at stake, the last thing she needed was to slur her words during the new product presentation, so she held off on the double martini. She tossed her shoulder-length brown hair back and thought about what her father always told her when she was a little girl; "Get up, do your best, and let God take care of the rest."

Well, dad, where was God when I went through that train wreck at Valiant two years ago?

She remembered his words when she lost her mom to a drunk driver at the age of thirteen. "I wish I could tell you it gets easier," he said then, "...but it doesn't. You'll always have a hollow feeling inside you." She flicked an ash over the rail. Her mom had given her the will to stand up and excel in the face of adversity, and without her, she probably would have never finished med school. She took a final drag on her Marlboro, taking comfort in the rush of nicotine. Stubbing it out with the toe of her Jimmy Choo high heel, her eyes drifted to a bright star in the western sky before she realized it was the planet Venus.

Through the hubbub of her surroundings, she heard the elevator doors open as someone approached from the hallway, and her research assistant joined her at the rail. She could feel his eyes on her, checking out her black sequin Givenchy gown while he jotted down some final notes for her presentation.

"Quick, Dr. Tremelle, what's another word for thesaurus?" he joked. From the corner of her eye, she could see he was grinning. "A hedge fund manager downstairs asked me if I knew who that beautiful woman was standing at the rail."

"Imagine that." She turned her attention back to the throng of guests pulling into the valet driveway two stories below. "You don't stop blowing smoke up my derriere, Dr. Talcott, I'm gonna float away like a hot-air balloon." She had a weakness for men who resembled Sean Connery in his earlier movies.

"So it's back to *Dr.* Talcott today. I was just getting used to Bruce."

"Let's be professional and use formal titles during the conference, shall we?" Bored with his hand-holding routine, she turned to her younger assistant. "They ready for me yet?"

"Ready to mic you in twenty minutes, and the teleprompter is set up-only as a guide, of course-as you requested." She was anxious, so he continued to prepare her. "Standing room only for our world-famous Director of Research." His eyes admired her from top to bottom. "Beautiful gown, quite shapely. Christion Dior or Givenchy?"

His grin seemed glib, but he was trying. "Givenchy. World famous, huh?" She eyed him skeptically through her black-rimmed Warby Parkers as she adjusted their fit. She'd once overheard him describe her to a colleague as "his sexy, demure doctor of biochemistry." He was needy, and his desire for more than just a professional relationship made her uneasy at times.

Talcott continued with his adulation. "Well, it is *rare* that a Director of Research can successfully guide a new potential blockbuster drug like edulimab all the way through Phase Three clinical trials in half the time allotted, and after surpassing endpoints by thirty percent."

"Potential blockbuster?" She thought about the $2.7 billion in preproduction backlogs. Grasping the metal rail tightly with both hands, she gave him a tight smile. "I heard our competitors at Biogen and ZTE Pharma were just *thrilled* about it. I'm sure they'll have their analysts and shills scattered throughout the audience to applaud our progress."

The sarcasm troubled him, but after working with her for ten months, he'd come to understand her moods. "As always, Dr. Tremelle, you're gonna blow them away."

She checked the incoming call on her phone. *Speak of the devil.* "It's Dr. Marchenko," giving her assistant an apologetic look. Pressing the talk button, "Anton, what a pleasant surprise," rolling her eyes. "How're things at ZTE?"

The ZTE Director of Clinical Research seemed surprised by her overly-pleasant tone. "Good, Katherine. I know you get ready to speak, so I get right to point." She winced at his English, knowing it wasn't even a third language for him. "As you know by now, we have FDA approval for Phase III trials on revlimuvant."

"So we've heard." There was a long pause as Tremelle tried to gauge the reason for his call. "Will you be in the auditorium for my presentation tonight, Anton?"

From across the courtyard, the portly Ukrainian cleared his throat and prepared to charm her with his thick Slavic accent. "Katherine, you know how much I love your presentations. Wouldn't miss for the world. You have great ability to captivate audience. Especially, *male* audience."

"But…," she interjected, waiting for his *caveat*.

"Yes, there is '*but*', not that there is anything wrong with *yours*."

"Let's keep my butt out of this, Anton. No reason to get lewd, if that's where you were going. What's on your mind?"

She heard him take a deep breath. "I've been asked to tell you we will file restraining order if you roll out edulimab before our suit for patent infringement is settled."

"My dear Anton, why didn't you just call our legal department? Why me? Why now?" attempting to shame him with the rhetorical questions. "You think suing us will help the millions suffering from Alzheimers?" Baiting him, she leaned her back against the rail and put him on speaker so Talcott could hear the mud their chief rival was slinging.

In a darker voice, Marchenko intoned, "After your involvement in that Valiant…ah, how you say…*train wreck* two years ago, you really want to preach me about what's good for patients, Katherine?"

"Leave it to you to dredge that up, Anton. You damn well know the psycho psychiatrist responsible for the patient's aberrant episode pled guilty to malpractice. He was lucky to avoid an assault conviction, so let's get our facts--"

"Which, I remind you, did not clear Valiant of wrongdoing, or did you forget about $360 million fine?" Marchenko refused to let up. "Wasn't it *your* testimony that put him in prison?"

Tremelle calmed herself, refusing to allow him to get her worked up with his reference to Dr. Hirt. "For the victim, and the drug's contrain-dications…I did what I thought was right."

"What's right is you don't rollout edulimab before we settle our suit." A long pause ensued before he added, "Don't say I did not warn you."

Surprised to hear his thinly-veiled threat, Tremelle stared at her assis-tant in disbelief as she muted the phone.

To lighten the mood, Talcott said, "Maybe we should find this guy before he posts his selfie to Face Book." She gave him a confused look. "You know. Like Van Gogh. Think maybe your smitten boy there is one sunny day away from cutting off his ear?" Suppressing a smile, she pretended she wasn't amused before unmuting the phone.

"Where are you, Anton?"

"Look across courtyard." She turned to see the sixty-two-year-old bald Ukrainian waving from the ground floor as he stood next to a huge man that could have passed for a four-hundred-pound gorilla. The bodyguard pointed up at her in an obvious attempt to intimidate her as Marchenko continued. "We just wanted you know we'll be watching, Katherine." The conversation made her feel dirty, like she needed a shower. After ending the call, the two men disappeared inside the building.

Talcott smirked. "You've got quite the fan club."

"Making friends wherever I go."

"Ignore those goons. They're just trying to rattle you. They know we have the superior candidate."

The two were startled by a voice behind them. "There you are, Dr. Tremelle." Their IT guy appeared, wearing his headset, accompanied by one of their security men. "We'll be ready for you in fifteen minutes… oh, and your makeup artist is waiting in your room."

"Thanks, Jerry."

The stern-looking security man stepped up. "Mr. and Mrs. McAllister asked for you from the lobby. Shall I send them up? They have a very special bottle of champagne for you. A Dom '57, they said to tell you."

"Tell them I'll meet them in my room in two minutes," she replied. The security guard tapped on his headset to deliver her instructions to the desk. Turning to her assistant, "Dr. Talcott, come with me. There's something I want you to do for me, and we don't have much time."

She led him to the elevator alcove and retrieved from a hidden pocket in her gown a small clear plastic case containing a transceiver the size of a dime. Making sure there was no one to overhear them, she said, "I want you to go right now and find Marchenko. Introduce yourself to him, be charming, then distract him and drop this bug in his coat pocket. Don't let anyone see you do it. Think you can do that for me?"

Surprised by her sudden cloak-and-dagger demeanor, he took the dime-shaped device into the palm of his hand and examined it. "Anything for you, Katherine."

"How many times must I ask you to call me--"

"Who's on the other end?" Talcott wanted to know.

She pushed the elevator call button. "Our head of security. Do it before we start. Gotta know what he's up to. I've got a bad feeling about those guys."

"You got it. Meet you in the back before you go onstage." She nodded and stepped inside the elevator, on her way to meet her friends as the doors closed.

Eager to protect his boss, Talcott headed for the north elevator to find Marchenko. Sidestepping the four-hundred-pound gorilla wasn't going to be easy, but for her, he'd do anything.

On the other side of the resort, Mark knocked on the door to room 361 for a third time in his Brioni tux while Stella stood beside him in her sequined gown. Looking forward to seeing their friend after two years in Bora Bora, she clung to the chilled bottle of Dom Perignon.

Hearing no answer, he put his ear to the door and checked his watch. "Katherine," shouting through the door, "…it's Mark and Stella. We're back, and we've got a surprise for you." He knocked again.

After watching the couple from down the hallway, a young man in a valet uniform approached. "Can I help you?" he asked.

"Trying to hook up with a friend," explained Stella, turning the business card over to check the room number. On it the concierge had scrawled "Room 361." "It's the right room," she confirmed.

On his phone, Mark scrolled to the hotel's main number and rang it. "Yeah, hi Melissa. Can you ring room 361 for me, please?" A moment later they could hear the phone ringing inside the room.

"Maybe she's in the shower," suggested Mark. Perplexed after the security guy told them she'd be inside, they stood in the hallway for a few moments as the phone continued to ring.

Suddenly, from deeper in the building, they were unnerved by the sound of a woman screaming hysterically. Then, a distraught hotel maid appeared in the hallway and ran past them toward the elevator holding a phone to her ear.

"C'mon. Let's check it out," urged Mark as they started for the elevator.

Tightening her grip on the champagne, she gave him a fearful look. "This is creeping me out, Mark."

FIVE

The CSI unit was finishing up with photos and cataloguing evidence as Detective Lieutenant Frank Foti slipped his hands into a pair of latex gloves. Squatting over the victim alongside his CSI tech, the twenty-year veteran of the Vero Beach Police Department focused on establishing the cause of death.

The grey-bearded detective examined the tiny trickle of blood that dripped from the back of her neck and shook his head in disgust. Closer examination revealed that a small sharp object had penetrated into her medulla, suggesting the unsub may have some knowledge of anatomy. From the blood's color, he guessed it was not post-mortem. The victim had two broken fingernails on her right hand, a burn mark from a stun gun, and the shape of ligature marks on her neck indicated the murderer was likely left handed.

His list of unanswered questions for the medical examiner was getting longer by the minute. After reviewing his notes, Foti stood and glanced at the laundry room entrance where he'd placed an officer to secure the site. Though the crime scene remained orderly, he noticed the gathering crowd was getting more curious.

Homicides on Orchid Island were rare, and so he was cautiously pacing himself, wanting to be thorough. A high-profile homicide like this was sure to bring a lot of attention to their little Mayberry-By-The-Sea,

32

probably even national media attention. Foti had placed two officers at the resort entrance to keep the media at bay and two more to keep the crowd behind the yellow crime scene tape and identify key witnesses.

The sight of a uniformed officer preventing McAllister from entering the laundry room caught Foti's attention. "Where are you taking her?" asked Mark as they loaded her covered body onto a gurney.

"The morgue for an autopsy," responded the uniformed corporal as he studied the man in the black Brioni tux. "Who are *you*, sir?"

Mark scanned the room to find the ranking officer in charge, wanting to get around this gatekeeper. "Sir, I can't let you in," said the officer. "Please stay behind the yellow tape until the detective calls for you. Are you related to the deceased?" doing a double take on Stella's aqua-colored Christian Dior gown and the bottle of champagne in her grip.

Mark wrestled with his emotions before meeting the officer's eyes. "Not immediate family, but she was our close friend."

"Katherine lived at our guest house here in Vero," offered Stella, wiping the moisture from her eyes. "We came to celebrate the introduction of her new Alzheimer's drug."

"I'm sorry for your loss, ma'am. Wait here. As soon as the detective is ready, he'll call for you. I'm sure he'll want to talk with you."

Overhearing the conversation, Foti was curious and studied the couple from across the room. "Corporal, what ya got over there?"

Pointing with his pen, "These folks knew the victim. She was living at their guest cottage."

"Keep them here. And John."

"Yes, sir."

"Send Officer Adami to collect a copy of all the footage from hotel surveillance cameras during the last 24 hours. Every camera in the hotel and on the street in surrounding buildings. After we've identified any suspects, crosscheck them with that new biometric AI program on loan from the FBI."

"Yes, sir."

Foti turned to the lead CSI tech as he watched him drop Dr. Tremelle's iPhone into a clear Ziploc. "Gary, when you get back to the lab, track and ID every call on her phone in the past week. Pull the PC card and make duplicate files. And run a complete crosscheck matrix of friends and contacts from her phone and social media."

"Yes, sir."

Foti squatted for a closer look at her fingernails and lifted her hand. "Looks like she put up a fight. Check her skin and fingernails for DNA. Let's find the dirt bag who did this."

"We'll bag 'em," Detective Locke assured him.

Flipping through the pages of his notepad, Foti stood to finish his interview with Dr. Talcott. He reminded himself that nothing is what it seems. Ignore your obvious conclusions, he told himself, and don't automatically trust your observations. What you see and what you hear are not always real.

He walked over to his witness. "Dr. Talcott, tell me more about this Anton Marchenko. Does he have any reason to harm Dr. Tremelle?" Recalling the conversation with Tremelle, Talcott looked rattled.

"Take your time, doctor."

Pressing his fingers against the electronic bug in his pants pocket, Talcott fought to stay calm. In his sadness and confusion, he blamed himself for not being able to find Marchenko as she'd asked, thinking that maybe she'd still be alive if he had. Still, he chose to keep quiet about the transceiver.

Talcott ran over the sequence of events in his head. It was all so confusing. Standing in the back of the room when the CEO announced Dr. Tremelle's death in the meeting room ten minutes earlier, Talcott felt sick and ran to the men's room to vomit. When he returned, he heard the CEO take the extraordinary step of cancelling Oconix's entire presentation. Amid the whispers of disbelief, most of the conference attendees had packed up their electronics and prepared to depart with so many of their questions still unanswered.

As he stood with Detective Foti, Talcott remembered her saying she had a "bad feeling" about this and shared her prescience with him. "She was afraid of him. He and his bodyguard were threatening her on her phone less than an hour ago. I heard them on speaker while I was standing next to her on the balcony upstairs."

Foti cocked his head and studied his witness, looking for cracks in his story. "And what is your relationship with Dr. Tremelle?"

Looking down at his shoes, he lowered his voice "Purely professional."

Foti watched him shift his weight and had a feeling Talcott was hiding something. "I'll need you to come down to the station to sign an official statement. Is this Marchenko a guest here in the hotel?"

"Not sure, but…he was standing in the courtyard."

Foti continued to study him. "Anything else?"

Overcome with emotion, Talcott shook his head and looked away. "Just seems like by the time we get everything figured out, we're too late to do anything about it."

Something felt a little off to the detective. "Meet me at the station in say…twenty minutes? 1055 Beachland. We'll get your full statement then." Talcott nodded.

The news of the homicide had spread through the island community like a raging wildfire, and news vans were crowding up and down Ocean Drive like they were covering The Rapture. Filled with a myriad of reporters looking to spin the next headline, the vans were parking all over the place, blocking alleys and driveways. To the locals and vacationers, it was a repulsive sight.

Foti stepped away from the scene to dial the hotel receptionist as he motioned toward Cpl. Banner. "Yeah, hi Melissa. Detective Foti. We met earlier. Need a room number for…uh," checking his notes, "…Anton Marchenko."

Melissa remembered their encounter earlier. "Are you that detective who looks like Ed Harris, the movie star?"

"Look, I appreciate the flattery, but I've got a homicide on my hands and I need your help. Tell me about Anton Marchenko."

"Yes sir," in a more formal tone. "Let me check the computer. We have a *Dr.* Anton Marchenko in room 302, facing the beach."

"Uh-huh. Do me a flavor, Melissa?"

"A flavor? Sure."

"I want you to ring his room and tell him there's a problem with his bill that can only be straightened out at the reception desk. Do that for me?"

"Like what kind--"

"Credit card problem...I dunno...be creative. Be a big help."

"I suppose I could."

"Good. I'll be there in two minutes-and let's keep this just between us."

"Yes sir."

Pocketing his phone, Foti approached the attractive couple standing in the hallway with the bottle of Dom. Ducking under the yellow crime scene tape, he displayed his badge as Cpl. Banner introduced the McAllisters. "Detective Frank Foti, Vero Beach Homicide/Robbery. You say the victim was staying at your home?"

"Our guest house," clarified Stella.

"We appreciate your help. Would you have any objection to a search of your guest house, Mr. McAllister? Personal records, computer, that sort of thing. May give us some leads."

Mark nodded. "I'd like to be there. I'm an investigative journ--"

"I know. I've read a few of your best sellers. I found them insightful. Can you meet me at police headquarters in twenty minutes to give us a statement about everything you saw tonight?"

"Sure," said Mark. He shook his head sadly. "Katherine was a brilliant woman, and my wife and I want to help find her killer." Hesitating, he asked, "How was she--"

"I can't discuss that with you." Foti regarded the well-dressed couple for a moment before reaching inside his tweed sport coat for a card. "I'm sorry for your loss. I heard she was well-liked. This was a singular crime, no evidence of robbery, no apparent signs of..." addressing Stella, "...I'm sorry, ma'am…of sexual motivation, so anything you can share would be helpful."

"Of course, detective," replied Mark.

"Call me Frank. See you in twenty minutes." After handing him the card, "Oh…and please don't touch anything in the guest house until I can get my CSI team in there."

Mark nodded. "Not my first rodeo, Frank. I know the routine. Turning to Stella, "I need a margarita after all this. Waldo's is on the way home, you wanna…"

"A gentle sea breeze and a Cuervo blended margarita. I might need more than one," she confessed, shaking her head. "Dear, dear Katherine."

Mark gave her a hug. "And maybe a third to toast our dearly departed."

Taking the elevator down to reception, Foti noted the security camera on the ceiling and the absence of any blood spatter on the walls or door. The unsub had been thorough in planning this, he concluded. Stuffing her in the second floor laundry chute after what looked like an ice pick to her medulla was silent, brutal and deadly. The image made him sick to his stomach.

As the elevator door opened, he spotted Melissa at the front desk, flashed his badge and did a double take. Reminding him of a demure librarian in her dark-rimmed Warby Parkers, her resemblance to Tremelle was uncanny. Foti waded through guests who were lined up five deep in a hurry to check out as word of the murder spread, and he overheard one refer to it as the "Bates Motel." Bellying up to the front desk, "So, Melissa, how'd we do with Dr. Marchenko? He on his way?"

She stopped what she was doing, walked over, and lowered her voice. "I'm sorry, detective, but he'd already checked out before I could call him.

Paid in cash. I was told he was in a hurry." She motioned for him to come closer. "One of the valets overheard him booking a two-room suite at The Driftwood Resort just down the beach. He had this huge scary guy with him…like a bodyguard. Is that helpful?" Foti nodded before glancing at the throng of reporters waiting outside.

"You bet. You make a copy of his driver's license?"

"We made a color copy of his passport. I remember it was Ukrainian."

Impressed, Foti raised his eyebrows. "Even better. Make me a copy?"

"Of course." Melissa's French-manicured nails danced across the keyboard to deliver the detective's request. "I'll grab it off the printer," pointing behind her.

"Thanks, Melissa."

Returning with the copy, "Can we keep this a secret?" pulling her hair back behind her glasses. "I'm new here and I love my job."

"Sure," he assured her. He studied the passport photo for a moment before folding it and stuffing it into his coat. "Oh, and if you think of anything else, here's my card. Direct line's on it."

"Okay." Giving him a quick smile, she read it before tucking it into her blouse pocket and turning to the next guest. "Who was next?"

Foti headed for the entrance, on his way to do what he disliked the most. After making a brief statement to the group of reporters and floating several "this is an ongoing investigation" and "I'm unable to comment on that" responses, he pushed his way through the crowd and headed for Ocean Drive. Walking a few blocks south to the Driftwood Resort gave him a chance to reflect on a conversation he had with his captain the day before. Captain Garrett insisted there be "no secrets and no agendas." That promise seemed a lot easier to keep yesterday, he thought, as he answered the call from Garrett.

"Frank, we're all over this at HQ."

"Yes, sir."

Garrett continued. "Look, I know how you get when the victim's a looker. There is no place for emotion here. I need you to be focused and on your best game, or not on the case." Garrett paused to let this sink in. "We owe that to Dr. Tremelle and her family, and to Oconix Pharmaceuticals."

Hearing his boss allude to Oconix as a victim, he sensed that his captain might be burdened with a political agenda. Political agendas always had a way of screwing things up and creating crosscurrents that were invisible until they blew you out the door.

"No worries, John. Everything by the book, straight down the fair-way," responded Foti.

Garrett sounded relieved. "Good. Now, what do you need?"

"Your security clearance for a full background on a Dr. Anton Marchenko. FBI, CIA, NSA, Interpol, everything. Along with known associates."

"I'll have it downloaded to your PC and phone immediately." Before he hung up, Garrett added, "Watch your step, Frank. Lotta eyeballs on this one."

SIX

Waldo's and the Driftwood Resort stand apart as one of the best-loved resorts and restaurants in Florida, and a favorite destination for many of the island gentry who valued a more laid-back venue with a unique history. Guests came from all over the world to enjoy what one of the original settlers in Vero Beach had created a hundred years ago.

In the 1920s, when Waldo Sexton arrived in Vero Beach and proceeded to build the Driftwood Inn, he set out to create one of the most extraordinary structures in the South. Sexton, founder of McKee's Jungle Attractions, also in Vero Beach, built his sprawling dream of driftwood, cypress logs and pecky-cypress paneling from the swamps of Blue Cypress Lake about twenty-six miles west of the beach. Townspeople who remembered the period describe Sexton pacing up and down the beach shouting verbal instructions to the crews who worked without written plans or blueprints.

The result was a two-story hotel with balconies everywhere surrounded by pole railings made of turned or peeled-log supports. Nothing seems to be completely square or level, and the main porch eases itself through shifts in level a little like a frozen wave.

Once Sexton finished the inn, he began to fill it, inside and out, with a mish-mash of objects ranging from ships' wheels to cannons. He gleaned the decorations from every corner of Florida, even as far away as Europe,

40

and included early Italian chests, plush sofas, and unique outdoor art and sculptures. The Driftwood affectionately calls this the "Menagerie of Monstrosities."

Certainly the most famous part of this menagerie is the vast collection of large bells from ships and locomotives. Some were purchased from missions in Mexico, others graced such proud locomotives as Old 97 of Virginia or the local line that ran to Key West. One of the bells belonged to Harriet Beecher Stowe. Anyone is free to ring a bell or two when the spirit moves them, and in earlier days at the Driftwood, one's popularity could be judged by the number of bells rung upon departure.

Nine decades after Sexton finished the famous landmarks, Lt. Foti opened the office door to the Driftwood Resort and was met by an amiable young man wearing a nametag that read "Zach." He looked familiar, but Foti couldn't quite place him.

"How can I help you today?" asked Zach as he was joined by another man at the desk.

"Detective Foti, Vero Beach Robbery/Homicide," exhibiting his badge. "You have a guest here named Anton Marchenko?" holding up the photo.

The men studied the photo, the older speaking first. "I'm Mike. Zach and I help manage the place. Dr. Marchenko checked in earlier today. He wanted something rustic and low-key, so we suggested the Wahoo Suite with his security guy. Why? What's he done? We heard police sirens earlier."

"Let *me* ask the questions. The other guy, big burly, tough-lookin'?"

"Yeah. Heavy Russian accent. Looked kinda rough with a pock-marked face."

"I need to speak with them urgently," feeling the weight of the Glock in his shoulder holster. "Can you take me to his room?"

"Sure," replied Mike. "Zach, you go ahead. I'll have Joe meet you there in case you need help."

A minute later they were standing on the rustic porch entrance and knocking on the pecky cypress front door. Foti noticed the name of the Wahoo Suite spelled out artistically in rope letters over the doorway. Looking up and down the rows of single-story cottages, it seemed appropriate that the suites were all named after colorful Florida game fish. An amiable young man stepped up to greet him.

"The two you're looking for are over at Waldo's having drinks," declared Joe. "Beachside table, big guys wearing expensive suits. Hard to miss."

"You've been helpful," replied Foti, handing them both a card. "Call me right away if you hear or see anything else unusual."

"Count on it," assured Zach. "Is it true that a woman was--"

"I really can't go into that," replied Foti over his shoulder as he headed for the seaside bistro just around the corner.

Billed as the quintessential "Last of the Great American Hangouts" Waldo's is where the food is great, and a favorite watering hole for folks when they felt like blending into a more laid-back "Key-Westy" beachfront setting.

Glowing in the candle light, the rustic ship's bell mounted above the rail shown in the light of the full moon at the beachfront table occupied by the two Ukrainians. Capturing the bodyguard's attention, the bell intrigued him, and he wondered what it sounded like.

"Don't even think about it," warned Marchenko in his Russian accent. "Try not to draw any attention." Bubba nodded, draining his vodka martini and turned to order another as the two heard footsteps on the wooden deck.

"Anton Marchenko?" asked Foti displaying his badge with one hand and carrying a chair over with his other.

"Da."

"Investigating a homicide. Got a coupla questions."

Marchenko smirked at the badge and looked up. "We're kinda in middle of something officer, and--"

"Detective Lieutenant," corrected Foti. "Yes I see. Very romantic, the full moon, candlelight and all. You two seem soooo close," he quipped, sitting down at their table in spite of Marchenko's objections.

"We can talk now, or at the station. Your choice."

Foti took a moment to size up his quarry, along with the bodyguard who sported a facial scare and bore such an uncanny resemblance to Luca Brasi of *The Godfather* fame. The two were beefy guys, Marchenko with deep set eyes and a ruddy face, and Yakovlev with all the grace of a silverback gorilla. He noticed the bodyguard take a deep drag on a black cigarette with gold lettering, then spotted the box of Treasurer Executive Black lying on the table. He remembered a conversation with a billionaire once who bragged that it was the most expensive brand in the world.

They were interrupted by the server. "Two vodka martinis," announced the bouncy young waitress as she set the drinks down. Turning to Foti, "And for you, sir?"

"Just a little privacy," he replied, placing a card on her tray. "Give my regards to Erich and Joe."

"Yes sir," her eyes growing large at the card as she stepped away.

Marchenko motioned for his bodyguard to stay calm as he leaned back in his chair and folded his arms. "What is it you need to know, detective?" By now, it was obvious that the two Ukrainians had the *right* to remain silent, but lacked the *ability* to do so.

He started with an easy question. "Do you own a stun gun?"

The two men looked at each other before Marchenko responded. "Nyet," he declared flatly.

With a smug look, "I'll put that down as a 'no.'" Making eye contact, "Witnesses stated you made a threatening phone call to the murder victim about an hour ago. We also know, as ZTE's Director of Research, you're Oconix's chief competitor in the Alzheimer's arena. That doesn't put you in a very good light, *doctor.*"

"Sure, I called Dr. Tremelle to wish her well tonight. I was sorry to hear what happened." Foti gave him a skeptical look. "If you check security cameras, you'll see I was in audience when--"

"*We* were in audience," interrupted Bubba.

"Witnesses are saying the call was threatening," insisted Foti. "Clearly, you stand to profit from her demise, yes? And how would you explain the fact that we've been able to identify your DNA on her hand?"

Marchenko's brow furrowed as he unfolded his thick arms and placed them on the table. "Bubba and I ran into her in the hallway, and I shook her hand to wish her well," he explained. "There were several witnesses."

"When was that?" asked Foti.

"About ten minutes before her presentation was to begin. Am I under arrest?" Foti didn't reply. "Do I need lawyer?"

Remaining pokerfaced, Foti ignored his question. "I'll need your passports."

Marchenko hesitated. "Next, you tell me to put honey in ears and fall asleep on anthill? I'm telling you the *truth,* detective."

"You're not telling the truth, doctor, you're selling the truth." Foti reached inside his coat and rested his hand on his Glock. "Don't make me bring you in. I guarantee you won't like it." It was a bluff, but it worked.

Holding his hand up, Marchenko changed his tune and turned to his bodyguard. "Bubba, go grab passports from my attache for detective. Let's show police we have nothing to hide."

The taciturn bodyguard got to his feet and guzzled his vodka martini as Foti stood with him. "I'll go with you to make sure you don't get lost." Sliding his chair in, "Thanks for the chat, doctor. If you'll pardon the cliché, don't leave town."

Marchenko frowned at the advice. "And if I do?"

Foti leaned forward on the chair, their faces only inches apart. "Then we'll have to get the FBI and NSA involved. *They* tend to ask a lot more embarrassing questions; your bosses, CEO, board of directors, people like that. Could get messy for you at work, put you in a bad light. I don't think you want that."

Taking Marchenko's silence for compliance, Foti turned to catch up with the bodyguard as he searched his phone for the incoming NCIC file on his prime suspect.

Interview Room #2 at the Vero Beach Police Department was an austere room with no windows, two-way mirror and large steel table in the center. A black digital recorder sat at one end of the rectangular metal table and HD cameras were mounted in two opposing corners of the acoustical tile ceiling. Seated at the table, Mark and Stella were still wearing their formal evening attire as they waited to give their statements to Foti.

On the other side of the two-way mirror, Stella caught the attention of rookie Det. Gary Locke as he stood in the hallway. "Who's the looker in the aqua evening gown?" he asked, peering through the glass.

"A woman who was married to a very unlucky man," replied Tech Officer Margo Violette.

"Whaddya mean, unlucky?" asked Locke.

"His third wife ran off with his second wife."

"You're joking, right?"

"Well, maybe about that, but I know for a fact that an author married his fourth wife."

"Stella Wilde?"

"That's right. Stella Wilde McAllister now. You missed your chance, detective," giving him a smug look.

"I still like her."

"Wait ten minutes," quipped Violette to discourage his interest. "I heard she's a real diva."

On the other side of the two-way mirror, Mark sipped his vending-machine coffee as his eyes swept the room. "They need to fire their decorator," in his best impersonation of a feminine interior designer. Waving his arm in mock disapproval, "It's all wrong."

Stella smiled at his impersonation and felt a little less inconsolable. Casually surveying the room, she agreed with her husband. "Yeah, I think I would have gone a different way here, too." The door swung open and Detective Foti quietly entered the room.

"Mr. and Mrs. McAllister. Thank you for coming." Mark nodded as Foti made himself comfortable in a seat across from them and set his file and notepad on the table. Weary from the day's events, he crossed his legs and sighed before he began.

"Forgive me, a long day," rubbing his eyes with the heel of his hand. "Look, I've been a detective for a long time, and learned that crimes like this aren't random. This homicide appears well-planned, and we've ruled out robbery and sexual assault as possible motives." He paused to gauge their reaction and gave them a stern look. "I'd prefer to interview you separately."

Stella glanced at Mark. "I'm not going to answer any questions unless my husband is sitting right here beside me. That's a deal-breaker."

She was resolute, and not wanting to lose the couple's assistance, Foti relented "All right, then. Did Dr. Tremelle have any enemies that either of you are aware of? Anybody that would want to harm her?"

"Not sure how to answer that." Stella rested her arms on the table and clasped her hands together, resigning herself to sharing her story with Foti. "We became friends when she helped with my addiction to ambienna and seraquim two years ago. When my late husband assaulted me." Foti glanced up at the cameras as Stella continued. "The drugs were prescribed to me by Dr. Christopher Hirt."

Foti's eyes widened and he leaned forward to hear more. "Yes, I remember that. He was convicted--"

"Of insider trading and medical malpractice, but got off on the felony assault charge. Dr. Tremelle was a witness for the prosecution but later recanted her testimony."

"Why?" asked Foti.

"Nobody knows," offered Mark, "...and she wouldn't say."

"Katherine refused to discuss it," confirmed Stella.

"You think she was threatened?" pressed Foti, jotting down the details.

"That would be my guess," responded Mark.

"By who? Hirt?"

"Possibly."

"Have either of you had any contact with Hirt since his release?"

"Why would we?" asked Stella. "We could never quite understand the cloak-and-dagger business of the biotech giants. Katherine did her best to steer clear of the power struggles and focus on her research."

"How so?"

Mark said, "She would often refer to her competitors as 'vampires... creatures that would suck her veins dry, crack open her bones, and...'"

"And what?" pressed Foti.

"And 'lick the marrow out' if it would get them the next blockbuster drug. Her words."

Foti massaged his forehead. "I see. Sounds like a charming group. Remind me to bring some garlic and a crucifix to their next meeting."

"We had her over for drinks and dinner a few times before we left for Bora Bora," continued Stella. "She appreciated the extra security measures we added to Villa Riomar and felt like she needed a safe house, especially after I was--"

"Kidnapped by Emilio Rosa" finished Foti. "Quite a story by itself. And you are, I presume, the Queen of South Beach?"

She gave him a cryptic smile but remained silent.

"Something about that case always puzzled me. Why did you try to save Dan from Rosa after he tried to strangle you?"

"I loved and pitied him," she confessed. "He always seemed so lost to me, always pedaling so furiously to keep from drowning in a...a cesspool of his own making." She hadn't shared her secrets with very many. Taking a deep breath, she stretched her arms out across the table and folded her hands together before she continued.

"Dan was all about the money. He thought it would buy him respect," she confessed. "In the final analysis, it didn't." Her eyes misty, she paused to gather her emotions. "He knew Rosa was coming for him. He said he wished he could offer me hope, but couldn't change what he'd done." Squeezing Mark's hand, "At the end, I got lucky."

"There's no luck here," declared Foti, impressed with her tenacity. "You're a tough lady, Stella. I read the FBI accounts. You fought hard for your life. And you got to keep it."

"We thought running a bread and breakfast in the South Pacific would help to put it all behind us," added Mark.

Foti was fascinated with her story. A heart this forgiving didn't often come with a woman so alluring. "So you offered Dr. Tremelle your guest house while you were away."

She nodded. "We needed a break, and it was a good fit…someone to watch over Villa Riomar. Someone we could trust."

Listening quietly, Foti leaned back in his chair and crossed his legs before posing another question. "So, this violent episode you had on hypnotic drugs…when you stabbed your former husband…ah…in self-defense, of course. Any repeat episodes?"

Emotional, she squeezed her husband's hand. "Not since ditching the wrong prescription. You *do* know that Dan was murdered by Rosa, right before my eyes."

"I'm sorry," replied Foti. For the fifty-two-year-old detective, it was a rare show of sympathy for a deceased gangster and his widow.

"Since Katherine's help with my therapy, I no longer use mind-altering drugs or SSRIs. Even the newer SNRIs are prone to cause harmful side effects." With a sly smile, "I'm learning how to avoid psychotics, whether in pill or human form."

"Lucky you," quipped Foti, not disrespectfully.

"Lucky? She questioned. "Maybe someday, when luck can afford me."

Struck by her unpretentious attitude, Foti took a moment to study the couple anew. "Look. I know you two have been through a lot, but here's my dilemma. This is a murder investigation, and I have to weigh all the possibilities. Just so we can eliminate you both as suspects, can anyone confirm your whereabouts between six-forty-five and seven-thirty tonight?"

Annoyed with his new direction, Mark leaned toward him. "Frank, we came here voluntarily to help you find out who killed our friend. If you need a character reference, check with Dominic Beretto at the FBI's BAU. He'll vouch for us...and tell you about cases we've worked together."

Foti considered this. "So we can eliminate you as a suspect, I still need to know where you were when she was killed," he repeated calmly.

"We were waiting at her hotel door with a bottle--"

"Did anyone see you?"

"There was a valet at her door with us," answered Stella. "Tall slender guy with short dark hair. His nametag said 'Serge'."

Making a note, he pressed to hear more. "Anyone else?"

"No one answered, so the three of us went downstairs when we heard the screams," explained Mark. "By then we knew something awful had happened."

"Okay," setting down his pen to reach into his pocket. "Look, I know it's late, and I appreciate your cooperation," sliding a card across the table. "Any other details you can remember, call me."

Mark stuck the card in his shirt pocket. Shaking hands, they stood to leave as Foti added, "I'll be over with my CSI crew first thing tomorrow morning."

Mark held up his phone. "Your number's in my cell, Frank. Let's find out who did this."

PART II

Wide is the gate, and broad is the way, that leadeth to destruction.

-MATTHEW 7:13

SEVEN

A week before Tremelle's murder in Vero Beach, the weather turned stormy in nearby Indiantown. A series of early-morning thunderstorms came in from the northeast as predicted, blowing southwest across Stuart. The bluster was unusual, as most of Indiantown's bad weather usually came from the southwest across Lake Okeechobee.

The nor'easter's winds and lightning shook Dr. Christopher Hirt's older two-story cracker house right down to the foundation, threatening to blow out the frail glass windows that rattled violently with the fury of the storm. Two years ago, it was the only rentable house available within walking distance of Raiford State Prison when he began his prison term and agreed to two years of pro-bono inmate counseling.

Hirt rose at dawn, awakened by howling winds and heavy rain. Gayane's *Adagio* from Khachaturian's ballet suite filled his head, the mournful tune providing a feeling of solitude to the dream just ended. In the dream, he was cut and bleeding, trying to make his way out of endless mounds of broken champagne flutes. As a psychiatrist, he was aware that the mountains of broken glass were subconscious reminders of his punitive surroundings for the last two years. In three more days, his undeserved penance would be over and he would be free to leave this God-forsaken place.

The rows of textbooks on the bookcase behind him were filled with most of the great thinkers and theologians of Western culture. Though he absorbed their words into his erudite mind years ago, he had failed to embrace the essence of the texts; the meaning of God, and the very substance of humanity and civilization. At his sentencing hearing, the judge declared that the Devil wanted his soul, and for the last two years, Hirt struggled with the veracity of the judge's assessment. On a quest for vengeance, Hirt's regression had become his new pathway to glory.

Tracking her, his fingers danced over the computer keys in a search of her favorite sites. He was having trouble locating her on Face Book, Instagram and Twitter. The hundred or so pages of her social media interactions already lying on his bookshelf didn't seem enough, and the media photos that popped up on Google brought on a brief fantasy of her coming to answer the door with just the stereo on. He wanted to own her, to anticipate her every move. To counter the power she wielded over him, he reminded himself that surrendering to the momentary peace of intimacy could be just as savage as any attack.

In his mind, Hirt reverted to yet another review of the events that led to his incarceration. Weighing the duplicity of evidence presented to him two years ago, a federal magistrate was deciding whether the psychiatrist who faced felony aggravated assault and insider trading charges should be granted pretrial release.

On one hand, there was the case of the Vero Beach psychiatrist held in high esteem by his neighbors and peers, a respected condo owner and community member who, with no children of his own, once wrote a check for a straight-A high school graduate's college expenses after learning of the student's financial struggles.

On the other side of the coin, there was the case of the heavily-indebted physician living a playboy-style life of luxury beyond his means, the misguided psychiatrist who abused his profession and the trust of his patients for egregious monetary gain. This was the man who took unfair advantage of those who suffered from depression and their addiction to SSRIs, hypnotics and other mind-altering drugs, all with little or no regard for the lives of his patients.

Hirt had become "totally depraved" in his pursuit of a lavish lifestyle in his penthouse at Village Spires, federal prosecutors alleged, as the psychiatrist stood opposite them in the courtroom weeks after his arrest wearing orange prison garb and shackles.

A philanthropic Vero Beach woman tried to kill her husband because of Hirt's sole desire to make millions from what he knew to be a drug wrongfully prescribed, they said, and his timing on shorting the stock of Valiant Pharmaceuticals was entirely "beyond coincidence." Prosecutors maintained that Hirt was far too dangerous to be allowed to continue to practice medicine, or even to be granted bail.

The magistrate who called the case that day "one of the most heinous and heart-wrenching of his career" agreed, remanding Hirt to the custody of federal marshals as his defense attorney prepared to take the case to trial.

In an abrupt turn of events during the fifth week of trial, an emotional courtroom scene unfolded when Dr. Tremelle inexplicably recanted her testimony regarding Hirt's knowledge of the side effects of ambienna and seraquim. There was unproven speculation of witness tampering and, as a result, felony aggravated assault charges against Hirt were dropped. A week later, a jury of twelve clinched his conviction on the remaining lesser charges. At the federal courthouse in Fort Lauderdale, jurors spent less than six hours to find the psychiatrist guilty on the remaining charges of medical malpractice and insider trading. With the short list of Hirt's "good deeds" considered, the Vero Beach psychiatrist received two years and a suspended license with the opportunity for reinstatement on the condition of performing pro bono inmate counseling during his incarceration.

"Let your experiences wash over you," he would tell his inmate patients, "...absorbing them like a sponge, then deny them. Have no expectations. Only then will you be prepared for what follows." Aiming the words at the hearts of the weak and the desperate, he refused to take his own advice out of resentment for having to provide it free of charge to criminally insane patients.

Disgusted with Indiantown's redneck surroundings, he'd been forced to live close to the Forensics Treatment Center for what seemed like an eternity. At the end of the week, he would finally be free to make his move to Delmar. Though the Vero Beach condo was only 90 miles northeast, it was worlds away in lifestyle. The century-old frame house he'd been living in was a far cry from the Village Spires beachfront penthouse he was forced to forfeit as part of his restitution and plea bargain for insider trading. He was indeed fortunate they hadn't found his main cache of wealth, his $19 million collection of near-flawless diamonds, a hoard that took him an entire career to build. The anonymous use of Bitcoin in his diamond transactions proved to be a fool-proof way of eliminating a paper trail.

No matter how dark Hirt found his patients' secrets to be, they were never as depraved as his own. Hurtful images of retribution smothered his brain. Techniques used in patient interviews came to mind, like "finish this sentence: no one knows that I…"

He thought of the last two years of his life as an unending date with battery acid. His resentment also extended to the reporters who focused solely on spinning events to create the next farcical headline. In so many instances, the media shouted the accusations but whispered the rebuttal. There could be no doubt that the hour would come where he would show them and set the record straight. Though peace-of-mind proved elusive for him, he found solace in knowing that vengeance was, indeed, a dish best served cold, and it was time for Vero Beach to pay up.

Standing at the head of the table, team leader Det. Lt. Foti pointed at the large glass façade that dominated the meeting room. The digital story-board was illustrated with color photos of suspects, key bullet points and persons-of-interest, all automatically uploaded from the NCIC database along with the tablets and PCs on the table as they became available in real time.

In the center of the storyboard was Dr. Tremelle's press photo, with her uncanny resemblance to Katherine Zeta-Jones. The victim's photo was surrounded by those of Dr. Christopher Hirt, Dr. Bruce Talcott, Dr. Anton Marchenko and his bodyguard, Boris Yakovlev. With the latest links and taglines appearing underneath each photo, the display was updated in real time by streaming data from the NCIC and the team's own computer links.

Stepping to the board, Foti tapped on Marchenko's image to enlarge it. "Currently, he's our lead suspect. Motive, opportunity, nasty personality, and now this. Got a bad feeling about this guy." The detective put a finger on the tag line that mentioned the presence of his DNA on the victim.

Sitting at the table, ranking officer Det. Capt. John Garrett contemplated the storyboard that seemed to ooze with such nauseating permutations. Somewhere in that mass of data was the truth, but some stories just refused to be easily told. People liked the truth delivered in nice neat packages, and this one looked it was going to get messy.

Foti continued. "By the way, captain, we've got an investigative journalist here in town who'd like to help in our investigation. Happens he was a friend of the vic."

"I heard some scuttlebutt about that. McAllister?"

"Yes, sir."

Garrett considered Foti's idea. "You trust him?"

"Yes sir, I do."

"Couldn't hurt. Heard he's got some keen profiling insights. Bring him in and keep him posted. Make sure he signs a waiver of liability and confidentiality agreement."

"Will do, sir."

Foti fixated on the daunting wall of information and looked around the table. "So, short of waterboarding our prime suspect, how do we sort this out?"

The team was quiet as they waited for Garrett's guidance. "Frank, here's what's bothering me. I'd hate to think your dislike of Ukrainians is affecting your objectivity here. And we still don't have a murder weapon." One by one, the two techs and Detective Heaton subtly concurred with Garrett. "How were you able to get a DNA match without a warrant?" he asked his lieutenant.

"Marchenko's DNA was on file in Interpol's database for a prior violent felony. Turns out, before he was a doctor, he was running guns for the Russian mob." Cocking his head, "I wonder how much he paid for his medical degree." Shrugging, he added, "Apparently, just about anything's for sale in the former Soviet Union."

Pushing the blonde hair from her eyes, Technical Officer Margo Violette flipped a page in her file. "Dossier says he's a research biochemist."

"PhD," clarified Locke as he tightened the knot on his tie. "Looks like mother was the invention of necessity."

Foti shot a confused look at him. "What?"

Annoyed with her coworker's continual misquotes of popular clichés, Violette chimed in. "He means--"

Garrett frowned, waving his hand in dismissal. "Never mind. Gary, get on with it."

Locke scanned his file and cleared his throat, launching into a summary of his findings to date. "I'll give ya the bullet points."

"Fine," agreed Foti. "Let's skip the clichés."

Locke nodded and pointed to the story-board photos. "Ligature marks on the neck suggest the unsub was left-handed, likely male. Broken fingernails on the victim indicate defensive wounds, so she likely put up a fight. Burn mark on the right side of her neck also indicates the unsub was left handed. At first we thought the puncture wound in her medulla might be from an ice pick. Then we noticed the faint scent of narcotics in her hair and, at first, we thought maybe it was from her shampoo.

But when we found traces of fentanyl in her blood, we determined the puncture was caused by a hypodermic needle, probably a fourteen gauge that delivered about ten ccs of pure fentanyl. More than enough to cause death within seconds."

"What are we officially listing as the COD?" asked Garrett.

"Acute fentanyl overdose leading to myocardial infarction and asphyxiation."

Detective Heaton looked up from his notes to make a final point. "The perp made no attempt to hide the needle mark, indicating he was in a hurry. My guess is Tremelle was overpowered in the stairway to avoid the security cameras."

Garrett nodded. "And our ME concurs with your forensic findings?"

"Yes, sir."

"Good work, Gary." Garrett surveyed his team for more evidence. "What else we got?" No one spoke up. "Okay, people, let's focus. C'mon," clapping his hands together.

Heeding his boss's call to action, Foti stepped up. "When I met with him at Waldo's, I noticed Marchenko's a lefty. He's got both motive and opportunity, and I'd say we have enough to bring 'em in for questioning," looking around the table. "His bodyguard, a big brute named Yakovlev, has priors as well. Kind of a Neanderthal, looks like he could take an hour-and-a-half to watch *60 Minutes*." Amused with the assessment, Garrett looked around the table for a consensus. Heaton and the two tech officers nodded in support of Foti's conclusion.

Garrett leaned back and stretched. "You'll never get the answers you want to hear...no matter who you talk to," he declared, pushing back from the table. "I'd like to avoid any diplomatic entanglements. Son-of-a-gun's probably halfway to the Ukraine by now."

Foti reached into Violette's file for the two Ukrainian passports, holding them up like they were winning lottery tickets. "Not without these."

"Good work, Frank," commended Garret. "All right. You and Dennis go bring 'em in," with a sweep of his hand, "...and remember, keep it right down the fairway. I don't want anything coming back on us. Let's try and keep the FBI and the Ukrainian consulate out of this one. Margo, you and Gary call the hotels and check the CCTV again. Find out where Marchenko's stayin' with that 400-pound gorilla of his and let's put him on a leash. Cross check his known associates and give Frank and Dennis all the support they need in the field."

Garrett gave the team a stern look and headed toward his office. "Gary, maybe you could brush up on those clichés."

"Preachin' to the congregation, boss."

"That's *choir*, Gary," corrected Garrett. "Preachin' to the *choir*. And don't talk to me again until you have something useful to say."

"Yes, sir."

EIGHT

The Howard Johnson's hotel hallway smelled like a high school locker room at the height of summer. Wearing sunglasses, Hard Rock Café T-shirt and faded blue jeans, Hirt crept cautiously down the airport hotel's corridor with his leather satchel, trying to blend in as he scanned the heavily-stained carpet. With a myriad of colors, it looked as though it had already been baptized with all twenty-eight flavors at one time or another. Eyeing the peeling paint and chipped plaster, the deplorable conditions made him wonder if indoor plumbing was a perc at the hotel.

A few feet from room 214, he turned to pace back and forth, listening for clues about the occupants before stopping to check his watch. Ten minutes ahead of his scheduled meeting time, he leaned back against the wall, lit a cigarette and thought about how best to handle the tip he'd gotten from his bag man Max Croaker.

Known in all the dive bars up and down the Treasure Coast for his tie-dyed shirts, short stocky build, beady eyes, and the psychedelic VW van, he had more shady connections than a two-hundred-foot oak tree. For years, Croaker was well-connected with Vero's subculture, and by the time Hirt met him in prison, the bag man already had a fifteen-year-long rap sheet decorated with drug busts, assaults, and robberies gone bad. But for Hirt, Croaker's street profile and countless dealer connections made him an ideal front man for helping the tarnished psychiatrist expand his network.

Resentful over having to ante up five bucks apiece for the fentanyl capsules, Hirt was sure the price would have been half that two years ago. The sourness faded slightly as he remembered Croaker saying the market in Vero was tight and the pills were now fetching fifty bucks apiece.

The local paper reported that demand for the fentanyl-laced fake oxycodone was so strong that New York and Florida had doubled law enforcement efforts and declared a public health emergency due to a spike in fentanyl-related deaths. In the past week, Federal prosecutors filed charges against a Florida smuggler caught at the Mexican border with seven duffle bags of fake oxycodone pills made with Chinese fentanyl in the latest sign that Mexican drug cartels were targeting U.S. addicts. In Hirt's mind, the victims were just another page in the stack of drug overdoses.

Stubbing out his cigarette butt on the frayed carpet, he approached the door to score his forty-thousand tabs of fake oxycodone.

At Waldo's on Ocean Drive, Mark checked his watch as he waited at the seaside table for Dominic Beretto, Supervising Agent at the FBI's Behavioral Analysis Unit in Atlanta. It was five-fifty p.m. and happy hour was just about to end as he ordered another half-price Cordon Bleu. Coming straight from a fundraiser, he felt overdressed in the black Brioni suit, not having time to change into something more casual.

After some chit-chat with his waitress, he sat for a few moments and sipped his cognac, listening to the ambient sounds of the bistro. The clinking of glasses, soft laughter and the sound of breaking waves on the beach provided the backdrop for mulling over events of the last few days. Someone dropped some coins in the jukebox, and the popular Righteous Brothers sixties hit "You've Lost That Lovin' Feelin'" filled the half-empty lounge. The tune had a magical effect on the patrons sitting at the bar, bringing back memories of a time that was perhaps more innocent, and maybe less complicated.

Weeknights at the beachside bistro tended to be more subdued, and the senior singles on the hunt for their next well-to-do spouse had not yet arrived for the mating game that colored the early-evening banter.

Like all married people, sometimes he entertained the idea of being single again as he met the gaze of an attractive blue-eyed blonde sitting at the bar. Maybe not today, but someday his idiotic flirtations would land him in hot water. Casting flirty looks wasn't always intentional, but now it was too late to avert her interest, her eyes flickering in recognition as she rose from her seat, martini in hand.

"Mr. McAllister," striding gracefully across the floor, "...Carolyn Hyde from the Save Our Turtles Foundation." Her hand felt soft and sensual in his grasp. "I wanted to personally thank you and your wife for your generous donation." Sticking to business, he pretended to be unaware that her eyes were asking for more than an introduction. From their brief phone conversation last week, he remembered Carolyn spoke a bit of French.

"*De rien*. Stella and I enjoy supporting worthy environmental causes. She'll be here shortly, if you want to..." glancing at his watch. Knowing how territorial his wife could be, he was hoping Carolyn would decline his polite offer to join him.

She sensed that her timing was a little off for anything other than a brief flirtation. "Uh, well...I'm meeting someone at the bar for dinner," gesturing over her shoulder. "I *did* want to meet you and offer you my thanks. Rain check, then?"

"You got it." Relieved, he smiled politely.

He turned his attention back to his anticipated meeting with Beretto and checked his watch again. Six o'clock. Beretto should be along shortly. His mood turned darker as he thought of his friend Katherine who'd taken her last breaths at Vero Beach Resort just around the corner. Still, he could make little sense of her murder. He felt a friendly pat on his shoulder.

"Knew I'd find you here. Join you?"

Mark turned to shake Beretto's outstretched hand as he took a seat and set his Ray Bans on the table. "How long has it been? Coupla years? Looks like Bora Bora's been kind to you, Mark."

"Thought maybe you stopped off for some donuts," leaning back to regard the FBI profiler. With salt-and-pepper hair, the special agent was fiftyish and sported a black polo and khaki Dockers, the sallow face and rugged good looks reminding him of a Clint Eastwood stunt double.

"You still dating the gangster's widow?" asked Beretto with a twinkle in his eye.

"Married the hottie. Only because she promised me an exclusive on her story," grinning at his FBI buddy.

"I'll bet!" The special agent turned serious for a moment. "I was very sorry to hear about your friend Dr. Tremelle. Even though she recanted it, I recall her testimony had its affect in bringing down Hirt."

They were interrupted by the waitress as she placed a napkin on the table in front of Beretto. "Can I get you something, sir?"

"Jameson on the rocks, and," focusing on her nametag, "…another cognac for Mr. McAllister, Melinda."

The waitress gave Mark a second look. "Thought you looked familiar. I'll be right back with your drinks."

With Melinda out of earshot, Beretto added, "Compliments of the FBI."

Mark continued. "After all that drama with Rosa and Hirt, Stella and I needed a long vacation. I heard they paroled him." He thought about his wife's concerns. "You're keeping tabs on him, right?" Beretto winced at the question.

"That's what I wanted to talk with you about. So far, it appears he's operating within the law since he resumed his practice, but it's a mystery how he stays so busy. Foti's men spot check his patients from time-to-time. Calls his office the 'Pain Free Clinic'. Look, you understand these sickos as well as any of us at the BAU, and I've already got a list of physician suspects long enough to staff a hospital. So, your perspective is always welcome."

"I can offer you my insights, Dom, but I doubt if my list of suspects is much different than yours."

"Don't sell yourself short."

Mark took a moment to reflect on what he knew. "Okay. At the top, I would put Marchenko, followed by Drs. Hirt, Talcott and Callaway. Pretty rough list. If they opened a practice together, I doubt if they'd be eligible for Medicare reimbursements."

Not unappreciative of his humor, Beretto gave him a tight smile and finished a notation in his notepad. "Hirt's got an alibi."

"You interview him?"

"Detective Garner did. Some slacker named Max Croaker and twelve other low-life pool players claim Hirt was with them at a west side bar named Kelley's Pub the night she was murdered." Foti rolled his eyes and returned to his notes. "Why Callaway?"

"Dr. Nancy Callaway headed up Oconix's Research Division before Katherine was handed the top spot by the CEO," explained Mark. "According to her, it was a bitter rivalry after Katherine threatened to blow the lid off Callaway's affair with her boss while her husband was in a hospice dying of Alzheimer's."

"Screwing her boss while her husband's on his deathbed? Ice water in the veins," was Beretto's diagnosis.

The author nodded. "Like the proverbial black widow, maybe Dr. Callaway wanted a head start on finding her next mate, even while her husband's brain was being biopsied," glancing at a familiar couple on the beach before continuing. "Katherine often confided in Stella when it came to personal matters. Apparently, Dr. Callaway had quite the reputation for screwing her way to the top." He paused for a moment as Steppenwolf's "Born To Be Wild" played from the jukebox in the background, amused by the irony.

"How'd the FBI get drawn into this?" asked Mark.

Beretto propped his elbow on the table and gazed out over the beach. "While the early bird gets the worm, it's the second mouse that gets the cheese," he replied cryptically. "A little different this time with Hirt. Not only are we trying to catch a killer, a killer we believe is a delusional psychopath, we're trying to prevent a potentially deadly drug from reaching the streets in quantity."

"And you think Hirt is part of that?"

Beretto shrugged. "Possibly, but can't get a warrant without probable cause." He took a gulp of his Jameson. "We believe Tremelle's murderer maybe trying to draw attention to his own perceived mistreatment...a delusional psychopath committed to playing out his ultimate vengeance. Hirt maintained his innocence during the entire malpractice and insider trading trial."

"I remember. So, is that your team's consensus on the unsub's profile?"

Beretto nodded. "We think it could be payback for having been wronged in some way. So, we think there's a connection between the fake oxycodone and Tremelle's murder."

Mark agreed with the assessment. "Well, whoever's behind it, they're putting fentanyl into fake pills and passing them off as legitimate prescriptions when they're actually fifty to a hundred times more deadly. So, the unsub's motive may go beyond uncontrolled greed."

Beretto added, "We're coordinating with the DEA, and Detective Foti is helping with the local legwork."

"Foti's a pitbull on steroids when it comes to high profile cases like this," commented Mark. "Who knows? Maybe he'll be our next sheriff."

Beretto grew philosophical. "Look, maybe I've blown out too many birthday candles to moralize on this, but let's not overlook the three thousand Floridians who died from fake oxycodone last year."

Mark pondered his point as he recalled the "comfortably numb" Moody Blues lyric. "Makes you wonder who's to blame for someone like Callaway, or Hirt, or Marchenko. Broken home? Babysitter drug addict? Society in general? Or none of the above?"

Their conversation was interrupted by Beretto's ringing phone. Noticing the absence of the caller's number, he figured it had to be a burner. Curious, he answered anyway.

"Beretto."

A man's voice asked, "Dominic Beretto...of the FBI?"

The agent gestured for silence. "Who's this?"

"The man who's gonna help you solve Tremelle's murder."

"I'm listening."

"Got your notepad handy?"

"Yup," reaching into his pocket.

"You might want to talk to a maid named Maria Ramirez at the Vero Beach Resort about a lovers' quarrel in Tremelle's room the night before she died."

"Maria Ramirez, huh?" jotting down the name, giving Mark a skeptical look. "Tell me, how'd you get this number?"

"Ain't technology grand?" The sarcasm was followed by an eerie silence as the anonymous caller hung up.

NINE

The day had gotten off to a rough start and promised to be as unpredictable as Foti's first day at the academy when he'd nearly gotten kicked out of Quantico for getting into a bar room brawl. Luckily, nothing that day had been broken except his pride.

Dr. Marchenko had called him earlier and demanded the return of his passport, but the detective had negotiated some conditions of his own, insisting on a "brief" Q & A at the station. Marchenko had reluctantly agreed and arrived at the appointed hour of five p.m. His entourage included his beefy protégé Yakovlev and a white-haired, soft-spoken gentleman he introduced as his attorney, Marv Goldstein.

Dressed like a crew of high-flying Vegas casino owners, the threesome arrived at the station in a shiny black Mercedes limo bearing a Ukrainian license plate, and Mr. Goldstein's voice seemed to match his appearance. Fluent in English and Ukrainian, and dressed in an expensive dove-grey suit, Marchenko's attorney seemed to provide the finesse lacked by his portly clients. He wore diamond and gold cufflinks and his shoes were of similar quality, crafted from lizard at about twelve hundred bucks a pair.

A uniformed officer ushered them into Interview Room #1 where Foti offered them nothing but a chair, making little effort to hide his disdain for oily Ukrainians and the attorneys who represented them. To balance the muscle in the room, Foti had beefy six-foot-four Sgt. Garner standing behind him as he set some terms for the interview.

"Mr. Goldstein, I'm going to interview Mr. Yakovlev separately after I finish with your boss. Please have him wait outside until he's called."

As Yakovlev started toward the door, Goldstein cautioned him. "Boris, speak to no one until I join you." The taciturn bodyguard dutifully nodded and reached into his shirt pocket for his special brand of black cigarettes as he turned to light up.

Foti was irked over the man's disregard for the non-smoking signs. "Mr. Yakovlev, this entire facility is a non-smoking area. You can smoke outside the building until you are summoned."

"What you do, arrest me for smoking?" Smirking, Yakovlev stepped into the hallway and lit one up as he headed outside.

Motioning for the men to sit, Foti waited until they were comfortably seated before addressing their point man. "Mr. Goldstein, do you also represent ZTE Pharmaceuticals?"

Adjusting the fit of his suit like a professor about to speak at his pulpit, Goldstein answered, "Dr. Marchenko and his employees are my only clients." Turning to Marchenko, Goldstein voiced something in Ukrainian, prompting Foti to reiterate his ground rules.

"Gentlemen, let's speak in English, with the clear understanding that any contrition would be viewed favorably later. Agreed?" Foti took their silence as tacit agreement. It was obvious the Ukrainians disliked being dragged into the interview as much as Foti disliked having to interrogate them.

After fifteen minutes of questioning, the interview turned out to be a repeat of Marchenko's original statements at Waldo's in which he denied having anything to do with Tremelle's murder. As proof of his client's whereabouts at the time of her death, Goldstein laid out on the table printed time-stamped photos taken by Marchenko and Yakovlev mingling with other conference attendees. Frustrated with having no valid grounds to hold the men, Foti prepared to return their passports before taking one last shot at exposing the truth.

"Dr. Marchenko, how many shares of ZTE Pharmaceuticals do you own, sir?"

Marchenko waited for his attorney's nod of approval before answering. "About one-hundred-fifty-thousand shares."

Foti raised his eyebrows. "So, at two-hundred-seventy-eight dollars a share, that comes to--"

"You do math," smirked Marchenko, shrugging again. "Is a capitalist country, no? I am guilty because I make money?"

Foti glared at him. "That gives you forty-three million reasons to take her out," raising his voice. "And how did the news of Dr. Tremelle's death affect the value of your company's stock?" With their main competitor's research genius now deceased, the question was clearly rhetorical. Marchenko gave him an uncomfortable shrug.

"How could my client accurately predict the market action of such a tragedy?" asked Goldstein. Tired of the stonewalling, Foti studied the men like two insects under a microscope, concluding it was time for a break. Knowing his captain had been watching the interview from the next room, Foti stood to regroup with Capt. Garrett, leaving Sgt. Garner and the uniformed officer to stand over his suspect.

In the adjoining room, Garrett eyed his lieutenant sternly. "We can't hold him, Frank. We've got nothing."

"He's dirty, John."

"Then get me some hard evidence. While we're young."

"I want to hold his passport for a few more days. At least he won't be leaving the country."

Looking impatient, Garrett folded his arms. "We don't need a diplomatic incident in our Mayberry-By-The-Sea here, Frank. Bad PR, and bad for business."

"By the time any complaint goes through diplomatic channels, I'll either charge him or return his passport. Five days. I'm tellin' ya, he's *dirty*."

Garrett unfolded his arms. "Against my better judgment, I'll give you three days. That's it. If we get any complaints, that's on you." The lieutenant nodded and returned to finish the interview.

Leaning over the table toward the seated Ukrainians, Foti was adamant. "All right. Here's what we're gonna do. You're free to go, but I'm holding your passports until we can completely clear you both. For your protection," he added.

Goldstein sat forward, placing his elbows on the table. "And there will be no criminal charges?"

"Not for now, pending the investigation. I'll need your clients to stay in Vero for the remainder of the week, just until we can clear a few things up."

"Is my client still a suspect?"

"Let's just say he's a person of interest," meeting Marchenko's eyes with a steely glare.

Clearly unhappy with the arrangement, the two Ukrainians stood to leave, giving Foti a surly look. No one was surprised when there were no gentlemanly handshakes offered. Stopping at the door, Goldstein added some pressure of his own. "If we don't have my clients' passports back by end of week, I will be filing complaint with American Consulate in Miami."

"Fair enough," answered Foti, gesturing through the two-way mirror to bring in their next person-of-interest.

After learning that Dr. Callaway was on her way in, the lieutenant ushered Yakovlev into the room for questioning. Following another twenty minutes of fruitless interrogation, Foti was ready to get off the Ukrainian merry-go-round and escorted them back into the hallway where Marchenko and Goldstein waited. Frustrated, he watched as the three left the police station, well-dressed, but unimpeded and uncharged.

Burdened with his inability to unearth new evidence, Foti stepped into the meeting room with his team for a consult to plan their next move. While his team pointed out that Drs. Callaway and Talcott had motive and opportunity, the lieutenant remained skeptical that either of them were capable of murder. Ravenous for clues, Foti sat on the edge of the desk and scrutinized the storyboard with his team.

Deeper into the rabbit hole they descended

71

Minutes later, Dr. Nancy Callaway entered the interview room with Foti while his team watched through the two-way mirror. The slender research physician was wearing a low-cut sundress and wedge heels that showcased her taut legs, and Foti was guessing it was an attempt to distract him. Preparing his first question, he sat on the corner of the table, focusing on her body language and facial expressions.

"Why didn't you tell me that you and Dr. Tremelle had heated arguments when we first spoke?" he asked calmly.

Glancing at the mirror, she crossed her legs slowly as if she were being interviewed by a TV talk show host. She appeared overly calm and answered matter-of-factly. "Our projects are typically run independently, so sometimes my apparent lack of candor...is really the result of being compromised by my not having all the facts." To Foti, she seemed slightly sedated, and from her dilated pupils and relaxed posture, Foti guessed the drug of choice to be a valium or two.

Hiding his skepticism, he encouraged her to ramble on. "Sometimes we find ourselves in awkward situations. When *men* are jealous of your success in the lab, it's because they covet it for themselves. But...when *women* want to take it from you, they don't care if they get it-they just want to deny it for their counterpart." Pausing, she offered her non-sequitur summary; "Sometimes institutions turn us against each other."

"Is that a confession?" asked Foti.

Startled, Callaway looked up at him. "Of course not. A dozen co-workers can vouch that I was seated in the auditorium before Katherine's death. Did we always get along? No." Taking a sip from her water bottle, she continued.

"My co-workers know that *I'm* the genius. Katherine got lucky when our CEO assigned her the more promising edulimab project. Genius isn't just one great idea. It involves thousands of hours of hard work." Mesmerized by the enormity of her ego, Foti recognized he was wading through the swamp of another clear case of the "God complex" and allowed her to continue. "I've been with Oconix nine years before

Katherine's arrival, longer than any other research physician, with four successful projects."

Foti cocked his head and gave her a skeptical look. "I understand you tried to take over Dr. Tremelle's last project, when your candidate in development was failing to meet the clinical end points."

"Where'd you hear that?"

"Dr. Talcott."

"Not exactly what I would call an unbiased source. You do know that Bruce and Katherine were lovers, right? They had an extremely volatile relationship, and I'm sure he'd love to pin this all on me."

Surprised, Foti was jotting down the details in his notepad, adding to his list of questions for Talcott. Flipping backwards through his pad, Foti stopped occasionally to decipher his own sloppy handwriting. Finished with his review, he slipped the notes into his jacket pocket as their eyes met.

"Anything else?"

"Yeah. Anyone ever mention you look like Clint Eastwood?" as she uncrossed her legs.

Foti smirked at her ploy. "Dr. Callaway, you're free to go."

Dr. Hirt sipped his expresso as he stood watching the sunrise from his third-floor office on the corner of Ocean Drive and Azalea Lane. Made from premium Illy expresso to ward off the yawning, and a splash of cognac to ward off reality, it had become a Monday morning ritual.

Across Ocean Drive, the wide expanse between Costa d'Este and Waldo's afforded him a colorful view of the sun rising slowly above the sea. The scene took him back to his misspent youth growing up as a surfer at Cocoa Beach High.

The reluctant son of an abusive father, his adolescence was scarred by frequent beatings from an alcoholic parent who couldn't control his temper; a man who would frequently kick and punch him, often without reason. Once, when he was five and had put too much jam on his toast at breakfast, Hirt remembered his father backhanded him so hard it knocked him out of his chair, the split lip requiring six stitches. The other small facial scar was on his forehead, a memento from being thrown into a window for forgetting to put his surfboard away.

The unending paternal abuse caused Hirt to grow up with a chip on his shoulder the size of a California redwood. To escape his restrained adolescence, he worked hard in high school, earning himself a college scholarship to facilitate the exit from the hamster wheel. Such were the childhood memories he tried to forget as he watched the sun climb higher above the horizon.

Shifting his attention to his immediate surroundings, the older offices of stone and concrete along Ocean Drive were originally built without ductwork and difficult to air condition properly. Even in January, the days were short but seldom cold, and the Florida heat and humidity could be uncomfortable even in winter. He could add a few window air conditioners, he supposed, but his affluent neighbors might object. Business owners were fanatical about appearances, and that might bring his illicit operation unwanted attention he could ill afford.

Hirt checked his watch. Seven-forty. Arriving before his staff, he was prepared to sign for the large oxycodone and Vicodin delivery due any minute. To fool any surveillance, he needed the legitimate shipments to provide the camouflage for what most of his patients really wanted; the heavy-duty stuff laced with fentanyl.

The shrill warning from the downstairs security buzzer interrupted his reverie. Glancing at the security monitor, he was pleased to see the delivery man leaning into the camera with four boxes in his arms. Within minutes, Hirt had the entire shipment secured in his two-ton Mesa safe well before his receptionist was due to arrive at eight-thirty. Satisfied with the contents of the delivery, he snagged the clipboard from Laura's desk to identify his first patient for the day.

"Duncan Hines?" he read aloud, thoroughly entertained by some of the aliases as he flipped through the schedule.

"Cake boy, huh?" laughing to himself. "Hope you got lotsa cash, cake boy."

Acting on the anonymous caller's tip, Foti headed west on Beachland Boulevard in his city-issued black Ford Explorer with Sgt. Garner. His sergeant was the proverbial strong silent type, and Foti took advantage of the sergeant's muted demeanor to give him time to think. They'd just finished a detailed twenty-minute interview with Maria Ramirez, chamber maid at the Vero Beach Resort and Spa. From the lover's quarrel the maid had described, his gut instinct had proven correct; Talcott was hiding something, and he was on his way to exposing the truth.

A light rain began to decorate his windshield and he hit his wipers. Losing larger in the less, his mind drifted to what his dying wife had whispered to him in the oncology wing at Indian River Medical Center. Five years ago today, Foti had no idea it would be the last day of her life. With her whispered words, she had breathed into his atmosphere a subtle malaria that he'd yet to shake.

Her last words brought back the empty hollowness inside him with the same raft of unanswered questions whenever he thought of her. Was her suffering any less because she valued goodness? Who were you that I shared a bed with? Was a friend to? He thought about her smile and the magic of her touch before turning away from her memory to refocus on the grisly murder case that consumed him today.

Questions. Lots of unanswered questions. A decorated officer who had risen through the ranks, his goal of retiring on a captain's pension remained in his sights. Some of his oversights made him feel like an underachiever who was looking back on his lucky breaks after they were gone, making him feel like he'd been given the gift of foresight retroactively.

His private pity party was interrupted as a car unexpectedly pulled out in front of him, bringing him back to the reason for his trip to Melbourne. As he tapped the brakes, he looked over at Sgt. Garner, who'd grown accustomed to his periods of deep thought.

To their right, the curved glass façade of Oconix Pharmaceutical swung into view. Slowing to make the turn into the main driveway, Foti was impressed with the curved four-story contemporary architecture and the guard-gate security, all very state-of-the-art.

After clearing the security gatehouse and parking the SUV, to Garner he said, "Let's find out what Dr. Talcott has to say about his murdered girlfriend."

"You got it, boss," slamming the door to punctuate his agreement.

Making their way inside the lobby, a muscular security guard wearing a Navy blazer called out to them as they approached the bank of elevators. Crossing the marble lobby to intercept them, the young guard with a military-style haircut proved to be more cooperative after Foti flashed his detective shield.

"Can I help you, officers?"

"Where can I find Dr. Bruce Talcott?"

"Southeast corner office, suite 401, I believe. Is he expecting you, sir?"

The detective gave him a half-hearted smile. "It's a surprise. You don't need to call him," as the elevator door closed. Foti and Garner stepped off on the fourth floor and found their way to Talcott's office. Tapping on the opaque glass door, Foti pushed it open to reveal the colorful backdrop, a panoramic view of the Intracoastal Waterway. Dressed in a black silk tie and white lab coat, Talcott was studying images on three computer screens when he glanced up and recognized Foti.

"Ah, Lieutenant Foti. What a surprise," swiveling in his chair to give Foti his full attention. "What can I do for you?"

"This is Sgt. Garner, and we have some questions, Dr. Talcott. Mind if we sit? Won't take long," taking seats in the leather chairs without waiting for an answer.

The doctor seemed annoyed with Foti's presumptuousness. "By all means, have a seat," gesturing toward the chairs with his hollow invitation.

"I'll get right to the point," declared Foti, pressing his palm on the desk. "Why did you lie to me about your relationship with Dr. Tremelle? Obstruction of justice is a serious crime, doctor."

"What do you mean?"

Annoyed with Talcott's dumb blonde act, Foti was losing patience. "Stop lying to me, Talcott. I could have Sgt. Garner here take you into custody if you like."

They were interrupted by the doctor's assistant who appeared suddenly in the doorway. "Everything okay here, Dr. Talcott?"

"Fine, Natalie," waving her off. "Will you close the door on your way out?" The men watched as the pert blonde in the lab coat did as requested.

Foti continued. "Just had an interesting conversation with a chambermaid at the Vero Beach Resort. She stated she saw you leave Tremelle's room after a loud argument the night before her murder. You were obviously having an affair with her." He leaned forward to press his point, raising his voice a notch. "Now, I want the *truth*! What happened between you two?"

Feeling cornered, Talcott planted his elbows on the desktop and ran his hands through his hair. "I didn't kill her...I loved Katherine." Foti continued to glare at him. "That night, she sent me to find Marchenko, and..." retrieving the dime-shaped transmitter from his top drawer, "...plant this on him." With his fingertip, he slid the device across the desk for Foti to inspect.

The detective studied it for a moment before reaching into his coat pocket for his evidence kit. With a pair of tweezers, he carefully grasped the tiny recorder and dropped it into a clear plastic baggie.

"I'll have forensics examine it," declared Foti as they stood to leave. "The origin of these kinds of devices is usually traceable. If you're *lyin'* to me again, Talcott, I'll be back with a warrant for you," looking around the room, "...and everything else in your waterfront den of iniquity, or whatever it is you do here."

Apprehensive, Talcott stood and extended his hand for a parting handshake. "Lt. Foti, I apologize for not telling the truth in our first conversation. I was nervous." Foti and Garner continued to stare at him. "Look, I want to find Katherine's killer as much as anyone, and I will do anything I can do to help. I mean it."

Opening the office door, Garner stepped into the hallway as Foti stopped with a parting remark. "For your sake, I hope so, Talcott." Gesturing toward the waterfront vista, "Nice view. Be a shame to replace it with four concrete walls."

TEN

It was a beautiful morning as they crested the Merrill P. Barber Bridge in their vintage white '53 XK 120. High over the Intracoastal Waterway, Mark downshifted and took a deep breath of fresh air at the very top. The couple enjoyed taking the classic Jag out for short hops around town, and along with the magnificent view, they were enjoying the sweet scent of salt air, the seventy-degree weather, and the deep-throated growl from the big V-8. Before leaving Villa Riomar, he'd tuned the four SU carburetors and put the Navy blue top up for her to reduce the windage inside the two seater. From the smile on her face, he could tell the V-8's vibrations and low guttural sounds were having their desired effect.

Cresting the big bridge opened up a breath-taking panoramic view of the Vero Beach Yacht Club and city marina to the north, and a vista of high-end waterfront residences to the south. The sunshine sparkled off the aqua water like a sea of gems, and the well-marked waterway was dotted with a string of sailboats, sport fisherman and trawlers meandering up and down the channel in no particular hurry, all in pursuit of their slice of paradise.

Entertained by an internet article on her phone, Stella made herself comfortable in the sumptuous Corinthian leather seat. Without looking up, she said, "We're having people for dinner tonight."

"You must get me the recipe," he replied, amused with her syntax.

79

She thought that was funny and hit his arm playfully as she read him a blog aloud. "Here we go, honey; a Chinese entrepreneur making some great points about social media. The guy's a former thoracic surgeon from Hong Kong."

"Really. My gut feeling is that he'll share the innards of his observations with us."

"You're hilarious."

Checking his fender-mounted rear view mirrors, he steered into the left lane as he prepared for the turn onto Indian River Boulevard. "Want to give me the inside scoop?"

Smiling to herself so as not to encourage him, "He says social media is creating a society that confuses popularity with truth. He says social media has become a group of advertising facing organizations and people that can't tell the difference between real news, fake news and opinion news." She looked up at him for a reaction. "How true is that?"

"You want the *truth*!!?" in his best imitation of Tom Cruise's famous line. "You can't handle the *truth*!!"

"Will you be serious?"

"Okay. If I must. Some of it excites me, and some of it scares the hell out of me. And sometimes I can't tell the difference either." He thought about Bitcoin. "Speaking of virtual vulnerabilities, think of all the fools pouring their hard-earned money into *faux* virtual currency only to have it disappear into the cyber void with an untraceable hack."

Scrolling with her finger, "Uh-huh. Check this out. He goes on to say that fake news is the cancer of our time and social media sites are the metastasis of our news flow that cause us to confuse a popular view with truth." Looking over at him, "Agree?"

Nodding, he thought about how true it seemed. "Very insightful, but how does he suggest we change it?" swerving to miss a minivan pulling into his lane. "Should we outlaw governance via Twitter?"

"Insist on verifiable truth and oversight. You already know I've boycotted all my social media accounts until they can guarantee my privacy."

"Don't hold your breath." He shot her a skeptical look as she continued.

"I read on the internet that this is about the war for attention. They're perpetually redesigning social media to actually up the dopamine levels in the brain, making it more addictive. Think about it. The more clicks, the more money."

"The only thing I'm addicted to is *you*, honey," squeezing her bare knee and steering her away from such *Weltschmerz* to get her to lighten up. Turning onto Miracle Mile, "You still worry about Hirt?"

"Not as long as he's not worried about me." Caressing his shoulder, "Besides, I've got you now."

Accustomed to having their XK ogled by the island gentry, he watched them passing in the opposite lane in their Mercedes and BMWs, waiting patiently for the traffic to clear before making the left turn into the shopping center. As the Jaguar approached the curb, Stella pulled out her compact and checked her makeup as she tidied up for her ten o'clock spa appointment at Ulta Beauty. Mark paid attention as she straightened her white short shorts and Navy blue halter top before getting out, knowing it was no accident that his fashionista had matched the Jag's colors so well.

Pushing his Jaguar cap aside, she kissed him and placed her finger over his lips. "Don't pick up any strays, Mr. McAllister," playfully grabbing his crotch, giving him a soft squeeze, "…and take good care of my toys."

"Honey, you know you're all I'll ever need," he replied, half-wishing she wouldn't let go as the engine puffed away in neutral like an expensive cigar.

"Pick me up in an hour right here, babe," stepping back to admire the classic car's elegant lines, "…and don't forget the Cordon Bleu on sale at Publix Liquors," as she sauntered inside.

His eyes roamed the half-empty parking lot looking for a safe place to park the Jaguar. Keeping the car in its perfectly-restored condition and away from runaway grocery carts was a priority as he slipped into an end parking space. Stopping to wipe a smudge from the fender, he smiled at a well-dressed couple on their way to TJMax.

"Haven't seen a good-lookin' XK 120 on the road for quite some time," complimented the older gentleman as he ambled toward the store. "What year is your Jaguar?"

"She was born in '53," replied Mark, claiming parental ownership.

Satisfied with the fender's sheen, he glanced up and was delighted to see that his favorite bench nearest the store's entrance was unoccupied. It was one of his preferred people-watching perches, and today the entryway was clear of people collecting for charitable causes.

No sooner had he taken a seat to keep an eye on his Jag when he noticed a stunning young woman stop and admire his car before she turned to scour the storefronts for its possible owner. As their eyes met, she pulled her honey-red hair back and began to walk toward him in a sultry way that would have done justice to any Victoria's Secret model.

Here comes trouble.

Dressed in skin-tight black tights and an aqua knit top that exposed her taut belly, she made a beeline for him in her Jimmy Choo heels. Lowering her Dolce Gabbanas to reveal stunning blue eyes, she gave him a knowing look, pointing at him with a manicured finger.

"You're that author guy, aren't you? Mark McSomething."

"Mark McAllister. And who might you be?" casually placing an arm along the top of the bench and leaning back as he admired her alluring freckled face. Up close, she looked to be no more than twenty-five.

"I'm Sam," placing her hands on her hips to showcase the diamond adorning her belly in a way that almost dared him to make a move. "Short for Samantha," she explained, swiveling her pelvis and pointing toward the Jaguar. "That your white sports car?" she asked in a Slavic accent.

"Yes, ma'am," adjusting his tan Jaguar cap as she stared at his wedding ring.

"Are you--"

"Married, but not buried."

Samantha waited impatiently for him to offer her a ride while an older woman dressed in tennis gear walked by and gave her a disapproving look. Moments passed before she said, "You know, for an author, you sure don't say much."

"It's because I'm dumbfounded by your beauty, Sam." That brought him the smile he'd been waiting for. "How did you recognize me?"

"From your book cover. And your...um, what you call...book signing at Barnes and Noble in Jensen Beach last month."

"Did I sign your book for you?" A rhetorical question, he definitely would have remembered meeting Sam.

"My Uncle Anton wouldn't let me," her full lips turning pouty. "He's very protective. He said you married gangster's widow, right? Queen of...of--"

"South Beach."

"So, where's your queen today?"

"Getting her hair done," pointing down the long walkway toward Ulta Beauty.

"Well, screw me sideways on pogo stick," giving him a big grin.

"Careful. I got a merit badge in that when I was in Boy Scouts." Enjoying her flirtation, he floated one of his best lines. "So, Sam, what brings joy to a beautiful girl like you?"

Samantha laughed. "So, take me for a ride in your white sports car, or I still looking for the man of my dreams?"

Curious, he cocked his head. "And how would you find the man of your dreams?"

With a sultry look, she took a step closer and softened her voice. "I ask him to look at me when he is kissing me here," caressing her pelvis.

Suddenly, he could see tomorrow's headlines: "WIFE SHOOTS HUSBAND-BAD HAIR DAY?" along with another million reasons why this was not a good idea. *Some days are like licking honey from a thorn.*

"Well, Samantha, as savory as that might sound, sometimes the fantasy is safer than the reality," he replied with a wry smile. "Let's save that one for another life so that we can at least live to see the end of this one. *Oui?*"

Not used to be being denied, she dangled her sunglasses and gave him that pouty look again. Seeing that his mind was made up, she brightened and extended her hand for a high-five. "*Oui.* Raincheck, then? You still my favorite author."

He wanted to embrace her and give her a big hug but wasn't sure if she'd let go. So he settled for her high five. "I am curious," she began, "...what are your hobbies?"

"Kegeling, collecting handcuffs, knitting, and erotic bird calls," with a straight face.

She thought that was funny. "We must go kegeling sometime, oui?"

He nodded, not quite sure if she understood what she was agreeing to. "By the way, Sam, I've been trying to place your accent. Where're you from?"

"Ukraine."

A light bulb went off in his head. "You must be Anton Marchenko's niece. The CEO of ZTE?" nonchalantly, trying to hide the awkwardness he felt over meeting the stunning niece of a murder suspect.

"Small world, yes?"

You have no idea, honey.

"He's famous research scientist." Impatient to get on with her day, she added, "I need food for my party tomorrow, but first I have something for you." Reaching into her tiny rhinestone purse, she handed him her personal card.

Impressed with the Coco Madamoiselle scent on the card, he read the feminine font aloud. "Samantha Marchenko. Fungirl1992 @ gmail. com." Subtley, he checked his own scent, hoping he was not exuding the "Eau de WD-40" that might be lingering from the earlier tune-up. "Nice touch, Sam," giving her card another approving whiff.

"*Appelle-moi*, Marky-Mark. *Enchante.*" With a royal wave, she slipped her Dolce Gabbanas back on and disappeared inside to score her party platters.

Wondering how many more fans he had like Samantha lurking in the parking lot, Mark sat on the bench, resigning himself to more mindful things. Enjoying the breeze on his face, he watched the sky changing colors, with wisps of dark cirrus clouds sailing rapidly across blue skies. It was another front approaching from the north, with the likely promise of cooler temperatures. When he was in the middle of the ocean, such sudden climate changes made him feel vulnerable as northern fronts were often the source of more inclement weather. Taking stock of his current surroundings, he reminded himself he was sitting on a bench outside Publix as he checked his watch and hoped Stella was running on schedule.

An older, shabbily-dressed man in jeans and torn shirt cautiously parked his battered bicycle next to the bench. Squatting, the bearded man fiddled with the plastic bags full of snacks, bottled water and clothing that hung from the bike. With a sunburned head, weathered skin and unsteady balance, the man looked to be in his seventies. "Is this seat taken?" he asked through broken teeth that looked as though they hadn't seen a dentist since 1965.

Mark had a soft spot for the homeless and patted the empty space next to him, remembering Reverend Eastbrook's suggestion that each member of the congregation should take in at least one homeless person once in a while. "Have a seat here, young man."

The old man smiled, revealing blue eyes and a weather-beaten face that had spent far too many winters outdoors. "Thank you, sir. Like your Jaguar hat."

Mark glanced at the man's sunburned head, and without hesitation, offered the cap to the man. "Take it. I have two more at home." The man's eyes opened wide, the old man overjoyed to have something to keep the scorching sun off his head.

"You shore?"

"I'm shore," handing it to him.

"Jeez, thanks, man," slipping the cap over what remained of his hair. "Fits perfik."

Curious, Mark asked, "What's your name?"

"Spencer."

"Mark," sharing a fist bump. "You look like you've traveled far, Spencer. Where you headed? The French Riviera maybe?"

"Yeah...well, got a lot on my mind," adjusting the fit of his new cap. "Lost my wife to cancer five years ago."

In a show of empathy, he met the old man's eyes and shared his late wife's tragic story. "Lost mine a few years back when she got run over by a dump truck hauling fifteen tons of sand. Company's name was 'The Sand Man'. Ironic, wouldn't you say, Spencer?"

The man nodded and continued to commiserate. "If I had the sense that God gave a fish, I would have drove my bike into a bus when she died."

Mark winced at his admission. "This town's scorched of life. Nothin' but a graveyard now. The music, the aroma of fresh food comin' out that door every time it opens, nickles, dimes and quarters they put in my jar, it don't mean nothin' to me now. Been some dark days."

Mark tried a different approach. "Should less respectable voices urge us to liquidate our stocks? Buy gold, canned goods and shotgun shells? And retreat to an abandoned missile silo in Idaho to await the end of days?"

The man looked confused, so Mark tried a different tack. "Seriously, though, we don't always know why people do what they do. We all look through our own window."

The old man nodded as parched lips formed the words, "That's fer shore."

"So, here's what you need to do to get back on track," continued Mark. "Think about being more receptive to letting friends and hope back into your life, Spencer." He watched the old man's eyes light up with the idea. "So, take care of yourself and let the light in, dude."

"You make it sound so easy, but it ain't," raising his new cap to scratch where the sunburn was making his head itch.

Mark continued and patted him on the shoulder. "And just by listening to me, you've already taken the first step."

Considering the advice, the old man began to feel a sense of accomplishment. "I'm gonna give it some thought," he promised.

Good," giving him another pat on the shoulder. "When life seems unbearable, simply choose to *stay*, in the hope that you will see the light again."

He watched Spencer nod and give him an inquisitive look. "You sound like a poet or somethin'."

"Close. Investigative journalist and screenwriter. And I was once as bummed out as you." Mark stood and checked his watch, knowing that Stella would be looking for him in a few minutes. He pulled a fifty from his pocket and offered it to the old man, hanging onto it until he had a firm deal. "This is for groceries, my good man. No booze or drugs. Agreed?"

Smiling through broken teeth, the homeless man acted like he'd just won the lottery. "Yeah, shore," inspecting the fifty like it was the first one ever printed. "Where ya goin'?"

"Gotta go check on someone. Take care of yourself, young man," giving him another fist bump. They parted company, Mark heading to the liquor store for Stella's Cordon Bleu while Spencer made a beeline for TJMax to pick up the raincoat he'd been in need of for so long.

From the corner of his eye, the old timer spotted a man in a parked Dodge Caravan peering at them through binoculars but thought nothing of it, the fifty dollar bill still holding his attention as he walked in the front door.

At the other end of the mall, Mark exited the liquor store with their favorite cognac just as she stepped out of the spa, her honey-red hair expertly cut to a shoulder-length coiffure. Looking radiant and feeling frisky, Stella met his gaze. "Hey there. You're a healthy-lookin' stallion. How do you stay so fit?" she asked coyly.

"I have a high-fiber diet."

Sidling up to him, "Oh? Consisting of...?"

"Wicker furniture," he replied with a straight face.

Touching his bicep, she gave him a coquettish look. "Sounds hard to swallow."

"Not if you blanch it."

"Uh-huh," smiling. "Do you have somewhere we could go?" her green eyes sparkling.

"Sure do. Need a lift?"

"Uh-huh." Grasping her outstretched hand, he guided her toward the Jaguar.

"You'll like the vibes," he promised.

Early afternoon the next day was another sun-filled day in paradise as tourists crowded the sidewalks and roamed the shops up and down Ocean Drive. The retired Michigan chiropractor was enjoying a chocolate almond ice cream cone from Kilwin's, his favorite beachfront ice cream shop, as he sidled down the steps toward the beach. For his wife who was sunning herself at the pool, he picked up a bag of gourmet chocolates and stuck them in the pocket of his walking shorts as a surprise for her when he returned. The portly geriatric was reminiscing about the fun they'd had during their two-week stay at The Driftwood Resort and planned to return again with his wife in November.

Ambling toward the beach for his mid-morning walk, he came upon a sign inside Humiston Park illustrating how to escape from a rip current as he tossed the wrapper into the trash. Curious, he posed a question to the two lifeguards he met yesterday.

"So, Erik, these rip currents, how dangerous are they?"

"Drag you out to sea and drown you if you're not careful," he explained, shifting his weight in the chair.

"That's why we've got the yellow warning flags up today," added Shaun, pointing at the flag flying from the stairway.

"Thank God we don't have those on Lake Mitchell," said the retired chiropractor. "Thanks for the tip."

Five minutes later, a quarter mile further up the beach, the retiree was savoring the last of his ice cream when something grotesque on the beach ahead caught his attention. As he got closer, he stopped in his tracks. Shocked by what he saw, he dropped his cone and fumbled for his phone, dialing the three-digit number for emergency services.

"911," declared the female dispatcher's voice. "What is your emergency?"

"I want to report, ah…what *looks* like a woman's body in the water on Vero Beach."

"Where on Vero Beach are you, sir?"

He spun around to read the sign posted on the stairway next to him as he shaded his eyes from the sun. "I'm standing next to a tall condo, ah… Village Spires."

"I'll need your full name, sir."

"It's Dr. Clifford Allen…from Cadillac, Michigan."

"Okay, Dr. Allen, stay there. They may have a few questions for you. I'm sending help now."

ELEVEN

Late the next morning, the sky had turned overcast as the head of the FBI BAU made the turn onto Ocean Drive in his government-issued black Tahoe. Feeling like he'd just rolled onto the set of "Lifestyles of the Rich and Famous", Beretto slowed his SUV, in awe of the stunning McMansions that formed The Ocean Estates of Riomar.

To understand the neighborhood the McAllister's had chosen in Vero Beach, one would need to understand that Riomar was simply one of the finest collections of oceanfront estate homes in America. It was not a neighborhood in an urban or suburban sense, but actually an exquisite collection of some of the finest beachfront homes available on the Eastern seaboard.

Predominated by old-money and bluebloods with time-honored social graces, The Ocean Estates of Riomar was defined by a gentile quality of life that deserved preservation. Seen as the quintessential triumph of substance over style, the enclave had become a mecca of sorts; a sanctuary for billionaires and Fortune 500 CEOs that sought to escape the mundane and nouveau riche further south on the Florida coast. He recalled what his late father was always saying; "...build your castles high, and dream, dream, dream." And so, some did, thought Beretto, as he turned to enter the security gate and rolled his window down to smile at the camera.

"It's Don Dadonda."

A few moments passed before he heard a familiar voice. "You're a funny guy, Dom. Sounds like bad news," replied Mark.

"Got time for an old friend?" The cast iron gate emitted a buzz as it began to swing open.

"C'mon up, Dom. Stella and I are grinding some fresh Guatemalan expresso."

Parking in what he presumed to be the villa's guest spaces, Beretto was particularly impressed with the long driveway's elegant checkerboard look formed by the large marble tiles meticulously separated by Bermuda grass borders.

Moments later, Beretto found himself seated inside at the expansive turquoise onyx island bar with a stunning view of the ocean. The demitasse of gourmet expresso he shared with the casually-dressed couple proved to be quite tasty and he asked for a refill. After complimenting the interior and exchanging a few minutes of polite chit-chat, Beretto got to the point of his visit.

"Look, I know you were joking earlier, but you're right. I do have some bad news. The BAU has now been given jurisdiction over the investigation, and we're working with Vero's finest on this." Sliding the satchel from his shoulder, he laid it on the bar top. "You two have a strong stomach?"

The couple gave each other a quick glance. "Why? What are we about to see?" asked Mark.

Pulling the file from his satchel, Beretto calmly opened it on the counter. "At first, we thought it could be an accidental drowning, or maybe the result of a strong rip current pulling her out to sea. But with her neck ligatures and the tox screen indicating a fatal dose of fentanyl in her system, we've ruled it the second in a series of homicides."

Beretto's voice softened as he turned to Stella. "We think you know the victim," as he spread the photos out for identification. "Phone records indicate you probably knew her well."

Stella pushed her demitasse out of the way to pull the photo closer and covered her mouth. "*Oh my God*, that's my fitness trainer...my friend

Kelly Ann. I just worked out with her yesterday morning." Shocked, she studied the photo of the shapely fitness trainer still clad in her workout gear. Her eyes welling, she was overcome with emotion as she stared at the photos.

"I'm so sorry," offered Beretto, covering her hand with his to console her as Mark held her close.

"Where'd they find her?" asked Mark.

"A retired chiropractor from Michigan found her washed up on the beach near Village Spires around one-thirty yesterday afternoon. As you can see, she was still wearing her training outfit." Beretto laid the photo down on the counter and leaned back. "Look, Stella, I know this is a shock, but do you know if Miss Granata had any drug addictions?"

Wiping away a tear, she replied, "Kelly Ann was a health nut. Wouldn't do drugs in a million years." Picking up the crime scene photo, she studied it more closely. "Looks like the same outfit she wore at our workout yesterday."

"What about enemies?" he asked.

"Really don't know of any," responded Stella. "She was very sweet, popular with just about everybody, especially the men at the gym. Never a harsh word for anyone."

"Boyfriends?"

Stella wiped her smeared mascara with a napkin. "Kelly Ann broke up with her last boyfriend about three months ago," staring out the window at the beach. "I think he moved to San Francisco to work for a software company."

"Did she mention his name?"

"Dylan something." Her brow furrowed with something else she remembered. "Wait," holding up an index finger, "...Kelly mentioned this retired older guy that was pestering her for dates at the gym. He liked touching her body inappropriately when they were training together. Kinda creeped her out, so she pawned him off on another female fitness trainer."

"Which gym?"

"Ultimate Crossfit on A1A in Indian River Shores," she replied.

"This guy got a name?"

"Yeah. She introduced me to him once. Even asked *me* for my phone number. He was always bragging about his big hands. Bruce Hat...feld... no, Bruce Hatfield. A real perv."

Beretto was carefully annotating all the details. "So far, there is no evidence suggesting a sexual assault or robbery with either of these victims. This could be something else."

Simultaneously, the two men looked at each other as they had the same thought. "Stella, I'd like to be able to tell you otherwise," said Beretto, "...but let's not overlook the fact that this maniac may be targeting you *and* your close friends. That's two girlfriends you've lost in less than three weeks."

"Have you found anything else linking the two victims?" asked Mark.

"Other than being good friends with Stella, no."

"Dom's right," she confirmed. "This doesn't feel like a...*co-inkydink*," turning to her husband. "I felt safer diving with man-eating sharks in Bora Bora than I do here today."

Beretto compared the crime scene photos. "The MO's are very similar," he observed. "Both were attractive women in their thirties...violent physical domination by the attacker...same-sized ligatures on their necks suggesting the unsub is a lefty. Also, both victims have fentanyl in their tox screen. Strangulation indicates the anger is of a more personal nature. I'm willing to bet forensics will find a needle mark somewhere on her upper torso and maybe a burn mark from a stun gun similar to Dr. Tremelle."

Mark articulated his profile. "I think we've got a left-handed white male, thirty to fifty, with unspecified anger issues toward women but no evidence of sexual motivation."

"Maybe he's impotent," she suggested.

To his wife, Mark said, "We need to look deeper into both victims' connections with you. Could be something more personal."

Beretto continued. "This could be some sort of revenge, a score to settle, or maybe he's working off some sort of hit list from a hangout where he could stalk them without being noticed."

"*Hangouts,*" she repeated, staring straight ahead, trancelike, raising a finger as she recalled recent phone conversations with the victims. "They both liked beach walks and hangin' with the lifeguards at Humiston Park Beach." Mark thought she might be on to something. "In the photos, their favorite pizza place was right there, too. Kelly liked taking selfies on the boardwalk, sometimes with the lifeguards chowing down on Nino's pizza."

Beretto stood up. "I think I passed a place called Nino's on my way here."

"Best pizza on the beach, just steps off the boardwalk," added Mark. "Anyone hungry for some good Italian while we check out the scene?"

"Not super hungry," said Stella, curling her hair around her ear before looking up to her husband, "...but I could use some company right now. Let's take the Range Rover. Can we stop off at our church?" Mark nodded, completely on the same page.

Beretto reached for his phone. "Meet you two at the boardwalk in twenty minutes then. I'll let Lt. Foti know where we'll be."

Det. Gary Locke carried a large brown bag of fresh take out from Casey's as he walked toward the white Ford Taurus parked on Azalea Lane. Seeing him approaching in the rear view mirror, Det. Heaton tripped the unlock button from the driver's seat.

"So, how was the movie?" asked Heaton sarcastically as Locke climbed in and shut the door.

Setting the bag of food on the seat, Locke smirked. "I took the long way around on Cardinal to keep a low profile," he explained. "Besides, good things wait for those to come."

Heaton gave his partner a disdainful look. "You mean good things come to those who wait, don't you?" grabbing the bag and pulling out his marlin dip and chips. It was the third day on the stake out for the pair, and things were getting a little chippy between the two. Tossing the quesadillas back into Locke's lap, "I thought we agreed to refrain from any more of your idiotic clichés."

Locke smirked again. "Any action with Dr. Pain Med while I was chasing down your lunch?"

"Not yet, but I counted six patients that are inside his office." Popping the Styrofoam top on his marlin dip, he added, "Let's eat before we make any arrests."

"You're the king of stakeouts, Dennis. Your call."

Famished after skipping breakfast, the two officers dove into their lunches as they kept a keen eye on Hirt's ground-floor entrance. An older couple walked past them sharing ice cream cones from Kilwin's, and across the street, a teenage couple in swimsuits and carrying skimboards made their way down Ocean Drive, giggling and playing grab ass with each other.

Unexpectedly, a heavy-set couple wearing tattered jeans and tank tops exited the clinic's stairway and surreptitiously glanced up and down Ocean Drive. Their suspicious behavior caught the officers' attention as the couple quickly turned the corner onto Azalea. The big bearded man with a head full of twisted corn rows stopped, looked around, and popped the plastic top off a pill vial before swallowing a mouthful and handing some off to his girlfriend.

Locke slipped into his best impression of a game show host; "So *Johnny,* what do we have for our two 'Addicts of the Week'?" With his hand on the car's door handle, Locke readied himself for a quick exit before Heaton reached out and stopped him.

"Wait. Let them get down the street a ways." The two officers watched until the couple reached the end of the block and out of sight from Hirt's second floor windows. "All right. Let's check'um out."

Dressed in street clothes, the two officers hastily caught up to the unsuspecting couple as they turned down an alley where their beat-up red F-150 was parked. The officers yanked out their chain-mounted badges as the surprised couple turned in response to footsteps. "Vero Beach Police. Stop and put your hands against the building," ordered Heaton. The couple quickly complied.

"What'd we do, officers?" the scruffy-looking man asked with an air of resentment as he and his female companion leaned against the building. After a thorough pat down from the two officers, Heaton pulled the vial of oxycontin from the man's front pocket.

"You got a script for these?"

"Yeah. In my left pocket," replied the man.

"Anything sharp in there, like needle or blades? Anything going to cut us?" as Heaton dug deeper into his pockets.

"No, sir."

The hefty woman wore her jeans so tight Locke had to struggle to get his hands in her pockets, and she turned to taunt him after he came up empty handed. "Was it good for you, officer?"

Ignoring her taunt, Locke spun her around to face him. "Let's see some ID." She produced a Florida driver's license that gave a Ft. Pierce address while Heaton inspected the man's license and prescription for narcotics.

"This your correct address in Ft. Pierce, Mr. Sweeny?"

"Yes, sir. Debbie and I just bought a new trailer there."

"Congratulations," responded Locke with a dash of sarcasm. Turning to the girl, "This your correct address in Ft. Pierce, Miss, ah...Debbie Saltrese?"

"Sure is. Harley and I live together."

"What're you doing up here in Vero, Mr. Sweeny?" asked Heaton.

"Doctor's appointment." Heaton gave him a skeptical look as he inspected the invoice for services rendered. "And this is what he charged you today? Eight-hundred-fifty-bucks for your script?"

"That's right," shuffling his feet and looking at the ground. "Our disability's paying for it."

"Who's the insurance company? Grabbit, Ripitoff and Run?" Locke gave him a big smirk, but Sweeny kept silent.

Rolling the vial of pills between his fingers, Heaton said, "These are a hundred milligrams. Maximum recommended dosage is one-hundred-five milligrams, and I just saw you take more than the prescribed dosage and share them with your mate." Looking more closely at the label, "And they're not supposed to be refillable."

"What're you gonna do, arrest me for exceeding the dosage and sharing pain meds with my girl?"

Heaton took a step closer. "No, but I might arrest you 'cause I don't like you." Studying the big man, something seemed a little off to the detective as he studied his dilated pupils. "Why do you need such a strong opioid?"

"What're you, my doctor? Got a bad shoulder. I'm on *disability*, man," feeling resentful.

"So, ya got the State of Florida paying for your opioids now, huh?" Heaton continued to eye him skeptically as Sweeny exchanged glances with his girlfriend.

"Got hit by a car. Look, can we go now? Why're you giving us such a hard time?"

Heaton stepped in to break it down for the couple. "We've had reports that The Pain Free Clinic's been selling illegal narcotics. You wouldn't know anything about that, would you?"

It was the girl's turn to get indignant. "We've told you everything, officers. Harley showed you his script. You can't hold us for no reason."

"What're you, his lawyer?" retorted Heaton. A standoff ensued as Locke noticed his partner's frustration and gestured for a time out. With the couple leaning with their hands against the wall, the two undercover detectives stepped to the curb to decide their next move.

Heaton shook his head slowly. "I was sure they were dirty."

Tired of a stakeout that was yielding no results, Locke felt it was time to move on. "Dennis, we got nothing. Let's let'um go. This is our fifth stop in three days. As much as I hate to admit it, it looks like Hirt's running a legit operation here. We've got no evidence of anything illegal. You know, like your favorite cereal, Nut'N Honey?"

"Don't be a wise ass." Heaton gave him a dubious look and glanced over at the couple waiting to hear their fate. "Yeah. Maybe you're right. We're oh for five. I'll call in to Foti, see if he wants us to extend the stakeout." Heaton withdrew a business card from his shirt pocket as they walked back to the couple.

"Okay, folks. Here's what we're going to do," as Heaton held out his card. "We're going to forget about your opioid abuse for today." He watched Harley make a face. "You're free to go, but in return, you're going to call me the next time you see anything out of place at The Pain Free Clinic. You can remain completely anonymous as long as you give me *all* the details. Agreed?"

"You want us to be snitches?" charged Sweeny.

Raising his eyebrows, "If you want your gravy train to continue, we ask you to be the intelligent, law-abiding citizens that you are. Right?" Heaton searched their faces for some sign of an understanding. Eager to accept the detective's proposal, Debbie stepped up to take his card.

"You got it, detective." Looking for a way out, she grabbed her boyfriend's hand. "C'mon, Harley. Let's head over to Mulligan's. I feel like a cheeseburger in paradise and an ice cold beer."

Heaton and Locke watched the two climb into their shabby F-150 and head down the alley toward Mulligan's at Sexton Plaza. Noticing the long look on Heaton's face, Locke smirked and offered his take; "Guess it ain't over 'til the fat lady belches."

"Jeez, Gary. I'm not even gonna grace that with a response." Giving him a disgusted look, "Do not speak to me again until you have something useful to say. C'mon. I gotta report in to Foti." From inside their Taurus, Heaton dialed the boss on his cell.

Lt. Foti sounded distracted as he answered Heaton's call. "Make it quick, sergeant. I'm on a crime scene."

"What's going on?"

Foti paused and lowered his voice. "Got another O.D. On Avenue "E" here in Ft. Pierce. Did you miss the call on your radio?"

"We were outside the car on a pedestrian stop." He could hear a woman screaming hysterically in the background. "Sir, we're in our third day of checking Hirt's patients. We've questioned five of his patients, and all had valid scripts. If he's our man, he's dealing the China white somewhere else." Heaton paused, looking for an angle. "What about that search warrant? Any progress?"

"Judge says we haven't met the probable cause threshold."

"You want us to continue here?"

There was a long pause as Foti thought it over. Despondent over the lack of progress, "No. You guys go home and get some sleep. I'll see you at the station in the morning. Eight sharp. And Dennis…"

"Yes, sir."

"You and Locke bring me some new evidence."

"Yes, sir."

TWELVE

Reviewing a lesson he learned three years ago, Beretto recalled the serial murder case in Gainesville, Florida as he drove toward Nino's and Humiston Park in his black Tahoe. Then, he needed the full cooperation of locals but failed to secure it from the clan of mistrustful rednecks. Four residents of a trailer park on the east side of town had been shot and killed with the same .357 magnum over a five month period, and the case had drawn national attention.

During the investigation, his boss constantly reminded him to keep a low profile and not rile the locals. Beretto remembered his exact words; "If you can't figure out a way to keep this low profile, I'm sure you'll enjoy working back home as an insurance adjuster."

Clan members of a small country church, who were aware of critical details about the murders, had withheld vital information out of mistrust of an FBI agent with a New York accent. As a result, one of his best agents was shot through the door in the ensuing shootout when they attempted to serve a search warrant on a man who turned out to be the perpetrator of all four murders. Beretto didn't appreciate having to explain what happened to the agent's widow, and it was a gut-wrenching lesson on the importance of gaining all the local support possible in a capital murder case.

In her white Range Rover, the McAllisters pulled up into an open spot directly in front of the church's stained glass window and headed toward a side entrance that led directly to the altar. Mark smiled to himself as he remembered joking with Pastor Cliff one day about adding a drive-thru for church members in a hurry to meet their T-times.

Inside, under the huge oak crossbeams supporting the cavernous transept, it was quiet, not a soul to be seen as Mark and Stella kneeled together on the cushions at the foot of the altar and prayed. Following five minutes of silent prayer, Stella looked up and touched his arm.

Out loud, he paraphrased one of their favorite prayers from Adam Hamilton; *"Lord, help us to be grateful for our lives, for what we have, and to stay out of harm's way. Help us remember that we don't need most of what we want, and that joy is found in simplicity and generosity. In the name of Jesus, Amen."*

"Amen," added Stella as she squeezed his hand.

A blue Bentley Corniche was vacating a parking space in front of Nino's as the couple pulled up, and Mark quickly slipped into the spot in front of the patio tables. Beretto and Foti were standing at the aluminum railing on the boardwalk fifty yards away as they surveyed the crowded beach goers playing volleyball, sunbathing, swimming and tossing the frisbee.

"Frank, thank you for meeting us," said Mark to the lieutenant as they approached the two officers. "Stella remembers both victims sending her selfies from this location. Thought we might check it out before we grab a pizza."

Foti nodded. "No worries. On my expense account."

"With the property taxes I pay, I'm sure the city can afford it," quipped Mark.

Beretto stepped up to him. "Mark, you know the local terrain. Before I leave the island, I thought I'd get a haircut. Any recommendations?"

"Sure. Coupla blocks north on Bougainvillea, just off Ocean Drive, you'll find Men's Hair by Suette. Cute. Excellent stylist. You'll like her."

Spotting the three lifeguards on duty at the beachfront office, Foti reached inside his jacket for the three-by-five photos of his top suspects. "Fellas," he said to Erik, Shaun and Vince as he stepped under their sun shade, "...Lt. Foti, Vero PD. Take a look at these photos and tell me if you've seen these men recently."

Spellbound by Stella in her short shorts and halter top, the three lifeguards removed their shades as she walked by. "Guys...guys," she's way over your pay grade," Foti holding the photos closer. "Over here... *these* photos," tapping on them.

"Sure," said Vince as he focused on the photos of Marchenko, Yakovlev and Hirt. Erik spoke first, tapping the photo of Yakovlev. "This guy looks familiar. I think he's the guy that a couple of high schoolers complained about one afternoon about a month ago."

"What'd they complain about?"

"He was ogling them close up with binoculars from the far end of the boardwalk," pointing north. "Kinda creeped them out, so I went over to talk to him, but he left before I could--"

"Real beefy bald guy with a beard?" Foti asked.

"Yeah, well, beefy and bearded, for sure, but he always wore a Nike cap, so don't know if--"

"Anything else you can remember?"

"Saw him climb in a black Maserati with a personalized plate."

"Remember what the plate said?"

"Yeah, Lovero...or something like that."

Finished making notations, Foti looked up at his witness. "Okay. Thanks, Erik. Guys, you've been a big help." The detective joined Beretto, and both headed toward the far end of the boardwalk.

"Stella," called Foti, waving her over as they began to inspect the area around the row of wooden benches that lined the boardwalk. Between the benches, they turned up a pack of fruit-flavored condoms, some breath mints, a tube of cherry Chapstick, a lone flip flop, and a Chicago Bears cap.

Near the last bench at the far end, something half-buried in the sand underneath the bench caught Stella's attention. Squatting, she brushed the sand away to reveal three black stubbed-out cigarette butts with gold lettering.

Looking up at Foti, she asked, "Who the hell smokes these?"

"I know who smokes 'em," replied Foti in an amusing southern drawl. "Treasurer Black Executive. High-dollar smokes from the U.K."

Foti being a Brooklyn native, she found his southern drawl especially entertaining. "Well, you gonna clue me in, Frank, or do I hafta guess?"

Foti squatted, carefully depositing the black cigarette stubs into a clear plastic baggie with his tweezers before looking up at her and continuing with his exaggerated southern drawl.

"His name's Bubba...and he ain't from aroun' these parts, missy."

Stella stood, brushing the sand from her shorts. "You're hilarious, Frank. We'll meet you inside Nino's. The maybe you can tell me who the hell Bubba is."

The McAllisters had found a large round table inside the restaurant with Beretto and Foti while the four enjoyed some genuine Italian. Holding up photos of Marchenko and Hirt, Beretto turned to Foti. "So, what's our strategy?"

"Follow the evidence trail."

From Dr. Tremelle's evidence file, Beretto held up a photo of Dr. Talcott. "Aside from the textbook answers, Frank, what about Talcott?"

"He may have had a lover's quarrel with Tremelle, but my gut tells me he's incapable of homicide. Plus, he's got an alibi that's been corroborated, and we have nothing to connect him to the second victim. He came clean on their relationship. I may decide to question him again."

"And Dr. Callaway?" continued Beretto. "Where're we at with her?"

"Lacks the physical strength our unsub has demonstrated in leaving severe ligature marks on the victims' neck before beating them. Callaway is also right handed. While she is definitely ethically challenged and had a heated competition with Tremelle for new drugs at Oconix, I'm not so sure she's capable of murder."

Beretto continued to shuffle through the suspect photos. "Okay. What about this pervert at the gym, Bruce Hatfield?"

"He's a lecherous old man, but at eighty-two, too old to even remember where he put his Viagra. The gym manager was pretty broken up about losing his most popular female trainer. Told me Hatfield hasn't been to the gym in a month."

Sharing the results of three days of surveillance, Foti said, "My two guys Heaton and Locke have been intercepting Hirt's patients for three days. He looks like he's running a clean operation out of his office."

"What about his Vista Del Mar condo?" Beretto asked. "What's he been running from there?"

Foti grimaced. "We've done a few drives by there, but my captain has his hands tied. Says we don't have the budget to stakeout both, so we chose his office thinking we could corner one of his mules."

Beretto wrote something into his planner before looking up. "The BAU may have someone available for the condo stakeout."

The two officers turned simultaneously to their investigative journalist. Pushing aside his unfinished lasagna, Mark placed his palm on the table. "This is starting to look more and more like a vendetta to me, and I do have a concern about Stella's safety," glancing at his wife.

Stella clasped her hands expectantly and waited for her husband to elaborate. "I'd like to suggest her name be left out of any police reports, as they are a matter of public record, and honey," turning to his wife, "...I think you need to be a little less visible in these investigations, because *if* my intuition is correct, and this *is* a vendetta, knowing you are involved will only serve to incite the perp's anger and accelerate his timetable." Mark paused and cocked his head. "Have you thought about taking a few months off in Bora Bora."

Stella listened to him carefully before she responded. "What about what you said earlier, about being in too deep to cut and run--"

"I've reconsidered."

"So have I," she said firmly, taking a deep breath. "Gentlemen, do I need to remind you that I've got five Expert Marksman Citations from the Dallas Gun Club? And...that I have a license to carry?" She leaned forward to make her point to each of the three men sitting at the table.

"I want to know who murdered my friends! I need to know who's stalking me as badly as *anyone* at this table," looking sternly at the men and thumping the table top with her finger. "I'm aware of the risks involved, so don't treat me like some ditzy blonde. You guys brought me into this, and you know what I went through on Rosa's yacht two years ago, so you know I can handle myself. *Now, I need some answers.*" Pausing, the room resounded with the sound of her silence. "Now, do *any* of you have any questions about my motivation?"

All three silently shook their heads before Mark turned to his wife. "I never doubted you, and I wouldn't have married you if you didn't have some spunk, Stella."

THIRTEEN

All through his years at Vero Beach High School, Max Croaker was a bit troubled, and his fellow students thought of him as kind of an odd ball. With scraggly white hair, stocky build and a face described as "funny looking" by his classmates, Croaker stood a mere five-and-a-half-feet tall, so they nicknamed him "Frodo", a nickname mentioned in five of his arrest reports. Croaker's lengthy criminal records spanned seventeen years and included attempted murder, robbery, burglary, drug possession and conspiracy to distribute narcotics.

In 2012, he was identified as the "prime suspect", and the only suspect ever publicly named by St. Lucie County Sheriff's detectives in the March 2012 abduction and murder of Angela Peyton. Peyton was a fifty-two year old Ft. Pierce dietician whose body was found the following day in an orange grove on the outskirts of town. Ms. Peyton had a long history of arrests for prostitution and possession of cocaine and methamphetamines. In light of her record, they were perplexed by her ability to secure a state license to practice as a dietician in the state of Florida.

Back then, Sgt. Marco Gonzalez was quoted as saying to a reporter; "We've done a thorough investigation of this case, and we're continuing to move forward until we find Ms. Peyton's killer. While I'm prohibited from discussing the details, I can say that Max Croaker is still a suspect in the homicide."

In the phone conversation, Gonzalez provided no clear-cut answers to reporters. This puzzled Vero Beach detectives who told reporters they still considered Croaker to be a "strong person of interest" in an eerily similar abduction and homicide of a Vero Beach woman that occurred four months earlier.

Sgt. Gonzalez declined to offer any other explanation, except to say that "...most of the information being disseminated on Facebook, Twitter and Instagram and other social media is not, in fact, accurate. These are people trying monopolize the spotlight for their one moment of fame using rumors and innuendo that only serve to muddy the water, or in other words, fake news."

Sadly, the Peyton homicide investigation seemed to slow to a standstill when Sgt. Gonzalez was shot and killed by a would-be bank robber in June, 2012 on the outskirts of Port St. Lucie. Rushed to the emergency room, Sgt. Gonzalez died in the back of the ambulance.

A *Sun Sentinel* reporter reinvigorated the case when she recently wrote an article asking about the mountain of circumstantial evidence which, seventeen years ago, was enough for detectives to convince a judge to issue warrants to secure DNA samples from Croaker. Prior to the recent *Sun Sentinel* article, the case had been buried for almost two decades before being reopened by St. Lucie County detectives who seized on the seventeenth anniversary of Peyton's murder after discovering new information that has yet to be shared with the public.

In television interviews seventeen years ago, an agency spokesperson told the reporter then that St. Lucie County detectives believed the prime suspect for Peyton's murder "...likely resides in Vero, is a suspect in another Vero Beach homicide, drives a psychedelic-painted VW bus with tires that match tracks in the grove, and stands about five-feet six-inches tall, which matches the height of the person in the PNC Bank ATM video." When the reporter asked why Croaker has not been arrested and charged with Peyton's murder, she was told by the agency spokesperson "...the evidence is primarily circumstantial, the detectives felt they needed more," and that "...there were some pieces missing from the puzzle."

According to the police report, Angela Peyton was launching a new career as a registered dietician and drove to her office for an appointment at six-thirty p.m. on the evening of March 26th. She was reported missing by a neighbor later that night when she came home at ten-thirty p.m. and found Peyton's apartment dark. Concerned, the neighbor drove to Peyton's new office on Seaway Drive where she found the lights on, the door unlocked and the phone lines cut. Peyton's keys were still inside and her new Subaru Outback was still parked outside. The victim's partially-clad body wasn't discovered until the next day in an orange grove where she'd been brutally stabbed twelve times and her throat slit.

According to Sgt. Gonzalez's original report, a withdrawal receipt found next to Peyton's body led detectives to a PNC Bank on Ocean Drive in Vero Beach, where the ATM camera produced a video recording of the unsub using her ATM card. Although the unsub wore a hooded sweatshirt wrapped tightly around his face and latex gloves, detectives were able to enhance the image revealing the user was Caucasian, about five-feet six-inches tall and drove a psychedelic-painted VW van.

The detectives also found next to Peyton's body a blood-stained tie-dyed shirt similar to the shirt worn over the hoodie at the PNC Bank ATM. This revelation prompted detectives to conclude that Peyton was likely alive during the trip to Vero Beach and was brutally murdered upon her return to St. Lucie County.

The *Sun Sentinel* report went on to say that Croaker has a lengthy criminal history and served thirteen years of a twenty-year sentence at Raiford State Prison for an attempted murder during a botched robbery at an Orlando motel.

In that case, the report said the judge who sentenced Croaker told him; "You seem to me to be deeply disturbed, and there is absolutely no doubt in my mind that it was your intention from the get-go to murder your victim."

Just before sunset seven years later, Max Croaker was behind the wheel of his dilapidated ten-year-old black Honda Fit on a drug delivery as he searched for an address on Avenue "F" in Ft. Pierce. Two years earlier, the police had confiscated his psychedelic VW van for evidence on a possession charge before dropping it off in his driveway in pieces where it still lay today.

Avenue "F" was a seedy, rundown neighborhood with six-foot tall chain-link fences, some topped with razor wire used to keep predators out and snarling pit bulls in. Vicious dogs that looked as though they hadn't been fed in days lunged at him as he passed.

With his pockets full of cash, he could be remarkably easy going, but being branded as a "career criminal" gave him few choices for employment. Being a dealer and bag man was all he knew. Hirt paid him well, and always in cash. It was a sick world, but he was a happy guy, he would say.

Croaker was a slow learner, but what he did learn was just enough to keep him on the streets and out of jail. He knew how to recognize a stakeout, like the one he'd just driven by on Avenue "D" two minutes ago. Come on, he thought, who sits in a white Ford Taurus on a street infested with drug addicts at six p.m. and reads a newspaper?

Something else he learned from the mentor he latched onto at Raiford; always carry a fully-charged phone battery everywhere you go, and promptly answer your phone. As an added precaution, Hirt set up a new phone procedure so all calls went to a dispatcher. The dispatcher was a third party who took the call, traced the number through a database of numbers to ID them, then returned the call from a different phone to confirm their request for drugs. In this case, it was either China white or oxycodone.

Like the popular song, Croaker "made enough money to buy Miami, but pissed it away so fast." Some of it went toward paying off past legal and medical bills, and with what was left over, the bag man enjoyed running up big tabs at Cobalt and Costa d'Este with his friends and frolicking with high-end hookers.

A news story on the car radio about a drug bust caught his attention, and he reached to turn up the volume.

"Customs officers stationed at the Port of Miami made the largest fentanyl seizure ever recorded in the U.S. today. According to U.S. Customs and Border Protection, a canine officer alerted other officers to the presence of 654 pounds of fentanyl hidden inside an eighteen-wheeler carrying mangos and papayas during a secondary inspection at the Miami port of entry just past noon on Saturday." Croaker pulled over and stopped in front of an abandoned crack house to listen to the details.

"'It's been sent for chemical analysis, so we won't know the purity until a much later date,' said Michael Nogales, the CBP Miami port director. Initial tests by the DEA indicate the synthetic opioid is eighty-to-one hundred times more potent than morphine.'"

"In addition to the fentanyl, officers also seized 295 pounds of methamphetamine hidden inside the sleeping compartment of the big rig.

The smuggling of both opiates has been on the rise in various ports of entry in recent years along the U.S. southern borders. Officers arrested the driver of the eighteen wheeler and handed him over to Homeland Security, the agency which prosecutes transnational criminal activity. As an extra precaution, the entire shipment of mangos and papayas was also destroyed."

So, he thought, the costs of certain fruits and opiates were headed higher. With such a huge seizure of fentanyl, surely the street value in South Florida was on the rise. He decided the opportunity shouldn't be underestimated and deemed the news important enough to break radio silence with his boss. At first, Hirt wasn't happy with the call that came in on his inside line.

"Dr. Hirt," he answered gruffly.

"Boss, 654 pounds of China white just got seized in Miami and--"

"I told you not to call me on this line."

"No worries. I'm on a burner." Croaker took a deep breath and continued. "I figure we could jack our price forty percent and not skip a beat. That's an extra sixteen grand on this load alone."

Hirt's attitude softened as he considered the opportunity. "How much coffee you have left for the weekend?"

"I'm sittin' on forty-two at the quoted price and destined for immediate appreciation."

Hirt was impressed by his bag man's use of words that exceeded two syllables. "Let me remind you we don't sell durable goods-we peddle perception, subject to market price fluctuations." After showing Croaker he was still better at throwing around nebulous business terms, Hirt relented. "Let's find out how much they like their coffee. Do it."

"You got it, boss."

"Oh, and I might have another muscle job for you."

"Let me know," he answered in a darker voice before hanging up. After laying out two grand for last night's threesome at Costa d'Este, Croaker was ready for some extra cash.

His main product was still narcotics, and up-selling should have been easy for him, but it wasn't. Although the drug addicts whose homes he entered could usually afford larger bags, they would rarely splurge on them because they claimed their habit was only casual. Sometimes they wanted to hang out with their dealer and share their grandiose plans for the future, but past experiences had taught him to keep it simple and avoid the temptation of fraternizing and becoming friends.

And so, in a way, Croaker was as much at the mercy of their drug-induced delusions as they were to his own pipe dreams.

FOURTEEN

Stella parked the Range Rover and tipped the security guy extra to keep an eye on it while their long-time Vero Beach friends Helene and Carl Finstrom helped them get organized aboard *Dream Girl*.

It was a quarter past sunrise and a balmy seventy-five degrees at the Pelican Yacht Club, and the foursome began to unload their provisions from the dock for the long weekend ahead. Helene was passing dive gear and extra tanks to her husband, who handed them to Mark for placement aboard the boat. When it came to heavy objects that could break loose in rough seas, the captain took extra precautions to make sure they were well-secured and snapped into their holders in the lazarette. Without instructions from the skipper, the crew worked efficiently to complete their tasks, having done so many times in the past.

The sun continued its ascent in the morning sky while seagulls circled the harbor, chirping their greetings and begging for a handout. With all the snowbirds back in town, Pelican Yacht Club was without a single vacant berth, and Mark noticed that even the clusters of mooring balls were fully occupied. Given their intended course south, he looked forward to flying the spinnaker in the light northeasterly that rustled through the palm fronds.

The couple waved at an interesting group of friends they knew from Waldo's who were busy provisioning a forty-foot Beneteau named *Blew*

By You berthed one dock over. The always affable T.J. and her young daughter Lisette were on the dock handing off supplies to Eddie and his colorful wife Whensday when the foursome paused to say hello.

"Where you guys headed today?" asked Whensday, setting a case of rum down on the cockpit seat, her skull and crossbones tattoo matching the one on her husband's bicep.

"South for some reef diving and shopping on Worth Avenue," replied Stella. "And you?"

"Just a day sail…out and around," responded Eddie, rubbing a hand through his short-cropped hair, "…and some fishing."

"May be a bit of plundering if'n we get our Jolly Roger raised up," added Whensday in a pirate's voice and giving a suggestive wink.

Finished clearing the gear from the dock, Helene, Carl and Stella hopped aboard *Dream Girl* and began putting food, spear guns and dive gear where it belonged. The bikini-clad women kept busy in the forward cockpit while Carl helped the skipper with stowage in the main cockpit aft. Proud of his new quad-band spear gun, Carl hoisted it to show his dive buddy.

"Mark, check this out. Riffe Mach 7, with a five-foot stainless spear, 400-pound test, thirty-foot graphite line. This'll snag those really fat groupers."

Admiring Carl's new gun, "Looks like the recoil could put you in the hospital. Just don't shoot any sharks with it. I don't want to have to stitch you up." Stepping to the pedestal, Mark engaged the starter and listened to the six-cylinder Perkins diesel sputter to life.

As the foursome made ready to cast off, a short stocky guy in his forties with scraggly grey hair and black cap appeared on the dock and aimed his phone camera at the crew. "Beautiful boat," he commented. "Mind if I snap a few photos?" Without waiting for an answer, the odd looking man clicked off five or six photos of *Dream Girl* and her four crew in quick succession. Then, without looking back, he scurried away toward the dock's entry gate like a land crab seeking a hole to hide in.

Mark had grown accustomed to having strangers photograph his wife, usually without permission, but he thought the man's peculiar appearance and odd behavior seemed strange. "Another secret admirer, girls?"

Coiling the staysail halyard, Helene replied, "Never saw him before. Probably some porn scout from Miami," watching her bikini-clad girlfriend stretching to unlock the spinnaker pole. "Maybe he just wanted a few snapshots of your luscious first mate there, captain."

With four hours of morning left, they cast off. Mark motored away from the piers and moorings toward the Ft. Pierce Inlet, moving against the flood tide. When they reached the inlet's mouth, he shut off the engine and turned into the wind to set sail. Each responsible for a sail, Carl hoisted the mainsail, Helene the staysail, and Stella readied to set the spinnaker as they turned southeast and cleared the outer marker. With all three sails billowing, Mark lowered the hydraulic centerboard to fourteen feet to steady her up, adjusted the boom vang, and headed toward the open waters of the Atlantic.

The sixty-four-footer skirted the farthest eastern reefs and shores of St. Lucie and Martin County, sailing past the St. Lucie Inlet where the go-fast Cigarettes and Scarabs jetted out to admire the Baltic's graceful lines. The McAllisters were comfortable with her, for she was an ideal club boat, versatile and good looking, without the glitzy look of Feadships and megayachts, the yacht epitomizing a nautical triumph of substance over style.

With the girls basking in privacy and sunning themselves au naturel in the forward cockpit, they stretched out on the cushions to enjoy the warmth of the mid-morning sun and the sounds of the wind and waves. Carl was busy making the deck shipshape when he shared an observation with the skipper. "Shoreline's so different down here. Seems like the further south we sail, the larger the oceanfront condos get."

From behind the wheel, Mark nodded. "Welcome to the land of concrete and condo commandos."

Off in the distance, the city of Jupiter rose up, with its tall redbrick lighthouse standing watch over the inlet. A hundred yards further north was a spit of beach where Mark and his late wife Carol had first made love at the water's edge, and he took a moment to relive the event.

After an hour under sail, the sun was passing behind intermittent clouds of light and dark grey as they cruised south along the coast. In the mood for a cold one, Carl went below and reappeared with a couple of ice-cold Becks. Without saying a word, the two thirsty men clinked bottles and toasted the day before draining them in five or six huge gulps. Carl checked their speed and heel on the instrument panel; seven knots with only nine degrees of heel. Impressed with the skipper's finesse, he asked, "How long you been sailing?"

Mark turned the wheel three degrees to port with his toes. "When I was five, my dad taught me to sail a Sunfish on Lake Mitchell near Cadillac, Michigan. A few years later, I traded the cold lake water for the warm salt spray when I graduated to beach catamarans in Miami Beach."

"You started early. I'm gonna grab us more refreshments." A moment later, Carl ascended the companionway stairs with the ice-packed cooler and set it on deck.

Hearing the clinking of bottles, Stella stepped into the cockpit. "May we join you?" In their bikini bottoms, the girls made themselves comfortable on the cushions as Carl opened the cooler.

"Who's ready for a cold one?" popping four tops with his opener.

Taking a healthy swig, Helene asked "So what's the plan, skipper?"

"Well, we know you girls want to hit Worth Avenue and try to max out your credit cards," smiling wryly, "...so I thought we'd put in to Palm Beach and grab an Uber."

Stella offered her approval. "Reading my mind again, captain."

"You two think five hours will do it?" asked Carl.

"We could max them out faster if that would help," quipped Helene.

Happy with the itinerary, Stella turned to her shopping partner and gave her a high five. "So, that work for you, girlfriend? And maybe a light lunch at Ta-boo with the guys?"

"*Gotta* swing by Gucci and Chanel," responded Helene, "...and I heard about this new place called Escada."

"Sounds like a plan," declared Stella.

Sitting in a stern rod holder, Carl's Penn Senator sounded off. "Fish on!" declared Carl as he handed his beer to Helene and leaped onto the aft deck.

"What you got on that line, Carl?" asked Mark.

Arching the deep-sea rod high in the air and cranking like a madman, "Hopefully not just my ballyhoo." Their question was answered when a colorful mahi-mahi jumped high into the air off their stern. "Yeah, baby!" raising the rod straight up, "...looks about thirty pounds!"

Stella grabbed the binoculars from the binnacle and focused them in time to see the multi-colored fish jump again. "Yeah, I'd say about a thirty-five-pound mahi-mahi. Way to go, Carl!"

As the four focused on Carl bringing in his dolphin, a thirty-foot black and white Scarab with twin black Mercury outboards shot past them on the starboard side at high speed. A short stocky man with scraggly white hair sat behind the wheel, while a middle-aged Latino girl waved from the aft bench seat.

"That guy," pointing at the driver and raising her binoculars, "... wasn't that the guy we saw on the dock at Pelican Yacht Club? The one who was snapping our pictures?" asked Stella. The Scarab headed north at high speed behind a plume of spray before anyone could be certain.

"You sure?" asked Helene.

"Sure looked like him," handing the binoculars to Mark for a look, but by then, the Scarab was too far north to ID anyone on board.

Using the gaff to hook the dolphin, Helen weighed it in at thirty-eight pounds. As Carl finished fileting it, they sailed into the Port of Palm Beach, slightly sunburned and ready to explore the city. Mark had reserved a berth on his phone, and the foursome tied up *Dream Girl* and set her fenders before going below to shower in one of the four heads.

After four and a half hours of shopping at Gucci, Chanel, Escada, and Brioni, the foursome enjoyed a late lunch at Ta-boo. Thirty minutes later, they sailed out of the Port of Palm beach into the open Atlantic, turning south toward their favorite reef off Delray. It had been a spectacular day of sailing, shopping and bar hopping, and after an easy sail south, they dropped anchor at their GPS coordinates one mile due east of the Linton Boulevard bridge just as the sun began to set.

The four broke out some cognac and toasted the day, watching the greatest show on earth; an offshore sunset with rose-hued clouds, a deep-blue fringe on the eastern horizon, and a moon just beginning to rise. With the grill smoking away on the stern rail, Carl lifted the lid to turn the fish and squeeze more fresh lime juice over the delicate filets.

"Fresh grilled mahi-mahi anyone?"

Lt. Foti and Sgt. Heaton drove north on U.S. 1, on their way to Melbourne to bring in Boris Yakovlev for a second round of questioning. After being informed of the growing mound of circumstantial evidence piling up against the Ukrainian, Capt. Garrett had consented to Yakovlev's detainment following the discovery of the Executive Black cigarette butts at Humiston Park Beach and the stalking complaints.

"We going in heavy, lieutenant?"

"Vests, side arms and ankle backups. Let's not take any unnecessary chances," replied Foti. "This guy reminds me of Luca Brazi."

"Yes, sir." Heaton looked confused. "Luca who, sir?"

"Luca Brazi, Corleone's hit man, you know...from *The Godfather.*"

"Oh, yeah, the guy who sleeps with the fishes."

Turning into ZTE Pharmaceutical's lush entryway, Heaton whistled at the flowering hibiscus, azaleas, and exotic palms lining the entrance. "Looks like they spent more on landscaping than they did on developing new drugs last year."

Shutting the Explorer's hatch and donning their vests, the two men checked their weapons before heading toward the entrance. What they didn't expect was to be challenged by the two burly security guards in black suits on the granite steps.

"Gentlemen, can I help you?" asked the muscular guard in a Russian accent as he stepped in front of the two detectives.

Foti held up the shield hanging from his neck. "Vero Beach Police on official business. Where would I find Mr. Yakovlev's office? Is he in this building?"

With an attitude, the beefy guard pointed straight ahead begrudgingly. "Our receptionist can tell you. Straight up those steps, Mr. Policeman."

Through the mirrored doors and inside the cavernous entry hall, they noted a number of security cameras positioned strategically throughout the huge lobby. Two female employees in white lab coats seemed surprised by the appearance of the detectives as they descended the grand staircase leading to a mezzanine level on the second floor. Prominently displayed on the thirty-foot wall to the right of the receptionist's desk were paintings that appeared to be original masterpieces by Kandinsky and Chagall.

The Paris Hilton look-alike at the reception desk smiled invitingly. "Gentlemen, welcome to ZTE Pharmaceuticals. Won't you sign in our guest registry?"

Foti held up his badge as he read her name tag. "Can you tell me where I can find Boris Yakovlev, Valentina?" Upon hearing his name, her smile quickly evaporated.

"One moment. I'll check." Tapping her earpiece and pushing a button on the console, she lowered her voice as Foti leaned on the granite counter to listen in.

"Dr. Marchenko, those two detectives are back and they're asking for Mr. Yakovlev." Foti could hear a man chattering instructions in Russian over her earpiece. "Yes sir," she said, redirecting her attention to Foti and Heaton. "Dr. Marchenko said he will be right down." She gestured toward the black leather loungers. "Would you like to make yourselves comfortable?"

"Sure," replied Foti. The detectives meandered over to the coffee table and perused the latest issues of *Psychiatry Today* and *Pharmaceutical*

Representative, pretending to read as they watched employees moving through the lobby. A number of attractive women in lab coats crisscrossed the lobby floor, curious about the two detectives wearing bullet-proof vests and sidearms.

Emerging from a private elevator behind the staircase, a confident Dr. Anton Marchenko smiled and walked toward Foti, extending his hand as if greeting an old friend. "Lieutenant Foti, what a surprise," nodding at Heaton, "…so, what can I do for you, detectives?"

Foti tepidly shook his hand. "We're here to see your bodyguard, Boris Yakovlev, or as you call him, 'Bubba'. He around today?"

"I'm afraid you have missed Boris. He was called away to Ukraine on family emergency."

Clearly not the answer they expected to hear, the two officers looked at each other. Heaton spoke first. "How can that be? We still have his passport." The detectives waited for an explanation.

Marchenko shrugged. "I try to tell you week ago, my cousin very well connected with Ukrainian embassy."

"Your cousin's in a lot of trouble, and we may have to extradite him," declared Foti.

Reacting to his threat, Marchenko reached into his shirt pocket and handed him a card bearing the name and contact information of the Ukrainian Ambassador in New York. Turning to leave, "Call this man at embassy if you have more questions. If there is nothing else, detectives, good luck."

FIFTEEN

Precisely at seven o'clock, bright orange streams of light broke through on the ocean's horizon off Delray Beach, and the sun broke above the skyline with spectacular brilliance. With the fresh scent of the ocean filling his nostrils, Mark stood on the bow wearing his teal dive skin, mesmerized by the spectacular sunrise. During the night, *Dream Girl* had swung around on her double anchors to face the steady seven-knot easterly breeze, and with seas of only three feet, the two men prepared for a great day of diving.

Gearing up together in the aft cockpit, Carl prepped his new Riffe Mach 7 spear gun, and Mark his proven Riffe triple-bander. The foursome had shared a late night of drinking amid hours of jovial banter, and Mark was pleasantly surprised that he didn't feel hung over given the quantities of liquor they consumed. Careful not to wake Stella and Helene, the two men continued putting on their gear and double-checked their equipment. Carl raised the red dive flag using the staysail halyard as Mark checked the lines to the two seventy-five-pound Danforths.

Both were experienced divers who liked to hunt solo and decided to head in different directions once they were underwater. Carl planned to head north along the reef face to search for grouper holes, while Mark would head south to a discarded tubular structure he called "The Cage."

Sitting on the gunnel, the two men checked each other's air supply one last time before plunging over backwards into the crystal-clear water.

The ocean become cooler as Mark descended into the turquoise depths toward the reef below. Behind him to the north, he could make out Carl's exhaust bubbles rising from the depths along the reef's top ridge. Prepared for an extended blue water hunt, Mark wore an overfilled steel tank with a forty-percent nitrox mix, an octopus rig, and an assortment of hunting gear dangling from six snap shackles attached to his buoyancy compensator.

Though dangerous and ill-advised by dive instructors, he was adept at skip-breathing, and was also proficient at controlling his heart rate underwater. If he stayed above seventy feet, Mark could squeeze out up to two hours of dive time without having to waste precious air decompressing, giving him even more time to locate the items on Stella's "shopping list," including fresh grouper, snapper, and-her favorite-Florida lobster.

Diving on a beautiful oceanic reef wasn't only physical for him, it took on a deeper spiritual meaning as he surrendered to a consciousness that superseded his own being. It was God, life, and love of Mother Nature all rolled into one beautiful kaleidoscopic experience as he imagined becoming part of the reef itself. Fascinated by the vibrancy and the incredible diversity of reef life, he felt protective, as if all the creatures were part of his family.

When he hovered in neutral buoyancy, reef diving made him feel like he was still suspended in amniotic fluid in his mother's womb. Feeling weightless, he was mesmerized by the colorful soft corals swaying back and forth in the mild current as he began his hunt. The myriad of clown fish, trumpet fish, striped grunts, French, grey and queen angelfish swimming in harmony with the sea fans offered a broad palate of spectacular colors. He thought of Gauguin's vivid portraits and often wondered how the famous artist would have painted these underwater scenes. Halfway up the reef wall, Mark spotted a medium-size nurse shark on a hunt of its own as it cruised in and out of rock formations.

To avoid a blood trail, he typically deferred the spear fishing until the end of his dive. Standing on the sandy bottom, he took a moment to double-check the lobster snare, game bag, mini-EPIRB and emergency regulator hanging from his BC. Lastly, he tightened the Velcro fasteners on his gloves and checked his compass bearings before turning due east toward the two seventy-five-pound Danforths dug into the sandy bottom.

His ear was tuned to the faint sounds of reef inhabitants scurrying about in the never-ending struggle for food and survival. He thought about men who liked to hunt deer with a high-powered rifle. The hunter has grace, respect, and purity of heart, and pumping a .308 slug into a defenseless deer just didn't qualify as a sporting event in his book. Hunting only seemed sporting to him if the hunter was in as much peril as the hunted.

Thrilled with the water clarity, he estimated the visibility to be about two-hundred feet as a large spotted moray eel slithered along the coral wall thirty feet below. The moray was followed by a curious school of yellowtail that swam up from the depths to greet him. As the lead shot weights in his BC and his steel tank carried him deeper, he spotted the shank and chain rode of the first anchor. The weather forecast had predicted an increase in wind and seas, and he wanted to place the two anchors on the windward side of the gigantic concrete slab that was set there two decades earlier by the Army Corps of Engineers.

Mark reached down and grasped the steel shank of the first anchor with his gloved hand and pressed the BC inflator button to give him lift. Bouncing off the bottom, he kicked hard like he was rebounding on the moon's surface with one-fifth the gravity, carrying the anchor ten yards forward to reposition it. After it dropped, he repeated the procedure with the second Danforth. Now, their anchorage was more secure.

Positioned in the middle of the half-mile long reef among the greatest concentration of lobster holes was "The Cage." The large metal structure was always the easiest of all the reef's features to identify on his boat's sonar screen. Within minutes, he scored three large lobsters before heading south against the mild current for the first half of his dive along the top of the reef wall. Then, he circled to the eastern edge where the large crevasses dropped off as they extended into the grey-green depths of the deeper water like giant fingers reaching toward the ocean's bottom.

Located on the backside of the reef seventy-five feet down, "The Rubble" was his next waypoint. Here, there were basketball-size chunks of odd-shaped coral mysteriously piled up as if a large backhoe had dug them up eons ago. Among the rocks was a cache of oversize lobster, and he was overjoyed to snare five of the largest in the group without much effort.

In neutral buoyancy at "The Rubble", he was disturbed by the sounds of a twin-engine boat hovering on the surface almost directly above him. Looking skyward, the hull of what looked like a thirty-footer with twin engines moved slowly south. Was the boat trolling across the reef without noticing his dive flag? To put more distance between himself and the sharp propellers above, he checked his compass and rode the light current to his next waypoint.

A hundred yards further north, he ascended over the top of the reef at about fifty-five feet before descending into a beautiful, sandy-bottomed underwater lagoon the size of a basketball court that he called "The Aquarium." There, the water was exceptionally clear and relatively motionless, and a myriad of sea anemones and soft corals of indescribable beauty ringed the entrance as they waved back and forth in the light current. Dropping inside "The Aquarium" and kneeling on the sand gave him the opportunity to scan the ten-foot-high coral walls that rimmed the perimeter. A large green spotted moray eel poked his head out of a coral hole, opening and closing his mouth to show his razor-sharp teeth as a warning to trespassers. Deeper inside the coral caves, Mark could also make out the antennae of several king-size bugs, any of which would make great trophies.

A great diversity of marine creatures both divine and deadly hid in the holes along the perimeter of "The Aquarium." Often filled with a dangerous collection of competing hunters that included black tip reef sharks, lionfish, moray eels and barracuda, Mark liked to think of it as his private seafood market. An occasional manta ray or school of tuna would sometimes find their way to the reef's edge and meander over the top in their hunt for a meal. One of his favorite sights were the groups of cuttlefish that would hover over the reef in formation like a squadron of aircraft suspended in midair.

Then he heard it again, the sounds of a twin-engine boat close by on the surface, only this time he couldn't locate it. Sounding like the same boat, it seemed like it was following his surface bubbles. Hoping it would move away, he turned his attention back to the caves where the lobsters were hiding. *Ready or not, here I come.*

On the hunt for similar prey, the huge moray continued to slither in and out of holes away from him, unaware of the huge spiny lobster Mark had spotted about twelve feet down the reef face. Releasing a stream of air from his inflator, he descended down to the sandy bottom, putting himself in a position ten yards directly in front of the monster lobster. Relaxing his breathing, he concentrated on reducing his heart rate and lowering his electromagnetic signature so he could get closer to the grand-daddy bug without alarming it. To his delight, the lobster responded to Mark's approach by creeping forward a few feet out of his hole. *What's on your mind, bud?*

Suddenly, out of the corner of his mask, he saw a large octopus with tentacles six feet long shoot out of a coral crevasse and lunge at him. He suppressed his instinct to unsheathe the razor-sharp dive knife strapped to his leg and dismember the beast, even as the animal's menacing beak pressed against the glass surface of his facemask. With his field of vision obscured, he was alarmed to feel one of the tentacles tugging at his regulator as he fought with the octopus to secure his air supply. In a surprise move, the creature pulled it out of his mouth and held it just out of his reach. *She must be protecting her young.*

Holding in his last breath, he was in a hell of a fix as he knelt on the ocean floor with the creature wrapped around his head, in control of his air supply. *Jesus, Joseph and Mary, give me back my damn regulator.*

A previous encounter with an octopus on the Great Barrier Reef years earlier flashed through his brain, and he remembered the key to surviving the experience lay in showing the creature that he meant it no harm.

With his last breath and one hand on his dive knife, his pulse raced as he struggled to remain calm. Making a last-ditch effort to avoid bloodshed, he firmly pushed the tentacles away from his body one at a time. The creature responded in kind by releasing his regulator and softening its grip on him. About to lose consciousness, he lunged for the regulator, grabbing it and reinserting it into his mouth. With stars whirling around his head, he took several long deep breaths of cool, sweet air.

In a surprise move, the huge creature squirted a massive cloud of black ink at him to disguise its retreat. With a fresh supply of oxygen coursing through his veins, he watched the octopus rocket back into the crevasse from which it had launched its ambush and disappear.

Unsettled by the attack, Mark maneuvered out of the black ink cloud into the clearer water behind him, thankful that he'd survived without having to kill such an intelligent creature. Relieved, he worked to regain his orientation and calm himself, looking toward the surface seventy feet up as his exhaust bubbles ascended.

He couldn't help wondering what Helene and Stella were doing topside as he watched his bubbles ascend and grow smaller toward the surface. He pictured them sunning themselves on the cockpit cushions, floating worlds away, chatting about their shopping experience on Worth Avenue yesterday or their last round of golf at Club Riomar.

His heart rate back to normal and no longer deprived of oxygen, his desire to bag the trophy lobster returned. Peering through the crystal-clear water ahead, he spotted his trophy-to-be, still waiting twenty yards away behind a school of yellowtail. The gargantuan lobster seemed unfazed by the life-and-death drama just played out on the sandy floor of "The Aquarium." In a defiant stance, it continued to sweep its antennae slowly back and forth, guarding the entrance to its lair.

Checking the reef wall ahead for any signs of the octopus, Mark moved in for the kill, now more determined than ever to bag the big bug. Extending his snare as he approached, he slipped the noose over the giant crustacean's tail and jerked hard on the cable to tighten the loop. Feeling like he'd snared a Sumo wrestler, the huge lobster grunted in protest as he wrestled it into his game bag with gloved hands and imagined the surprised look on Stella's face when he presented his trophy to her.

Another eighty minutes of hunting lapsed, and there was still no sign of Carl. Six more good-size bugs joined the others in his game bag, bringing his count to fourteen. *Thanks for playing, fellas.*

From the depths, two playful porpoise emerged, swimming up close to check out his bulging game bag as he pulled it nearer to protect his day's catch. When he reached out to touch them, one of the mammals nudged his hand as if to say hello before disappearing into the depths.

The two-foot-long lobster had torn his dive skin during his struggle to corral it, and Mark could feel his mac-daddy bug working hard to escape its nylon prison as he double-checked the clasp on the bag. With enough air left for one final gamefish run, he strained to stretch and lock all three bands on his spear gun before beginning his final leg along the soft corals on the top of the reef.

Starting at 3,300 PSI, his air gauge now read 635 PSI, barely enough for what he had in mind. After encountering three large sharks earlier on his dive, he thought about the risks of leaving a blood trail from a wounded fish. Though his catch bag was getting heavy, he still had enough room for one or two gamefish and began skip breathing to conserve his remaining air.

Cruising another fifty yards along the reef top, he passed a few medium-sized hogfish meandering through the soft corals before spotting a large black grouper darting between holes. Just out of range, Mark settled in behind a group of sea fans to camouflage his approach. Groupers were more elusive than hogfish, so he'd have to be on his toes to bag it. A trophy black grouper to match his monster lobster would be a nice addition to the menu, and the one in his sights looked to be about twenty pounds. He waited patiently and burned through another ten pounds of nitrox before he saw the grouper emerge again. Mark descended below the edge of the reef and made his approach at a right angle to optimize his shot. *C'mon out, Mr. Grouper. You're on my wife's shopping list.*

As the grouper emerged again ten feet away, he had a clear shot, took aim and squeezed the trigger. The stainless steel spear hit the fish just behind the gill plate. It was a perfect shot, and he pounced quickly before the grouper could roll over on the bottom and push the spear out. Holding it against the sea floor with his flipper, he extracted his spear and stuffed the grouper head-first into his packed game bag. *Welcome aboard.*

Straining to stretch the three bands and reload his spear gun, he heard a strange sound like escaping compressed air. Something hard and heavy impacted the side of his buoyancy compensator where the lead shot weight bags were located, knocking him sideways. Stunned, he reached around to feel a spear lodged firmly in his BC and caught a glimpse of the shooter-a diver in a black wetsuit swimming rapidly away using the sea fans for cover. Mark pulled hard on the spear to dislodge it before realizing his BC was leaking a stream of air bubbles. Checking his console, his air gauge was reading zero, and the nitrogen saturation gauge indicated he had already crossed into the yellow warning zone. Without enough nitrox to chase the diver who had just tried to send him to Davey Jones's locker, he prepared to surface.

Mark had to get topside fast if he wanted to live to dive another day and prepared for an emergency ascent with the spear still lodged in the side of his BC. With his last breath, he spotted the anchor's chain rode and followed the line upward, careful not to ascend faster than his bubbles, the air in his lungs expanding as he angled toward the surface. His tank and BC empty, his lungs screamed for air as he neared the top.

"Huuhhhhhhh," taking a huge lungful of air as he broke the surface a hundred feet from the bow, overjoyed to see the sky again. Without knowing if sharks had followed his blood trail to the surface, Mark took one last look into the depths below to make sure. Exhausted, negatively buoyant with a hole in his BC, and treading water with the full weight of his equipment, he was eager to get to *Dream Girl's* stern swim ladder.

The sound of high-speed engines caught his attention as he raised his mask and looked south toward the distant boat departing the area at high speed. Unable to identify any details, all he could see was a high white plume of water as it raced south. Looking up, he saw Stella kneeling on the swim platform as she leaned over and dropped the swim ladder.

"Honey, are you okay? You were gone a long time." Peering over the edge, her bare breasts dangled six feet above him like two beautiful ripe peaches in the morning sun.

"You've just given me two more gorgeous reasons to get aboard," he said. Spitting out sea water, "Got us enough seafood to last us a month." With his fins on the bottom rung, they managed to lift the over-stuffed game bag into the boat. Almost weightless in the water, he estimated it contained over a hundred pounds of seafood as they hoisted it aboard.

"Where's Carl?" he asked.

"He's already on his second dive. Helene is with him. You should see the groupers he scored." She got upset when she saw the two-foot spear protruding from his BC. "Honey, you've got a *spear* in you. *What on earth happened to you down there?*"

Once aboard, he sat down heavily on the cockpit seat cushions, banging his tank and the two-foot spear against the bulkhead. Bothered by the blood, she watched it drip off his equipment onto the teak deck as he wriggled out of his BC and harness. Staring at the red droplets, then the spear, she was relieved that it had not penetrated any further than the lead shot weights. "So...the blood--"

"From the fish, not mine." Gesturing at the spear, "Diver in a black wetsuit took a shot at me. First time I've ever been shot at underwater."

Troubled, she knelt down in front of him. "Could it have been an accident?" she ventured.

Shaking his head. "Not likely. The shooter waited until I was preoccupied and my gun was empty." Giving her a grave look, "I think someone wants me off this case."

A thought occurred to him. "While I was down, did that twin-engine Scarab come around? You know, the one we saw off St. Lucie Inlet yesterday? With that runt at the wheel? I think it may have been the one I just saw heading south at warp speed."

"I heard a twin-engine boat a while ago, but it was at a distance. I was half asleep." Her face turning pouty, "I had a dream that you weren't coming back. Let's head back when Carl and Helene return." She thought about the weirdo photographer at Pelican Yacht Club. "You think that guy followed us from Ft. Pierce?"

He shrugged. "It's possible."

Something odd sticking to his shoulder caught her attention. "And what's this?" peeling off an octopus sucker from the back of his dive skin and turning it over in the palm of her hand.

"Not all the wildlife was friendly," he said. "Giant octopus turned my dive into," taking a deep breath, "...an encounter of the wrong kind." She stared at him in disbelief. "*Jesus*, Mark, you had one helluva dive!"

Glancing at his wriggling catch bag full of creatures trying to make their getaway, "The price you pay for fresh seafood, I guess," giving her a brief smile. "Let's get the catch bag on ice and into the big cooler. First, can you bring me the first aid kit from the starboard cabinet in the galley?" He began stripping off the rest of his equipment. "I need to rest for a moment," tilting his head back onto the seat bolster.

Stella stood and pirouetted, sashaying toward the cabin entrance to tease some life back into her dog-tired diver. Playfully pointing to starboard, she stopped and posed like a model. "Starboard is on the right, right?"

"Stop it. And while you're down there, can you bring me up a cold beer? For medicinal purposes," his smile turning into more of a wince.

Twenty minutes later, Carl and Helene returned with their catch bags brimming with snapper, grouper and lobsters. With the sailboat rocking peacefully in a ten-knot breeze and light seas, Mark had fallen asleep in the master cabin, still exhausted from his ordeal with the octopus and the mysterious diver in black.

So, after hearing of his ordeal, they all agreed to allow the captain to finish his nap while the girls made plans in the forward cockpit. While Carl kept watch, Stella brought Helene up to date on the two murder investigations, and she was shocked to learn that there could be a connection between today's spear gun attack and their help with the investigations.

Below deck, Mark was busy dreaming about Stella in a beauty contest. He dreamt that the first prize was one million dollars a month for the rest of their lives, enough to fund another extended circumnavigation.

In his dream, he was suddenly aware that the crowd applauding his wife onstage consisted entirely of dead SWAT team officers and deceased drug dealers chasing him in black wetsuits. Terrified, he began running toward the beach and calling out for her as he looked back over his shoulder. He ran as fast as he could, fearful the crowd of dead drug dealers would catch him as he searched for a path between the gleaming high-rises and condominiums to make his escape.

But there was no way out.

The sprawling mass of huge concrete buildings blocked his view of the sky, and there was no road, no alleyway, or even a beacon of light to lead him to safety.

In the dream, he ran frantically as the sand beneath his feet was disappearing under waves of cold sea water rolling in, slowing his escape. When it reached his ankles, he realized the tide was coming in much faster than usual. When the water reached his waist, it was impossible to run, and his legs ceased moving, immobilized by the freezing water.

Looking skyward for warmth from the sun, there was his answer: the water had turned frigid because the sprawling condos had become so massive that the sun's rays were being blocked out by huge concrete buildings thousands of stories high.

His dream morphing into a nightmare, the frigid sea water rose up to his neck as he fought to catch his breath. He felt stabbing pains throughout his body from the shockingly-cold ocean and floating all around him were the corpses of SWAT teams and the cadavers of dead pelicans and seagulls. Crying out for help, he pushed away a hand from one of the cadavers. It wasn't a cadaver, but Stella's touch that caused him to awaken and open his eyes.

"Honey, you were having a bad dream. It's okay, just a bad dream," she said softly, caressing his cheek.

He reached for her hand. "Promise you'll never leave me."

"Promise," running her fingers gently across the lines of his face. "Rest. You've been through a lot today."

"Are Carl and Helene back aboard?" he asked.

"Yeah, and they scored some goodies. They couldn't believe the size of your mac-daddy lobster. We had a photo op with it. Carl figured you'd want to get underway and is making preparations."

"You've been filling them in?"

"Over a couple of cognacs."

"You let Dominic know what happened?" guessing she had called him.

She nodded. "He was concerned, and I told him we'd meet him late tomorrow. He suggested you preserve any prints that may be on the spear by putting it in a garbage bag."

"That's just what I was going to do."

Uncomfortable with the obvious conclusion, she asked, "You don't think it could've been an accident, and the guy just freaked and took off?"

Mark thought about it. "It's possible," but his instincts were telling him otherwise.

Her mood changing abruptly, she'd been waiting for the right time to spring her idea. "Honey, I've been thinking. Mulligan's is offering twenty-five thousand in cash for the winner of their next bikini contest, and Helene and I want to enter. Carl says we'd be shoo-ins. It's only a hundred bucks apiece to enter." He thought about his dream and winced.

Giving him her best Hollywood smile, "Whad'ya think, cowboy? Will you sponsor me?"

SIXTEEN

Monday morning was passing uneventfully for Mark, apart from a slight headache as he drove in Stella's Range Rover to the Vero Beach Police Department. Speculating that the headache was likely brought on by the nitrogen narcosis from his dive yesterday, he figured it could also be a result of the stress he was under. Rare was the day when he would desire a cognac so early in the morning, but today was one of those days.

On his way to meet Foti and Beretto, he was deeply concerned with the danger he and Stella were facing. Mark was torn between his desire to catch this homicidal maniac and his desire to protect his wife by taking her out of the unsub's crosshairs. He blamed himself for underestimating the risks of providing assistance in the murders of Dr. Tremelle and Kelly Ann Granata, but he and Stella were undeterred in their belief that the victims and their families deserved justice.

What had once made him feel worthy to his friends in law enforcement was now making him feel concerned for the safety of everyone he knew. This unsub had hijacked his life, and Mark realized that as long as the killer was still at large, he wouldn't be at peace with himself. Strangely, he hadn't felt that way before the spear gun attack off Delray Beach.

Uncertain as to why this revelation was born today, he supposed that revelations were indeed like that; all of a sudden, one day, they just slap you across the face, and unannounced, the truth collides with you, whether you were looking for it or not. What he would do about it was what occupied his immediate attention today, and that depended quite a bit on what Beretto and Foti had to say. Stepping up to take on an increasingly dangerous role, his intuition was telling him the killer may have already decided to provide that role for him.

Beretto met him at the security door to the CID and looked him over for signs of wear. "So, how is Aqua Man feeling today?"

"Like maybe I should buy my seafood at Publix from now on. I could have the guy behind the counter toss it to me so I could say I caught it."

"Uh-huh. Might live longer, but look at the fun you'd miss," flashing a broad grin. He regarded the black plastic bag containing the spear in Mark's grip and gestured to the forensics officer. "Margo," handing her the bag, "...fingerprints and origin on this, pronto. We'll be in the conference room. Feel free to interrupt with your analysis."

"Yes, sir," she said, doing a U-turn in her lab coat and safety glasses as she headed to the lab.

"Lt. Foti's in the conference room," said Beretto, "...along with a new member of our team I brought in from Atlanta. She says her idea may bring you a bit more aggravation."

"Did you tell her I'm already married?"

Beretto laughed. "I see you haven't lost your sense of humor."

"My bravado, maybe, but never my sense of humor. So, what's her name?"

"Special Agent Gwen Madani. Been on my team for three years."

"She good?"

Reaching for the conference room door, "Ninety-eight percent conviction rate. I'd like to hear what you think of her ideas."

As the door opened, an attractive dark-haired woman in a tight-fitting skirt was standing at the head of the table as she spoke to Lt. Foti, D.S. Garner, D.S. Heaton, and Tech Ofc. Locke who were seated around the big table with their tablets. Beretto and McAllister quietly took a seat at the opposite end as Madani nodded at the newcomers and continued her update.

"And so, over the past decade, this is why the subject of serial murders has attracted more of our attention in law enforcement. It may not be as bad as the epidemic suggested by the headline news stories they're spinning, but it's alarming that such a small number of offenders are responsible for so many wasted lives and so much widespread fear." Madani paused to look around the room and take a sip from her bottled water before she continued.

"Typically, though we think not in *this* case, the serial killer is a white male in his thirties who objectifies his victims encountered near his work or home. These killers tend to be psychopaths who may satisfy personal needs by killing their victims using physical force."

Det. Sgt. Garner posed a rare question; "Agent Madani, clarify something for me. What is it that you think is different about this unsub?"

"Good question," she continued. "In my study of the case files, this killer is demographically similar to the mass murderer in that this serial killer kills victims he knows using deliberate actions and methods-in this case, lethal chemical injections of fentanyl. He is executing them in the most lethal and convenient way. It is also my belief that he is sending his future victims a message in the order they are executed."

"What are the similarities that you see in motivation, and can you tell us more about the order of execution?" asked Mark.

"Sure. The difference of timing that separates serial from mass murderers could also camouflage strong similarities in their motivation. Both types can be understood within the identical motivational typology of power, revenge, profit, and terror."

"And so, what specific motivational type are we dealing with here, Gwen," queried Beretto.

"The unsub we're looking for is a brutally sadistic white male between thirty-five and fifty-five who gets off on the victim's fear, and her resistance allows him to push the limits of torture even further. In this case, immobilized with a stun gun, choked, beaten and then drugged."

"And the motivation?" repeated Foti.

She replied with conviction. "I believe that not only are we trying to catch a delusional psychopathic killer bent on some sort of revenge for his own perceived mistreatment, he may be intentionally sharing clues about his future victims to terrify them. He appears to be goal oriented, driven by rage, and uses power to control his victims, making them feel totally helpless. My guess is his rage has been suppressed for years, which makes his methods of torture extremely brutal." She paused and looked around the room to encourage questions.

"What about his timeline," asked Heaton. "When do you think he'll strike next?"

"Good question," replied Madani. "We believe this unsub is becoming increasingly driven to revenge and more volatile with each victim. He acts on compulsion, a need-based desire, and understanding his needs will be the key to capturing him."

"What about the fentanyl," asked Mark. "How does that play in?"

"Separately, our efforts to prevent deadly drugs from reaching the streets in quantity may lead us to this unsub as I believe it is a drug of convenience for him. And so, there's that connection."

"A rolling rock gathers no grass, huh?" interjected Locke inopportunely.

Bewildered, the officers looked at each other. Confused, Madani said, "Not sure I'm following--"

"Don't mind our resident clown of clichés," said Heaton as he stared at Locke. "I think he was going for--"

"Coffee," interrupted Foti. "Gary, bring us six coffees. Yesterday."

"Yes, sir." Embarrassed, Locke timidly left the room to get coffee for the group while the other five used the break to catch up on their notes.

Foti leaned back and crossed his arms, impressed with her profile of the killer. "Do you see a pattern in his victim selection?"

"I do, and it doesn't appear random. Both geographic, which we've plotted on this Google map," pointing at the digital storyboard, "...and also by social media, or social proximity, illustrated on this spider web chart."

As he studied the intricate illustrations developed by Madani's team, Mark realized his wife was right in the cross hairs of both the spider web chart and geographical map depicting Orchid Island. "Why do you think he's moving in this direction?" he asked, trying to suppress his anxiety.

"I think he enjoys terrorizing his future victim. It's a power play," responded Beretto, "...like a cat playing with its mouse."

Madani leaned against the edge of the table and confirmed her boss's observation. "Exactly." She regarded the six men sitting at the table one at a time, then fixed her gaze on Mark whom she guessed was trying to avoid an uncomfortable conclusion.

Madani was about to ask the investigative journalist a question when forensics officer Violette entered the conference room with her PC and a four-page fingerprint analysis.

She handed it to Foti. "We could only get a partial, sir." Violette leaned over to explain her results. "We narrowed it down to three possible suspects with the most likely one on top," as she pointed at the screen, "... who also has a lengthy rap sheet going back three decades. The pneumatic spear shaft was generic, but we're checking digital POS footage from the few dive shops that carry this item." As she straightened, she added, "All of it's been sent to your phones and tablets."

Foti looked up at her. "Good work, Margo. I knew you weren't just another pretty face," as he handed the hard copy to Beretto, who examined it carefully before handing it to Madani.

"Take a seat, Margo," directed Beretto. "We may need you again." Violette took a seat, adjusting her PC as the other officers reviewed the fresh data on their screens.

Locke returned from the kitchen with a tray full of fresh coffee, milk and sweeteners which he quietly set in the center of the table before meekly taking his seat.

Finished with her own review of Violette's report, Madani took center stage again as she perused her computer. "I suggest we focus on the Google map and social media spider web chart. Also, we've identified three possible suspects for the spear gun attack who could also be fentanyl distributors." She lowered her gaze to Mark. "Only one of them has a lengthy record, is a designated career criminal, and is about the height and weight you've described."

She made a few entries on her tablet to transfer the data and pointed at a color photo appearing on the digital storyboard. The scraggly grey-haired man in the tie-dyed shirt looked vaguely familiar to the team of Vero Beach detectives.

"Gentlemen, I give you Max Croaker." She looked at Mark. "You think you can positively say this is the guy you saw?"

Everyone's eyes turned to Mark as he stared at the photo. "I'd like to say yes, but I can't say for certain. I hate to disappoint you guys, but…"

Beretto leaned forward with his arms on the table. "Mark, you know how important this is. How about Stella. She get a better look at this guy?"

"That's doubtful. She was busy loading supplies during the only time we saw him close up on the dock at Pelican Yacht Club."

Clearly disappointed, the group looked to their lead detective who was preparing to say something. "It was about eight years ago," mused Foti, "…I remember this dirt bag. He was the prime suspect in the murder of a hooker in St. Lucie County. The detectives on the case gave a mountain of evidence to the state attorney, but they declined to prosecute him, claiming it was all too circumstantial."

"That's right," added Garner, "…I used to play softball with the lead detective on the case, Sgt. Marco Gonzalez, 'til he got himself shot and killed in a bank robbery in Port St. Lucie." A rare look of sadness crossed his face. "Great ball player, even better detective. Relatives claimed they bungled the case--"

"I don't believe that," interjected Foti.

"Neither do I," continued Garner, "…and after Marco was gone, St. Lucie County put the case on the back burner."

Studying Croaker's case files, Heaton weighed in. "Croaker's still a suspect in a Vero murder that occurred four months *before* Angela Peyton's murder in Port Fierce."

"Port Fierce?" questioned Foti.

"Force of habit, boss," explained Heaton.

"Actually, it fits. Port Fierce," repeated Foti.

Beretto had been listening attentively and offered his summary. "So, we've uncovered a career criminal, this 'dirt bag', as you say, Max Croaker, who is now the suspect in *four* separate murders?" holding up four fingers. "All here on the Treasure Coast?"

"Where there's smoke, there's fire!" declared Locke, finally getting one right, to the amazement of the group.

Reading the faces around the table, Beretto clarified; "That's not smoke, Gary, that's a *raging forest fire!*"

Madani looked first at Beretto, then Foti. "With the homicides of Peyton, Tremelle, Granata, and this other woman in Vero, you think we have enough for a warrant?"

Foti shook his head at Beretto who nodded in agreement. "This one's a little thin," replied her boss, "... so I doubt if the judge would approve it, especially given the fact that the St. Lucie County judge refused to approve the arrest warrant years ago when the evidence was fresher. But we can start the affidavit and see what we've got, even though a lot of it is circumstantial."

"Okay, then," declared Foti loudly. "Margo, you and Gary keep digging on Croaker."

Violette typed away on her keyboard. "Already on it, boss. This guy's *real sketchy*, but he pops up on the grid here and there."

Foti continued. "Dennis and Greg, when Margo and Gary locate this dirt bag, I want you two to put a 24-hour surveillance on him." The two officers looked up from their computers and nodded.

"Do we share with our brothers in St. Lucie on this one?" Heaton wanted to know.

"I'll leave that to your discretion. Now, let's put a net over it. I need to know where he sleeps, eats and who he meets with. All right, let's go!" clapping his hands together.

"Everyone, find another gear! Lives at stake here!"

SEVENTEEN

In her early twenties, well before she'd developed a more definitive set of moral values, and almost nine years before she became a Vero Beach police officer, Margo Violette found herself caught up in a glitzy Boca lifestyle that she would just as soon forget about. Today, it seemed like a whole other life on a planet far far away.

On one of those days nine years ago, Margo stared out the window of her central Boca Beach condo overlooking Red Reef Park as she watched a group of surfers carving up the waves. They reminded her of the young men she'd been engaged to when she naively pursued men for love instead of money. With another sip of chardonnay, her thoughts drifted to the terms of endearment often used to gain her favors over the years, and the gifts of diamonds and jewelry that went along with the promises. The diamond rings she'd returned without remorse, with the exception of one she kept for sentimental reasons. It was a ring given to her by a guy named Jimmy Sheister, one of the few guys she'd almost been in love with.

Always broke, Jimmy Sheister struggled for years as a singer in bars and restaurants, almost starving until he started doing voice overs for political campaigns. His fortunes began to change, with more work than he could handle, and he became quite successful with his new-found career of vocal art, as he called it.

Gradually, he made his way onto the airwaves on primetime television doing voice overs for campaign commercials. Ironically, Sheister couldn't stand politics and held the senators and congressmen who employed him in such low esteem that he refused to vote for them. She had come to admire him for recognizing the hypocrisy in what he did and admitting that he hated his job. Margo thought it took a man with integrity to recognize there were few things in today's world that were as deceptive as a sixty-second campaign commercial.

After living a dichotomous life for years, Sheister began to develop deep psychological issues with the hypocrisy he was caught up in, even entertaining suicidal thoughts that he would sometimes share with Margo. As she watched a man she admired squander his God-given talents as a singer to provide a wealthy lifestyle for her, she realized that she was at least partly responsible for his conundrum. Often, she faced the same self-inflicted dilemma; she could be idealistic, or she could be wealthy, but she didn't see a way to be both. It was a sad dilemma for her at such an early age.

Earlier in their relationship, she felt guilty about the jewelry, the Benz, the waterfront house on Biscayne Bay, and all the extravagant shopping trips, all provided by a job that Jimmy hated. After their break up, Margo saw her choices with even greater clarity when she learned of his suicide the night he put a shotgun in his mouth. She missed him, but had already made the decision to move up the food chain with men who were more affluent. Growing more appreciative of the finer things money could buy, her collection of seventy-six Hermes and Luis Vuitton handbags was the envy of every woman in her narcotics anonymous class.

After the Jimmy Sheister fiasco, Margo decided that she was indeed a player and set out on a new path to secure her own financial independence. Given the often superficial valuations that Americans placed on women's beauty, she took what looked like an easy road and set out to monetize her looks and sex appeal on the internet.

After having a professional website created, she was ready to implement her lucrative plan to perform "private dances" for older gentlemen of power and wealth; men whose carefree use of Viagra as a recreational drug made them so incredibly eager to make appointments on her website. She played on their need to reinvigorate their dwindling sex lives, and her business plan consisted of hooking up with the octogenarian billionaires whose gigantic egos demanded the intimate company of a former Playmate of the Month. And so Margo's path to financial independence changed course with the easy money she figured to make by hooking up with elderly "generous gents."

On the net, Margo came across an old geezer named Anthony Bellarosa. Mr. Bellarosa had described himself as a "generous gent who enjoyed private parties." He posted photos of himself on "ManlyMillionairesClub. com", photos that Margo guessed were likely taken shortly after his college graduation. After spending ten minutes with him in a private chatroom, he expressed an ardent desire for a private show after she emailed him a link to her website, complete with a digital collection of photos from her Miss September layout. When Mr. Bellarosa began babbling on with her about doubling up on his heart meds, she was quick to dismiss it as a cheap attempt to feel sorry for him and reduce her fee.

"How do I know you're not some violent lunatic psycho?" she'd asked him in the online chatroom, a question that had become standard in her qualifying process. Turns out that Mr. Bellarosa had developed a deep infatuation with the former Miss September and wouldn't take no for an answer.

When she succeeded in enticing him into doubling his offer from five to ten grand, she was all in with a "lap dance to die for." With his wife away for a week at a spa in Palm Beach, they decided to hook up at his luxury high-rise at Aragon for their tryst. Anticipating tight security at the upscale condo, she went in wearing a disguise using her stage name "Sherry."

It was just before eight p.m., and apparently, Mr. Anthony Bellarosa's condo had a few New Yorkers on the payroll. As she pulled to a stop at the security gate, a large and quite hairy Homo sapiens appeared in the head lights of her S550, then leaned into her open window, the dark blazer not quite concealing his shoulder holster. A scary-looking man, he had an unpleasant face which seemed a pretty good match with his demeanor.

"Can I help ya?" he asked her in a strong Brooklyn accent.

"Yeah. Da Violettas ta see da Bellarosas," smiling and wondering if he was paper trained.

"Okay. Be justa minute, Mrs. Violetta. Gotta call ya in."

"Dat's poifeckly okay." After the huge man retreated inside the guard post, his knuckles almost dragging on the ground, the gate opened.

Clearing the guardhouse and the hulking horror show, she chose an out-of-the-way space in guest parking. Scanning the security marquee for Bellarosa's listing, she picked up the entry phone and pressed the talk button, peering into the security camera in her Dolce Gabbana sunglasses, Donna Karan floppy black hat, red wig, seven-inch Jimmy Choo heels and *faux* fur coat. As it rang, she checked her Rolex. It was exactly 7:59 p.m.

"Yeah? Can I help ya," asked her date in a thick Brooklyn accent.

Margo made eye contact with the camera and waved. "Sherry. Miss September. For our eight o'clock appointment."

"Ah…wait a sec. Miss September's a blonde. You're a redhead. Who're you, honey?" Bellarosa seemed annoyed.

Making a face, "Honestly, Tony. I thought it would be fun to wear a disguise. C'mon. Loosen up a little."

With the Viagra beginning to have its desired effect, "All right. C'mon up. Apartment 508. End of the hallway."

What a toad, she thought as she hung up the phone. She heard the electronic lock release and pulled the door open, entering the glitzy marble-columned lobby. Riding the mirrored elevator to the fifth floor, she noticed two more cameras from under the brim of her hat and avoided looking directly into the lenses. As a tease for whomever was watching, she opened her fur coat to straighten the seams on her fishnet stockings. Exiting the elevator, she spotted her mark standing two doors down the hallway. The pot-bellied board member was dressed in a blue smoking jacket, flannel boxer shorts, and wearing the worst toupee she'd ever set eyes on. For God's sake, she thought, she'd seen better rugs at Family Dollar Store.

Bellarosa stood expectantly beside his open door at the end of the hallway chomping on a huge stogie. "C'mon in, *Sherry*," his eyes feasting on her as he waved her in. The portly man gloated over his trophy date as she stepped past him into his living room and invited her to get "more comfortable." Margo placed her coat, hat, wig and sunglasses into a nearby suede chair. The Aragon director removed his jacket to reveal a wife-beater tee shirt as he dropped his ponderous rear end into the suede couch and prepared for a "lap dance to die for."

Regarding the surrounding Louie XIV décor, she couldn't help noticing a generous stack of hundred dollar bills sitting on the marble end table. "That for me?" she asked.

"Make me a happy guy and it's all yours, honey," flicking the ash off his stogie into the gold-colored ashtray. "Can I fix you a drink?"

"Thanks, Tony, but I had three before I left," she said, smiling. "You know, to get in the mood. Almost hit a palm tree on the way in."

"Well, okay then. How 'bout a dance to start things off?" He sat back with his arm on the edge of the couch to admire her tight-fitting thong, fishnet stockings and high heels as she set her I-pad down on the coffee table and pushed the play button. Gato Barbieri's *Europa* flooded the room, the sexy saxophone music setting a sultry mood for her dance. Keeping eye contact with him, Margo began a slow grinding motion, and within moments, Bellarosa was mesmerized by her pelvic gyrations.

Putting on her best erotic dance, it was a sexy routine she perfected during her years as a pole dancer in a burlesque club before becoming Miss September. She couldn't help wondering how many Viagra pills he'd popped to jump start his manhood. As she placed her hands on his bare thigh and squatted down suggestively on his knee, Bellarosa's face suddenly turned bright pink, and the big man lurched forward, grabbing at his heart, his cigar dropping onto the floor.

"AARRGGGHHH!" Bellarosa's eyes glazed as he clutched his chest, his head slumping lifelessly over her shoulder and pinning her in an awkward embrace.

"Oh my God!" With both arms, she pushed the huge man off her and onto the back of the couch. Standing over him in her high heels with her hands on her hips, she squatted to see if he was still breathing. The huge man gurgled and moaned her name.

"Tony???" Desperate to revive him, but having skipped the CPR course that was recommended at her last DUI class, she straddled his body in her high heels and began bitch slapping him across the face to try and revive him as she acted out a scene from a Sharon Stone movie.

"Tony, wake up!!" grasping his jaw and shaking it back and forth, a maneuver she'd learned from an online tutorial on National Geographic Channel about training gorillas. "Wake up!" From her experiences with guys who liked it rough, Margo bitch slapped him a few more times before stopping at the sight of foam forming at the corners of his mouth.

Frozen with fear, she was clueless as to what to do next, desperate for a way to avoid being blamed for his heart attack, or whatever the hell was making his mouth foam. With no response from Tony, she dismounted the unconscious condo director and paused to straighten the seams on her fishnet stockings before putting on her wig, fur coat, hat and sunglasses, pocketing the fat stack of hundreds from the coffee table. Her eyes scanning the condo for a phone, she spotted his cell on the kitchen counter and dialed 911.

"911.What is your emergency?" asked the female dispatcher.

"I think Mr. Bellarosa is having a heart attack!" she blurted. "*Please,* send an ambulance to Aragon on Boca Beach! For God's sake, he has foam coming out of his mouth!"

"Please calm down, ma'am. Can you tell if he's breathing?" Margo could hear shouting on the dispatcher's phone in the background.

Flustered, she approached her unconscious date and began bitch slapping him again. "WAKE UP, TONY!" she yelled, becoming frantic as she thought about the prison term for manslaughter, or even worse, death by lap dance. By now, she was out of her mind with fear and considered hanging up, but the dispatcher returned before she could end the call.

"Hang on," said the dispatcher. "We got someone off their meds here. I need to confirm the address there, honey."

"I don't know exactly," said Margo in a panic. "South on A1A. Aragon. Just look for that aqua-colored condo on the beach. Number 508...I think," as she picked up his lifeless wrist to check for a pulse. "Please hurry! He's going limp on me." She heard another round of loud voices, then some laughter in the background.

"Okay," said the dispatcher. "I got Aragon, South Boca Beach, number 508. Stay with me, ma'am. What's your name?" Margo's heart raced with fear. "Ma'am? I need your--"

Margo hung up. Petrified, she wiped her prints off the phone with the edge of her stockings and slid it across the marbled counter where it fell, clanging into the stainless steel sink. She was startled to hear a very strange voice coming from the bedroom that sounded like a little old lady singing *Rock of Ages* in a falsetto.

"Rock of ages...cleft for meeeee....rock of ages, cleft for meeeee! SQUAWK!"

Dressed in her Jimmy Choo high heels, fishnet stockings, fur coat, wig, Dolce Gabbana sunglasses and Donna Karan floppy hat, she crept cautiously down the travertine hallway toward the bedroom, fearful of who or what she was about to confront and petrified at the thought of a possible witness.

"Hello, is someone there?" fear causing her voice to crack. Peeking through the bedroom doorway, she could see no one. Then the singing repeated.

"Rock of ages...cleft for meeeee....rock of ages, cleft for meeeee! SQUAWK!"

Her heart beating wildly, she peeked inside the master bedroom where she saw a large gilded cage hanging from the ceiling with a white cockatiel inside. The bird's crest stiffen as it turned around on the perch to face her.

"Scored a lap dance to die for! Lap dance to die for!" squawked the bird. "Hi, I'm Perry. Perry's a rock star! Perry's a rock star! What's yer name? What's yer name? SQUAWK!"

Her world had taken a hard left turn into the land of the surreal. Not believing what she was seeing, even less of what she was hearing, she lowered her sunglasses in astonishment as she leaned against the door jamb. *"Oh my God!"* she said in amazement.

"Oh my God! Oh my God!" repeated the cockatiel. "Wake up, Tony! Wake up, Tony! SQUAWK! Got some cash for ya, honey! Take the cash! Need a date, honey? Better call an ambulance! SQUAWK!"

Margo grabbed her purse and i-Pad and ran to the front door as fast as her Jimmy Choo high heels could carry her without breaking a heel.

"Perry's a rock star! Take the cash! Better call an ambulance!" squawked the cockatiel from the bedroom as she slammed the door behind her.

Leaving the bizarre scene behind, she exited Aragon in her S550 through the service entrance and hit the gas on A1A, driving north at double the posted speed limit. Feeling like a character in a Stephen King novel, she nervously checked her rearview mirror for cops as she distanced herself from the insane asylum she'd just left. Reaching for the pint of Cuervo in her glove box and unscrewing the cap, she accidentally spilled some on her wig and guzzled almost half the bottle before spotting the flashing lights approaching.

Directly ahead, a red and white Palm Beach County ambulance raced in her direction at high speed, sirens wailing and lights flashing. She was guessing it was Bellarosa's ride to the ER. The ambulance was followed by a black and white Boca police car as she slowed her Mercedes and yielded to the emergency vehicles passing her, almost running over two teens on skateboards just south of the Boca Inlet Bridge. *It was only a lap dance, for God's sake. Didn't mean to kill the poor bastard.*

After the emergency vehicles passed, she punched the accelerator and the big Benz lurched forward, crossing over Boca Inlet Bridge. She recalled her last high dollar booking at Aragon on the day that big perv

Craig Stewart had booked her nude performance last week. Repeating in her head were the same words that formed the new banner at the bottom of her website; "A Lap Dance To Die For."

Speeding north on A1A, she thought it might be a good idea to limit her future liabilities by adding a disclaimer to the website recommending a recent EKG before booking a lap dance. The idea triggered thoughts about adding liability insurance to cover future lap dances, and Margo made a mental note to call her agent for some quotes.

Then, Perry's unforgettable performance of *Rock of Ages* popped back into her head as she freshened her lipstick in the rearview mirror at seventy miles an hour and checked again for cop cars. Unable to get the tune out of her head, she began to sing the lyrics out loud again, trying to mimic the cockatiel's falsetto.

"Rock of ages….cleft for meeee."

EIGHTEEN

By Wednesday, Hirt and Croaker had moved another three pounds of fentanyl, sold mostly to dealers in Ft. Pierce, Port St. Lucie, and Vero Beach, who put it on the streets all over South Florida. There were two more deaths reported from fentanyl overdoses, one in Vero, and another in Port St. Lucie, and although Hirt and his bag man had heard of the fatal O.D.s, they continued to dismiss the people that died as just another overdose in a pile of death certificates.

It was the last day in January, and though the daylight seemed short, Croaker noticed the days were getting longer. It was okay with him; his most profitable work was done under cover of darkness. At five-thirty p.m., the sunlight was already fading, but he didn't need or even want much light for his meeting with his informant at the old abandoned Hale Groves warehouse.

Croaker's street sources told him the cops had him on their watch list, and he was fanatical about keeping his name off any official records, living small, off the grid, down low and under the radar. Croaker put the utility bills in his landlord's name and reimbursed him monthly from his stash of cash when he paid the rent, and the lease at Vero Estates was in the name of a shell corporation. Sometimes his paranoia would take hold, and he thought about transporting his stash of cash and drugs to a new hideout, but for the time being, he stayed hunkered down.

As the sunlight faded, he walked past the old Hale Groves gatehouse, now used to store old fencing and signs. The dark green camouflage outfit made him feel invisible, and he liked wearing it to meetings with new snitches. He noticed the brick pavers that once formed the entrance to the warehouse had been dug up, and the floral landscaping that once welcomed visitors had been overgrown by scraggly weeds and brambles. A long line of earthmoving equipment sat idle parked single file along the perimeter.

He thought about her, and he still had mixed feelings about what he'd done. The woman caused him so much pain that the agony had to end. Dismissing her as just another hooker the world would forget about, he continued to make his way toward the rear of the warehouse, stepping around the heap of rubble where new footers had been dug. He heard a noise and saw a shadow moving in his direction.

"Ola." Croaker's informant had stepped from behind the half-wall ten feet in front of him wearing a black Toyota cap and dark sunglasses.

"Ola, hermano," he replied, their pre-arranged greeting. "Whatcha got for me, Louis?"

"A thousand bucks worth, mi amigo." Though it was unlikely Louis was his real name, or that he was even Puerto Rican, he didn't care. As long as the intel was fresh and useful, he could be as anonymous as he liked.

"A thousand bucks?" queried Croaker. "So, what do I get for that?"

"You get to stay in business and out of jail, mi amigo"

It occurred to him Louis might be trying to shake him down, so he put his hand on the Browning .45 auto stuck in his waist band. "You better explain that one to me. We wouldn't want to have a misunderstanding."

Carefully, Louis continued. "Lt. Foti and his crew got it in for you. You know he ordered a 24-hour tail on you and looking to get a warrant."

Though it disturbed him, Croaker acted cavalier. "Yeah? So, what else ya got?"

"Also, some hot shot named Beretto from the FBI is onto you, and they've teamed up with Foti. You might want to stay off the grid and keep low, bro."

Croaker's eyes widened. "You makin' fun of my height?"

"No, sir, mi amigo. Just a suggestion."

Unfazed, the bagman was used to having heat on him. He thought of an angle. "Can you get me photos of Foti and his crew?"

Louis held out his hand and rubbed his fingers together, mimicking the feel of money. "I might be able to do that," stepping closer. "Need some juice here, bro. Got a big family to feed." Nervous, he shifted his weight from one foot to the other and waited.

Reluctantly, Croaker pulled out a wad of cash and counted out $700, then stuck the rest of it back in his pocket. "I'll give you another $800 when you bring me the photos. We good?"

Louis stroked his chin. "I think the intel's worth more, bro."

Intuition told him Louis had a nose for fentanyl. "Plus a gram of uncut China white."

Knowing he could make twenty-times its value, Louis considered the gram of fentanyl a generous bonus. "Done. I'll call ya when I have your package, bro," stuffing the cash and drugs into his pocket. "You want those in color or black and white?"

"What do you think?" Croaker stared at him.

"Color, then."

"Next time, we'll meet at a new location. Keep diggin' at this, Louis, and I'll make sure your family is eating steak."

Nodding his understanding, "I'm deep down the rabbit hole, boss," Louis assured him before disappearing around the back of the warehouse.

Croaker stepped in the opposite direction, pleased with his deal. It was almost dark as he headed toward his ten-year-old Honda Fit parked in the swale outside the fence.

He had no idea how close they were getting.

On Thursday, Heaton and Garner decided to tip off St. Lucie County detectives about their investigation of Croaker, naming him as the prime suspect in the murders of Tremelle and Granata to spur them into action and on the search warrants in the Angela Peyton case. With the two counties working together for the first time, the noose was tightening. If captured, it was likely Croaker would be denied bail with the capital murder charges and the flight risk he posed, making it easier for detectives to build their case against him. The fear of an acquittal might explain why the St. Lucie judge had been so reticent in issuing the search and arrest warrants years before. Having only one shot in a capital murder case, prosecutors wanted to make sure they would have enough evidence to convict him.

Then there was the matter of Mary Walter's murder in Vero Beach in 2012, only four months before the Peyton homicide. Among those puzzled by St. Lucie County's reluctance to prosecute Croaker for Peyton's murder was Vero Beach Police Capt. John Garrett, who was then a lieutenant. He remembered the details of the Peyton case vividly.

In the unlawful death of Mary Walters, who was then thirty-nine, the victim was home alone when she was abducted from her Vero Beach waterfront condo across the canal from Mr. Manatee's. Forced to drive her red 1990 Honda CRX at gunpoint to a Melbourne ATM to withdraw a stack of cash, she was then forced by the killer to return to Vero and withdraw an additional $3,500 from a drive-through teller. Garrett remembered that her abandoned car was discovered in the parking lot of a raw bar in Ft. Pierce with her bank withdrawal receipts lying on the seat. Four days later, her brutally beaten body was found in an orange grove in west St. Lucie County.

In an update with Foti Thursday morning, Garrett was welcoming any new insights from his lieutenant. "Does this ring a bell, Frank?" clasping his hands and propping his elbows on his desk.

Foti recalled the case. "I'll never forget the similarities in the two homicides," he replied. "Captain, in my thirty years on the force, they're the only two cases I ever worked where the perp forced the victims to drive to their ATMs to withdraw cash, then drove to a remote area and beat them to death. Barbaric. And in both cases, the victim's car was left in a parking lot." Foti sat back in the black leather chair and crossed his legs as he recalled more details. "With both victims, Croaker's home was a short walk from the abduction points."

"And, in both cases," continued Garrett, "…lab results confirmed the killer wore the same brand of latex gloves." Remembering the bookmark, Garrett rotated his PC to show his lieutenant. "Check this out, Frank. A gofundme account is offering $75,000 for information leading to the arrest and conviction of Peyton's killer. As if we didn't have enough reasons to nail this guy."

"There are too many coincidences, Garrett replied. "We can't let whatever St. Lucie County does-or doesn't do-to deter us from naming Croaker as a person-of-interest in the Tremelle and Granata cases."

"I agree. I have a feeling I know what our brothers in St. Lucie County might say; killer's motivation is different this time. And they'll say Walters and Peyton are *older* cases, *and* they'll take time, we want to do this the *right* way, etcetera, etcetera." An idea came to him. "Can the department get enough cash together for a sting on Hirt?"

Garrett sat back and considered the idea. "How much you think we'd need to bait him?"

"I'm thinkin' we'd have to offer him at least fifty percent over street value, so probably at least $100,000. And a real convincing undercover player. What do we have in the evidence lockers to work with?"

Garrett checked his computer for the last several drug busts involving cash confiscations that were pending trial. "Let's see," scrolling down two years, "…Bobby Lee Gifford, $32,000…Ferguson, $15,000…Drago, $24,000…Morgan, $12,000…Juarez, $48,000." Looking up, he added, "I'd say we have enough."

"Hirt's got a lot of connections on the street. Let's bring in a new face so we don't scare him off, a u.c. from Palm Beach County." Foti cocked his head. "You think we can get Sheriff Bradshaw to lend us one of his?"

Without hesitation, Garrett responded. "I like your idea. Bradshaw owes us one from December when one of our guys stepped in for their team. I'll make the call."

Garrett stood and pressed his fingertips onto the desktop to make his point. "Frank, *find* this killer and bring'em in! And use whatever resources we have, but *do it!*"

As he approached his 45th birthday, Mark had come a long way since the days of jetting around the Delray and Boca waterfront bistros with his hair on fire aboard his twin-turbo *Momentum*. Wanting less noise and vibration from his boats, nothing but the tranquil sounds of sweeping winds and water seemed as soothing to his soul these days. Stella liked to say the touch of grey he acquired made him look more distinguished as he aged "like a fine Bordeaux."

It was mid-afternoon on Saturday, and Mark was on his second margarita, de-stressing at Waldo's, "The Last of the Great American Hangouts." Trying to put the week's events behind him, he was enjoying the sun and sea breeze while Stella was out shopping on Ocean Drive with her girlfriend. Dressed in his Bora Bora tank top, Nike cap and cargo shorts, he sat on a barstool at the patio bar, hanging out with the bartenders and watching guests come and go.

The band of the day, "Twenty-One Hearts, One Beat" was on break after their last song, Jimmy Buffett's "A Pirate Looks at Forty." He and Dalton were enjoying the party animals parading past the bar, thoroughly entertained by their comments. Scanning a few recent photos on his iPhone of Stella, Mark came across a stunning photo of a special beach in Moorea that he wanted to share with his buddy.

"Dalton, what's your email? I'm gonna send you a photo you'll want to hang onto. Maybe wallpaper your desktop or something with it."

Dalton leaned across the bar top so he wouldn't be overheard. "Keywasted7289@gmail.com."

"How appropriate," said Mark.

Dalton floated one of his favorite questions as he prepared two daiquiris for a couple sitting at the end of the bar. "So, what's the craziest date you ever had before you married Stella?"

The margaritas had put him in a playful mood as he thought about some of the crazier rendezvous that came to mind. "I met this one girl at Cobalt one night. Smokin' hot, very feminine, great dancer. Turns out she was a *shemale*."

"In Vero? Yeah? And you found out how?" Grinning, Dalton was all ears.

"Well, in the interests of full disclosure, she told me before we got too romantic and even invited me to feel her…ah, her implants--"

"You didn't!"

Mark took a sip of his margarita before continuing. "Well, when we were sitting at the bar, I saw something stirring that made me nervous."

Dalton broke out laughing. "So, marriage was out of the question?"

"Well…I guess. So, later, I took the shemale thing off my bucket list," trying to keep a straight face.

"I took the bucket list off my bucket list," quipped Joe who was passing by to check on things.

Mark continued. "Uh-huh. So after that episode, my confidence took a nose dive and I decided to stop even thinking about love on the first date."

Dalton gave him a skeptical look. "So, how'd that work out?"

"I decided to skip the first date."

"Uh-huh."

"But that didn't work, so I just stopped dating."

Dalton didn't look convinced. "Yeah, right."

"For two whole days."

"Heard that." Dalton waited to hear more as he polished a highball glass. Mark was thinking about more of his dry spells, back when he'd been stranded between wives and sailboats.

His walk down memory lane was interrupted by a heavy-set girl carrying a daiquiri with one of those little pink umbrellas stuck in it. She sported a gold tooth, leopard-print bikini, and straw cowboy hat with a button that read "Bite Me" as she made her way toward Mark like a linebacker through the crowded bar.

As a lifelong J.C. Penney's Gold Card member, Bobbi Jo Jenkins was pretty certain she knew what high fashion was all about. With her gaze fixed firmly on Mark, it looked like she was having hot flashes as she fanned herself with the color brochures from The Vero Beach Wine and Film Festival as she sidled up to him.

"Hi, honey. I'm Bobbi Jo Jenkins from Paducah. What's *yer* name?" she asked in a hillbilly Kentucky twang as she looked him up and down like he was the flavor du jour. Without waiting for an answer, she focused on his Nike cap. "Nike, is that a I-talian name?"

Wincing from the attention, he decided to have some fun with Bobbi Jo. Apparently, she didn't have much of an eye for details, otherwise she might have noticed the wedding ring he was wearing. He had perfected a whole bag of tricks he used to deflect such unwanted advances. With a slight frown, Mark removed his cap, pretending to check the spelling of "Nike" on the front.

"Oh, this?" pointing at the lettering. "Well, not exactly," he explained, testing her gullibility, "...my name's Mike. It was custom ordered, and they misspelled my name, so I didn't have to pay for it," straight-faced. Putting his cap back on, "I guess it's become a popular name 'cause I see it everywhere these days." Bobbi Jo blinked a few times, unable to sort it out, and tried again.

"So, Mike, what's yer sign?"

She made him feel like he was being drawn by an invisible tractor beam back into the seventies. "I don't believe in astrology. I'm an

Aquarius, and we're very skeptical," trying hard to keep a straight face. The irony seemed lost on her, so he tossed her another curve ball.

"They called me 'Hannibal the Cannibal' in the slammer."

Bobbi Jo wrinkled up her nose in distaste, but didn't take the hint and moved in closer, seemingly unaware of the important concept of personal space. "That's so, ah...cute I guess," doing her best to look beyond his faults. "What were ya in jail fer, Hannibal?"

With a deadpan look, "I was driving drunk and hit a dear, ah...well...a dear old man with my car."

"Oh, dear."

"Exactly."

"Whad'ya do?" she asked.

"Well...I left a note, and..."

Bobbi Jo laughed so hard she snorted like a wild boar. Convinced he would make a big hit at her trailer park, she began to plot a way to get him to her next pig roast at her double-wide in Paducah. Frowning, he tried again to discourage her and held up a few napkins from the stack on the bar.

"Bobbi Jo, do you think these napkins smell like chloroform?" A horrified look crossed her face, and Bobbi Jo's maternal instincts finally took a back seat to her concern for her own safety. Clueless about how to respond, she headed on down the row of bar stools toward the next available hunky guy.

Relieved, Dalton was chuckling in amusement. "We have a *wiener.*"

"Jeez. Thought she'd never move on," admitted Mark, exasperated with the woman's tenacity as he took another sip of his margarita and entertained less weighty issues.

"You know you're a redneck if your home has wheels but your car doesn't," joked Dalton.

Mark chuckled to himself as he glanced over at Bobbi Jo putting the moves on one of the regulars he knew from the dive shop. "Ten bucks says she thinks that professional wrestling is real but the moon landing was faked."

Freed of the tyranny of unwanted attention from girls wearing "Bite Me" buttons, the two returned to their favorite game of selecting the next Miss Vero Beach from the throng of women on the pool deck. Spotting a TV-producer friend of his sitting in a lounger on the far side of the pool, Mark decided to wander over and say hello.

Wherever he was introduced, people remembered meeting Big Bob Stanley. With the body of a weight lifter, Big Bob was a statuesque six-foot-six and two-hundred-eighty pounds and still spent ten hours a week working out at the gym. Showing few signs of age, his physique hadn't changed much since he boxed professionally twenty years ago. With a ruggedly handsome face that carried the reminders of every glove that cut him, his chiseled facial features and imperfect nose had borne the brunt of many a fighter's punch. After twenty years around the ring, his experiences had sculpted him into the successful fight promoter and TV producer that he was today.

This afternoon, Big Bob was nursing a hangover. Lounging at the pool with his laptop, he labored at crafting some new scenes for his Spike TV reality fight show called *My Family's Greatest Hits*. For scrappy pre-schoolers, his staff had proposed the spin-off of a less violent, sanitized version called *KOs for Kids*, and his teleplay writer was preparing it for debut on Nickelodeon next month. Reminding himself that content was king as he straddled the lounger with his laptop between his knees, Big Bob heard his name being called.

"Big Bob Stanley, how the hell are you?" asked Mark. "You stayin' here at the Driftwood?"

"Marky-Mark McAllister!" Big Bob stood and gave him a bear hug. "Yeah, well...two weeks ago, I bought one of the corner penthouses. Just like you say in your last novel, our own 'Mayberry-By-the-Sea.' I haven't seen you since we hooked up to watch that weird wildlife documentary that debuted at the Met five years ago."

"Oh, that Michael Moore film? I've seen better film on teeth," quipped Mark, taking a seat in the adjoining lounger as he glanced at his video.

"You working on something new?"

"Yeah, I got a new show with Spike TV, and a possible spin-off. Like to get your take on it sometime."

They were both distracted by two bikini-clad hotties wearing purple spiked hair as they sauntered by on their way to the beach. Big Bob was particularly fascinated. "Make you wonder where life on this planet is headed? So, what are you up to these days, Marky-Mark?"

"After seven novels, I seem to have gravitated to investigative journalism."

"What kind of writing pays the most?"

"Uh…hmmm. I'm thinkin' ransom notes," with a twinkle in his eye.

Big Bob laughed. "Walked right into that one, didn't I?"

"Actually, I'm lending a hand in a couple of homicides with the FBI and Vero Police right now." Not wanting to ruin the mood, he avoided sharing the details.

Out of the corner of his eye, Mark noticed Special Agent Madani waiting at the bar with a drink in her hand. Earlier, she had called him to tell him that Croaker had fallen off the grid, and that the VBPD and the BAU were clueless about his whereabouts.

Mark excused himself after sharing a fist bump with the TV producer. "This won't take long, so when you finish with your video editing, c'mon over to the bar for a top-shelf margarita. I'm buying."

"Count on it. Say, thirty minutes?" Mark nodded and headed back to the bar to meet with Madani, promising himself that he'd stick to business with her.

Refocusing his attention on new scenes for his video show, Big Bob straddled the lounger and went back to work on his teleplay. Oblivious to the guests drifting past him toward the beach, some passed by searching for an empty pool lounger to settle into. An attractive middle-aged woman in a bikini and floppy hat caught his eye as she sashayed toward him. Delighted to see him out by the pool again, she gave Bob a big smile.

"Hi, Bob", said the shapely woman as she spread her towel out on the adjoining lounger. Peering out from under a huge floral beach hat that matched her bikini, she extended her hand and smiled. "It's Esther…

Esther Hershfeld…from that wild wine and cheese thing last week. How are you?" fluttering her eyelashes. He looked up, a little confused, unable to recall the event. "You were showing me the video clips of your TV shows from your phone and licking chip dip off my belly. Remember?"

"Oh, yeah…Mrs. Hershfeld…good to see you again," trying hard to recall if he'd done anything really embarrassing. "Sorry, a little distracted…working on some new scenes to my TV series."

"Sure, go right ahead, honey." Esther smiled and made herself comfortable on the lounger as she stretched out and began to slather sun tan oil all over herself. Thinking that perhaps her hint had been too subtle, she glanced furtively at him and continued smoothing the oil suggestively over her legs.

"Ever since my husband passed away last summer," she said, "…I've been hoping to find a man with strong hands to do this for me. Howard didn't like getting his hands greasy," she explained. "He said it made it hard to hang onto his walker."

"Uh-huh," responded Bob absentmindedly, eyes still focused on his laptop as he reworked one of the scenes. Desirous of his full attention, Esther was getting flustered, now more determined than ever to become the focus of his fantasies. After all, she was an attractive widow with a great body and healthy libido. Why shouldn't she be able to have some fun with a big strong man? Howard sure as hell wasn't going to give her what she needed, buried under two tons of granite at Beth El Mausoleum.

"So Bob, do you think it's unusual for a doctor to fondle a woman's breasts during an examination?"

Big Bob was slowly warming up to her and went with the flow, entertained by her creativity and her unquenched desire for his attention. "Well, yeah, unusual if he's a podiatrist," he quipped. "Why? Did your doctor cop a feel, Mrs. Hershfeld?"

"Yeah, that's what I'm trying to tell you. I think he's a perv." She smiled mischievously. "I gotta admit, though, I kinda liked it."

"Ya goin' back for another check-up, Mrs. Hershfeld?"

"Dear, dear Bob. Since you've slurped chip dip off my belly, I think you know me well enough to call me Esther." She continued applying a heavy coat of oil on her legs in exaggerated strokes, hoping she wouldn't have to spell it out. When she was sufficiently oiled up, she reclined on the lounger, getting more comfortable and covering her face with her floppy hat.

In a sultry voice she said, "Let me know when you're ready to get wild with that chip dip again. It was the most fun I've had since my kids spilled Howard's ashes on the floor at the Ben and Jerry's in Boca."

Not sure if he'd heard her correctly, he stopped in mid-keystroke to regard her. *Crazy is the price of that ride.* She'd finally succeeded in getting his full attention and stretched out invitingly on the lounger. "Uh... sure, Esther. And here I thought cougars were an endangered species. What flavor chip dip do you like, honey?"

"Guacamole," she said in a muffled voice from under her hat. "And it's on sale this week at Publix. Two for one."

A sucker for a playful looker with a sense of humor, he made a mental note to add guacamole dip to his shopping list, quite certain that he wouldn't find Esther's suggested use of the condiment anywhere on the container.

Wondering just how far she'd go, "I like your sense of humor, Esther. Let's drop some acid and play Twister sometime."

She lifted her hat and sat up on her elbows, smiling. "Honey, I thought you'd never ask."

NINETEEN

At seven-forty-five a.m. on the following Monday, Hirt stood facing the ocean on the third floor of The Pain Free Clinic with his windows open as he watched a spectacular sunrise. The sound of crashing ocean waves reaching their final destination was lulling him into a reverie of recent events.

Enjoying his second demitasse of expresso, he was pleased that Croaker had delivered to him color photos of the entire Vero CID unit. In case they had the balls to call on him at his office, he'd made a digital file of each member so he could view the images at his desk top to avoid any surprises.

Hirt smiled at the thought of the money he was making. The street price of fentanyl had risen over thirty percent since he'd been out of Raiford, while his price had risen only ten percent. With fentanyl sales so much more lucrative than heroin and cocaine, he was glad he'd made the transition to dealing in the most profitable drug on the planet. Now all he needed to do was keep his shadow banker in line.

Rereading the *New York Times* article that lay on the credenza, Hirt wondered how the reporters had gathered their facts. The article stated that a kilogram of heroin could be purchased for $6,000 and sold for as much as $1.6 million. *Yeah, what planet is that?* The article went on to explain that the reason for this vast difference in pricing is the potency of uncut fentanyl. At fifty times the potency of heroin or other opioids, profitability could be stretched quite lucratively.

Checking his schedule for the day, he was impressed that Laura had set up an average of seven appointments an hour. After their talk last week, she made it a point to step up her game after he offered her a modest per patient stipend.

Hirt spent the next thirty minutes online and on the phone shopping the global diamond market, looking to add to his $22 million horde of high-quality stones. Primarily of VVS quality, it was a large and growing collection he'd accumulated over the last ten years. With investable cash profits of over a million a month, the drug-dealing psychiatrist was gravitating more toward additional investments in diamonds rather than stashing it in offshore bank accounts that were expensive to launder and left a paper trail. Ruling out gold bullion and currency because of weight and bulk, he'd become enamored with the beauty of the stones and the ease of transporting them while fancying himself as somewhat of an expert.

Halfway through the day, with a waiting room full of patients, his assistant brought him a bearded, scraggly-looking man wearing a tattered leather jacket covered with underworld insignia. The thin bearded man exhibited all the physical signs of a drug addict, including burns on his fingers and cracked lips. He held a Walmart bag close to his body and introduced himself as Daniel but was unable to produce any form of personal ID. That part bothered Hirt, and he dug deeper to identify the customer.

Nodding politely at the scraggly man sitting across from him, the doctor was cautious. "So, Daniel…what's your surname?"

Daniel nervously shifted his weight in the seat, obviously uncomfortable with the question. "Does it matter?"

Hirt regarded him suspiciously. "As a physician, the Federal government requires a certain amount of basic information about my patients, including their medical records. I want to help you, but--"

"*But*, you need cash or insurance, right?" interrupted his patient. Slouching in the chair, the man calling himself Daniel listened with a glazed look over his eyes, impatient with the doctor's bureaucratic nonsense. "Look, doc. Let's cut to the chase. My pancreatic cancer is untreatable and the pain is killing me. I'm only here to get the strongest pain meds ya got."

Reaching into his Walmart bag, he removed ten bundles of $10,000, each wrapped with a rubber band. Daniel set the bundles on the doctor's desk one at a time as he rattled off the names of three of Hirt's patients as references. "Don't need a receipt or any records, doctor. Will you help me?"

The psychiatrist stared at the large stack of cash, conflicted over how to handle Daniel, not fully trusting his story. "I might be able to swing some oxycontin for--"

"That stuff doesn't do it for me. *I* need the China white...the fentanyl, doc. That's what *I* need. So, why don't you just reach inside that big safe there and give me what I need?"

Feeling pressured, Hirt responded cautiously. "Sorry, Daniel, but I have to ask you this: are you a law enforcement officer, or associated with law enforcement in any way?"

Visibly upset with Hirt's insinuation, Daniel raised his voice. "Are you kidding? Look at me. You think I'm a *cop*!?"

Hirt studied the man like he had three heads. "You haven't answered my question, Daniel, if that's your real name." Gesturing at the pile of cash, "And where'd this money come from?"

"Income tax refund!"

Things were getting heated as the two continued to raise their voices. "You don't look well enough to even have a job," responded Hirt. "Look, I've got an office full of patients and I've gotta ask you to--"

Concerned with the loud voices, his assistant stuck her head in. "Everything okay here, Dr. Hirt?" Laura's eyes widened at the sight of the bundles of cash on his desk. "Do we need security here, doctor?"

Hirt shook his head. "Daniel was just leaving. He was under the impression that we're a cash vending machine for illegal drugs." Closely eyeing the cash, he shooed her away with a wave of his hand as his greed took center stage.

Hirt lowered his voice. "How 'bout this, Daniel: unless you want the Vero police to know about your stash, I suggest you leave one of those bundles with me as insurance so you can keep the rest."

Facing off, the two men glared at each other across the desk before Daniel called his bluff. "Now you wanna extort money from me? Really, doc? This the way you treat your patients?"

Standing abruptly, he scooped the ten bundles back into his grey Walmart bag and angrily tossed the desktop candy dish in Hirt's face. *"You can go screw yourself, doc!!"*

Storming past Laura and an office full of patients with his bag full of cash, the scraggly man turned in the doorway as he exited The Pain Free Clinic. "Good luck, everybody!" pointing toward Hirt's office. "This guy's as mean as a snake and as crooked as they come!"

Following Daniel's stormy departure, Laura took it upon herself to calm the remaining patients. She reassured them The Pain Free Clinic was there to provide them with the best possible patient care, and all the pain meds they needed, provided they had the insurance coverage or the cash to pay.

Four hours and twenty-six patients later, Laura put a call through to the busy psychiatrist. "Dr. Hirt, it's your personal banker. He says it's important. Shall I put him through?"

"Tell him I'll call him back on a different line when I finish with this patient. I do need to talk to him."

"Okay, I'll--"

"And be sure to get his private number, Laura."

"Yes, sir."

After filling a patient script for oxycontin, Hirt called him back in a better mood. "Damon, how's the weather in Miami? You taking good care of my hard-earned cash?"

From a twelfth floor office in the Brickell Plaza overlooking Biscayne Bay, Damon picked up his private line. "Well, to answer your first question, my ten-year-old son's favorite lapel button reads, 'The Weather Is Here, Wish You Were Beautiful.'"

"You're a funny guy, Damon."

"By the way, our bank foreclosed on a gorgeous bayfront condo right around the corner, and we have it priced to sell fast. You have an interest in waterfront real estate, Dr. Hirt?"

"What do you have east of Miami Beach?"

"Ocean."

"And the price?"

"It's free, Dr. Hirt."

"I'll take all you got."

Morgan chuckled, trying hard to hide his disdain for doctors who treated the Hippocratic Oath like their personal doormat. "By the way, what kind of doctor are you?"

"Pathologist. You don't want to see me," he quipped. By the same token, Hirt didn't care much for bankers who stooped to laundering drug money, especially when they charged him a whopping fifteen percent.

"Uh-huh…"

Hirt continued in a more business-like tone. "My receptionist told me it was important. What's up?"

"Sounds like you're busy, so I'll get right to the point. It's about our arrangement, Dr. Hirt. The directors are increasingly uncomfortable about the attention you've been getting from the authorities, and the added risk that means for us. Consequently, they want to raise your fee to twenty percent to properly compensate the bank for this. Please understand that I mean you no offense."

Annoyed, Hirt stayed calm. "None taken. So, Damon, where are you hearing about this so-called attention I'm getting? I mean, Dade Tropical Bank has been a laundry bank *long* before I became a client. No offense."

"None taken. We have reliable sources on the street and inside law enforcement, some of which, as you know, we've shared with you. And, ah…I hope that's been of some help to you."

"It has, but I'm not in a position to delay our deal, even for a few days, nor will I agree to a five percent increase in fees. And, on the outside chance that I get some kind of freeze on my assets, that's obviously not going to help either of us."

"Well, the board of directors here appreciate your situation, but, as I've said, with this added attention from law enforcement, they want to be better compensated. You do understand we can't afford to attract the, well...*wrong* sort of attention."

"Neither of us want that, right? So, you're saying an additional five percent would put us back on track?"

"The board would feel more comfortable in going forward with the additional compensation."

A pause ensued as Hirt weighed his position. "And fifteen percent of my money isn't enough?"

Morgan was getting annoyed. The sound of silence lingered on the line, until he reiterated, "I think we've answered that question."

Hirt continued. "You know, I'm getting the feeling that it's not the risk that's bothering the board, but, well...it feels like you're putting the squeeze on me, maybe taking advantage of the situation."

"Dr. Hirt, I'm sorry that you feel that way, but it's really not the case. Our twenty-percent fee would be a fair price for what you're getting."

Waving off his next patient, Hirt spoke calmly. "Damon, we both know that what I'm *getting* is a bank that's been in the laundry business for decades, and a board that's made some investments that are going south so fast that they need *my* cash to deflect the anger of current investors. C'mon, you've got one director right now under indictment and pending extradition to Canada."

Hirt's assessment was met with more silence. "I do my homework, too, Damon. What, you guys think I wouldn't check you out?"

"We've had a few loose cannons from time to--"

"Let me break it down for you, Damon. Here's the deal I'm prepared to make: if we can't move forward with our original deal, I'm afraid some of Dade Tropical Bank's Greatest Hits may be heard in places you don't want them to."

"Dr. Hirt, we stood by you when--"

"Talk to your board, Damon. You have about an hour before I leave at five p.m." His voice took on a menacing monotone. "A man who doesn't know his role in this world doesn't deserve to stay in it."

Annoyed, and now two patients behind schedule, Hirt hung up and buzzed Laura on the intercom to let her know he was ready for his next patient. Another forty minutes passed as Hirt rushed through nine patient screenings and dispensed ten new prescriptions. At 4:45 p.m., he rang Croaker.

With his feet propped up, the bag man was in a good mood, lounging in air conditioned comfort in his new 37-foot Winnebago parked at the Pelican Yacht Club in Ft. Pierce. Thanks to the club's head of security, he had all the wi-fi and power he needed from two 50-amp shore power cables running from the marina. Picking up his burner phone, he answered Hirt's call on the third ring. "What's up, doc?"

"Don't be a smart ass, Max. I'm not in the mood," pausing to sign three more opioid scripts. "Did you finish moving?"

"As of an hour ago, boss. Everything moved over and feedin' off the grid at Pelican Yacht Club. Only set me back two grand a month plus a coupla grams of China white for Diego."

With Croaker, Hirt was constantly having to re-evaluate his risk. "Does *anyone* there know who you are?"

"Funny, all these millionaires runnin' around on their sportfish, con- gratulating each other on being masters of the universe. I'm just the lowly night watchman here."

"Alright. Stay low, Max."

"You makin' fun of my height again?"

"You know what I mean. What else?"

"Wanted to give you a heads up. We may have a problem with the Disciples, you know, that biker group I told you about a coupla weeks ago."

Thinking he could pose a quick fix, "Yeah. Dante's gang. We used to do business in Miami years ago. What kinda problem you having with him?"

"Coupla their guys tried to take a few of my buyers with a cheaper product down south. One of my guys got the crap beat out of him, but he'll live. We're golden on the Treasure Coast, but down there, things can get a little rough. Might hafta hire some muscle to--"

"Listen, before you do that, let's drop our price, just temporarily. Only with certain buyers, and only if you have to compete until we can reach an understanding. We can afford it. We got a 4,000 percent mark-up. We'll put the squeeze on'em while I talk to Dante."

"Our biggest buyers in Miami and Lauderdale tell me we've got the best stuff, so a little discount from time-to-time might work. I'll try it on."

"Yeah. Let me know how that goes."

"What else, boss?"

Hirt checked his notes on the conversation with Morgan. "Listen, I need you to do something for me. Write this down: Damon Morgan, C.F.O., Board of Directors at Dade Tropical Bank on Biscayne Boulevard, Miami."

Jotting it down on an empty cheeseburger bag. "Yeah, okay. Got it. You need him to disappear?"

"No. Don't hurt him. I need all the dirt you can get on Morgan and his crew. Yesterday. This is important, Max. Don't screw it up. Get on his good side."

"How you suggest I do that?" he asked, taking a healthy swallow of his Bud Light.

"Feed him bits of fake intel on me, be his buddy, send him a birthday cake, flowers, a butt plug, whatever he needs. I don't care. You know how to schmooze, and you know how to vet online. I need *all* the heavy dirt on this guy and his directors. No questions asked."

"What's so urgent about Dade Tropical Bank?"

Sometimes Croaker exasperated the hell out of him, but Hirt just chalked it up to all the hallucinogens that shrank his brain to the size of a walnut thirty years ago. "What did I just tell you? *No questions.*"

"Okay, boss. I'm down the rabbit hole."

TWENTY

"Plausible deniability," declared Foti to the officers seated at the conference room table. The lieutenant was in an early morning face-to-face with Garrett, Beretto, Heaton and Garner who were waiting for him to elaborate.

"That's what keeps these partners-in-crime together, yet separate," continued Foti. "Right hand stays clean in plain view above board, the left, under the table, does all the dirty work. Hirt's at the top of our list of China white dealers, and if it *is* him movin' the weight, he's got a bag man bouncing around somewhere unloading this stuff and making him a fortune while he stays clean. I'm bettin' that man is Croaker. We know they were buddies in Raiford."

Garrett folded his hands together. "We've had continuous surveillance on Hirt with nothing to show for it, and now a failed undercover operation yesterday. It looks as though he's running a clean practice, Frank. Sheriff Bradshaw claims this undercover was the best he's got in Palm Beach County, and the man put a chunk of cash on the table with no results. Is it possible that you're wrong about him?"

"Hirt fits the profile," said Foti, with Beretto nodding in agreement.

"What about Marchenko and Yakovlev? Last week, they were number *one* on your list."

"Yakovlev's still in Ukraine," explained Foti, "and we don't have an extradition treaty with them. With Marchenko, we just don't have enough on him beyond his Ukrainian rap sheet. By the way, he's got a new body-guard, so somethin' tells me Yakovlev's not comin' back."

Garrett looked disappointed. "What else?"

Foti nodded at his two sergeants. "Dennis and Greg's sources point to Hirt. My two forensic computer techs tell me they've seen large intraday spikes in his bank balances, but then they're back to normal by the end of the week."

With a dour look, he continued. "As of last night, Croaker's disappeared off the grid. His last known residence in Vero Estates was cleaned out and wiped down sometime in the last day or two, but we found twenty grams of China white hidden in a bedroom wall that he must have forgotten about."

Det. Heaton offered an update. "When we interviewed his neighbors, they were clueless. CSI did find a pair of Nike tennis shoes buried under a wheelbarrow at the house that matched shoe prints found in the grove where Walter's body was found. The shoes were soaked in bleach, so any DNA evidence was destroyed."

Exasperated, Foti made a face. "He's gotta be *somewhere*, backstroking in that cesspool of his."

Sgt. Garner stepped in to update the group. "Eye witness interviews confirm Croaker was seen hangin' around Ultimate Fitness, the gym where Kelly Granata worked. I interviewed the manager, and he identified Croaker from photos. Manager claims he never officially joined the gym, but he *did* manage to creep the girls out."

"What about that spear McAllister pulled out of his B.C. Anything there?" asked Garrett.

Heaton shook his head. "Any identifying marks, including the serial number and manufacturer, were ground off with a grinder like the one we found in Croaker's garage. That act in itself speaks to motive. Margo pulled all the area point-of-sale videos, and we vetted two leads, but nothing panned out, so another dead end, captain."

"I'll let McAllister know," Foti said to Beretto. "With this mountain of evidence, we should be able to get a warrant on Croaker."

Listening patiently to the officers' commentary, Beretto broke his silence. "So far, it's fairly circumstantial. Agent Madani updated her profile of the unsub, and she's still convinced the fentanyl trafficking and the Tremelle and Granata homicides are *linked*. We figure out how he's movin' the China white and laundering the cash, we can take down the whole crew."

Looking around the table, Beretto concluded the team was in general agreement. "One clue at a time, like a big jigsaw puzzle, we're putting the pieces together. We need those search warrants, but for that, gentlemen, we do need probable cause."

Catching the end of the meeting, Tech. Ofc. Locke stuck his head in the door. "Just a hop, blip and a thump away, right guys?"

The group shook their heads as Foti glared at him. "Not helpful, Locke. Be careful. You're approaching the twilight of a spectacularly dismal career. Get my drift?"

"Yes, sir. Sorry, sir."

While the FBI and Vero's finest were having their morning powwow downtown, Mark was in the middle of a five-mile beach jog. The tide was out, and he was in the mood for one of his longer runs, his feet barely touching the sand as flew along the eroded shoreline like he had wings. Lost in thought, it occurred to him that the ebb and flow of recent events seemed to mimic the forces eroding the coastline, always building up and tearing down as they changed the look of the shoreline. What would the tides bring him today, he wondered?

Given the dark events of the past few weeks, he thought it would be wise to add a safe room to Villa Riomar and decided to run it by Stella when she returned home from shopping with Helene. He worried about her, but after seeing how well she handled the new Glock 29 she carried, he had a bit more confidence in her safety.

As he ran, the stories he reviewed earlier on the internet took him back to his college years when he was married to the mob and working for his ex-father-in-law. Back then, he was dropping off suitcases full of cash and picking up bolita tickets from men whose faces looked like they'd been kissing lug nuts off eighteen wheelers, and whose names all ended in vowels. For those dubious deeds and other questionable activities, he stood to gain the hand of Mr. Fiore's beautiful daughter, Melissa, but it proved to be a stormy and short-lived relationship.

His ex-father-in-law was a guy named Tony Fiore, a caporegime, or capo, a rank used in both the Sicilian Mafia and the Italian-American Mafia. Mr. Fiore was a made member of the "Teflon Don's" family, a/k/a Mr. John Gotti. Fiore lived in an upper-middle class neighborhood in Coral Gables with his wife Lucille and their two precocious daughters, Melissa and JoAnn, until one day, Mark came along and swept Melissa off her feet.

His future father-in-law was a card-carrying member of the Teamsters Union who played pool in his home with the mayor of Miami once a week. Proud of his Sicilian heritage, Tony enjoyed making his own wine and insisted on importing the hottest Sicilian peppers to spice up his wife's dishes. He took pleasure in making cappuccino four times a day with an expresso machine custom designed in Italy.

During the mayor's visits, Mark would often witness the transfer of large amounts of neatly-bundled cash and knew not to ask any questions. It was rumored that Tony Fiore was one of the few guys that could tell you where all the bodies were buried, even that of a former friend named Jimmy Hoffa. As it turned out, it was a secret that died with him.

With all that went on with his Sicilian in-laws, Mark learned to pay attention to the good *and* the evil omens. To protect yourself, you best put three coins in the fountain and exactly three coffee beans in the sambuca. His father-in-law would always say "You had to respect it because you never knew for sure." Mark thought it all sounded kind of pagan, but when you're married to the mob, you did what you were told. So, he learned to keep his opinions to himself and lived to tell about it.

His summer jobs with his father-in-law were going well until one of Tony's lieutenants, a guy named Giancarlo Genovese, was busted with three pounds of cocaine and $147,000 of cash in his pockets on a street corner in downtown Coconut Grove. The police had the chutzpah to seize his family's house, his yacht, his three exotic sports cars, even the antique expresso machine.

When the *Miami Herald* got hold of the story after making the connection between Genovese and Gotti, the whole thing spiraled out of control. The front-page story led to two murders and six arrests in a matter of days, heralding the beginning of the end for Gotti.

He remembered his ex-father-in-law's advice; "You gotta be damned careful what you say to reporters. They're always twisting things around, looking for a headline. You think they're looking for the facts, but they really just want a good funny story. That's what they like-funny."

When Tony Fiore went out for a pack of cigarettes one day and never returned, nobody was laughing. After his father-in-law disappeared and Melissa announced she was ready to start a family, Mark decided it was time to return to the university and finish his education. Either that, or learn to speak Italian and play pool with the mayor.

Looking back on the crazy stuff he did when he was married to the mob, it occurred to him that though we are handiworks of our past, we don't have to be confined by the mistakes of our youth.

Flying over the sand on bare feet, he wondered what the tide would bring him today.

Deciding she wasn't going to let two local murders force her to stay home in fear, Stella was enjoying the day shopping on Ocean Drive in Vero Beach. It was her favorite locale to shop on the Treasure Coast, with all the charm and quaintness, without the pretense of Boca and Worth Avenue. As an added precaution, today she was packing her new Glock 29 automatic, a gift from her husband. Joined by Helene for a girl's day out, she too was enjoying the absence of pushy crowds and the glitz that characterized South Florida shopping venues.

The two just finished previewing the Vendorafa Collection at one of their favorite shops, Veranda, the collection featuring elegant hand-hammered gold and mahogany jewelry. Allison and Angie had also shown them Michael Wainwright's new award-winning Pompeii collection. They were having fun, strolling down the crowded boulevard in their Yves St. Laurent sun dresses, carrying on like a couple of schoolgirls with their dad's credit card.

"You wanna go by Studio Gabriella?" asked Stella.

"Isn't that place more for fashionistas who can't afford the Humane Society Thrift Shop?"

"Yeah, I guess. Their stuff is a little frumpy."

Stella had a better idea. "Let's go to Tiffany's next. I wanna show you something you're not gonna believe, girl!"

"What? The Chippendale Dancers performing live onstage?"

Stella opened the door to the upscale store and gave her a mock rebuke. "You naughty girl. C'mon. You're in for a fun surprise!"

After exchanging greetings with the young female clerk, they stopped in the center of the store to behold a vending machine fully stocked with the brand's signature fragrance in various sizes. Amazed with the marketing, Helene was ready to test it.

"This is so cool!" She punched in her favorite selection, swiped her card, and stood back as she watched the machine gently carry it down to the velvet-lined tray for removal. Delighted with the dispensary, Helene quickly opened the package, spritzed some on her neck and offered the bottle to Stella. "Try some?"

"On my wrist," replied Stella, "...just a little. Mark enjoys a different scent on me," smiling mischievously.

"Well, sure, girl," giving her a half-spritz.

"The vending machine is just one part of an innovative retail experience that we offer," said their clerk, pointing to the back of the store. "There's also a personalization station, called #MakeItTiffany, where customers can draw whatever design they like on an iPad and then have it copied directly onto their Tiffany swag. Getting your initials engraved is so last year," she explained, feigning boredom.

"Well, hell's bells, Stella, we gotta try that too!" declared Helene. For a fraction of a second, she thought she saw a scraggly-haired man in a tie-dyed shirt pointing at them through the window. When she did a double take, the man had disappeared. Thinking that it may have been just a reflection from the street, she let it pass.

The female clerk continued with her presentation. "The store also has plans to host a range of immersive experiences, from performances to styling sessions. We'd be pleased to update you if you'd like to enter your email."

"I'll pass on the email," replied Stella cautiously, "...but I can stop by again next week. I live here on the beach."

"Sure," responded the clerk. "People like having their shopping experience enriched, instead of just shopping. Our customers love to be entertained."

"Funny, that's what my husband's always saying about his readers," said Stella.

Joining the crowd on the sidewalk, they trekked toward their next stop as Helene turned to check the crowd following behind. "You look worried, girl," commented Stella. "What's up?"

"I didn't want to creep you out, but I think I saw him."

"Who?"

"That stocky grey-haired guy that took our photo on the dock at Pelican Yacht Club last week."

Grabbing her arm, Stella pulled her off the sidewalk. They stopped in a shady spot that looked like an intimate enchanted garden in front of Veranda. Apprehensive, Stella scanned the street in both directions.

"You sure?" she asked Helene, looking up and down Ocean Drive. "There're a lot of billionaires around here that look like they just stepped off a fishing boat in Key West."

"Not positive, but…" Uncertain of what she actually saw, Helene gave her a shrug.

"Tell you what, girlfriend. When we finish shopping, unless you have other plans, I'm taking you target shooting at the Vero Police Benevolent range with the new Glock 29 that Mark bought me. It'll give you a whole new piece of mind, girl."

The idea put a twinkle in Helene's blue eyes. "Actually, that sounds like fun. Not that I want to shoot anyone. Carl and I've got some experience with skeet shooting, but toting a shotgun around town might raise some eyebrows."

"If you like it, maybe you'll get one for yourself. It's got a great power-to-weight ratio." She studied her friend for a moment, then waved her arms at the steady stream of shoppers. "Look around us. We're in a very public place here, girlfriend. No worries. Plus, I've got this," patting the bulge in her purse.

Feeling a little safer, Helene began to relax, and the joy of shopping on a cool sunny day on Vero's Ocean Drive returned. "Okay. Let's go see those two new collections, shall we?"

The two resumed their walk toward the jewelry shop. Inside, Claire stood waiting to greet them and gave Stella and Helene a hug. "Hey, girls. So good to see you two. Won't you join us in previewing the stunning Mizuki's Pearl Collection?" With a wave of her hand, she guided them to a wall display.

"How gorgeous are these?" exclaimed Helene, admiring the gold hoops with a magnificent black pearl balanced on the bottom.

"Cosmic. Love the design," agreed Stella, holding them up in the light and then up to her ear. Favoring the look, Helene nodded in approval.

"Could I get a pair with one white and one black pearl?" she asked Claire. "My husband adores black pearls."

"Sure. Whatever your heart desires, girls, and if you don't see what you want on our displays, I'd be delighted to custom design something for you."

"Okay. I'll take this white and black pair and think about your suggestion."

Carrying the earrings to the checkout counter, Claire rang them up and placed them in a velvet-lined box before dropping them into her signature shopping bag. She glanced at the man standing near the doorway staring at Stella. "Is he with you?" she asked the two girls.

"Who?" asked Helene.

"The guy right..." turning toward the doorway, but the man had disappeared. Stella and Helene looked at Claire for an explanation. "There was a guy standing right there," pointing at the doorway, "...staring at you two. I thought he must be with--"

"What'd he look like?" asked the two girls almost simultaneously.

"Well, I didn't mean to alarm you," replied Claire, somewhat perplexed, using her hands to describe him. "He was kinda short, colorful shirt, scraggly grey hair. Do you know him?"

Their eyes widening, the two girls looked at each other before Helene strode briskly toward the door, their mood changing from joyful to cautious in the blink of an eye. "Thank you, Claire, I'll enjoy the earrings," grabbing her shopping bags and rushing toward the door behind Helene.

"Anything I can do to help?" asked Claire, baffled by her sudden change in demeanor.

"Thanks, Claire. I got this."

The two girls strode back onto the sunlit sidewalk, wading through a throng of shoppers to try and ID their mysterious stalker, almost colliding with a young girl pushing a baby stroller. Using their hands to shade their eyes, they scanned up and down Ocean Drive for a sighting of the short creepy guy in the tie-dyed shirt who was stalking them.

Stella reached into her purse and pulled out her phone, autodialing her husband and listening to his voice mail. "Honey, call me right away. I think we're being stalked by that creep from Pelican Yacht Club," clutching her bags and purse. Waving at Helene returning from her reconnaissance jaunt halfway down the block, she added, "…and don't worry, I've got my Glock with me."

As she hung up her phone, Stella was startled to see a casually-dressed Dominic Beretto exit his black SUV with a slender female officer. As they approached from across the street, she noticed that they were both armed. Unusually stern, he said, "Stella, you and Helene need to go home right now. Your stalker's here somewhere. Agent Madani and I got this."

Stella nodded and turned to Helene with an inquisitive look. "You still want to blow off some steam and do some target shooting?"

"More than ever. You and me, girlfriend. Let's do it."

TWENTY-ONE

The public be damned, but blessed be their unquenchable demand for public records, thought Hirt as he studied his computer monitor. Amazed with the detailed information, the balding psychiatrist was pouring over the schematics of Villa Riomar's floor plan, conveniently made available to the online viewer and displayed on his PC.

Continually surprised by what he thought was private information available on the internet, he was able to access the architect's blueprints required by the county as part of the request for a building permit. Using maximum magnification to study the details, he was keenly interested in the estate's entry points. The floorplan even identified the type of material and thickness used in the construction of each wall, floor and ceiling. With this information, planning an intrusion would be a piece of cake.

In the middle of his research, his burner cell phone rang. He knew it wasn't a robo call because only a handful of people had the number. The phone displayed a 305 area code, and now he remembered calling the leader of the Disciples the day before. Maybe Dante was interested in smoking the peace pipe after all.

A big player in the coke and meth trade in Miami, Dante was known on the street as a fearless man, and Hirt had learned from reliable sources that he had the brains and the chutzpah to do just about anything for a buck. Short for Dantoyevsky, Dante was a muscular man of few words, with chiseled facial features and deep ties to the Russian mob. Telling himself he could play chess with the best, Hirt hoped he wasn't exposing too much of his crew by laying his cards on the table with the Russian.

"What's up, brother?" ventured Hirt.

A pro in body language both on and off the phone, Dante listened to Hirt's breathing and nonverbal sounds to ferret out any fear or weakness over the phone. "I, ah…heard you had deal for me. What you have in mind, *brother*?"

Hirt sensed it was time to be direct. "Look. We've got a lot in common, you and I, and I understand your business. Let me ask you this: if I could increase your profits by fifteen to twenty percent in the China white trade, would you be interested?"

"Go on."

"I'm prepared to offer you my uncut China white for the same price you're paying for that *Borax* you're pushing around town, no offense intended. You could jack your price at least fifteen percent. No turf war, no one gets hurt, and we both make more coin without skipping a beat. Sound good?" He could almost hear the wheels turning in Dante's head.

Listening to Hirt's tone, Dante thought he could smell the scent of desperation. It was a good opportunity to step up the quality of his product, and Dante leaned back in the soft leather chair to deliver his low-ball offer. "I like to try, and if good as you say, I buy five kilos for $400,000 cash to start."

Dante's offer was a full fifty grand under what he had in mind, so Hirt stalled him as he worked some math in his head. The extra cash flow would save him at least that much on the cost to launder the proceeds and would serve to open the door to a more profitable relationship. "I'll split the difference at $425,000, but that's as low as I can go on five kilos." Hirt held his breath.

Following a long premeditated pause, Dante responded; "Agreed, as long as it uncut."

"Pure as the driven snow, Dante. Straight from the hills overlooking Beijing." He had no doubt that Dante was quite capable of all sorts of deadly deeds. Someone once told him if you crossed him, he'd kill you and your entire family, and *then* he'd go to work on you.

"No need to come in heavy," assured Hirt, "...I am a businessman, not a thug." Still, to protect himself, he wanted a public place to meet and had a spot in mind. "You're in Miami, I'm in Vero. So, I could meet you halfway, at the hotel bar at the Hyatt Place on Lakeview in downtown West Palm."

"I know it."

"Ten o'clock tonight work for you?"

"Da. Come alone." The line went dead as Dante ended the call.

Not exactly a rousing rendition of prosaic oration, the psychiatrist realized that Mr. Dantoyesvsky had, indeed, lived up to his billing as a man of few words.

Upon her return to Villa Riomar, a visibly upset Stella spent what seemed like an inordinate amount of time lying in bed, naked as a jaybird, telling Mark all about her shopping spree with Helene. She told him about her cat-and-mouse game with the stalker and how they worked off their frustration target shooting at the pistol range. And, how Beretto had unexpectedly showed up, aware they were being stalked, and ordered the two to head home for their own protection.

Pointedly, she asked Mark, "How did he know where I was? Did he use me for bait?" Mark didn't have an answer.

She was anxious, confused, and in need of her husband's soothing touch. Plus, she was pretty frisky from firing her Glock. Why does shooting make me so randy, she asked herself. And so, he did what any red-blooded husband would do under such circumstances; he made love to her. At first, she moaned and groaned, then fell into a sensual rhythm and began to really enjoy herself. Between momentous moments, she gasped a few words in French that he didn't understand, but they sounded quite sexy, maybe even a bit bawdy.

Afterward, as they lay panting on the bed, uncustomarily separated by a few feet of sheets and her laptop, Stella said, "I think we should go away for a while. Take a vacation."

"You mean together?" he kidded.

Moments went by while he waited for a polite chuckle from her, which never came. Instead, she remained serious. "Of course together. We've got to get out of here, Mark. Today. Before it's too late."

She was on one of her crusades, and he knew what she meant by too late. His intuition was telling him it was already too late. "Stella, we can't leave now. We're right smack in the middle of this. There's too much going on."

She looked away and lay there in silence for some time, wanting to ask him; what do you do about those fissures in your soul where your doubts peer out? But she didn't.

Instead, she asked, "You remember two years ago, when I asked you if we could go away for a while? You remember what happened?"

He nodded. It was a night that he'd just as soon forget about, a night that ended with a body count. "That was different, Stella. You were another man's wife then," vividly recalling the shootout off the coast of Islamorada involving Emilio Rosa, his thugs, and her late husband Dan Wilde.

She turned her head on the pillow to face him. "Don't forget I asked."

There was an ominous silence that settled between them like a thick fog, a heaviness that seemed to last a long time. They both watched the shadows of the swaying palms dance around the room and across the bed before he broke the calm.

"I was thinking about building a safe room for us. Whad'ya think?"

The idea lightened her mood, and she rolled closer, nudging him with her bare knee. In spite of their dangerous adventures and occasional acts of free-spirited abandonment, they both wanted to live long enough to enjoy their friends, each other, and the wealth they'd accumulated. "I think it's a good idea. When do we start?"

"Dom recommended a friend of his from Atlanta, a specialist. I'll call him later today." He glanced at the computer lying at the foot of the bed. "What were you looking at on your laptop?"

"I was double-checking all the social websites to make sure I was off." Sitting up on her elbows, "So no one can track us. I mean, how *the hell* does this guy even know where I am all the time?" Unable to provide her with an explanation, he was confident Beretto and Foti's team were getting closer to a solution. He didn't answer, so she pressed.

"You still think I'm paranoid?" she asked.

Reaching for her, he rolled over and looked deep into her stunning green eyes to share the truth. "No, baby. As a matter of fact, I'm beginning to shun the internet as much as I used to embrace it, especially when it comes to our personal stuff. I would prefer we expurgate as much as we can."

She gave him an inquisitive look. "Expurgate?"

"Redact. Edit." His response brought into focus the delicate balancing act between his need for personal privacy and the necessity of portraying his public image as a writer.

"*Now* we're on the same page," she said, giving him a quick kiss. "For a moment I thought we were experiencing page fright." She sat up and reached for her lap top. "Oh, hey," refreshing the screen, "…I came across something you should see. Check this out," scrolling to an article she'd bookmarked earlier. "You're never gonna want to borrow money again after you read *this,*" she remarked, paraphrasing the article from a major wire service.

"We've never had to borrow money," he said.

Of course, she was aware of this, but continued reading anyway, convinced the article would underscore her point. She'd always been more impressed with the ugliest of truths than with the prettiest of lies.

"A massive breach of mortgage data that exposed the personal financial information of more than 60,000 potential borrowers has raised some important questions about what happens to all the disclosures consumers make after they apply for and are granted home loans, car loans and the like. Who protects our Social Security numbers, tax returns, credit and bank account numbers when the servicing rights to these loans are sold and resold to other companies?"

She looked up to see if he was paying attention before continuing. "Borrowers would hope that all that very personal data remains padlocked and sequestered far out of the reach of criminals cruising the internet. In this case, tens of thousands of mortgage borrowers had all their private data exposed to identity thieves trolling the internet, and the victims had no idea their information was exposed, and most of them may still not even know about this breach."

"How did this happen?" he asked.

Tracing a finger across the screen, "It says a server configuration error at Gatorland Partners in Gainesville, Florida was to blame. Gatorland Partners is a consortium that owns a group of auto dealerships in southwest and north central Florida. They're still on probation by the IRS and FBI. It goes on to say that not only was there no lock on the files by the time the servicing rights were sold for the third time, but these ultra-sensitive files weren't even protected by a simple password."

Mark reacted by writing on the bed with an imaginary pen. "Dear diary; just when you think you've heard it all. Incompetence at the highest level. Where were the original applications made?" he asked. "So we know who to avoid."

"Wells Fargo, Citigroup, and HSBC. And some other mid-size lenders. They're already denying any responsibility for the breach because they claim that they neither own nor service the loans. Says this happened three weeks ago, and victims are already finding that criminals used their data to open new credit card accounts and new mortgages."

Sitting naked and cross-legged in front of her computer, reading an eye-opening account of yet another failure of internet data privacy, Stella knew how to keep his attention. "Says here victims should do what they did in the Equifax hack and take advantage of any free credit-monitoring services offered, like freezing your accounts and locking your credit reports." Making a face, "Yeah, right."

Mark shook his head. "So, after the horse has already left the barn, they suggest you lock the door? That pretty much it?"

She nodded, grabbing her toes and stretching her legs. "Remember back in 2017 when the security researchers rang the alarm about Russian hackers infiltrating our power grid? They had evidence that the hackers even had direct access to an American utility's nuclear control systems; kind of a sobering revelation, yeah?"

"And they uncovered Russian hackers interfering with our elections in 2016," he added. "The state-sponsored hacking is getting scarier by the day. In March of 2018, I remember researchers uncovered a huge hack by Iranians where they stole 31 terabytes of intellectual property from several U.S. universities worth about $3 billion."

Throwing a blanket over it, they were stringing all the hackings back together like a giant patchwork quilt. "Let's not forget," noted Stella, "…that gigantic Equifax hack in 2016 when millions of private credit accounts had their personal data exposed to identity thieves in North Korea, Iran and China. A year later, 150 million accounts exposed at Under Armour, another 340 million at Exactis, and millions more at Face Book, Twitter and Wells Fargo. Where does it end?"

"It doesn't," concluded Mark, "…unless we step back and refuse to play. It's time our government realized that cyberattacks could make thermonuclear war obsolete."

"My dear author, can I quote you on that?" she asked.

In the middle of their cyber rant, Mark's phone rang. He recognized Beretto's number. "Hey, Dom. Stella says thanks for the rescue. Did you get him?"

Beretto sounded uncharacteristically subdued. "I'm sorry to say he slipped through the perimeter we set up on Ocean Drive. He's a tricky SOB, but we're checking out some leads. We'll bag'em. How's Stella?"

"Frazzled, but she'll be okay. She and Helene sharpened their skills at the shooting range."

"That's my girl."

"We're gonna go ahead and build a safe room. Can you text me your guy's contact info? We want to move on this."

"It'll be on your phone in five. I'll call you when I have more news about our stalker." Upon reflection, Beretto thought that sounded a bit stiff. "Better yet, why don't you and Stella meet us for a drink at our hotel tonight?"

"Where're you stayin'?"

"Costa d'Este."

"Perfect. They've got a great jazz band Saturday nights. Say, eight o-clock? We can catch up and blow off some steam."

"Si, mio amico. Until then."

Still upset with his predatory banker, Hirt was rarely able to set aside his own ego when it came to business deals. But with Morgan, with an ego the size of Utah, he decided it would be a good move. Compromising with the greedy money launderer could make them both more money. Dialing him up, he heard the phone ring four times before Morgan answered.

"Dr. Hirt. Glad you called. You were on my list to call today."

"Uh-huh," replied Hirt with more than a little skepticism.

"How are you, doctor?"

"Every day a holiday, every man a king." Morgan laughed politely as Hirt continued. "Got an idea."

"Like Ross Perot, I'm all ears."

Ross Perot? Rest in peace, that took him back a ways. "Well, Damon, I think we might be able to move beyond our impasse on the fee structure. Here's what I'm proposing: if I agree to increase the cash flow to Dade

Tropical Bank by another ten percent within thirty days, you can damn well afford to keep my laundry tab at fifteen percent."

Morgan was mulling over his idea, knowing full well the other directors would likely agree to his offer. But he just couldn't resist messing with a physician who trampled all over the Hippocratic Oath as if it were something to wipe one's derriere with. "Sounds good. I'll run it by the Board and get back to you."

"Wait. Damon. You and I know it's a good deal for us both. It's either this or I switch to a new bank that's hungry to make fifteen percent on my cash. And you don't need the banking regulators breathing down your neck, right?" An uncomfortable silence ensued as Morgan weighed the thinly-veiled threat.

"Thirty days you say?"

"Yup." Wishing his response had been less glib, Hirt waited for Morgan's reply.

Convinced he still had the upper hand, Morgan took his time to respond. "All right. Let's get back on the same page. I'll agree to your offer, providing, of course, you meet that quota within the specified thirty days. With the extra cash flow, the directors will be more agreeable to managing the added risk you bring. No offense intended."

"Good. You get to stay on my Christmas list."

A dubious honor at best, thought Morgan. "Remember, thirty days. Use a bonded courier this time. We don't want any of it to get lost, do we, *doctor*? "

TWENTY-TWO

Dressed in a blue sport coat and grey slacks, Beretto sat on the barstool next to his attractive protégé, Special Agent Gwen Madani, who wore a black skirt and cream-colored shear blouse. Taking some rare time off, the pair of FBI profilers took delight in the jazz quartet's live performance in the hotel bar at Costa d'Este. Beretto glanced outside toward the beach, the long dark shadows making a familiar scene look mysterious as the twilight descended over Vero Beach, ushering in a new mood for the evening.

The subtle sounds of Channel Light Vessel flowed over them like a river of syncopated rhythm, serving to ease the day's stress. Curious to hear what new intel Mark and Stella had to share about the homicides, they sat with their backs to the bar, keeping an eye on the entrance.

Beretto couldn't help noticing the looks Madani was getting from the single men in the crowd as he reflected on her talent of leveraging her feminine attributes to gather information. Though he often felt like a protective father, Beretto thought she looked quite alluring in her black leather skirt, silk stockings and low-cut cream-colored blouse.

The crowded interior was growing darker, the clinking of glasses and conversation blending in with the soft laughter and approving sounds of admiring patrons as they basked in the subtle sounds of the alternative jazz group. The crowd was savoring the pastiche of music that permeated the club with the harmonic dissonance and sharp intelligence of a new sound for Vero Beach.

Relishing the euphoric combination of her second Johnny Walker Black and the live performance, Madani looked forward to meeting the author again in a more relaxed environment. There was just something about him that she couldn't quite describe.

Beretto was nursing his second margarita, mildly entertained by the disapproving twitters from patrons that assumed he and Madani were an intimate couple. He supposed having his arm around the twenty-nine-year-old's waist when they arrived fifteen minutes earlier might have contributed to the erroneous conclusions. Ignoring their judgements, he discretely watched his pretty colleague enjoy herself on the barstool as she twisted her body in rhythm to the sensuous beat. Someday, his idiotic flirtations would get him in trouble. Admittedly, there were times when he wished that dating a colleague wasn't so completely taboo within the ranks of the FBI.

Having a naturally suspicious mind, Beretto continued to nurse his margarita as he subtly licked the salt from the glass's rim. With his peripheral vision, he checked for others who might be admiring his protégé's sultry moves. The jazz quartet went on break as the congenial young bartender noticed his empty glass and leaned across the bar.

"Can I get you another margarita, sir?"

As he was about to reorder, Madani nudged him. "Dom, they're here."

To the bartender, he said, "Give us a minute."

With their eyes on the bar's entrance, the FBI duo watched as the McAllisters glided through the brass doors and made their way to the hostess desk. A popular pair at Costa d'Este, the couple searched the room for a place to perch before spotting Beretto and Madani at the bar. Easing their way into the crowded bistro, the couple garnered ample attention as the throng made room for the couple, Stella in her semi-sheer blouse and skirt, Mark in his black tight-fitting outfit.

Beretto and Madani stood, the two couples exchanging pleasantries, and Mark thanked the FBI agents again for their interdiction with Stella's stalker as he smiled and gave Madani an appreciative look. "Gwen, if more agents looked like you, culprits would be standing in line to surrender."

Flattered, she shook his hand. "If only it was that easy, Mark," her sultry brown eyes signaling more than a professional interest.

Not to be outdone, Stella balanced his play by extending her hand to Beretto. "How's my Clint Eastwood stunt-double?"

"Thank you for making my day," was his droll reply. "Why don't we grab a table outside on the patio where we can talk more privately?" Turning to Mark and lowering his voice, "There've been some new developments."

Here was a man, thought Mark, who obviously enjoyed life, which was understandable for a law enforcement officer who knew firsthand how abruptly it could end. As they walked outside, he asked, "So, how did he slip away, Dom?"

Beretto sighed and let a meaningful few seconds pass before answering. Mark felt like he may have sounded too accusative with his question. "We just didn't have enough manpower to set up an effective perimeter. It was just me and Madani."

Despite his cavalier attitude toward their meeting venue, Mark was more than a little concerned for his wife's safety as he led her outside with his arm around her waist. Beretto led them to the only empty four-top on the patio deck, and it was situated on the far corner with a view of the beach. The tables were expertly built of teak, and, running his hand over the finish, the workmanship reminded him of the fine joiner work throughout the interior of *Dream Girl*.

As the four made themselves comfortable, the group was thankful for the privacy afforded by an end table as Beretto cleared his throat to speak. Placing his hands flat on the table, he made his announcement; "A Federal Judge has *finally* issued an arrest warrant for Croaker. Now, all we have to do is find him."

"We're hoping he rolls," added Madani. "With the new intel we have, we're convinced he handles most of the China white trade for Hirt. If we offer Croaker a plea bargain in exchange for his cooperation, the plausible deniability thing falls apart and we'll take down the whole crew."

Their server had made her way across the patio deck, the college-age girl with her hair in a French twist and wearing a nametag that read "Randi." She did a double take on the foursome as she took their drink orders, trying to figure out where she might have seen them before.

After she'd left, Mark turned to the two agents. "What would a deal for Croaker look like if we can catch him alive?"

"Not *if...when*," corrected Madani. "When facing the death penalty, ninety percent of serial killers will choose life in prison in a federal penitentiary-especially in max security where their safety can be guaranteed."

Until now, Stella had stayed silent, listening to their conversation, the ambient sounds of the nearby bar, the mellow jazz, and the sounds of a crowd enjoying the entertainment. After hearing Madani's prediction, Stella looked out at the beach with a forlorn look, turning her attention to the blinking lights on the ocean's horizon and the stars and crescent moon, as if searching for a better answer. Something was off key, and it was all starting to sound too glib for her.

"What about the families of victims that want to see him pay the ultimate price. Would they have a voice?" she asked.

Knowing she wanted justice for her two murdered friends, Beretto had an idea of what she was feeling. "Of course they would. But a judge would likely see that Croaker would have more value to law enforcement as a way to bring down Hirt and his entire crew than as a corpse. A plea deal would be more likely."

Stella noticed their server returning with their drink orders. Setting them down, she asked, "Would any of you care for anything else?"

Handing her a fifty, Mark replied, "A little privacy for now. This is for you. Give us about twenty minutes before you check back, yeah?"

Grasping the fifty, "Of course, sir. Thank you."

Mark looked around the table at his entourage. Raising his snifter of Cordon Bleu, he proposed a toast; "Some ships are wooden ships, but those ships may sink. The best ships are friendships, and to those ships, we drink."

Lifting her glass of Glenfiddich, in a sobering voice, Stella addressed what was on her mind; "And...to absent friends." Quietly, she'd been watching Madani making eyes at her husband and decided it was time to demonstrate some territoriality.

After taking a healthy swallow of her single malt, Stella leaned closer to her husband, glancing at Madani as she whispered in his ear. "You told me once that I'm the only one you want to sleep with. Remember?" playfully pulling him closer.

"I only said that because all the others kept me awake all night," he said with a grin.

Having made her point, from then on, Stella noticed that her FBI rival had apparently conceded her the high ground. The rest of the evening went more smoothly as Madani wisely turned her amorous attentions to easier game.

Sunday, Hirt drove his Porsche Turbo to South Beach Park to ogle the sixteen-year-olds prancing around in their skimpy Brazilian-cut bikinis. Lying in the shade with his back against a palm tree, the balding sixty-two-year-old psychiatrist had furtively spent an hour taking videos and photos of scantily-clad young girls using his new iPhone's telephoto lens.

Still, the inappropriate entertainment did little to assuage his obsession for *her.*

Around lunchtime on the next day, Hirt found himself at The Wave inside Costa d'Este Resort waiting for a certified registered nurse anesthetist named Rita to join him for lunch. Hirt wasn't big on daytime outings away from the office and was rarely seen in such a public place. But on the phone, the CRNA had promised him information that sounded like it could be quite lucrative and insisted on meeting him at a popular bistro.

Ironically, Rita was not only a fentanyl addict and a regular patient of his, she also dispensed fentanyl patches at the community hospital. Usually prescribed for cancer patients in extreme pain, the patches weren't nearly as potent as the China white he distributed, and he was happy to oblige her addiction if her intel was valuable.

A popular place for lawyers, doctors and other business professionals, The Wave bustled with waiters and bartenders preparing for a busy lunch hour. Perfect for their discrete meeting, he'd chosen the place for its dimly-lit interior and the high-backed booths that afforded him the extra privacy they would need. From his booth on the end of the row, he carefully surveyed the restaurant for undercover cops while sipping his daiquiri and keeping an eye on the front door. Customers were drifting in, mostly a mix of professionals and retirees looking for a refined sense of hospitality and willing to pay up for it.

Behind the bar, the vibrant underwater videos of oceanic reef life formed the backdrop as the young male bartender got busy creating the specialties of the house. The video images echoed the brilliant colors of the large salt water aquarium situated just inside the entrance. In a world of their own, images of clownfish, pygmy sea horses, blue tangs, damsel fish and sea anemones waved back and forth, displaying their brilliance like colorful city lights aglow in a nocturnal sea.

Turning to check the procession of patrons, Hirt noticed a thin, not unattractive woman dressed in blue-green hospital scrubs step inside. A bit frazzled, it was obvious she was searching the room for a familiar face.

"Rita?"

Hearing her name, she turned and clutched her purse. "Dr. Hirt. Thanks for meeting me."

Looking to draw as little attention as possible, Hirt stayed seated. "Won't you join me?" gesturing at the empty seat across from him in the booth. Giving him an apologetic smile, they shook hands as she sidled into the seat.

"Sorry I'm late. Couldn't find a place to park," she explained. "Had to make three passes around the parking lot to find a spot."

"No one seems to be in a big hurry here in 'Heaven's Waiting Room'," replied the psychiatrist with a smirk. He took a moment to regard her. Aside from her gaunt face and slender build, few would guess she was an addict. Recalling her bi-monthly office visits from the hundreds of patients he dispensed opioids to, Hirt remembered her incessant requests for stronger doses. Her addiction brought into question her reliability as a nurse anesthetist *and* a tipster, and so he told himself to be careful.

"What'll you have, Rita?"

Eyeing his daiquiri with the little umbrella, she felt ready to relax, but wanted to present a responsible image to the doctor. "That looks good. I've got to be back at the hospital in forty minutes," setting her purse beside her, "...so I'll just have one."

Another functional addict, he thought. "Sure," waving over their server and doing a second take on Rita's hospital nametag. "So, 'Book' is your last name? Was your mother a librarian or something?"

"Actually, my dad wrote children's books when I was a kid," she explained. "Later, he became a copy editor for his publisher," placing her napkin in her lap.

Something was gnawing on him. Hirt had learned to trust his instincts and had a sudden urge to reconnoiter the restaurant. "Rita, will you excuse me? I'll be right back." Standing, he headed toward the men's room, giving Rita more time to collect her thoughts.

It seemed like her whole life, Rita struggled to reconcile her spiritual beliefs with her opioid addiction. Diagnosed as an INTP personality by her psychiatrist, she often had little understanding of decisions made on the basis of a person's feelings, a personality trait her husband could never understand. Her "bitchy side", he called it. She found herself constantly striving to achieve logical conclusions to issues while ignoring the importance of emotions. And because she was often out of tune with how people felt after a disagreement, she found herself relinquishing her own personal boundaries to meet the emotional needs of others.

In her twenties, she learned that sex always seemed to work the best to close the emotional gulf, and her husband had discovered this early in his relationship with her. So their fights would inevitably lead to steamy make-up sex, sometimes even violent lovemaking, which explained why her husband was never reluctant to pick a fight with her. Ironically, her husband's predilection for arrogance and confrontation with her was rewarded in a way uncharacteristic of normal husband and wife relationships. She knew it wasn't normal, but loved him anyway. His "steamy hot mess", he liked to call her, and it was about that time she'd discovered the euphoric escape that fentanyl offered.

"So, Rita Book, R.N.A., why are we here?" asked Hirt, suddenly reappearing and sliding back into his seat.

"Well…certain things make for interesting conversations," was her cryptic reply.

Interrupted by the arrival of their waiter, they ordered a round of drinks and two orders of grilled blackened dolphin before Hirt removed his reading glasses and glanced around the room again to make sure they weren't being overheard. Rita Book followed his lead.

"On the phone, you mentioned some valuable information," extracting an envelope from his coat pocket and placing it on the table, "…that you would exchange for five grams of this." Hirt kept his fingers on the envelope as he watched her nod. "If it's good information I can profit from, you can take it home with you. Agreed?"

Leaning forward, she nodded and glanced from side to side, nervous with what she was about to say. "You know who Dr. Nancy Callaway is?"

"Yes, of course, the new Director of Research at Oconix, filling in for the late Dr. Tremelle." Intrigued, he glanced at the beach before re-establishing eye contact. "What about her?"

Rita leaned closer, keeping an eye on the envelope. "Two days ago, we performed a laparoscopic cholecystectomy on Dr. Callaway, and there were complications that required us to extend her care--"

"She had her gall bladder removed?" he asked, watching her nod again. "I'll bet she was a lousy patient."

"Yeah…she was. It's true, doctors *do* make lousy patients, present company accepted. She gave us one personal order after another, spent her waking hours telling us what we were doing wrong, so…we upped her meds to give us some peace and quiet."

Hirt thought this was amusing. "Why did she have her gall bladder removed?"

"It was partially necrotic. As her CRNA, I was in charge of her post-op care. Anyway, yesterday, while she was heavily sedated on morphine, she got very chatty and let something slip out, saying she was gonna be a *very* wealthy woman after the Oconix buyout." She leaned back from the table as their waiter served their entrees.

Hirt struggled to disguise his interest as he reflected on the last piece of inside information he traded on. Though the Valiant collapse had made him over $2 million in put option profits which he was forced to relinquish, it had also cost him two years of pro bono work at Raiford after he was convicted of insider trading. Concerned with the accuracy of the information, he asked, "How long has Dr. Callaway been at Oconix?"

Checking to make sure their waiter was out of earshot, "Since about the time I passed my nurse anesthetist boards thirteen years ago. That's enough time to accumulate a lot of stock and make a lot of friends there, wouldn't you say?" She glanced again at the envelope.

Cocking his head, "You invested in stocks, Rita?"

Surprised with his directness, she gave him a direct answer. "Apart from my 401-K, I have a modest trading account. Got some Abbvie, Pfizer, AT&T, a few other high-dividend blue chips. I like watching CNBC on my lunch hour in the hospital cafeteria." Leaning forward, in a whisper, as if she were trading secrets over her neighbor's fence, "I did buy 300 shares of Oconix *on margin.*"

So, she got skin in the game, he thought, stroking his bald head. On margin, no less. "You have a favorite analyst?"

"I like David Chu," she replied.

Recognizing the name from the CNBC line-up, he tested her sense of humor. "David Chu? Oh…the sandwich analyst."

She laughed. "*That* was funny. Actually, I think he covers the trending topics."

Taking a sip of his daiquiri, he continued to study her as their entrees were served. "How sure are you of your information on Oconix?" Aware that the biopharma company was one of the movers and shakers in new and novel medications for a wide range of oncologic and psychiatric disorders, Hirt knew there were ample reasons for a possible buyout. But he was still concerned about the timing.

She took a healthy swallow of her drink, then set her glass down. "I know what I heard, Dr. Hirt. I'm not going to give you bad information. You've been taking good care of my pain meds, and I'd like to continue being your patient." She thought of something else. "What you may not know is that Dr. Callaway is on very good terms with the CEO over there, and….ah," leaning forward again, "…I think they're sleeping with each other."

Hirt sat back and rubbed his ear. "Now *that's* interesting." He let a meaningful moment pass before pushing the envelope across the table. "Take it. I think you've earned it." Without hesitation, she snatched the envelope and quickly stuffed it into her purse. "When you come up with anything else like *this* little tidbit, there's more where that came from, Rita Book."

Nervous, she checked her watch and looked around the restaurant. "Obviously, we need to keep this between ourselves, Dr. Hirt. If anyone else found out I was passing on confidential patient information, I could lose my job."

"That makes three of us. I'm schizophrenic." His attempt at levity did little to dissuade her fear, so he leaned forward and put his hand on hers. "You have my promise, Rita. We never had this conversation. No worries."

Raising his glass for a toast, "Here's to new heights in medicine, and another 500 shares of Oconix." Of course, Hirt had no intention of limiting his purchase to just 500 shares. His whole life, he'd placed mostly small bets, and the house usually won. But when that right opportunity presented itself, you bet big, and maybe you take the house.

Raising her glass, she went with the flow, pretending like they'd never spoken about it and glanced at her watch again. "Got ten minutes to get back, so I'll have to leave you," tossing back the rest of her drink. "Thanks for lunch, doctor, and the…ah…" patting her purse.

Giving her a garish wink, "Thank *you,* Rita. See you at our next appointment. Let me know how you like that stuff."

Hirt was a man with a chip on his shoulder the size of a giant sequoia, and he was pleased that the intel from the meeting would even things up for him. Heading off the reservation again, he was determined to make up for the Oconix put option profit that was taken from him and paid as restitution two years ago. Like an inactive volcano about to erupt, the deep pool of resentment welled up inside him as it became clear there was only one course of action, and he was convinced it was brilliant. He would pay his broker one of his rare appearances since it was only two blocks away.

After paying the check, the once-heralded psychiatrist was hoofing it toward the Morgan Stanley office on Ocean Drive. Congratulating himself, he felt prescient about setting up a fee-based wrap account that would allow him to avoid any additional commissions on trades.

A new blue-grey Bentley convertible stopped for him as he stepped into the crosswalk, the well-dressed older man behind the wheel waving him across. With a covetous look toward the stately car, Hirt vowed to make enough money on this trade to buy *three* Bentleys. It was his chance to even the score and game the system, and *this* time he planned on keeping the money. Pushing open the tall glass door with an attitude, Hirt stepped into the hallowed halls of Morgan Stanley and looked around for his broker as he smiled at the receptionist. "John Hale in?"

"Yes, sir," the receptionist turning in her seat to see if he was free.

"Thanks, Kathleen, I see him." Spotting the young VP sitting alone in his office, Hirt tapped on the glass as he hung up the phone. He'd always wondered if it was the Hale Groves family money and their connections that propelled him to his vice presidency at such an early age, or if it was a real ability to make his client money. Hale was a sharp dresser, looking dapper in his dark blue pin-striped suit and coral-colored tie.

Recognizing the owner of The Pain Free Clinic, Hale was cordial. "Dr. Hirt, c'mon on in," gestured the VP of investments, "...make yourself comfortable."

"You busy, John?" stepping inside.

"Not a bit. Just returned from lunch. What can I do for you?"

"Bring up my account and tell me my total balance," as he made himself comfortable in the oversize leather chair. "Gotta make this quick. I've got a lobby full of waiting patients."

"Of course," Hale replied. "You've got $500,040, about half in Pfizer, and half in cash." Hale recalled the $500,000 wire transfer from a bank in the Caymans that funded Hirt's account a month earlier. Anticipating further instructions, the vice president knew it was usually a waste of time to present recommendations to him, so he sat back and waited patiently to hear what his client had in mind.

Hirt was tempted to leverage his long position in Oconix with call options, but because he couldn't be sure of the timing on the buyout, he was hesitant. Options had an expiration date. Mulling it over, he remembered the SEC had made a big deal of his overly aggressive short-dated put options in the Valiant scandal and had used them to support their claim of inside information. He decided a long stock position would be more defensible, using no margin, and more in line with his usual investment style.

"What's Oconix Pharmaceutical trading at today?" asked Hirt.

"Oconix is...last trade was $39.32," averting Hirt's gaze. "Took a big hit when they lost Dr. Tremelle recently. She was their Director of Research and responsible for most of their past blockbuster drugs." Looking up from his computer, "We have a sell rating--"

Hirt shook his head and held up a finger, stopping him in mid-sentence. "Does your firm have an investment banking relationship with Pfizer?"

"Yes, but--"

"How 'bout Oconix?"

"Well...no, but that has--"

Hirt smirked at his answer. "Convenient," he replied with obvious sarcasm, an implication that his broker was less than pleased with. Waving his hand in dismissal, "All that doesn't matter, John. Here's what we're gonna do," sliding forward in his chair and meeting Hale's inquisitive gaze. "Sell all the Pfizer at the market, put the proceeds and all the cash into Oconix, market orders."

"You want to do this now?"

"Yes, of course now. Is there any other meaning to 'market order'?"

Feeling like he'd been admonished by his third grade teacher, Hale repeated the order and did as he was instructed, waiting for the executions before looking up at his client. "Dr. Hirt, you now own 12,717 shares of Oconix," he announced, feeling a little uncomfortable with such a large order of a sell-rated stock. With a note to the file, he made it a point to classify the trade as "unsolicited." Knowing his client had an enviable track record with pharmaceuticals, Hale sat back in his chair and took a moment to study him.

"Dr. Hirt, I gotta be honest with you. It's important that your relationship with our firm continues to be profitable, but this is a sizable bet on a poorly-performing biopharma. Their pipeline has lagged since they lost Tremelle. If I may ask...what do you see in Oconix?"

Hirt avoided looking him in the eye, preferring instead to look down and pretend to brush something off his Nike cross trainers. "Nothing but upside, and I don't think it gets any cheaper. Now, I've got to get back to my patients."

Extending his hand, the doctor stood. "Thank you, John. Call me at noon for the next few days, let me know what Oconix is doing. I expect to be very busy with patients and may forget to check my account."

Hale entered the notes into his tablet. "You can count on it, Dr. Hirt. And thanks for the business."

Feeling smug, Hirt stopped at the side bar in the lobby to make himself a cup of coffee from the Keurig machine. Stirring in the Coffee Mate and sweetener, he glanced around the lobby at a few geriatrics sitting in the overstuffed chairs, absorbed in reading the *Wall Street Journal.* Ah... the herd mentality.

Fitting the lid, he mused about his trade. *Easiest million I'll ever make.*

TWENTY-THREE

On a partly-cloudy day in early February, Stella noticed the afternoon weather was becoming more spring-like as the brief showers became more frequent. After spending most of the morning working out in her home gym, she had some fun racing Helene to the top of Hawaii's famous Diamond Head using the 3-D virtual workout program on her new Peloton exercise bike.

With gardening on her agenda, she peered out her kitchen window at Villa Riomar to see if the light rain had stopped. The blue skies further south were sweeping toward their villa, and by the time she was finished with her glass of Camus, she hoped the sun would be out. The flying drones were still a nuisance to her, especially when she was *au naturel*, but there were fewer of them ever since her husband had pointed a shotgun at a few that had gotten close enough to count her freckles.

Today, to the disappointment of the high-tech voyeurs who operated those drones, she had reluctantly acquiesced to Mark's plea for more modest gardening accoutrement. He was away, attending a directors' meeting at the Pelican Yacht Club, but his loaded twelve gauge continued to lean against the front loggia wall in case she needed it.

For now, the light rain seemed all too fitting given her muses on the dearly departed, but she refused to allow her spirits to be dampened. She thought about a conversation she had with her father years ago when he mentioned an unnamed guest would be sailing with them the following day. The guest turned out to be Dominic Beretto, then a Special Agent before his appointment to a supervisory position at the BAU, and a guest who'd since become an indispensable friend.

Of the people and things that she felt most optimistic about back then, her father was always adept at thinking outside the box and laying out options she hadn't considered. She missed his sage advice. Today, the most relevant advice seemed to be coming mostly from her two friends in law enforcement, Beretto and Foti, and she wondered where it would lead. Of course, her husband was still her most trusted source of advice, and would remain so to her dying day. In tough situations, he had proven to be a man who believed in a four-star heaven, someone who gave a damn about what you do here on earth.

But of all the clear and present dangers facing her today, none seemed as chilling as the unidentified serial killer that continued to stalk her. She found herself asking how it was that she could be the captain of her fate, but never quite the master.

The urgency was real, and Beretto needed to say very little to persuade the Safe-U four-man team to fly out from Atlanta the very next day. And so, at the behest of her special friend who headed the regional BAU, the three-man team at Safe-U had amazed everyone by completing the construction of the McAllister's safe room in less than four days.

While the safe room installers were busy doing their thing, Mark had arranged for the completion of a concrete privacy wall around Villa Riomar to protect Stella from prying eyes while she cultivated her greenery. Though she still preferred to tend her flowering garden and edible plants *au naturel*, the couple reached a compromise in which Stella agreed to wear her bikini bottom, and on certain days, sometimes even her top. Whenever craftsmen and laborers were present, the hot-blooded woman in her secretly enjoyed moving around the jobsite among the men, especially if they were younger and bare-chested. Often, she would catch them looking at her as if she were a fresh, double-cheese pepperoni pizza.

Stepping outside, she noticed the rain had stopped, the sun shining again as she strode through her freshly-watered garden. With her vegetable garden in bloom again, she wandered through, taking her time to admire each new sprout and bud. Since it's planting, Stella's garden had survived two gale-force thunderstorms, along with a host of creepy caterpillar pests that were bent on turning her cultivation into a month-long smorgasbord. Proud of her handiwork, she put her gloves on and squatted to pull a few weeds from between a row of plants, pleased with how the basil, carrots, peppers, eggplant and tomatoes were looking.

A Monarch butterfly landed on her index finger. It was a fortuitous omen, and she carefully raised it up to admire its beauty. "You're welcome to hang out with me today," she said to the butterfly slowly fanning its wings, "...just make sure to go next door when you're ready to lay your caterpillar eggs. Yeah?" Her interlude with the butterfly ended when she heard a car approach. She peeked over the top of the privacy wall to see their landscaper trimming hedges along the driveway with hedge shears and a half-pint of rum sticking out of his back pocket.

"Looks good, Hector. You're going to save that Myers 'til after you're through, right? We need those hedges nice and straight."

"Si, Mrs. McAllister. Entiendo. Mas tarde," patting his pocket in agreement. Stella had a soft spot for the man since learning of his wife's Alzheimer's disability, often tipping him with a C-note on Fridays so he could take his wife and five kids out to dinner.

Five years before, Hector made the headlines when he defended a girl in a tavern in Sebastian from a would-be rapist. She was a defenseless eighteen-year old barmaid from Fellesmere, and Hector wound up serving three years in Raiford for attempted manslaughter when the rapist almost died from the pummeling he inflicted on him. It was an act of chivalry that forever endeared him to the McAllisters, and one of the main reasons they'd found a place for him on the payroll.

A black GMC Denali with U.S. Government plates pulled up to the entry gate, the tinted window rolling down to reveal a smiling Dominic Beretto. Waving, Stella reached for the remote gate controller and pressed the green button. Not expecting company, she brushed herself off and donned her sheer black wrap as the Denali began to make its way up the long Chicago brick driveway.

"Hello, Dom. Watch'a up to today?" as the casually-dressed FBI agent exited the SUV with a gun and badge on his hip.

"Stella, that's got to be the most becoming *gardening* outfit I've ever laid eyes on," striding up to her.

"Well…you won't find it at Home Depot," she said. "It would ruin the look with one of their orange aprons. I was gonna surprise Mark tonight with a fresh homemade salad from our garden," wrapping her cover-up a bit tighter.

"I can only guess at what he likes for dessert," winking. "Got to admire your relationship. The only people I remember making happy in my two marriages were the divorce attorneys."

Entertained with his candor, she found it unusual for a ranking FBI agent. "Okay. Now that we got that out of the way, I know you didn't drive all the way out here to compliment my gardening attire."

Walking her up the brick driveway, he smiled. "Though that *would* be a good enough reason in itself for a drive out here." Stopping at the top of her driveway, "I wanted to inspect your safe room with you and make sure everything is set up right."

Stella nodded. "Yeah, good idea. I'd like to get your take on that. Some of the gauges looked a little confusing, especially the CO2 scrubbers."

"Calibrated correctly, the gauges are very accurate. I'll show you how they work." Beretto turned and pointed at a black car parked beside the road a block south on Ocean Drive. "See that black sedan? He's one of ours, and will be there mostly at night for a while." Turning back to her, "And don't be alarmed if you see him follow you around town. Lt. Foti and I decided to beef up your security. I left your husband a voicemail about it."

"I'm grateful. Makes me feel safer with you two watching our backs." The sun went behind a cloud, and her intuition told her Beretto was holding something back. "Level with me, Dom. What else is going on? You have some new intel on our suspects?"

He shook his head. "I wish we did." Seeing her disappointment, he rested a reassuring hand on her shoulder. "Look, Stella...these guys play rough, and they're elusive. The manhunt continues for our number one suspect. We have his boss under surveillance, and we're close to having a search warrant."

"Croaker and Hirt?" she asked.

Bretto nodded. "Don't underestimate them. You're doing all the right things, Stella. You two just need to stay low until we find them. I suggest you drive different routes and vary your routines for a while." Offering her some encouragement, "This safe room was a good idea." He noticed the shotgun leaning against the loggia wall. "You doin' some skeet shooting in your garden?"

Finally, he had her smiling. "You're hilarious. It's for those damn drones. You think I *want* to be on You Tube?"

"What, in this high-end neighborhood, they don't allow anti-aircraft missiles?"

She thought that was funny. "Believe me, if they did, I'd install a few in my garden and the back patio."

"I bet you would."

"Yeah, well...shotgun's too big for my purse, so my loving husband got me a new Glock 29." She watched as the crow's feet around his eyes crinkled.

"Are you messin' with me?" he kidded. "You licensed to carry?"

"No, to drive, silly. But I don't drive in my house."

Beretto enjoyed her humor. "Uh-huh. Now that we've got that cleared up, let's take a look at your safe room, shall we?" leading her to the front door.

Stella reached for the handle on the five-inch-thick mahogany doors, "Toast our new safe room with a drink?"

"Yeah, sure. You have any of that Cordon Bleu around?"

"Sure do," cocking her head at his choice of libation. "Breakfast of champions, yeah?"

The two detectives were on undercover assignment at The Wave at Costa d'Este. Dressed in floral Tommy Bahama shirts, jeans, Ray Bans, and flip-flops, the two detectives were giving a stellar performance as long-lost Jimmy Buffett fans on their way to Margaritaville. From their table on the patio deck outside, Heaton had a partial view of the inside table where Hirt sat with the slender nurse dressed in hospital scrubs. He and Locke were guessing it had to be some kind of drug connection.

Careful not to turn his head, Locke asked, "Who's the nurse he's with?"

His peripheral vison served him well as he wrapped his hands around his cheeseburger. "No idea, but she looks nervous, keeps checking her watch like she's gotta be somewhere. Looks like a hospital ID tag she's wearing. My guess is she's on her lunch break at the hospital."

"Ya know, Dennis, we've had this dirtbag under surveillance for almost two weeks now, and this could be our first break. We know where he's headed, so I say we follow her. See if she's dirty."

Heaton gave his partner a slight nod. "He just pulled out a fat envelope and set it on the table. Whatever it is, it sure got her attention. That's gotta be drugs or some kinda bribe." After a pause, "Looks like things are heating up."

"Maybe it's the alcohol. My gut tells me this is the day he slips up."

Tired of sharing meals, crossword puzzles, fruitless searches, and sleeping in their car, Heaton and Locke were both ready to take their investigation to the next level. "I hope you're right, partner," Heaton replied. "If the lieutenant keeps us on surveillance, I'm gonna ask for a car with a vibrating recliner."

"Dream on. My wife says she's gonna divorce me unless I spend more time with her and the kids."

"Yeah?" commiserated Locke. "Tell me about it. Mine mentioned a new friend named 'Peter' yesterday. When I asked her who 'Peter' was, she went to her bedside drawer and held up her vibrator. "'Meet Peter Fitzwell,' she says."

After sharing their chuckle, Heaton glanced at his partner with a rare look of empathy. "We need to nail this scumbag and close this case," followed by a fist bump. "Lives at stake."

A few more minutes ticked by before either spoke again. "All right, don't turn around," said Heaton, "…she just stuffed the envelope in her purse. Looks like leaving behavior, so let's get ready."

Catching their waiter's attention, Locke gestured for the check and handed him a credit card. After clearing their tab, Heaton and Locke quietly waited for their mark to depart. "She's headed for the front door. Let's go around the side," suggested Heaton in a low voice, "…and watch her from the car. I'm betting she's headed to the hospital or a clinic nearby."

Striding briskly to their white Taurus, the two detectives watched Rita Book climb into an older blue Subaru Outback and make a phone call. Locke asked, "Shall we take her here?"

"No, Hirt could see us. Let's follow her. We'll take her in her employer's parking lot."

The blue Outback pulled onto Ocean Drive and turned right, heading toward Beachland with the two detectives following closely. Driving under the speed limit, she was easy to track, and obviously unaware that she was being followed. From his cell phone, Heaton called in the subject's tag number to Officer Violette at the Vero CID.

Setting her coffee down, "Tech officer Violette."

"Margo, run this tag. Florida, NXJ 57R."

After a few moments on her keyboard, "That car is a 2009 blue Subaru Outback registered to Mrs. Rita Book, 1990 15th Avenue, Vero. Except for a D.U.I. two years ago, she's clean."

"Copy that, Margo. Did you say Rita…Book?"

"Affirmative. She's a CRNA at the community hospital."

"She's a what?"

"Certified registered nurse anesthetist. She dispenses narcotics to patients."

"Copy that. Looks like she's been dispensing some to herself. Requesting a K-9 unit meet us at the hospital. We're gonna pull her over there."

"Roger your request. Be about eight minutes. Hang on. I got the lieutenant in my other ear." Following some background chatter, "The lieutenant's on another line but wants to know what you're doing."

"Copy that. Hang on." Heaton could hear Foti in the background. "You can tell him we've got a good lead on Hirt and may be about to bust one of his dealers."

"I'll let him know. I'll see if I can expedite the K-9 unit. Margo out."

The two detectives followed their CRNA north on Indian River Boulevard. Pulling in front of the Subaru, they cut her off and blocked her in after she entered the hospital parking lot. Locke hit the car's blue lights and the two detectives walked back to the Subaru with their badges displayed. Completely unnerved, Rita Book rolled her window down, embarrassed about being pulled over in front of her fellow employees who were just returning from lunch.

With her best dumb blonde act, she asked, "Was I speeding, officer?" Then it dawned on her that it was the same two men that were watching her eating lunch at The Wave. Only then did she think about the white envelope in her purse.

"Hands on the wheel. Do not reach for anything," instructed Heaton sternly. In her rear view mirror, she watched the K-9 unit pull in behind her. Heaton stood imposingly at her driver's-side door. "Ma'am, will you please turn off the ignition and step out of the car?"

Book reached for her purse, and fearing she was about to hide evidence, Heaton barked at her. "Ma'am, stop moving. Is that your purse?"

"I was just gonna--"

"Leave your purse on the seat and exit the car," repeated Heaton sternly, placing his right hand on his Glock to show he meant business. "Keep your hands where we can see them."

Distraught, Book did as she was told. "What's this all about, officer?"

Heaton corrected her. "It's 'detective', ma'am, and I think you already know what this is about."

Locke opened the passenger side door for the K-9 officer and watched him walk the eager dog toward the front seat. "Find," he said. After sniffing around the inside for a few moments, the German shepherd began barking, his nose pointing at the purse lying on the front seat.

"We got probable cause. Gary, search the car," said Heaton. The K-9 officer pulled hard on the leash to reign her in and instructed her to heel. Sasha obeyed, and the officer gave her a beef-flavored treat as the dog sat obediently and waited for further instructions.

"Willie, write me up a detailed report on your K-9's inspection, will you?"

"I'll have your report ready for you in about ten minutes, detective."

Ignoring the steady stream of rubberneckers drifting in to the hospital parking lot, Heaton knew the stop was about to uncover some contraband. "Ma'am, I'll need you to step over here to the front of the white Ford Taurus."

"Bingo," declared Locke from inside the Subaru, holding up a Ziploc plastic bag full of white powder. After walking over her purse and ID to Heaton for further inspection, he broke out the colorimetric field drug test kit and inserted a tiny portion of the powder into the receptacle. Shaking the mixture, it turned a bluish-purple as he nodded at Heaton. "Testing positive for fentanyl, Dennis. Looks like about five grams."

Heaton nodded at his partner as he stood with the nurse and examined her Florida driver's license. Slipping it back into the clear plastic enclosure, "Is this your current address, Mrs. Book?"

"Yes…I was just going back to the critical care unit and--"

Tossing her purse back to Locke, Heaton lowered his voice. "Might be awhile before you're dispensing *any* narcotics to *anyone*," releasing the handcuffs. "Mrs. Book, you're under arrest for possession of an illegal controlled substance. Please turn around and place your hands behind you." After he adjusted the cuffs and patted her down, she broke down, sobbing quietly while Locke stood beside his partner and read her Miranda rights.

"I have to pick up my daughter from school," she pleaded. "Where are you taking me?"

"To the Vero Beach Police station for booking," replied Heaton matter-of-factly, walking her to the rear door. "Maybe you can call someone from there. Watch your head, ma'am," as he placed her in the back seat of the Taurus.

Looking at his partner over the top of the car, "Gary, did you find anything else?" Locke shook his head. "Okay, lock it up and hop in, partner. Good work."

PART III

We will now discuss in a little more detail the
Struggle for Existence.

-CHARLES DARWIN
The Origin of Species

TWENTY-FOUR

After her booking and fingerprinting, Rita Book sat in an austere, windowless interview room, handcuffed to the table as she thought about the mess she was in. Fearful that she was overdue in paying for her sins, and upset that her life was about to radically change, she waited for the arrival of her attorney, hoping he could show her a way forward that didn't involve suicide.

The past was another story. What's done is done, and you couldn't change it, she thought, but maybe you could find a way to break from it and leave the worst behind. Unfortunately, her love for the euphoria that fentanyl brought her had overruled her preference for a cash payment. Facing up to the harsher consequences of addiction was far worse than her D.U.I. conviction two years ago when her daughter left to live with her father at his North Lauderdale beach condo.

The steel door to the interview room swung open, and Detectives Heaton and Locke shuffled in, still dressed in floral shirts, blue jeans and flip flops. Taking a seat opposite her at the table, Heaton opened her file as the two detectives took a few moments to evaluate their detainee. "Would you like a cup of coffee, Rita?" asked Locke.

The pleasantry was unexpected. "Coffee with cream and sugar would be nice," studying her restraints. Locke started for the door, and since the officers seemed conciliatory, she was inclined to ask for more. "Can you please take these shackles off me?" raising her chained wrists. "Promise, I'll be good."

"Unfortunately, felony charges dictate we keep you restrained, Rita," explained Heaton. With a stern look, he continued. "You are being charged with felony possession of five grams of fentanyl, and you're also facing a felony charge of conspiracy to distribute," with a sympathetic look. "You're facing from ten to twenty years in prison, and the permanent revocation of your nursing license, along with the possible loss of parental rights. Do you understand these charges and possible consequences?"

She'd never felt so humiliated. "Yes," she murmured as Locke returned with three cups of coffee and set one down for her. Taking a soothing sip of the creamy liquid, Rita eased back in the chair. "Thanks for the coffee. My attorney is on his way here to explain my options."

"Options?" Heaton looked at her like she was from another planet. "Your options, Rita, are ten to twenty years in prison and the loss of your nursing license and daughter...or...you go to work for us. Cut and dry. That's it."

"What do you mean?"

"You're caught up in a bigger fish fry, Rita." Heaton slid a photo of Hirt across the table. "This is the man we want. The man you had lunch with. For conspiracy to commit murder, for distribution of a controlled substance, aggravated assault, and numerous other crimes. We think he's involved in the murders of at least two women."

Locke leaned forward. "Will you help us make Vero Beach safer?"

Before she could answer, a clean-cut man in his forties wearing a dark blue suit and red patterned Hermes tie barged into the room. In an authoritative voice, "Don't answer that, Rita." Turning to Heaton and Locke, "I'm Peter Decker, attorney for Mrs. Book," holding out his business card. The two detectives eyed it suspiciously.

"I'm instructing her *not* to answer any more questions," continued Decker. "We've set a bail hearing for ten a.m. tomorrow morning, at which time she will likely be granted bail." Decker noticed the photo of Hirt before Heaton could tuck it back into the folder. In a scolding voice, "Detectives, you know better than to question my client without an attorney present."

Heaton waved his hand, and without meaning to, he answered contentiously. "Save it for the jury, counselor. She's been read her rights." Not wanting to cross swords with her attorney, the detective reconsidered his approach before standing to make his point.

"Look, Mr. Decker," with his hands on the back of the chair, "...we're trying to stop a murderer and known drug dealer," looking at Decker and then at Book. "The man who passed these narcotics to your client is a suspect in two violent murders already and may be planning more. While we have no particular axe to grind with Mrs. Book, other than the drug charges, if you can convince your client to cooperate, we could be far more lenient with the charges she's now facing."

Decker considered the detective's conciliatory tone. "How lenient?"

"Hirt is the man we want, and Vero P.D. will use any and all legal means to bring him in. You want to be the key that opens the lock?"

Struck by the detective's sincerity, Decker was weighing the pros and cons. "Can I have a few minutes alone with my client?"

Heaton nodded his understanding. "We'll be back in ten minutes," gesturing for Locke to follow him outside before turning back to Decker. "If you'd like to save your client years in prison, and her nursing license and parental rights, convince her to be cooperative. Like I said, we have some leeway here that might prove to be very beneficial for Rita." Pointing at the clock on the wall, "Clock's ticking."

While Decker and his client spoke privately in the interview room, Heaton and Locke spent the next ten minutes sitting in Lt. Foti's office. The two briefed their boss on the situation with the Hirt case, the surveillance at Costa d'Este, the arrest, and the appearance of Rita Book's attorney. The turn of events made Foti realize this was the break they'd been waiting for. He led his two detectives back into the interview room to make the accused an offer she couldn't refuse.

"Mr. Decker, Lt. Foti, Vero C.I.D," shaking hands with the attorney and taking a seat across the table. "Detectives Heaton and Locke have just briefed me on the circumstances surrounding your client's arrest for possession and conspiracy, and it is my feeling they've done an admiral job of explaining our priorities here."

"So far, they've been very forthright, except for the issue of probable cause in the search of my client's car," ventured Decker. "It was an illegal search."

Foti gave him a skeptical look. "Look, Mr. Decker, I've read the reports. I've been a police officer for thirty years and a detective for twenty," crossing his legs. "I've been fully briefed on those details, reviewed the procedures they followed, and I think we're well beyond that point, counselor. But, if your client agrees to cooperate with us, we're prepared to reduce the charges to misdemeanor possession, a twelve month probation, maybe some community service, with a plea of no contest, maybe some time in rehab. Given her ties to the community, we could move for a recognizance bail on her behalf. In other words, she can have her life back. Now, that's about as sweet as it gets, wouldn't you say?"

Surprised with the plea bargain details, Decker raised his eyebrows at the generous terms and gave an encouraging look to his client as her eyes lit up with hope. "Ah…one more thing. She'd like to keep her job at the hospital. What about her nursing license, lieutenant?"

"Well, that's up to the hospital," replied Foti, "…but we could put in a good word for her since she's not had any prior drug offenses. In these types of cases, that often makes a difference."

"I appreciate your candor in the matter, lieutenant," checking his client's disposition for approval. Book leaned over and whispered something in his ear while the three detectives waited for more signs of they could come to an agreement.

"Ah…one more thing. We ask that the bail hearing be reset for four o'clock this afternoon. My client would like to spend the evening at home instead of in jail to explain all this to her daughter."

Detailing the terms of the plea bargain in his notes, Foti looked up at Decker to close the deal. "I think I can persuade my captain to agree to that, provided we have Mrs. Book's *full* cooperation." Shifting his attention to her, "Anything else?"

Checking her watch, she brought her final concern front and center. "It's three o'clock. Could you send a non-uniformed officer by my daughter's school to pick her up? I don't want her to be frightened. She'll be alone at the parent pick-up at three-thirty after band practice."

"We can do that," he said emphatically, making a final notation. "I could send one of our techies. Are there any other conditions that we need to discuss?"

Rita Book shook her head and glanced expectantly at Foti, then at Decker. "If the police can promise these things, I'll agree to full cooperation, Peter."

"Including testifying in open court against Hirt?" asked Foti.

"Yes," she replied.

Rolling his eyes in relief, Decker clasped his hands together. "Gentlemen, we have a deal," shaking hands with Foti.

Foti handed his notes on the plea arrangement to Locke. "Gary, have the agreement drawn up with these provisions right away, and notify the county prosecutor."

"Yes, sir," said Locke as he left the interview room.

By the time five o'clock rolled around, Judge Francis Carpazio had granted Book a recognizance bail bond at the behest of the Vero P.D. and county prosecutor. After leaving the courthouse together in the light rain, Book and Decker were en route to the hospital in the attorney's Mercedes to pick up her car. Pulling up next to her blue Subaru Outback, Decker idled his 500 S and turned to face his client.

"Rita, we got you a *great* deal. It's all gonna work out. Now, I want you to get a good night's rest tonight. Don't discuss this with anyone at work tomorrow. I'll call you when I have the date for your arraignment." He leaned across her to open the car door and handed her his card. "My cell number's on it, Rita. Call me if you need me."

Heading for home in her Subaru, it had been a helluva day, and Rita Book couldn't see how it could get any worse. But it did.

Fifteen minutes later, she entered the front door of her home. "Laura, I'm home, honey. Where are you?" her voice echoing through the empty house as she tossed her keys onto the credenza. After searching the house, she discovered Laura had cleaned out her clothes closet and all her makeup from her bath and vanity. Reading a handwritten note lying on her daughter's bed, her eyes welled. The note from her daughter said she was tired of living with a drug addict and had left to live with her dad. Heartbroken, she wiped a tear from her cheek.

Attempting to appeal to his better judgment, she dialed her ex-husband's cell. After three calls without a response, Rita left a voicemail, pleading for him to let her know their daughter was safe. Sitting on the edge of the bed with the note in her hand, she was badly in need of something to soften the blows of the day.

A believer in the occult, she went downstairs to try and calm herself by playing tarot cards. Shuffling the deck three times to ensure an accurate prediction, she drew the Devil card on the first play. Dissatisfied with the grim forecast, she shuffled them again, this time expecting better results. On the second play, she drew the Tower card. Distressed over the outcome, she stacked the deck neatly on the dining table and abandoned the notion of finding any answers in the tarot cards.

She needed something strong to calm her nerves and reached for her bottle of oxycodone to ease the pain. Swallowing two 250 mg tablets, Book chased them with a giant swig of vodka and waited. Twice the normal dosage, she didn't care. As the minutes ticked by, she found herself adrift in a sea of euphoria, the opioid making her feel like she was floating somewhere on the edge of the universe. She felt isolated, alone in her thoughts, and completely disconnected as she peered into the darkness outside her window. Before she fell asleep, her last thoughts were images from the tarot cards as she found herself trapped inside a flaming tower trying to escape the devil's wrath.

At a little after nine o'clock on that same warm humid night, a full moon rose ominously outside her window. Waiting patiently for a cloud to obscure the moon, a man in a black cap dressed in green camouflage gear crouched in the bushes outside the old wooden two-story house. When the lights went out, he waited another thirty minutes to make sure she was soundly asleep before approaching the house. As the moonlight was dimmed by passing clouds, the man hunched over like an orangutan and crept cautiously to the side of the house to remove the wood lattice that guarded the crawlspace.

He knew all too well these old turn-of-the-century wooden homes were usually in such a state of disrepair that serious maintenance issues posed unseen fire hazards. Older plumbing, pipes and leaky gas connections were often the culprit. On all fours, he pushed the cobwebs aside, making his way through the tight crawlspace with a small flashlight. As expected, the wooden floors built on stone pilings had exposed copper gas lines underneath. Following the lines with his flashlight, he could see they led to the underside of the kitchen floor and could easily be punctured with his Swiss Army knife. Any large accumulation of gas was very susceptible to explosion from a spark from another source; a gas water heater, or an air conditioner starting up, like the one that sat fifteen feet away. Using the Phillips head attachment, he pushed hard with the heel of his hand, silently puncturing a hole in the thin copper line. His dirty deed done, he listened to the sound of escaping gas.

In the darkness, a dog began to bark a few houses down, then he saw a car drive slowly by. There was a noise from inside the house, and he turned off his flashlight and froze, listening intently to the sounds above him as the sweat trickled from under the wool cap and into his eyes. The sounds of someone snoring and the soft hiss of escaping gas were all that he heard. Eyeing the air conditioner sitting a few feet from him, for now it remained silent, but he had no way of predicting when it would kick on. Quietly, the man in camouflage crawled out from under the floor. Wiping the cobwebs from his face, he scampered for the safety of the bushes on the vacant lot across the street.

Crouching behind the hedgerow, he waited. Five minutes ticked by, then ten more as the air conditioner stood silent. The neighbor's dog continued to bark, and a pick-up truck full of teens drinking beer and playing loud music cruised the street in front of the house before continuing down the road. After a few more minutes, he began to question his plan, wondering if she'd turned off her air conditioner.

Suddenly, the compressor kicked on, and he ducked instinctively. Sparked by the electric motor, within seconds a huge fireball engulfed the wooden house and the explosion knocked him backward into a chain link fence. Sure that no one inside could have lived through such a violent explosion, he stood, dusted himself off, and began to jog toward his car, hoping to be mistaken for someone fleeing from the fire.

The following morning, the *Press Journal* carried a front page story about the fire that incinerated the old wooden house downtown, killing Mrs. Rita Book and injuring three of her sleeping neighbors. In the article, there was no mention of her arrest earlier on the same day, and the Vero Beach Fire Department classified the cause of the fire as "…a gas leak likely caused by poor maintenance, pending further investigation." The article mentioned Book's years of service to the community as a CRNA at Indian River Community Hospital, and as a devoted mother.

The article also mentioned investigators were puzzled by a number of burnt tarot cards found in the ashes around the victim's house.

TWENTY-FIVE

A t the police station the next morning, Foti was in early, channel surfing on the nineteen-inch color TV that his late wife had given him for his office. Despondent over the local reports of the overnight blaze that killed their key witness, he'd already watched three separate accounts of the downtown fire and Rita Book's demise as he caught up on the news. Social media and TV reporters were now describing the tragedy as "suspicious, pending further investigation."

Flipping through the channels to find out what else was going on in the world, he settled on a curious story on Bloomberg News that was highly relevant to his murder investigation. It was a news report about the stock buyout of Oconix Pharmaceuticals by rival ZTE for $97 a share. The Bloomberg reporter stated it was a 215% premium to Oconix's closing price yesterday, and the news prompted him to revisit the related profiles on his PC.

The report brought him back to Dr. Katherine Tremelle, their first homicide victim. The news of the buyout made him wonder if Garrett had made the right decision to pull him off the investigation of Marchenko and Yakovlev when he declared them "no longer persons of interest." Had their actions helped instigate the takeover of Tremelle's company? Was it all about the money, or was there something else going on beneath the surface?

Suddenly, an irate Capt. Garrett strode into Foti's office and threw the morning paper down on his desk. "That's three dead women in three weeks, Frank," pointing at the headline. "Tell me you've got something on this."

Distressed by his boss's anger, Foti glanced at the headline and set his coffee down as he met Garrett's angry stare. "Cornering these two guys is like trying to catch a pair of eels with a spoon." Garrett was impassive as Foti continued. "John, if I had come to you yesterday and asked for round-the-clock protection for a woman we'd just cut a plea deal with for possession, what would you have said?"

Garrett stroked his chin and considered his lieutenant's question. "Honestly, I don't know, Frank. Even if you'd told me we had a potential witness that was willing to testify against Hirt, that nurse's arrest earlier in the day was never made public. How the hell did anyone find out about it so fast?"

"Hirt and Croaker have a lot of sources on the street. Probably more than we do."

Garrett offered a different slant. "Maybe we have a leak."

"It's a possibility, but I'd like to think--"

Pointing a finger, Garrett gave him two new orders. "Hang on. Here's what we're going to do. First, I want you to put around-the-clock surveillance on Hirt. I know we're stretched thin, but if he wasn't responsible, my gut tells me he had a hand in it." Foti nodded in agreement. "Then, I want you to have our C.I.O. bring me the background on all our officers who have access to our internal data base."

Disgusted with losing their key witness, Garrett picked the paper up and read the headline again before thwacking it on the desktop loudly. "Lotta eyeballs on us right now, Frank. Get back to me as soon as you have something."

"Yes, sir," replied Foti. It was one of those mornings when nothing seemed to go right for him. He thought about how Book had died. Maybe it would be a blessing to be blown up in his own house. Better yet, maybe he'd like to die on his own boat, one like the McAllisters's had, maybe buried at sea. But the thought of dying at his own desk upset him to no end. If he could choose how and when he was to die, he would want to be a ninety-year-old man shot by a jealous young husband who had caught him in bed with his teenage wife. He got up and poured himself another cup of coffee. Tempted to make it an Irish coffee, he held his impulse in check. Foti sat back down and watched the sun burn off the haze outside as he decided if the teenage wife was a blonde or a brunette.

His daydream was interrupted when Det. Garner appeared in his doorway. Not usually excitable, something definitely had him stirred up this morning. "Boss, one of our undercover guys just busted a coke dealer in Winter Beach who sells used RVs."

Foti set his cup of coffee down, expecting to hear more. "Okay. Anything else?"

"The dealer's a three-time loser, so to suck up to us and avoid the mandatory three-strike sentence, the prisoner gave the uc a tip about a short sketchy guy with beady eyes who paid him $92,000 in cash for a Winnebago a few days ago. Turns out the dealer used the same pile of cash to try to score the coke from our uc."

Foti raised his eyebrows. "Could be our guy Croaker. And you found this out how?"

"I play softball with the uc. He's a buddy of mine."

"Go on."

"Yes sir, and this is the really interesting part; the guy first offered to pay for the Winnebago with uncut China white, but the dealer said he needed the cash. Thought you might be interested in interviewing him."

"You're damn right I am!" standing and rounding the desk corner eagerly. "Where's this RV coke dealer now?"

"Interview Room #2. They just finished booking him, and he's cooperating."

"Well, hallelujah. We got a description of the Winnebago?"

"I believe so, sir."

225

Tech officer Violette was next to appear in his doorway. "Lt. Foti, sorry to interrupt, but Special Agents Beretto and Madani are here to see you."

"Okay, Margo." Meeting the FBI agents in the hallway, "Frank, Gwen, we've got a new lead in the Croaker case. I think you two should sit in on this. I'd like to get your take on this guy."

Beretto nodded. "Sure, Frank. I think we can all agree this fire last night was no accident."

Nodding, "Yeah, we're on the same page. Walk with me."

Intercepting him before he entered the interview room, Detective Locke caught up with his boss. "Sir, I just spoke to the team investigating the Book fire. They found a hole punctured in one of the copper gas pipes under the house, and it appears to have been put there deliberately."

"What, like last night?" replied Foti. "Why am I not surprised?" To the FBI profilers, "Dom and Gwen, we're heading into an interview with a coke dealer we busted for possession. He might have some new information on Croaker. Claims he sold a man matching his description a Winnebago."

Caught up in the sudden flow of testosterone, Madani asked, "Do we have a tag number and description?"

"I think we do," said Foti.

Beretto tapped him on the shoulder. "Let's go interview this guy."

Most employees of the Vero Beach Police Department knew very little about the system administrator, and most weren't sure what it was about technology that attracted certain types of people while frustrating others. Studies have shown there are generally three kinds of personalities in the workplace: Type A, Type B, and then there's Type IT. The last type are regarded as a breed apart from the rest, and Sakhil Patel was certainly no exception from your typical middle-eastern geek. In his thirties, dark-skinned and slightly overweight from indulging in vast quantities of pizza and Coke, he was a whirlwind of energy and seemed entirely devoted to the VBPD's data network. But he did have some secrets.

Raised in India, but born in Pakistan, all would agree that Patel was a dedicated administrator, often working twelve to fifteen hours a day to keep their IT systems up and running. Maybe it was all those electrons spinning through the millions of miles of cyberspace that he found so fascinating. Or, maybe it was being cooped up in a cubicle that deprived him of sunlight and human interaction with his fellow techies and officers. One thing they did know about him; he liked getting paid time-and-a-half to keep the VBPD systems up and running.

Though his co-workers found him always polite, he had no true friends at the police station. Patel's attitude was simple: Friends? Who needs 'em? That's why God created computers. To earn the unqualified trust of the Department, he was the kind of guy that would volunteer to do the 48-hour server upgrade over the weekend and have it up and running by six a.m. Monday morning. It was these demonstrations of skill and sacrifice that had earned him the unquestioned trust of his co-workers.

Patel relished technical certifications that served to boost his respect-ability, which he prominently displayed on his cubicle walls to impress his co-workers. He excelled at writing network security subroutines in binary code to protect against logic bombs and nefarious query language intrusions to the Department database. He particularly enjoyed the blank stares that such descriptions of his work produced from his co-workers, which tended to reinforce how indispensable he was to the Department.

But Sakhil Patel had a hidden chip on his shoulder and a secret agenda, a double-deadly combination because money was his top priority; money, and relaxing with a line or two of China white in his central beach apart-ment. Raised by his maternal grandparents in New Delhi, no one knew that his parents were killed by an American drone in Pakistan the year he was born. He'd managed to keep this dark secret from everyone, lest his allegiances be questioned, especially at such a bastion of patriotism like the VBPD.

Using Louis as his contact name, Patel was typically ambivalent about sharing highly-sensitive police information with a stocky, peculiar-looking man he knew only as Max. He could always count on Max to pay him either in cash, his first preference, or his drug of choice, China white. So when Patel called Max on his burner phone about how the police were tipped off on his Winnebago, Patel was expecting a generous fee, this being the second time he'd saved Max from arrest.

At a quarter after six, an hour before sunset, Patel rang Croaker on his burner phone. "What's up, Louis?" asked the bag man.

"Got some very important intel for you, bro. Need to meet right away."

"How important?"

"A thousand bucks worth."

Digging into his pocket, Croaker pulled out a wad five times that amount to make sure he could cover it. He happened to be on South Hutchinson Island finishing up on a sizable delivery to a dealer who'd driven up from Miami for the score. "Meet me at the 4090 Ocean Villas on Ocean Drive in fifteen minutes. It's a construction site. Wear your hardhat for cover."

"Yeah, I know it. See you in fifteen. Gotta make a stop at the Ace Hardware on Beachland."

Ten minutes later, Croaker rolled up to the Ocean Drive site and stopped next to the unfinished pool, parking his rented Chevy Cruze out of street view between a stack of pavers and a large fork lift. The bag man sat for a moment behind the wheel, listening quietly for confirmation that workers had left for the day. Satisfied he was alone, from the front seat he grabbed the white paper tube that mimicked the look of rolled-up architectural plans, his hard hat, and his .45 automatic before heading toward the unfinished first floor villa.

Because of the warrant, Croaker had changed his appearance by shaving his head and growing a beard. The bagman stopped to admire his reflection in the window, the hard hat, tank top and faded jeans adding to his impersonation of a construction worker. Proud of his chameleon-like abilities, he smoothed his beard and adjusted the hard hat in the reflection, the hardhat fitting snugly over his shaved head. A car approached, coming to a stop on the gravel parking area nearby. It was a blue Corolla, and the driver flashed the headlights before stepping out of the car.

"Ola, Max." His eyes concealed behind dark sunglasses, Patel stood and straightened his yellow hard hat. Seeing he was alone, Croaker waved him around the unfinished concrete block wall for their face-to-face, away from the prying eyes of any locals driving by on Ocean Drive.

To his snitch Croaker said, "Louis, this intel better be good for a thousand bucks."

Wanting the quick cash, Patel thought of Croaker as his new ATM as he squared off with him. The unfinished installation of a new server upgrade at the station was waiting for him, and he promised to have it up and running by 6 a.m. the following morning, so he got right to the point. "Max, the coke dealer you bought your Winnebago from gave you up. The cops have your vehicle description, but not your tag number."

Surprised by the news, he acted nonchalant. "Yeah? Go on."

"You might want to move it, have it painted, or trade it out of the county. You know they have a warrant out for your arrest now, right?"

Croaker looked away and shifted his weight before making eye contact with Patel again. "How old is this intel?"

"For Indian River County, the A.P.B. went out four hours ago, but for some reason, no other counties were notified."

"Why's that?"

"My guess is that it was an oversight. Either that, or Vero Police don't want to share the intel. Maybe they want sole credit for the bust."

A burning question had been nagging him since his last meeting with his snitch. "How do you know all this stuff, Louis?"

"I've got direct access to the VBPD's mainframe and all their servers. Plus, I hear things around the Department, conversations between officers." Meeting his eyes, "Things that help you stay profitable, and out of jail."

'Uh-huh." Not super tech savvy himself, Croaker wondered if the software was available at Walmart. "What kind of software you use for this?"

Proud of the surveillance system he helped to develop, Patel did his takeaway. "It's a program available only to law enforcement." To heighten Croaker's interest, "I also have access to a cell phone surveillance program that can identify any person's private phone number, hack it, and monitor texts and voice messages. But, I have to be able to show cause to use it, so it involves more risk."

Here was something Croaker could put to immediate use. "So, if I give you a name or two, you can tell me who and what they're saying and texting?"

"Correct."

"To anyone?"

"Correct. As I said, it's risky, so I gotta get paid."

"What else ya got for me, Louis?"

Croaker watched his snitch shake his head. "That's all I got for now. Isn't that enough?"

Without answering, he reached into his pocket for the roll of Benjamins and peeled off five bills. "I'm gonna have some names for you on that phone hacking program. Keep up the good work, Louis. Here's five hundred cash…." reaching into his other pocket, "…and a gram of uncut China white worth another thousand. You can cut that ten-to-one and it will still give you a helluva buzz."

Taking the cash and the baggie of China white, Patel nodded his approval. "Okay. I'll call ya when I have something else." Patel walked quickly to his Corolla just as the sun dropped below the horizon. Looking around the jobsite, he could feel the twilight begin to cast an eerie look over the half-finished walls and piles of debris. In a hurry to sample the goodies, he climbed back in his Corolla and left the construction site.

To avoid being followed, Croaker lurked inside the concrete walls for awhile. Within the shadows of the building, he watched to make sure Patel cleared the area before entering his rented Chevy and heading for his Winnebago at Pelican Yacht Club. Making a beeline for A1A south, he had a plan that involved a pal in Port St. Lucie who ran a used RV business. Maybe a Mercedes would be a better fit for a man of his wealth.

To find out what he had available that would fit his needs, he rang him up.

TWENTY-SIX

The following day was another warm one, and Mark found himself running north on the beach at mid-morning under a partly-sunny sky. It was low tide, and to keep himself quick on his feet for his five miler, he had a light breakfast of half a banana and a double expresso with a splash of Cordon Bleu. The powerful waves sweeping up the beach had him reminiscing about some of the more memorable voyages he shared with Stella aboard *Dream Girl* as he jogged toward Vero's only pier. Euphoric from the endorphins and the sea breeze on his face, there was one vivid memory in particular that stood out.

They were on a colorful South Pacific passage almost three years before. He remembered it was spring in the South Pacific, and he found it impossible to forget the exotic landscape and turquoise waters of Tahiti, Marquesas and French Polynesia. From the lush, green slopes of the high islands to the pink sand and palm-lined atolls that surrounded lagoons bluer than the purest of cobalt blues, he still thought of French Polynesia as the ultimate paradise.

Like many sailors before him, Mark liked reading up on the history and cultures of his destinations, often sharing his research with his wife. He learned the early Polynesians were an adventurous seafaring people who displayed highly-developed navigational skills. Genetic research and archeological findings indicated they colonized previously unsettled islands by making very long passages in primitive dugout canoes, only adding sails to their craft around the thirteenth century.

What he found particularly interesting was that early Polynesians were also accomplished celestial navigators who steered by the sun and the stars. They were often able to detect the existence and even the location of new islands by skillful observations of cloud reflections and bird flight patterns. One Polynesian word in particular that kept reverberating in his head was the name given by early native navigators to a star or constellation used as a mark to steer by; *kaweinga*. Over the centuries, it was a word that had acquired several meanings among Polynesians, all having to do with either spiritual or maritime direction. Stella liked using the word as a double entendre in their private conversations, sometimes referring to it as a "Mark to steer by."

According to his studies on Polynesian culture, by 1280 AD, archeological evidence suggested entire small villages of Polynesian explorers had set sail in their primitive catamarans and succeeded in settling the vast Polynesian triangle. He recalled Stella tracing with her fingertip the Polynesian triangle on a chart, pointing out that it was anchored at its northern corner by the Hawaiian Islands, the eastern corner by Rapa Nui, which later became known as Easter Island, and finally the southern corner in New Zealand. By comparison, other archeological timelines indicated the Vikings colonized Iceland about 875 AD, and there were suggestions that early Polynesian seafarers even reached the South American mainland at about the same time.

Three years ago in July, after almost two weeks of blue water sailing south from Hawaii, Stella and Mark caught sight of the northeastern-most shores of French Polynesia as they approached Hiva Oa, the first island in Marquesas. After being confined aboard for thirteen days of sailing open seas, they'd been dying to stretch their legs with a good run. The Marquesas is the most remote chain of islands in the Tahitian archipelago and it's usually the first point of land that every boat crossing the Pacific from the Americas sees. Towering above the deep blue waters of the Pacific and unprotected by any atolls, he remembered the stunning mountain peaks of the Marquesas that seemed to lift high into the air from the depths of green tropical valleys as they approached the islands.

During his runs, he relived those idyllic weeks like they were yesterday. The congenial natives had been very intrigued with the lifestyle of an American author and his beautiful wife, so Mark and Stella generously shared the personal details of their lives, their travels, and other pleasantries in lieu of tipping, a practice discouraged among most native Polynesians. It was an arrangement that worked like magic with the good-natured locals who were so completely entertained by the couple's personal stories. When it came to entertainment, the indigenous tribes understood reciprocity. One of the customs that fascinated them was the native Polynesians dancing and twirling lit torches to tribal drums in the light of giant bonfires in their celebration of the French National Holiday.

On that particular passage, he'd been anxious to set sail for Fatu Hiva, but Stella persuaded him to accept an invitation to a wedding at Taipivei where 900 guests (half the town) were invited. One of the villagers owned a bus, so more than thirty party animals and yachties climbed aboard for the trip past Anaho Bay to Taipivei where the entourage stopped to pick flowers. He remembered giving one of the pink and yellow tiares to Stella to put in her hair, and further down the dirt road, everyone stopped to enjoy fresh mangos and guava. There were plenty of coconuts, but you had to be careful under the coconut trees; local Marquesans will tell you that more people get killed by falling coconuts than by sharks.

As Vero's only pier grew larger on the horizon, he realized he was craving a few days on the high seas with his first mate. The week they'd spent in Fatu Hiva had been an unforgettable stopover. Famed for its stunning coastal scenery and lush landscaped cliffs right out of a dream, Fatu Hiva was truly incredible. One of the most popular destinations in the Marquesas, they spent the first day on Fatu Hiva exploring the island's coves and waterfalls filled with clear waters ranging in hue from turquoise to the deepest of cobalt. With the cloudless skies, azure lagoons, kaleidoscopic tropical coral gardens and a mind-blowing array of colorful fish to entertain them, Mark and Stella spent much of the second day snorkeling for black pearls around the boat's anchorage.

He remembered all the island banter about the Black Tahitian pearls, the "black gold of Tuamotus", where 90% of the world's black pearl production could be found. The natives called the rainbow-lipped oysters Concha Nacar, and the black pearls from these oysters were the most sought-after in the world.

As with most of the outer Marquesan islands, rustic townships like Fatu Hiva were all on the larger islands, thankfully having escaped the upheaval of major development. For hundreds of years, they remained sites where time seemed to stop altogether.

Caught up in the reverie of their French Polynesian travels, he almost tripped over a sandcastle in his path. To keep him from falling, the heavy-set well-endowed mother of the architect rushed toward him like a '55 Buick with oversize bumper guards, nearly tackling him before he recovered his balance.

"Sorry," he shouted over his shoulder, recovering his stride, "…didn't want to wreck your son's sandcastle."

Reaching his halfway point, he rounded the concrete legs of the pier and made a decision to propose a weekend of sailing with Stella involving the consumption of large quantities of alcohol. With their second wedding anniversary coming up, the Abacos were calling to him. He made a mental note to call Connie at Southern Wine and Spirits to arrange a secret delivery of a case of Cordon Bleu and a case of Camus to *Dream Girl*, along with a dozen red roses to celebrate.

In the early afternoon on the same day, Hirt was sitting in his office, buried in Medicare paperwork. There was a lobby full of patients waiting, and another at his desk when his receptionist buzzed him. "With a patient, Laura. What's up?"

"There is a Mr. Hackett on the line from the SEC."

"Tell him I'm busy and to call me in October."

"He says it is most urgent that he speak to you."

Indignant, he replied, "Find out what he wants."

"I *asked* him, Dr. Hirt, but he says he needs to speak to you *personally.*"

"Oh…all right. Tell him to hold while I finish with my patient," adding his signature to the opioid script on his desk with an illegible flourish. The patient grunted a thank you and snatched it from his hand like it was a ticket to immortality as he buzzed his receptionist.

"Laura, you can put him through now."

"Yes, doctor." Hirt heard a click, then a nasally male voice which he disliked immediately. "Dr. Christopher Hirt?"

"Yes."

"My name is Leonard Hackett, an investigator for the Securities and Exchange Commission."

"Uh-huh."

"I'd like to stop by your office and discuss an important matter with you."

"Look, I'm very busy today. What *kind* of matter?"

"A very serious matter regarding your purchase of a large number of Oconix Pharmaceutical stock *forty-eight* hours before they announced a buy-out."

"Why? Is this illegal?"

"I'd rather not get into that over the phone."

"Why not, Mr. Hackett? Are your phones bugged by the American Society for Profitable Trading?" Hirt waited for a gentlemanly response, or a good-natured chuckle, but he heard only silence. Apparently, Hackett had no sense of humor. "Okay, then…what about next Tuesday, at--"

"I'll be at your office in thirty minutes, Dr. Hirt. I expect you to be there. Please set aside an hour for our visit. Thank you."

There was a click as the phone went dead. "Unbelievable," he said to himself as he buzzed Laura back. "Please clear my appointments from two to three today, and when Mr. Hackett arrives, keep him waiting twenty minutes."

"Yes, Dr. Hirt."

Hirt stood and walked to his third floor window. Looking down on the millionaires and billionaires milling about on Ocean Drive in their determined search for shopkeepers to relieve them of their cash, he grappled with his new predicament.

By the man's tone, and the sheer arrogance with which he conducted himself, it was obvious that Mr. Hackett of the SEC thought he was pursuing a criminal matter and had a tiger by the tail. But all he was doing was pissing in the punchbowl, and it would be quite entertaining to watch him quench his thirst with it. He expected them to bring up his prior conviction for insider trading, and he was ready for their assault on his power and prestige, as well as the $729,000 in short-term capital gains he pocketed from the Oconix stock sale.

At two-fifteen, Laura showed Mr. Leonard Hackett into The Pain Free Clinic's office. The SEC investigator was one of those rare people whose telephone voice precisely matched his appearance. After the customary limp handshake, Mr. Hackett showed the doctor his credentials, which identified him as a Special Agent, not just an investigator. From his past investigation for insider trading, Hirt knew the difference; this man was with the SEC's Criminal Investigation Division.

"What was it that you so urgently needed to discuss, Mr. Hackett?"

Indifferent to his question, Hackett sat down, crossed his legs and withdrew a small notebook from his breast pocket, perusing it without looking up as he proceeded at the speed of smell. The discourteous act annoyed Hirt, who briefly entertained the thought of throwing him out the window. But after getting hold of himself, he concluded they'd just send a replacement.

Hirt took a moment to regard his adversary. He wore an ill-fitting, light-blue polyester suit, the sort of suit that a state prison would issue to a prisoner after completing a long period of confinement. The suit did little to hide the bulging ankle holster strapped to his right ankle, or his Timex watch, Argyle socks, clip-on tie, and short-sleeved shirt. Even his haircut looked like a flea market special. Hirt was tempted to ask him if the suit came in his size, but the man was already pissed off and seemed intent on using every opportunity to try and ruin his life.

Hirt's patience was running thin. "Mr. Hackett, I have a lobby full of waiting patients. Do you need help finding something in that notebook?"

Finally, he looked up at Hirt. "It's Special Agent Hackett, Dr. Hirt." Reading from his notebook, "Several days ago, you bought 12,717 shares of Oconix Pharmaceutical at $39.32 a share. Two days later, on the morning they announced a buyout by ZTE Pharmaceutical at $97 a share, you sold all of it for $96.65 a share, resulting in a short-term capital gain, a *very* short-term gain, I might add, of $729,065." Cocking his head, "How did you know about this buyout, Dr. Hirt?"

Wouldn't you like to know? With his elbows on the desk, Hirt clasped his hands together. "I didn't, of course," smirking at his tormentor. "That would be insider trading and illegal, would it not?"

"The same illegality didn't seem to stop you a few years ago, Dr. Hirt, when you made over $2 million buying put options on Valiant a few weeks before they announced some very bad news, which just so happened to involve *you* and one of your patients." Hackett did little to hide his sarcasm.

Hirt could feel the resentment welling up inside him. "That was an uncharacteristic mistake, a mistake that I paid dearly for, Mr. Hackett. I was not about to repeat such a mistake, so this time, I did my homework and bought an underpriced stock at just the right time." Chin in hand, Hackett glared at him as the doctor held up his palms in mock supplication. "I mean, you gotta get lucky sometime, right?"

Shifting his weight, "Be honest with me, with the understanding that a little penance now could be viewed quite favorably later. Who do you know at Oconix, Dr. Hirt?"

"Not a soul."

Clearly annoyed, Hackett continued his fishing expedition. "So, Dr. Hirt, you expect me to believe that, following the unsolved homicide of Dr. Katherine Tremelle, which precipitated the huge drop in Oconix... that you just stumbled into this trade as well? Two days before a buyout was announced?"

"Yup," said the psychiatrist, perhaps a bit too glibly.

Visibly upset at his flippant reply, Hackett abruptly stood and leaned forward with his palms on the desk. "This could go very badly for you should you choose not to cooperate with us. The SEC has the power to subpoena your computer and phone records, which *we will do* unless you are more forthcoming, doctor. And, we do share our findings with the FBI and the IRS."

In defiance, Hirt got to his feet, Hackett standing his ground. "Do you honestly expect me to make it easy for you to try and ruin my life, Mr. Hackett, which I believe you will try to do anyway? If you have any proof that I have violated the law, then I demand to see it. Now!"

Hackett kept his cool and lowered his voice. "Given the circumstances, I couldn't possibly think of anyone *less* deserving to profit from these two trades." Pointing his finger, "The SEC will find out the truth, Dr. Hirt, and when we do, rest assured, you'll be going to prison for a very long time. Good day."

Without saying another word, Special Agent Leonard Hackett of the SEC opened the door and stalked out of Hirt's office. As he passed Laura, her open mouth and wide eyes showed her surprise at what she had just overheard.

Despite his belief that the SEC had no proof of his guilt, Hirt was still disturbed over the possibility of another huge fine and spending more time in a federal prison. The fact remained that he knew no one at Oconix, or their underwriters or investment bankers, and a direct link with anyone at Oconix would be almost impossible to prove. Even his conversation with Rita Book over what her patient may, or may not have said, was technically considered hearsay in a court of law. What a shame it was, he thought, that the CRNA was no longer available to share her testimony.

Feeling better, Hirt buzzed his receptionist. "Laura, send in my next patient, will you?"

TWENTY-SEVEN

At seven forty-five p.m., the sun had begun to set as Croaker drove north at a speed under the posted limit. In a good mood as he tooled along on A1A in his late-model Mercedes RV, he thought about his new source of intel inside the VBPD, and it made him feel invincible. To look more like a tourist, he sported a handmade palm frond hat hand woven by Bibble, a colorful man he met at a bar around the corner from Reno's RV lot in Port St. Lucie. On his way back to Port Fierce for a large delivery of China white, he smiled as he thought about the fifteen grand in profit he was about to pocket. *Come and try to unravel the enigma that is me.*

To keep the cops off his trail, the Idaho license plate displayed on the 34-foot RV was a tag Reno had given him from a different owner who was recently deceased. And knowing his pal Reno the way he did, the cause of death was unlikely from old age. From his own deceptions involving tag swapping, Croaker concluded the tag adorning his new diesel-powered RV would be almost impossible to trace. Down to his last half-kilo of China white, he rang up Hirt on his new burner phone to arrange for a supply drop as he steered the big RV with one hand.

From his office window, Hirt looked down on the throng of tourists and shoppers milling about on Ocean Drive as the call came in, resentful at the thought of all the Wall Street moguls trading on inside information who weren't being persecuted by the government. He picked up his burner phone to talk with his bag man.

"Where are you, Max? I heard the cops in Vero have a warrant and a county-wide APB on you."

"Yeah, I know. Heard that from my new source. I thought about leaving for California, but we're making way too much money."

"Look, Max…I need you to stay cool and under the radar or it's both our asses." In a pleading tone, "Why don't you work your connections further south for a while until things settle down in here in Vero?"

"No worries, doc," reaching to turn down the AC so he could hear. "Got a new ride, a new tag, a new look and some profitable new connections." In a lower voice, "These guys can move some weight, so I need some more, ah…coffee." Pausing, he almost forgot before to mention his new snitch. "Oh, and I've got a new informant *inside* the cop shop, this time, and he's got access to phone surveillance software."

Hirt's voice took on a more casual tone as he disguised his interest in this last bit of news. "Yeah, no worries, cowboy, I'll hook you up with as much coffee as you need. Tonight, usual place, nine o'clock?"

"Okay. Got enough cash for the usual amount."

"Okay, but first, tell me about this new source you've got. You say he can hack into phones?"

Croaker hesitated. "I dunno, chief. This one I may want to keep just for myself."

Knowing how valuable the intel could be, Hirt decided it was time to play hardball. "I'm not askin', Max. You want this stuff tonight or what?"

"So, it's like that, huh?" Sometimes Croaker felt powerless, resenting being controlled by a man who refused to get his hands dirty.

"'Fraid so, Max." His admission was met with stone cold silence. "Look, Max…I got a lot goin' on right now. I could use a source on the inside to protect us *both*. We're a team, right? If you get popped, who's gonna be around to post your bail and give you safe harbor? Help you with your defense and legal fees? Dante?" The psychiatrist stood at his office window watching the twilight settling over the beach, waiting for an answer he knew he wouldn't hear.

He needed that source. "You wind up in the slammer, Max, you're gonna need someone to watch your back." What he was really thinking was that perhaps the symbiotic nature of plausible deniability had outlived its usefulness and maybe it was time to cut away the dead weight.

Croaker was resentful, his carefree mood now ruined with Hirt's threat to cut him off. "Doc, I stuck with you when no one else--"

"Max…for once…shut up and listen to me." Croaker went silent as Hirt continued. "We've made a ton of money together. But, right now, you've got the FBI and Vero detectives all over you, which could lead them to me. With the risks we're *both* facing, I'm sticking my neck out by keeping you supplied. You want this stuff tonight? Then we're going to share the intel from your new source. It'll be good for both of us. Now, for the last time, I'll ask you nicely. What's your contact's name and cell number?"

Backed into a corner, and running out of options, Croaker reached into his shirt pocket for a piece of paper with his informant's number. Slowly, he read Patel's number over the phone, realizing he'd made a huge mistake by mentioning it at all.

"He goes by Louis, but that's not his real name."

"Got it," confirmed Hirt. "Congratulations, Max, you're still on my payroll. See you at nine tonight." Then the line went silent.

Making the left turn from A1A onto Seaway, Croaker headed toward the Kampground of America RV Park on U.S. 1 as he reflected on the contentious conversation. He'd always let Hirt do his thinking for him, and maybe he was right. Sharing access to his informant may actually work better for them both.

Hungry, he pulled into the parking lot at Dave's Diner just off Seaway and parked the RV off to the side. Locking it, Croaker was ready for a few cold beers and some of that world-famous comfort food as he ambled toward the 24-hour diner still wearing his Bibble palm frond hat.

At work in his second floor office at Villa Riomar, Mark grabbed his cell phone and tapped on the number listed for Southern Wine and Spirits. It was Thursday, and this time Connie's delivery would be to *Dream Girl* berthed at Pelican Yacht Club right around the corner from their liquor store in Ft. Pierce. The parties at the villa and on their yacht proved popular with their friends and were occasionally a little on the wild side, but so far he hadn't lost anyone overboard.

So far.

"Southern Wine and Spirits. Connie speaking."

"Connie. Mark McAllister. Been awhile. Good to hear your voice."

"Yes, it's been awhile." Pausing to express her condolences, "I was very sorry to hear of your late wife's passing. Carol was a real gem and the consummate entertainer."

"Thanks for your kind words, Connie."

"Okay. I know we've made a few deliveries to you this year at Villa Riomar, but I don't think I've seen you since Carol's memorial service at Holy Cross. I heard you remarried. Your wife's name is Stella, right?"

"Attention to details is why I enjoy doing business with you, Connie. I'm planning a surprise weekend outing with Stella to celebrate our second anniversary aboard *Dream Girl*, so I'll need a few things."

"Just like your novels, forever the incurable romantic. Remember that wild Fourth of July yacht party aboard *Dream Girl* three years ago when you hired Taylor Swift to perform onboard? And Carol and Taylor were sharing the mic and singing karaoke together?"

"Yes, that was a lot of fun." Mark also had a brief recollection of the confrontation below deck that night when he'd caught one of the rock star's security men snorting coke and threatened to throw the 350-pound man overboard. "Fat chance," the man had said, not intending to be funny.

"How can I help?" asked Connie.

"Okay. Here's my list, and I hope you've got it all in stock," referring to his tablet. "For delivery to *Dream Girl*, below deck, one case of the 2016 Camus Napa Valley Cabernet, Stella's favorite cab."

"Check."

"A case of the Cordon Bleu XO, our staple cognac."

"Yes, I remember."

"And a dozen of your freshest red roses for display in a crystal vase on the teak dining table in the main salon."

"Got it all in stock," Connie assured him, checking off the inventory listed on her tablet, "…and to help you celebrate, I'd like to offer you ten percent off the total and free delivery. Is a Baccarat vase acceptable?"

"Perfect. Connie, you're a sweetheart," giving her his debit card number for payment. "Also, when you're there, will you check and make sure the air conditioners are set on 79 degrees? The controls are on the teak bulkhead at eye level just above the bronze sea water intakes. Don't want those roses to wilt."

"Sure. I've made those notes to the delivery request. I won't forget."

"You'll need the security codes to the electronic dock gate at Pelican Yacht and for the main hatch keypad on the yacht. These are for your use only. Stella likes to change them every week as a precaution."

"I don't blame her for being careful. I heard about the murders." Concerned, she asked, "Did she know the girls?"

"I may be able to talk with you about that someday, but right now, they're active investigations. Ready for the keypad codes?" Sounds of static interference could be heard on the phone, and Mark assumed it was on Connie's end as she reached for a pen.

"Sorry. Didn't mean to pry. Go ahead."

"No problem. Dock gate code is 7-1-3-5-6, and main hatch is 6-4-3-9-asterisk-8." She repeated the codes to make sure she had them written down correctly. "We're all set, Mark. Sounds like fun. When are you casting off?"

"Probably around nine on Friday morning."

"So, I'll make the delivery for late Thursday afternoon. Will that work for you?"

"Perfect, Connie. Stella's nuts about roses, especially when they're fresh cut."

"Our florist flies them in daily from South America. Thanks for your business, Mark."

After he ended the call, Connie's condolences had triggered a reverie of his late wife's memorial service, her comments dredging up images of Carol that he'd been struggling to let go of.

It was a solemn but uplifting affair, as memorial services went, and her untimely death from a collision with a sand-filled dump truck had devastated him. The service at Holy Cross was well attended, and Monsignor Monaco had presided over a touching service for his beloved wife, Carol Nutter McAllister. Without judgment, and with great reverence, the Monsignor spoke quite well of his late wife; how she was spiritual, yet born to be wild. Thankfully, the Monsignor made no mention of the naked bar-top dancing and other wild affairs that colored her life. So, he guessed the check had cleared.

In the next few days after her memorial service, he spent hours poring over photos, blaming himself and wishing he could have patched things up with her before her untimely death. If he had, maybe there wouldn't have been an accident. His friends reminded him that it had been Carol's affair with Stella's late husband that precipitated their rancor, and he thanked God that Stella was there to soothe the unrest that still churned deep inside him.

TWENTY-EIGHT

Later in the tourist season, the RV parks on the Treasure Coast were usually filled to capacity. Using an alias, Croaker was fortunate to have found an open space at the Kampgrounds of America off U.S. 1 in Ft. Pierce. His Mercedes RV was nestled among seventy other campers and RV enthusiasts toward the rear of the park. There, the pine trees were taller and the shrubs thicker, providing a good place to hide out until he could formulate more long-range plans.

By the light of a full moon, Croaker parked the rented Chevy Cruze next to his RV. It was three a.m., and he'd purposely left the lights on in the RV to make it appear as if someone were home while he conducted his business with Hirt and a fentanyl dealer in Melbourne. The rain came while he was away, and the roller-furling awning remained extended out over the charcoal grill along with the two aluminum beach chairs he'd bought at Walmart. Resting on the patch of weeds and grass that passed for landscaping, he was disturbed to see that the lawn furniture looked like someone had rearranged it.

The humidity enveloped him like a hot wet blanket as he quietly stepped out of his car with his bag of Slim Jims and Coca-Cola. Exhausted from the drive, he stopped to gaze up at the rising moon, careful not to wake his sleeping neighbors before unloading his cargo of eight bricks. Eerily bright, the moon illuminated the surrounding landscape and neighboring RVs with an unearthly glow, transforming the natural colors into silvery shades of white and blue. He was surprised when the interior lights came on in the vintage Airstream parked next door and a man called out to him.

"Stan, you're back!" His assumed name, it took Croaker a moment to realize his elderly neighbor was addressing him through the screen door as he stood in his boxer shorts holding a fly swatter. "It's Joe. I met ya earlier. How's yer mom doin'?"

Then he remembered the made-up story he told Joe about visiting his dying mom at the hospital. "Ah…she's better," was all he could think to say to the old timer. Joe looked as though he had more to say, so Croaker ambled over to see why his neighbor was up so late.

"Ya missed all the excitement, young man!" said Joe, waving the fly swatter.

"What excitement?" Croaker took a few steps closer.

"The cops came by, knockin' on everyone's door, botherin' us, askin' for IDs, registration and stuff," missing a mosquito with his swatter. "They never leave ya alone." Joe looked a little confused. "I thought getting old would take longer."

"I hear ya, Joe. When were they here?"

"Guess it was around nine o'clock, after you went to visit your mom at the hospital. They asked me if I knew ya."

Concerned, he moved closer to the RV's steps and put his hand on his .45. "What did you tell them?"

"Well…ah…" scratching his head, "…I told 'em ya just got here, and yer name's Stan Miller. That's yer name, right?"

"Yup." Getting anxious, Croaker surveyed the surrounding campers illuminated in the moonlight to see if anyone else was stirring. It was quiet, only the hoot of an owl in a nearby pine tree broke the silence. Sensing that the old man had more details to share, he took a step closer to the screen door. "What else can you tell me, Joe?"

"Well, they had a perticular interest in yer bumper stickers," absent-mindedly scratching his groin. "Oh…and they asked me why you had those extra containers of diesel fuel strapped to the back."

"And you said…what?"

"Told 'em I had no idea," shrugging.

"Thanks, old timer," pulling his cell phone out of his jeans pocket and walking back toward his RV. Forgetting what time it was, he dialed his informant to find out if the Vero police had expanded the APB. He heard the phone ring sixteen times with no answer. Hitting the redial button, he tried reaching the man he knew as Louis but the phone continued to ring. Then he remembered it was three in the morning, and it was unlikely that any of the other Kampgrounds of America would be answering either.

Too early to call anyone, he would use the next few hours to grab a nap, organize his stuff, and get the hell out of dodge at first light.

Four hours later, Beretto, Madani, Foti and Garner were speeding down U.S. 1 in Beretto's black GMC Denali with siren blaring and lights flashing. Right behind the Denali, Locke and Heaton were following with the rest of the county SWAT team in the SWAT van. Foti had asked Violette to stay behind at headquarters to coordinate logistics and computer queries for the team.

Determined to catch Croaker before he could slip away again, Beretto was doing eighty-plus and using both southbound lanes to dodge slower traffic. The team had gathered twenty minutes earlier and grabbed their SWAT gear when the call came in from St. Lucie County deputies on a possible ID on Croaker. Assuming the murder suspect was armed and would do anything to avoid being captured, the team was going in heavy, with Heckler and Koch MP5s, Glock .40 cal. sidearms, as well as smoke and stun grenades. Aware that Croaker vowed he would never go back to prison, they were expecting a violent confrontation.

Beretto turned to Foti sitting in the back seat. "Why the hell did the deputies wait this long to contact us? They were at his RV *hours* ago."

Yelling over the siren, "Their in-vehicle laptops were down, so they had to wait until they got back to the station to run the prints."

Madani shouted over the siren, "At least the deputy at the scene was smart enough to lift a print from the door handle before they left. A shame they didn't process the prints sooner. We'd have him in custody by now." With all the weaponry around her, she feared the showdown would end badly. *Men have such an appetite for bloodshed and slaughter.*

The SUV's radio squawked to life as Violette's voice came over the VHF. "Base to BAU4, Capt. Garrett wants to know your 20."

Madani picked up the mic. "Copy that, Margo. We just passed into North Ft. Pierce, heading south on US 1 about five miles from the scene. What's up?"

"Copy. Be advised we got a call from St. Lucie County deputies on the scene. They report the subject has fled less than two minutes ago and have activated their aerial surveillance unit."

Overhearing this, Beretto slammed his hand on the wheel in anger and turned off the siren and lights, pulling over in a strip mall parking lot. Sgt. Garner reached out the window and motioned the SWAT team to follow suit.

Madani handed Beretto the mic. "Which direction did Croaker go, Margo?"

"They don't know, sir."

"Does *anyone* have eyes on Croaker?" he asked.

There was commotion in the background as Violette responded. "That's a negative, sir."

"Do we have a description of the vehicle?"

"Yes, sir. Deputies report that our subject is in possession of a black and tan Mercedes RV. Subject left behind a Chevy Cruze at the RV park."

"Copy that," responded Beretto. Madani displayed a street map of Ft. Pierce on her tablet as precious seconds ticked away. Leaning over to show him, she traced the routes with her finger.

"Dom, look. There's only three ways outa there. Seaway southbound, Causeway northbound, and Orange Avenue SR 68 westbound," handing the tablet to Beretto.

Realizing they still had a chance to set a perimeter, Beretto reached around the seat to share the map with Foti. "Frank, let's set up roadblocks ten miles from the scene in each direction and form a perimeter, here, here...and here," pointing at locations on the map. "You know the area better, so I'll defer to you. You agree?"

Foti laid his MP5 on the floorboard and leaned forward to study Beretto's plan. "I do. We've got to contain him and keep him from getting on the interstate. If he gets on I-95, it'll be harder to intercept him in rush-hour traffic without the possible loss of innocent lives. You're in tactical command, Dom. I think it's our best shot."

Grabbing the mic, Beretto barked his orders. "Margo, ask Capt. Garrett to co-ordinate the St. Lucie County Sheriff roadblocks ten miles out from the scene on Seaway and North Causeway. Our team will take the shortcut to SR 68 and set up a roadblock just east of the I-95 intersection. Let's do this *yesterday*. Lives at stake. Copy?"

"Copy that, yes sir."

Beretto handed Madani the mic as the SWAT team in the SUV behind them waited for further instructions. "Gwen, let Heaton and Locke's team know what we're doing. Tell them to get the spike strips ready." Turning the siren and lights back on, Beretto steered the SUV toward SR 68 westbound. "We need to take him in the RV before he gets on the interstate."

After another six minutes of dodging slower traffic, Beretto and Foti had the two teams position the SUVs in a defensive V-shape on SR 68 in a way that blocked both westbound lanes just east of the I-95 intersection. Capt. Garrett had two more St. Lucie County sheriff's deputies join the group to help enforce the roadblock, and within minutes they were directing passenger cars as they approached in a single lane. Motorists were cooperating, but the rubberneckers were slowing things down as the deputies guided drivers around the spike strips.

Standing behind the Denali for protection, Foti spoke into his shoulder-mounted radio. "What about that chopper, Margo? They got eyes on Croaker yet?" There was some chatter in the background, followed by her voice.

"In their search pattern, they've identified two possibles, both heading west with the traffic toward your 20. They're closing to get a better visual. Wait." There was more garbled radio chatter, then Violette's voice again. "Sir, the pilots have confirmed that one of the RVs approaching your 20 is a black and tan Mercedes, and the driver is accelerating."

Foti grabbed a pair of binoculars from the SUV and trained them on the oncoming vehicles in the westbound lanes of SR 68. "Dom, I think I see him," adjusting the focus, "...I'd say...maybe a mile out. He's really movin'."

Beretto waved his arm as he positioned himself behind the SUV. "Gwen, I want you here beside me. Frank, what's he doin' now?"

Adjusting the focus, Foti squinted into the binoculars, but the intermittent sunlight from the east was causing the image to fluctuate as clouds passed across the sun. "He's still coming."

"Men," yelled Beretto, waving at the deputies, "...move the spike strips further east down the road another fifty yards." Turning to Foti, "At that speed, we need more room to stop him." Surveying the placement of vehicles and the men with sniper rifles, Beretto yelled, "Everyone, take cover and get ready!" With almost a dozen guns aimed at the oncoming RV, the officers crouched behind their vehicles, hoping they could stop Croaker before impact.

"Dom...looks like he's doin' over a hundred now," lowering the binoculars. "He's not gonna stop," concluded Foti. "Who are we kidding? We're gonna hafta take him out." To the two SWAT teams behind the SUVs, he yelled, "Aim for the tires! Watch your background-we've got civilians out there!" Waving at the deputies, "Get those cars off the road!"

As the sun passed behind a cloud, horrified motorists ducked for cover, some looking on as the RV rocketed toward the blockade at over a hundred miles an hour. Knowing their vehicles would offer them little protection against the heavier RV, the team members tensed with fingers on the triggers.

Seconds before impact, Croaker thought of a plan as he spotted the deputies moving the spike strips. Choosing a level area in the median, he swerved the big RV toward the grass and felt it plow into the swale. The front wheels lifted briefly, losing contact with the grassy surface before straightening out and giving him control again. Streaking by the spike strips deployed on the pavement, Croaker was plainly visible in his palm-frond hat and tie-dyed shirt, laughing hysterically as he maneuvered the RV past their first line of defense,

When Foti and Beretto saw that he'd managed to steer around the spike strips, there was no other choice but to give the order to fire. Eleven weapons of various caliber and lethality blazed away simultaneously with several rounds hitting the right front tire. At that moment, Croaker lost his ability to steer and the RV careened out of control, almost tipping over precariously as he accelerated before the RV righted itself and smashed into the massive concrete support column at a hundred miles an hour.

A huge fireball erupted as the RV exploded on impact, the containers of diesel fuel strapped to the rear sending a gigantic ball of flame high in the air. It was a horrific detonation that shook the ground and could be heard as far away as downtown Ft. Pierce. Chunks of aluminum, steel and glass shot in all directions as the SWAT team and deputies hunkered down behind the SUVs, protected by the helmets and riot gear they wore. After silencing their weapons, the officers waited for the explosions to subside before searching the wreckage for survivors. There were no signs of life in the flaming wreck.

With flames towering above the overpass, traffic on it had ground to a halt as Madani stood gaping at the burning vehicle. Had they done the right thing but with the wrong results? While her instinct as a human being was to protect and preserve life, her intellect as a police officer told her the world would be well rid of Mr. Max Croaker. Though shocked by the outcome, the BAU agent struggled to think of anyone who would actually miss him.

There were those who would say the government may have wanted Croaker to face the judgment of society, not the judgment of those who lacked the moral and legal right to end someone's life. Conflicted over the savagery of what had just happened, Madani wavered as she tried to balance the rights of the families of the four murder victims against the rights of the accused. So, she wondered, was this justice?

Standing out of harm's way as the flames engulfed the RV, Foti and Beretto also wrestled to calm themselves after the unavoidable violence. For them, it was exhausting and inconclusive, since now they would never know if he had acted alone.

Surprisingly, the rear bumper of the Mercedes Benz RV had been blown off in the explosion and lay in the grass, largely intact. One of the partially burned bumper stickers was still legible. Approaching the wreckage cautiously on foot, Foti, Madani, Beretto, Heaton and Garner were close enough to read the charred lettering through the flames;

IF THEY THINK YOU'RE DEAD
THEY'LL LEAVE YOU ALONE

PART IV

At two hours after midnight appeared the land at a distance of two leagues.

-CHRISTOPHER COLUMBUS
Journal of the First Voyage
October 12, 1492

TWENTY-NINE

By eight-fifteen on that same Thursday morning, the press had already gotten hold of the story and pandered to the crowds by making a headline of Max Croaker's demise. Over the years, Croaker had been a suspect in several Florida homicides, the news reported, asking why he hadn't been arrested. With all of the unsolved murders, there were still a lot of unanswered questions.

The mindless internet tabloids raised the question of whether the string of murders was over, an online survey even asking; *Are the area murders over? Vote yes, or no.* Out of thousands of respondents, sixty-nine percent said yes, eleven percent said no, and twenty percent were undecided. Inevitably, horrific images of the exploding RV found their way onto You Tube as the question was hotly debated among tens of thousands on social media and ultimately became one of Google's most searched topics of the week.

If Croaker had survived to be tried by the press or social media, it would have been a brutal lynching.

Unfamiliar with the news of the day, the McAllisters were in the sun-filled kitchen at Villa Riomar preparing one of Stella's favorite break-fasts, a cheese and souffle omelette, when the call came in from Beretto. Recognizing the number, Mark set the knife down on the onyx counter and pushed the talk button. "Dom, good of you to call. What's the latest?"

257

"Turn on your TV or computer. We got him."

"Who?" signaling to Stella to switch on the kitchen TV.

"Croaker."

"He's in custody?"

"He's dead," replied Beretto without emotion. "Twenty minutes ago, he drove his RV into a concrete bridge support at over a hundred miles an hour attempting to escape. The only way we could stop him was by shooting out his tires."

Mark was both stunned and relieved. "I'm putting you on speaker so Stella can hear," hitting the button. "You think it's over?"

"Speaking as a professional…no one here is happy that he died before he could tell us everything he knew. We're still not sure if he acted alone."

A pause ensued as Mark and Stella exchanged glances. It wasn't the answer they wanted to hear. Processing the optics, Mark replied, "Well… we all knew he wouldn't be taken alive. Probably didn't feel a thing." He thought about his buddies at the police station that put themselves in the line of fire.

"Anybody hurt besides Croaker?" A bystander had captured the moment of impact on their cell phone camera, and Stella covered her mouth as she watched the horrifying explosion pictured on TV.

"Nope. We were lucky," replied Beretto with relief. "Probably would've been a lot worse if we hadn't gotten out in front of him with a roadblock. There would've been more casualties. How's Stella taking the news?"

"In stride," turning to check her reaction.

Emotional over the news, Stella gazed out the window at her caged cockatiel basking in the sun on the loggia. Her eyes welling, she hoped it could all be over and wondered if her life could now return to normal. Turning away from the sunlight streaming through the window, she met her husband's eyes as he stepped closer to give her a hug. "Let me talk to him," reaching for his phone.

"Congratulations, Dom," wiping the wetness from her eyes. "I seem to be a magnet for murdering psychopaths."

"No worries, Stella. You're certainly not to blame. You could easily have been his next victim. Now, he's gone for good." He listened to her sigh. "The FBI will always have your back," he promised.

"In Dom we trust. Listen, can we take you and Agent Madani out to dinner tonight?" glancing at her husband, who nodded in approval. "Tomorrow, we're heading out on *Dream Girl* for a seven-day sail to celebrate our anniversary. So tonight may be our last chance to see each other for a while and thank you for all you've done."

"Many happy returns to you both. Hang on. Lemme see if Gwen can join us." After some background discussion, "She says she looks forward to it."

Still, the question lingered. "Level with me, Dom. Do you think this is over?"

He wanted to reassure her, give her some peace of mind that an evil man of such malicious intent had been vanquished. "Well, Stella...he fit our unsub profile to a "T", and we've eliminated our number one suspect. So, let's continue to be vigilant...and count our blessings."

"Spoken like our next Secretary of Homeland Security." She took a deep breath. "Okay, then. From your lips to God's ears. Cocktails at seven, dinner at seven-thirty. We'll meet you at The Tides. They've got a nice dance band there."

"Sounds good. Save a dance for me."

Dawn came too soon after a late evening of dinner and drinks with their FBI friends. Mark and Stella had risen early Friday morning to gather their things and organize their equipment for a week of celebration aboard *Dream Girl*. Needing a getaway, their itinerary included a dive on the third reef off Delray, an underwater formation flush with snapper, grouper and other gamefish. Then they planned to sail across the Gulfstream to Marsh Harbour on the Bahamian island of Abaco for gunkholing and more diving.

Speaking softly between themselves last night, the subject of money came up. He remembered what she'd said about the luxury of having a nearly unlimited bank account, admitting that some of that luxury was due to her dearly departed dad.

Her late father was a legend in the semiconductor industry and generally regarded as a genius. James Dodge had become a billionaire at the age of fifty-five by inventing a series of smart programmable chipsets used in everything from accelerated visual computing to artificial intelligence. Stella was his only heir, and he'd left his entire multi-billion-dollar fortune to her, together with rights and royalties to over a hundred patents. She and her heirs, should she choose to have any, were set for life.

"You know the money is irrelevant, mon cherie," she'd said with a knowing smile.

He supposed that if your maiden name was Dodge, then maybe what she said was true. One of the benefits of the super-rich, and being on the right side of the grass, was the ability to make acquisitions and write a large bank cheque without having to worry about it clearing. Although he didn't consider himself super-rich, he appreciated the convenience of having a wife who was.

This morning, when he saw that she'd packed the homicide case files for their week away, he came to realize just how overdue she was for their getaway. Though she did her best to rise above it, the past few weeks of unrelenting stress had been hard on her. True to his word, he would take her to his promised sanctuaries, the vibrant worlds she enjoyed exploring. He would bring back her playfulness, and her sense of adventure were some of the things he loved most about her.

For the McAllisters, *Dream Girl* had always been a home away from home, their starship to other galaxies, a magical time machine that could transport them to a better state of mind. With Croaker's demise, and for the first time in weeks, the couple weren't as preoccupied with the possibility of having to take refuge in their new safe room. Instead, they would take refuge in the boundlessness of the high seas.

Mark had always enjoyed tinkering with the mechanical and electrical systems on the boat, but he enjoyed sailing her even more, especially during episodes that only a female first mate can enhance. Every experienced sailor knows a sailboat requires a bit more seamanship than a motorboat, and knows it's advisable to have at least two seasoned sailors aboard. But with Stella as his first mate, he never felt the need for additional crew. Nonetheless, he always took the time to check the sheets and standing rigging for signs of wear, and to check for spare parts. Sailing third-world countries, one thing he learned was that spare parts were hard to come by.

In the sky over the marina, seagulls swooped and circled, and a light breeze rustled the surrounding palms on another sunny day in paradise. In preparation for their Bahamian adventure, Mark and Stella began unloading provisions and equipment onto the dock, dressed in their usual yachting outfits-cargo shorts and tank tops.

As they did so, Don and Katy, a friendly retired couple they'd met at one of the yacht club socials, stopped by on their way to the clubhouse to admire the sixty-four-foot Baltic. The couple shared a colorful story of sailing their sloop in the summer waters off Nantucket before wishing the McAllisters a *bon voyage,*

Stepping over the lifelines, Stella jumped down into the aft cockpit to organize the equipment while Mark parked her Range Rover in the club's long term parking lot. Sorting through the gear, she decided which things to keep topside and which to secure down below. Proud of her new pneumatic spear gun, she held it up to admire the design. She liked the way the four attached twenty-eight-inch spears snapped into place around the cylinder and looked forward to testing it on the Delray reef. After setting it next to Mark's triple-bander Riffe in the lazarette, she got busy with the work of making ready to sail.

After locking up the Range Rover, Mark stopped to check the sea water discharge from the AC ports before boarding, pleased to see that the four water-to-air units were working properly. Preparing to spring his surprise, he thought about the red roses that Connie had put aboard, knowing they would bring his wife a lot of joy at a time when she really needed it.

As Stella busied herself collecting the dock lines and fifty-amp shore cables, Mark jumped into the aft cockpit and entered the security code on the alarm keypad. Rolling the dodger back and snapping it down, he slid the companionway hatch forward and stepped down into the main salon to check on his surprise.

The magnificent floral arrangement contained by the crystal Baccarat vase presented the roses in all their splendor, as if they'd just been picked. It was a stunning display, and Connie had taken the time to anchor the vase with a non-skid base to prevent it from sliding across the teak table. Pleased with the arrangement, he called out to his wife.

"Hey, matey…when you get a chance I'd like to show you something." Peeking out the companionway hatch, he watched her placing the coiled power cables into the stowage under the cockpit seats. Mark extended his hand to help her down the steps. "Got a surprise for you."

Grasping his hand, "Is it part of your anatomy?" she teased. Seeing the bouquet of red roses sitting next to a case of Cordon Bleu and a case of Camus on the dining table, she was taken by surprise. "Mark…honey… they're beautiful!"

"Happy anniversary, Stella," bending her over backwards and giving her a huge Hollywood-style kiss.

"What…no card?" Teasing him again, she knew her husband wasn't big on cards. He liked to say it was best said with the lips, which invariably made her blush. Lifting a bottle of cognac from the box, he peeled off the seal and poured the magical elixir into two snifters

Lifting his glass to her, "Here's to the husband…here's to the wife… may they remain…lovers for life."

"I love that toast!" Clinking glasses, she tossed the double shot back in one gulp. "Perfect!" Gasping for breath, "Wow," licking her lips, "… can we get outa here now so we can get naked?"

In a pirate's voice, "You betcha, matey! Single up all ye lines, prepare to lower the yardarm and cast off!"

Following her captain's orders, Stella stowed the four fenders in their holders on deck, casting the bow, stern and spring lines aboard as Mark started the engine and engaged the bow thrusters to move them away from the pier. Clear of the pilings, he put the main propulsion in gear.

Out Ft. Pierce inlet they headed on a slack tide, and when they cleared the last marker, they set sail in pleasant three to four-foot seas. Switching places with her, Mark hoisted the mainsail, then the staysail, then set the genoa. The Reckmann roller furling systems made setting the sails a piece of cake for the short-handed crew. Stella swung the huge stainless steel wheel slightly to port and brought the yacht to a 170-degree bearing to smooth the fluttering sails. On his way back to the aft cockpit, he double-checked the fasteners which held the rigid hull inflatable Zodiac in place on the foredeck davits. Finding them nice and snug, he jumped back down to the cockpit to join his first mate.

Smiling mischievously, she asked, "Will you take the wheel, honey? I'm gonna get comfortable." He obliged her, knowing he was about to be presented with the best view on the high seas. Taking the wheel, he watched Stella strip down to just her thong bottoms, lay out invitingly on the cockpit seat cushions, and extend her shapely body as she applied a skin moisturizer that made her skin sparkle in the sun. Enjoying one of her favorite games, she loved testing him to see how long he could endure her teasing. His mind adrift with her sensuous behavior, she reminded him of a golden goddess, her alluring vision triggering a daydream.

He imagined himself at the helm of the sixty-four-foot Baltic heading west toward the pink-sand beaches of Bora Bora. With a setting sun on the horizon, the Navy-blue hull was cutting majestically through the aqua-colored waves. He pictured the Jolly Roger flying at the top of the mast and his crew busy at their tasks; Taylor Swift holding his snifter of cognac, Charlize Theron performing calisthenics on the foredeck, and Penelope Cruz massaging his neck. *Sorry Javier, but it's my daydream.*

His fantasy only served to wet his appetite for her touch. For an instant, he searched the horizon for nearby vessels, and seeing none, he considered setting the autopilot and staying on his current course so he could ravish her where she lay. But, leaving the helm unattended was not the decision of a prudent captain, so he restrained himself, allowing Stella to continue working her magic.

There was a nice easterly blowing, and soon *Dream Girl* was doing ten knots on a brisk beam reach. The modified winged-keel was designed to give the yacht added lift at almost any speed, and so their starship was taking off. Sensing a wind shift, Mark looked at the sagging tell tales and steered five degrees to port. The sails smoothed out, filling again as he reminded himself the Florida weather could change at the drop of a hat.

Sitting up in a sultry mood, Stella surveyed the coastline, shading her eyes with her hand and rubbing her thigh with the other. "How far are we from the reef?"

"Should be there before sunset. You in a hurry to get somewhere?"

Smiling broadly, "Honey, you *know* where *I* want to go."

Yes, indeed I do. Feeling things heating up, "Well…you know what Jim Morrison said…"

She looked expectantly at him with her cat-like green eyes as she continued to rub her shapely thighs. "Of 'The Doors'?"

"Is there another?"

"So…what'd he say?"

"He said, '…the best part of the trip was…the trip to the best part.'"

"Uh-huh." Putting her fingertip to her lips, "I'm gonna go below. Can I bring you some cognac for breakfast, *mon capitaine?*" As she stood, she gave him an inviting smile and peeled off her thong, dropping it on the cockpit seat suggestively, giving him no doubts about what she had on her mind.

He cocked his head and looked at her. "Well…when you put it *that* way…"

The warmth of the sun on her skin was making her feel frisky. She turned to make sure he was watching as she flounced her hips and sashayed below deck. The two snifters and open bottle of Cordon Bleu rested on the teak dining table right where they'd left them earlier. As she gathered them up and turned to ascend the companionway steps, she heard a strange noise that sounded like it came from the port side berth. Curious, she set the cognac and glasses down on the table and made her way forward to the closed teak door.

"Anyone there?" she called out. Maybe she had imagined it. Wanting to make sure the port side berth was empty, she quietly pressed the French handle downward and slowly swung the door open. A strong medicinal smell filled her nostrils. From the doorway, the cabin appeared to be vacant, but at second glance the bedding looked disturbed, as if someone had recently slept there. She stepped into the stateroom to investigate.

He'd been coiled up and waiting ten hours for her. Without warning, he sprang his trap from behind the door. Before she could call out for help, she felt a soft wet cloth reeking of a strong, sweet chemical cover her mouth and nose tightly while another arm grabbed her in a choke hold, pulling her head back violently.

"Scream, and I'll break your neck." He tightened his choke hold and pressed the trichloromethane-soaked cloth tightly against Stella's face, forcing her to breathe the noxious fumes. Kicking furiously and struggling to break free, she emitted a muffled squeal as he pulled her backward onto the berth, hitting his back on the railing. Sensing her attacker was in pain, with one foot pushing down on the berth, she pushed herself as high as she could off the berth and landed a heel on the headliner with a loud "thump" before he could restrain her legs with his own. Struggling against her stronger assailant, precious seconds ticked away as she was forced to breathe the noxious fumes.

Hearing the impact of her foot against the headliner, Mark mistakenly thought she'd gone forward to loosen the hatch tie-down dogs in the forward berths to improve the air flow below. Seated at the helm, he bent down and looked forward down the companionway, unaware that she was struggling for her life. He yelled down the companionway; "Stella, be careful with raising those hatches. We're doing thirteen knots now. I don't want them flying away on us."

After another two minutes of silence, he wondered what was keeping her. He adjusted course five degrees further south on a wind shift and watched the Simrad digital speedometer increase to fourteen knots. Listening intently for her response, all he could hear was the wind whistling through the sails and the hull slicing through the waves. She should have responded by now. He heard another thump from the forward berth.

"Stella?" Again, there was no answer. Yelling down the companionway toward the bow, "You gonna leave your skipper high and dry?" Even if she'd stopped to relieve herself and freshen up, she was taking too long.

Deciding to go below, Mark did a 360-degree scan of the horizon to check for other boats. He could see three distant sportfish heading out to sea, away from them. Deciding to risk it and leave the helm unattended, he felt compelled to see what was keeping Stella and engaged the autopilot.

Stepping toward the main hatch, Mark caught a whiff of a strong, medicinal-smelling chemical. Had she somehow dropped something from the medicine cabinet? Intuition told him something wasn't right. Backtracking, he turned around and lifted the aft lazarette cover. Sifting through the locker's contents, he pushed aside a bang stick and his three-bander spear gun to select Stella's short-stock pneumatic gun to arm himself. On the outside chance there was trouble, he wanted to be ready. Inserting the spear, he pressed the tip against the teak stringer and pushed down hard to load it into the pressurized chamber. Then, he stepped down the short flight of teak stairs to see what was keeping his wife.

"Stella?" Warily, he stepped forward into the salon.

"Son of a-" he cried out, not seeing the broken snifter lying on the floor in time. The thin piece of curved glass had penetrated his heel, and he was leaving bloody footprints on the teak and holly sole. As he bent over to extract the piece of glass, he noticed the roses scattered on the salon floor.

Before he could stand, he felt an immense blow to the back of his head. In extreme pain, a galaxy of stars spun around his brain as he fell to the floor. Before passing out, he caught a glimpse of a bald man holding the Baccarat vase by the neck and wondered how on earth he'd gotten aboard.

THIRTY

Feeling like a speeding freight train was running through his head, Mark slowly regained consciousness. He thought he'd heard Stella calling out to him over the groan of the diesel engine further aft. Diesel engine? When he left the helm they were under sail. Unsure of how long he'd been out, he could feel the engine's vibrations through the floor in his bare feet and realized his wrists were restrained with his arms raised over his head. Groggy, he opened his right eye, trying to focus, then his left to see a trail of blood on the floor's mosaic tiles. It was his own, he remembered, as he vaguely recalled cutting his foot on a broken cognac glass.

Raising his head, he faced the bleary image of Dr. Christopher Hirt standing over him holding his wife's pneumatic spear gun in his left hand, and a syringe in his right. In a sheath strapped to his leg, Hirt wore a nasty-looking survival knife. The man who'd tried to kill his wife and cash in on her death two years ago stood over him and gloated.

"Neat little spear gun you got here, McAllister. Did you think you were gonna use it on me?"

Still partially drugged, Mark struggled to respond coherently, only managing to mutter something even he couldn't understand.

"That's what I thought. Focus on what I'm holding," said Hirt in a menacing tone. Slumped on the toilet, Mark was propped against the bulkhead with his arms raised, held there by stainless steel cuffs attached to the teak grab bar. He recognized it as the starboard guest head because he was the one who refurbished it three years earlier. Surveying the decor, it was complete with the tile mosaics, Italian marble counter, and a decorative bronze mermaid relief adorning the mirror. Glancing at his cuffed wrists, he recalled how well he had attached the teak grab bar when he installed it. With its six half-inch stainless steel screws, it was strong enough to handle two men his size. His tendency to build things to last forever wasn't helping him today.

"Good news and bad news, McAllister. Good news is, you and Stella may live to see this through. Bad news is, she's gonna be my new yacht slave." He took a step closer. "A beauty like *her*...why should you have all the fun?" Hirt continued to pointedly tap the tip of the spear gun against Mark's bare knee as he stood over his victim. With the drugs wearing off, the welts on his face and bruises on his head began to throb painfully. Out cold from the blow to his head, he had no memory of being injected with the fentanyl.

Hirt could see he was coming around. "Did you think you were going to escape in your La-La-Land safe room?" he taunted. "Yeah, I know... you thought it was a big secret."

He didn't reply.

"Tell me, how's a guy like you score a girl like that?"

Again, no reply.

Bleary eyed, he looked up at his antagonist. "Where's...Stella?" he asked, his brain on fire and his face throbbing.

"Oh...she's in the *other* guest bath, of course..." pointing through the open door across the companionway, "...just across the hall from you. So...you're neighbors, you two." To torment him, he added, "I did put her thong back on...after we were finished...but, I had to gag her to stop her from screaming."

Angry, Mark replied, "Hurt her, you piece of crap, I'll hunt you--"

"Shut up, Mr. Big Shot Author," shoving him hard against the bulkhead and putting the spear tip against his throat, "...or I'll pump you up with more fentanyl."

His brain began to function again, and he regarded his captor anew. It was clear that challenging the sicko wasn't going to work. "What do you want, Dr. Hirt?" he asked in a more subdued voice.

"Oh, so now we're being polite?" Hirt squatted to look into his eyes. "Maybe some justice. You may recall it was your wife's testimony that sent me away for two years."

"After you prescribed a drug that you knew would make her violent." Hirt listened, interested in what he had to say. "After she stabbed her husband in self-defense, you collected millions in the stock market from her adverse reaction." Emboldened by Hirt's silence, Mark lowered his voice. "You killed Dr. Tremelle, didn't you?"

With a tilt of his head and raised brows, he casually acknowledged the accusation. "You have any idea what it's like to be forced to counsel perverts and scumbags on death row for two years...while you two were living it up in Bora Bora?"

"Your own doing, doctor."

"Well, maybe it's *my* turn for a little fun. Or...maybe I just need a ride to a reef off Boca on your sailboat."

"How did you get aboard my boat?"

Hirt was smug. "You're far too trusting with your passcodes. And since your wife made herself impossible to track on social media, she forced me to use software that hacks phones. Ain't technology grand?"

In his half-drugged state, Mark was able to read through the tea leaves. It pained him as an investigative journalist, and a person who once welcomed social media, to finally recognize that the internet's advances were failing to provide the benefits they were once expected to deliver. With his life now at risk, it was painfully obvious to him that the hacking of personal data, including his own, was growing exponentially.

All along, Stella had been right. Private data and personal information were being commercialized and weaponized at an alarming rate. Like

Hirt, it was the inhumane and malevolent actors who were gaming the system, facilitated by technology in ways not intended by its creators. The increasing number of malevolent actors manipulating the platforms was spreading like a cancerous growth, unable to be contained because maybe it was too late to turn it off. All this, while the publically-traded stocks of those same creators marched higher with the hefty profits from ad sales. Mark wished he'd listened to her sooner.

Reveling in the helplessness of his victim, Hirt continued. "So, Mr. Best Selling Author, here's the deal," getting right in his face, "...do what I tell you and behave yourself...everyone gets to live a nice long life. I like a man who stays put." Pulling a black pouch from his pocket, "This will help you relax." Raising the syringe to eye level, he tapped on it as Mark noticed what appeared to be a bite mark on his left hand.

Glaring angrily, Mark tested the strength of his restraints. "Stella must've had a pretty good reason to give you *that* little memento, you impotent piece of cow dung. What did you do to her?"

Unable to defend himself, Hirt stuck him in his exposed tricep with a healthy dose of fentanyl, then stepped back to watch the opioid take effect. Within seconds, a flood of euphoria washed over him, rendering him speechless.

"Nice high, huh?" slapping him on the shoulder, the spear gun banging against the vanity. "Gotta go check on some things, so behave yourself and you might get your boat back." Putting it back in the pouch, Hirt tucked the syringe in his pocket. He used his thumb to raise Mark's eyelids and examine his pupils. Then, he shut the door and went topside to check the horizon for any incoming vessels.

In the port guest head across the companionway, Stella was in an opioid-induced state of unconsciousness, her hands cuffed overhead to the grab bar like her husband. Her lip was hurt and her neck badly bruised, but she was feeling no pain as her drug-induced dream unfolded.

In her dream, she sat at the window seat on a train passing through the countryside as it sped past rows of houses with children playing in the yards. They were beautiful, grassed yards with short white fences and trees with swings, occupied by those whose lives she wondered about but never lived. Curious, to herself she questioned what they did, what they said to each other, what they had for breakfast, and if they were living happy lives. She kept telling herself not to look, but she looked anyway, in spite of her own admonitions.

In her dream, she remembered confessing to a bald man wearing a white lab coat and stethoscope that she wasn't the woman she used to be. She'd changed because she had a good husband now. But she couldn't find him-or her clothes-as she realized she was sitting next to him naked.

From the vibrations coursing through her body and the noise it made, she knew she was riding a diesel-powered train that was winding its way along the river through the green countryside. When the man in the white lab coat tried to force himself on her, she screamed and tried to fight him off, but the passengers on the train weren't helping her.

Terrified after repeating the same scenes over and over, she emerged from her dream dripping with sweat. She opened her eyes, and from her view through the boat's porthole, she could see it wasn't a river, but a vast body of water streaming by. Listening to the familiar clatter of the diesel, it sounded louder now that she was conscious. Focusing on her surroundings, she wished she was living the life of one of those strangers playing in the yards that she passed on the train.

But she wasn't, and she dreaded what her tormentor had in mind for her next.

Unfamiliar with the workings of sails, halyards, sheets, lines, blocks, outhauls, travelers, vangs and winches, the psychiatrist was a bit over-whelmed by all the gadgetry needed to sail the yacht. It had taken him a while to figure out how to furl the boat's three sails without being pulled from the cockpit and thrown overboard by the sheets. Then, he figured out how to use the winches. Not being the kind of man who appreciated the art and skill of harnessing the wind to propel the vessel, the yacht seemed so much simpler to operate under power. After all, he was a psychiatrist, not a sailor with the experience of a yachtsman like McAllister.

After a thorough search of the navigation cabin earlier, he found the main engine key, and in the V-berth, he found thirty thousand dollars in a safe that he managed to break open with a crow bar from the engine room. In the teak drawers, he found hollow points for a 9 mm and ammo for a .223 caliber assault rifle, but no guns. Rummaging through the fridge and galley cabinets, Hirt was disgusted with finding mostly vegetables.

"I didn't climb to the top of the food chain to eat carrots!" he said out loud. He did help himself to a bottle of cognac and two bottles of Camus.

The afternoon had turned partly cloudy and the wind had picked up to a steady fifteen knots. Smug about pirating *Dream Girl,* Hirt sat at the helm in his Viagra cap, T-shirt and shorts as the yacht cut through the light seas at six knots on a southeasterly heading. Avoiding other vessels, the offshore boat traffic had been relatively light the last few hours, with half a dozen boats moving east toward deeper water. He continued to monitor Ch.16, confident that his mutiny was succeeding. Hirt had brought enough fentanyl to keep his victims incapacitated, but he was still undecided about sparing their lives.

Still, he would save her for last.

After some tinkering, he'd been able to access the tutorial on the autopilot's touch screen while he worked out the logistics of his rendezvous. Glancing behind at the boat's wake, he smiled to himself, feeling prideful as the sixty-four-footer was practically sailing herself. With the autopilot engaged, he was able to take his hands off the wheel for the first time and focus on his hand-held GPS as he set a way point on a reef off Boca.

The coordinates he entered were accurate to within one meter;

Latitude 2623.5213 north,
Longitude 8003.9197 west

The waypoint he had picked was a two-century-old wreck located in twenty-eight feet of water on a reef only two hundred yards from shore. Believing in the value of redundancy, he wrote the coordinates down on the back of a scrap of paper with a waterproof Sharpie and stuck it in his back pocket for safekeeping. By his calculations, he would be there by nightfall. Given its shallow depth and location, the wreck was the perfect temporary hiding place for his $21 million in diamonds. In the event of his capture, Hirt was convinced the police would never think to search underwater, and because it was so close to shore, he could snorkel to it if he had to.

Representing his entire life savings of twenty-three years of drug deals, excessive fees and fraudulent Medicare reimbursements, the cache would be hidden if he was captured before he could buy himself a new identity. Believing his plan to be pure genius, he was pleased with his choice of diamonds to preserve his wealth, since the precious stones were so much easier to transport than gold bullion or currency. Hiding the treasure inside a rusty steel pipe buried in a coral hole under the wreck was the perfect disguise. With a weight of under twelve pounds, the two-foot-long pipe filled with diamonds could be easily pulled from the bottom using a line from any surface vessel.

If only they knew where to look.

At his present speed, he figured there were a few more hours before arriving at his waypoint around sunset. Surveying the horizon in all directions, he was beginning to appreciate the mystique of sailing before going below to check on his two prisoners. On the way through the galley, he snatched two water bottles and two Snicker bars.

Putting his ear to the door, he heard only silence before swinging it open. When Stella saw him standing in the doorway with her spear gun and survival knife, she let out a muffled scream and jerked on her restraints to show him she was ready to defend herself. She was surprised when he stuck the survival knife back in its sheath and waved the bottle of water in her face. Over the steady drone of the diesel, she listened to what he had to say.

"I'm not gonna hurt you, Stella. I'm gonna remove your gag," in a calm voice, "...but if you scream, we're gonna have another go-round. Nod if you understand."

She continued nodding as he placed a Snickers bar on the vanity counter in front of her and gently pulled the duct tape from her mouth. Firmly chained to the grab bar, she gazed at him with her emerald-green eyes, her strawberry-blonde hair a mess. He was trying hard to resist the allure of his topless prisoner.

"C-c-can...I have some water?" she begged.

"Sure," unscrewing the cap and setting it on the counter just in front of her. "*After* you answer some questions for me." Reluctantly, she nodded again. "I need the keys for the Zodiac...and I want you to tell me where the guns are."

Cocking her head, "So you can use them on us?"

"If I was going to kill you, you'd already be dead, Stella."

"We thought we might need them at Villa Riomar, so Mark and I took them home," she said with as much sincerity as she could muster. "I honestly don't know where he keeps the keys to the Zodiac."

"Uh-huh," grabbing her by the jaw, "...why don't I believe you?"

She noticed he liked staring at her breasts and thought of an angle. Submissively, "I kept my promise and answered your questions, Dr. Hirt. Now...will you keep yours?" She glanced again at the water and candy bar.

"Maybe," tipping the bottle for her to sip from. She guzzled half the bottle before he jerked it from her mouth, purposely spilling some on her breasts. Watching the water trickle down her abdomen, he bent over to lap up the water, licking his way down her belly.

"*Please*...stop!" Her body writhing in disgust, she endured the indignity as long as she could before yelling loudly, "Mark, please tell him where the guns are!!" Startled by her outburst, Hirt stopped his slobbering and listened for an answer.

Knowing she was in trouble, Mark yelled through the closed door, "They're at home!" Though it wasn't true, he was betting the secret panel concealing the guns behind the staircase was so perfectly crafted that Hirt would never find them.

Struggling to rid herself of the repulsive man, she yelled across to the starboard head again. "Get off me!! Mark will you tell him where the keys to the Zodiac are?"

"Tell him to come talk to me!" yelled Mark.

Hirt raised his head from her pelvis and looked into her eyes. "Gonna go talk to your husband. If he doesn't tell me where the keys are, I'll be back for more refreshments." Opening the teak door, he turned to her with a crooked smile. "You should know when you've been licked."

"Okay, Mr. McAllister, you're up," opening the teak door to the starboard head. "If you want to keep your wife from being ravished again, you'll tell me where those keys are."

"Look, Dr. Hirt--"

"We're being polite again, huh?" with an angry look. "Tell me what I want to know, or I go back next door," jerking his thumb over his shoulder, "...and you can listen to your wife scream some more." They felt the yacht shudder, the diesel engine changing its pitch as if shutting down. Expecting Mark to explain what was happening, Hirt stared at him.

"Either some contaminants in the fuel filters," ventured Mark. "...or that spaghetti seaweed clogging the impellers." Hirt studied him with a skeptical look. "It happens. I can help you with that." Hirt continued to stare at him as the diesel resumed its standard pitch. His offer failing to impress his captor, he added, "I've got thirty thousand in cash I'll give you if you let us go."

"Already found it. I'm a wanted criminal, probably with a price on my head. Anyway, why should I trust you?"

"Because all I care about is keeping us alive." Hirt continued to listen to his pleas. "Look, we don't care about your escape plans. Let us go in the Zodiac, and we'll leave you alone...and I swear, on the life of my kids--"

"You don't have any kids."

"On the life of my mother and father--"

"They died in a car accident years ago. What…you don't think I do my homework?"

"Okay," he pleaded, "…I swear on Stella's life that we will tell no one about you. That you drowned at sea…whatever you want us to say. Just let us go topside, and I'll tell you where the keys are. You can cast us adrift with life preservers. We'll say nothing about you. Truly, we mean you no harm."

"That why you're helping the cops with solving the murders?"

"I'm an investigative journalist. It's what I do." He attempted to express himself with his hands, but they'd grown numb from the lack of circulation. "It's nothing personal."

"But it is, isn't it? Personal?"

Mark didn't reply.

"You not only knew about all of it, you aided and abetted it." Mark knew Hirt was right, and there was no avoiding what it was.

He replied this time, in a calmer voice. "If you spare us our lives… we'll help you escape. Please let us go. So far, you've done nothing to us that we can't forgive." *Except for the murder of three or four women.*

Hoping that there might be a shred of decency left in the psychopath, he was digging deep to exhume some semblance of an act of contrition from Hirt. Desperate, he knew it was a tall order for a serial killer.

Needing time to think, Hirt decided to re-dose them with fentanyl. Gaping at the syringe, Mark knew there was no way of avoiding the sting of the needle as it penetrated his bicep. *Got to figure a way out of this before he overdoses us.*

"Need to keep you two sedated," said Hirt, pointing it in the air to refill it from the vial. With the syringe in one hand and his other on the door handle, he turned with a warning. "Keep it quiet down here and you may get your boat back. Or maybe, you get the Zodiac."

In the companionway, he put his ear to the door and listened. He could hear her praying before stepping inside to dose her. When he entered, she went silent and looked at him, her emerald green eyes seeming to stare right through him to his very soul. "I'm sorry that I testified against you. I did it to help you be a better doctor."

"Uh-huh," he replied, now completely confused, his plans for her coming unraveled. He wondered if she truly believed in what she said, and wondered whether she was a goddess, or a demon like himself. Accepting the inevitability of her situation, she became less confrontational as he injected her again with a modest dose of fentanyl.

Blinded by her beauty, but conflicted over his desire for vengeance, he'd overlooked her spirituality. Her eyes closed as she went limp. *You should be praying to me, honey. I'm your God.*

Hirt returned topside to check their course and scan the ocean for incoming vessels. In command and seated at the helm gave him a brief feeling of prosperity once again as he reminisced about his life before his conviction. He missed parading through the pages of the Vero Beach shiny sheets with socialites and swim suit models half his age. He missed making three hundred an hour pandering to the psychobabble of island gentry rock stars, and he was tired of bowing to the Mc*Whatevers* and the *Something*fields that ran the show in Vero Beach. While his current plan was a huge gamble, he was certain the outcome would guarantee him a languorous retirement.

They motored on, and later in the afternoon, he was pleased that the wind and seas had diminished, making it easier for him to access his drop point. Studying the distant coastline through the binoculars, he could make out the massive concrete towers that formed the bulk of Boca's oceanfront condos. Further south, near the mouth of the inlet, he could see several boats of various sizes heading in from a day at sea.

Hearing the high-pitched whine of outboard engines behind him, he turned to the view in his wake and focused the binoculars on a fast moving small craft approaching from astern. The boat seemed to be heading north toward Boca Inlet. As it speeded toward him, he sharpened the focus.

On its hull he spotted the distinctive green and white insignia of the Palm Beach County Sheriff's Office.

THIRTY-ONE

The sheriff's patrol boat was a fast-moving thirty-foot T-top powered by three Mercury outboards and heading right for him. Through his binoculars, Hirt could see two uniformed officers at the helm and estimated the patrol boat was moving at about 50 mph east-northeast of *Dream Girl.* He switched the VHF back on, and at first he heard only the routine traffic of fishing and dive boats hailing one another. The only vessel in his immediate vicinity was the sheriff's patrol boat, which continued to cruise on an intercept course.

With the sun just beginning to set, Hirt was hoping the deputies would bypass him as they headed into port to call it a day. He had a fleeting thought of searching for the yacht's registration papers in case he was stopped, then realized he wouldn't have enough time. He unhooked the spear gun from his belt and hid the knife and contraband in the backpack, then stashed the items and his .45 under the cockpit seat to keep them out of sight. After stowing the weapons, the VHF squawked to life.

"*Dream Girl, Dream Girl,* this is sheriff's patrol off your port quarter. Do you copy?" The deputy's voice sounded routine, without any sense of urgency, which was somewhat of a relief to him. Through his binoculars, he could see both wore side arms and were watching him through their binoculars.

The question was repeated. "*Dream Girl, Dream Girl*, sheriff's patrol, approaching from your stern. Do you copy?"

Reaching for the mic hanging from the binnacle post, Hirt wanted to answer the officers promptly to ward off the possibility of an inspection. "Sheriff's patrol, this is *Dream Girl*. Copy you." Pretending to be a responsible yachtsman, he raised his arm and waved at the two deputies, giving them a broad, insincere smile.

The sheriff's patrol boat slowed and steered toward the sailboat, matching the larger boat's speed and course as the taller deputy reached under the deck and dropped two attached fenders over the starboard side in preparation for tying off.

"*Dream Girl*, sheriff's patrol. Heave to for a safety check and state your name, business and port-of-call." Hearing the order struck dread into him as more static poured from the radio and he pondered a response. Pulling back on the gearshift lever, Hirt reduced power and put the engine in neutral as he thought hard about a reply, trying to decide if he should use an alias or the owner's real name. He made a decision and responded calmly.

"Sheriff's patrol, *Dream Girl*. Copy your request. This is Mark McAllister. My wife and I are heading south to Key West on a pleasure cruise. We're out of Vero Beach…sir." Adding the "sir" was a nice touch, he thought.

By now, the patrol boat was abeam and closing at a slower speed, apparently with the intention of rafting up. Hirt watched it approach, still on a parallel course and close enough to see the two officers discussing what he presumed would be their next course of action, his fate hanging in the balance.

Uneasy over having the two armed policemen discover his true identity, he saw the deputy lift his binoculars again, prompting him to smile and wave a second time. With the sheriff's patrol boat so close, he was surprised when the flashing blue lights activated along with the shrill sound of the siren. Raising the cockpit seat just enough to slip his hand around the .45, his heart raced with the thought of shooting the two deputies.

The radio squawked again. "All right, *Dream Girl*. We've got a Code 3 in Boca Inlet. We're sure everything's in order aboard your vessel. Remember, safety first. Have a good one." Hirt breathed a sigh of relief as the boat turned sharply and headed away. He watched the deputy stow the fenders as the patrol boat accelerated and returned to its original southwesterly heading, the three Mercury outboards whining loudly.

Part of him was thankful he wouldn't have to shoot two Palm Beach County deputies in cold blood. He looked northwest at a view of the sun setting as it descended below a cadre of high rises, giving rise to a mosaic of rose-hued clouds. About to be treated to a nautical sunset, he started the engine and pushed the gear shift forward. The transmission clanked in protest as it engaged the propshaft, and the yacht moved forward in the gathering twilight, now only three miles from the reef drop point.

A black fringe began to form on the distant horizon, and the rising moon in the east together with the gulls gliding over the sea were painting quite a portrait. He engaged the autopilot and stepped away from the helm to check on his hostages, hoping they would still be unconscious from the earlier dosing. Descending the companionway stairs, it occurred to him that he still hadn't figured out how to launch the rigid hull inflatable Zodiac by himself. Eighteen feet long, he figured it had to weigh at least 1,200 pounds with the attached outboard, batteries, and gas tanks.

Deep within his twisted mind, a plan was unfolding that involved a bit of trickery.

Less than an hour later, Hirt was studying the illuminated touch screen of the Simrad bottom profiler in order to confirm the coordinates displayed on the GPS in his hand. Only pinpoint accuracy would ensure he could find and recover his fortune when the coast was clear. To minimize any unwanted attention as the yacht approached the coast, he turned off the navigation lights, and with the partial crescent moon overhead, he had just enough light to complete his mission.

The interior lights on the row of oceanfront condos two hundred yards away seemed to flicker on and off as residents moved about inside the high rises. With night descending, and all the boat's lights extinguished except for his navigation instruments, the sea had an eerie feel to it as he approached the reef.

The wind and seas were still relatively calm, but the humidity was rising and the radar indicated light rain approaching from the southeast. The drop coordinates were within easy reach, and with the tide now flooding, he would have to make the drop quickly or risk losing control over the sailboat's movement. Moments later, he saw the wreck's profile appear onscreen while he guided the sixty-four-foot Baltic one foot at a time over the reef. With his eyes on the screen, he eased the throttle forward to counter the rising tide and align with the precise drop point.

When the depth finder registered twenty-eight feet, he switched on the yacht's underwater lights and turned with his binoculars toward the beach to see if he'd attracted any attention. Nothing ashore was moving except the palm trees that swayed in the light breeze and the thin trail of distant headlights from the vehicles making their way along A1A. Earlier, he'd raided their equipment locker for a set of snorkel gear in preparation for his descent on the reef.

His heart skipped a beat when he peered over the side into the crystal clear water to see several large fish swimming over his designated drop point. His pulse quickened at the thought of sharks in the area as he tied off a long line to the cleat amidship and wrapped the other end around himself to ensure he stayed connected to the sailboat. Climbing down to the teak swim platform on the stern, he slipped the mask and snorkel over his head and tightened the fins before hyperventilating and taking a final lungful of air. Then, he jumped overboard with the steel pipe under one arm and the long dock line looped around the other.

At seventy-nine degrees, the ocean water off Highland Beach felt a little chilly. In the shimmering lights and shadows that alternated between day and night, he could make out the details of the jagged coral and the decaying ribs of the wreck as he descended deeper. Standing on the top of the reef with his fins flat on the coral, he reached out to touch the keel, the center piece of the wreck he'd come so far to see. To his left, he spotted a hole within a coral crevasse that was the perfect size to conceal his cache, but before he could plant it inside, he was forced to surface for another lungful of air.

Catching his breath as he broke the surface, he could see the reef teeming with life beneath him, some predators, and others their prey. The meanderings of a wayward nurse shark caught his attention, swimming in and out of crevasses in the shadowy lighting, and he kept a wary eye on it as it prowled the reef for dinner. He dove again into the shimmering water, swimming through the shadowy patches of light and darkness. Finding himself surrounded by a vast assortment of colorful reef fish, the scene reminded him of the Costa d'Este fish tanks at his lunch with Rita Book. Poor Rita, he thought as he swam toward the crevasse. If only she'd kept her mouth shut. Reaching the crevasse, he carefully wedged the pipe deep into the hole in such a way that it was hidden from view.

Satisfied with the placement, he looked toward the surface, ready for another lungful of air. Suddenly, he came face to face with a reef shark less than three feet from his mask. Terrified, Hirt panicked and shot straight up toward the lights of the boat, ascending as fast as he could, his eyes glued to the shark that first circled, then pursued him to the surface.

Unable to wrest his eyes from the shark as it pursued him to the surface, Hirt was ascending in such a state of panic that he hit his head on the teak swim platform, almost knocking himself unconscious and swallowing mouthfuls of sea water. Fearing for his life, and now bleeding from his head, he managed to grab the handle on the stainless steel swim ladder and pulled hard to unfold it. Still in panic mode, he climbed the ladder, threw the fins onto the deck and scrambled aboard just as the shark breached the surface two feet from him. The gruesome beast rolled onto its side and glared at him with the black lifeless eyes of a hungry predator that had missed his mark.

Mark could feel the yacht accelerate as he woke from his drug-induced slumber, the clickety clack of the diesel engine and footsteps on the deck above sounding familiar. Peering out the starboard porthole, he was surprised to see the brightly-lit high rises standing within a few hundred yards before realizing the yacht was heading due east, back out to deeper water.

What was their crazy psychiatrist up to, bringing *Dream Girl* so close to land, he wondered. Had he picked something up or dropped something off? Now, they were moving back out to sea at a brisk pace, picking up speed as he watched the lights along A1A recede into the distance. Assuming Hirt couldn't hear him over the noise of the engine, he called out to her.

"Stella. Can you hear me?"

There was no reply.

Fearing that Hirt had drugged her again, he called out to her. "Stella, are you awake?" This time there was a muffled response, her voice emitting an unintelligible rely. He couldn't handle the thought of Hirt hurting her again and dug deep within himself to reassure her.

"Honey, as God is my witness, we *will* survive this nightmare," he declared to her. "Our faith will get us through this. *Don't* give up." Again, her response was muffled.

Mark knew Hirt wanted to launch the Zodiac but was uncertain as to why. Of one thing he was certain; he would never be able to launch the Zodiac by himself. The rigid hull inflatable boat, or RHIB, with the attached outboard, battery and inboard gas tanks weighed over 1,200 pounds and could only be lifted off the forward davits using the main halyard operated by one person, while another with a guide line pushed it to the side and over the lifelines. Mark concluded that Hirt wanted the RHIB for one of two reasons, neither of which made him feel comfortable.

Weary from his close encounter with the shark and slamming his head into the swim platform, Hirt couldn't keep his eyes open any longer. He needed to eat something and dress the gash in his head. Checking the fathometer revealed only a hundred-fifty-feet of water beneath the hull, too shallow for what he was planning. He made a decision to drop anchor, get some sleep, and give it another go in the morning.

After switching off the engine, he rummaged through the stowage under the seat and found a large waterproof flashlight with a lanyard which he could have used earlier on the reef. He swept the bright beam around the deck to test its strength, up into the night sky, the beam revealing an empty black ocean beyond the rail. Miles further out on the horizon, he could see the lights of a passing cruise ship, and in the blackness suddenly felt more alone than ever. Out in the darkness a mile from shore, he didn't care if his two victims yelled their heads off. No one would hear their screams.

With the flashlight, Hirt staggered forward on the deck to the bow pulpit to drop the anchor. There was a catch latch on the chain rode, which he released before pulling the pin that secured the one-hundred-fifty-pound Danforth. He unwrapped the chain rode from around the windlass and grabbed the shank of the huge anchor, pushing it off the pulpit rollers and stepping back to watch it plunge into the black depths below. After the anchor had dragged more than two hundred feet of chain and line overboard, it stopped when it hit bottom. Giving the anchor line three twists around the windlass, he then secured it on the anchor cleat.

With midnight fast approaching, the light rain arrived. The anchor line pulled taut as he stood on the bow, and he could see it was holding. He aimed the light up in the air to measure the downpour, then back on the deck as he watched it rinse away the blood stains that spotted the deck. Exhausted, he went below to dress his head wound, fix himself a tuna sandwich, and swill some of that Cordon Bleu.

THIRTY-TWO

The National Crime Information Center (NCIC) is the U.S. central data base for tracking crime-related information. It was created in 1967 to be an information sharing tool of the FBI and is interlinked with federal, tribal, state and local agencies and law-enforcement offices throughout the fifty states. Created in 1967 under FBI Director J. Edgar Hoover, the purpose of the system was to create a centralized information system to facilitate information flow between the numerous law enforcement branches. The NCIC system had its drawbacks, notably those that came to light during the 9/11 attacks when critical intel should have been shared, and since then, law enforcement officers would sometimes question its accuracy.

Staring at the screen of computer monitors at his desk inside the Atlanta BAU Regional Headquarters, Beretto was wondering if the NCIC figures were correct. Could the elimination of a single drug trafficker actually account for a forty-percent drop in fentanyl-related overdoses and crimes in the East Central Florida counties?

Impressed with the latest figures, Beretto pressed the intercom button on his desk phone. "Gwen...come in here for a second. Got something to show you."

Beretto couldn't deny he liked working with his younger female team-mate, and he was instrumental in her last two promotions. Her dedication to a strong work ethic and analytical skills helped the BAU team produce consistent results. As she entered his office, Beretto pivoted the screen around so she could look on. The snug-fitting Dolce and Gabbana black pantsuit she wore complimented her figure and looked quite professional, and one of the characteristics he admired about her was how she utilized her looks to further their investigations.

Madani leaned over his desk in her low-cut blouse to view the data. "What's up, boss?"

Trying to look beyond her obvious attributes, Beretto pointed at the screen and shared his data. "Since the demise of Mr. Croaker, that area of Florida has experienced a forty percent drop in fentanyl-related crimes and overdoses," continuing to summarize the data, "…and, a one-hundred-dred-percent drop in homicides. I think you should know when your work makes a difference, Gwen."

"Thank you, sir, but it wasn't just me. We're a team, right?" She thought of McAllister, and as she thought of him she felt her groin tingle. Needing an angle, she made a suggestion. "Why don't I call Mark McAllister? His insights were helpful, and I'm sure he'd appreciate knowing that his wife is safer now."

With a twinge of jealousy, Beretto gave her a stern look. "You *do* know he's happily married, right? And on their yacht celebrating their second anniversary."

"Of course, sir." Exiting his office, she smiled and gave him a subtle wink. "I'll let you know what he says."

It was eleven-thirty a.m., and the sun was almost directly over the top of the mast as Hirt lay in the cockpit. He awoke to the sounds of a phone ringing in the navigation cabin and an empty wine bottle rolling around on the deck. Stretched out on the cushions in the aft cockpit, he had passed out from over indulging in cognac and an entire bottle of Camus the night before. His head throbbed as he sat up and checked his bandage, amazed that he'd slept through the entire morning.

Watching a lone Hatteras heading southeast on the horizon, Hirt remembered bringing water and granola bars to his two hostages last night. Then, his dream about Stella came back into focus. The fantasy made him realize that he still struggled to reconcile his feelings of both lust and revenge for her, and it made him want to be more cautious.

In his dream, he was sitting in her giant Jacuzzi tub full of warm bubbling bathwater at Villa Riomar when she entered the master bath wearing only a skimpy black Victoria's Secret nightie. A pair of sparkling emerald earrings that perfectly matched her green eyes dangled from her earlobes. In a flash, she was out of her lingerie and straddling him eagerly, and when they were finished, exhausted, Stella's legs were strewn in the Jacuzzi like a broken doll, one foot hooked on the tub's edge, the other leaning against the faucet, her dripping strawberry-blonde hair draped across her face in a lopsided tangle.

From the dream, he remembered her exact words; "Un…believable," she panted between her gasps for air. "That was fantastic." The dream excited him so much he worked to remember every detail.

Curious to find out who had called McAllister's phone, Hirt went below to the navigation desk where he'd hidden the phones. He was surprised to find McAllister's phone unlocked as he put his ear to it and listened to the recording of Special Agent Madani's sultry voice;

"Mark…it's Gwen Madani. How's my favorite author? Dom and I are back at BAU headquarters in Atlanta. We wanted you to know that, because of your help in cornering Croaker, fentanyl-related crimes are down forty percent in your area. On a…ah…more personal note, I'll never forget the dance we had at Costa d'Este. Stella's a lucky woman. Have fun on your anniversary. Call me when you get this message."

The voicemail confirmed his suspicions that the two were helping the FBI with their investigation. Annoyed with their deception, Hirt made his way to the helm and started the diesel engine, listening to its character-istic clatter and leaving the shift lever in neutral. Checking the Zodiac's mounting on his way forward to the anchor windlass, he activated it with the foot switch and began coiling the line into the locker as the windlass hoisted it aboard. Within a few minutes the large anchor was seated in the bow pulpit and secured with a large cotter pin. Free from its anchorage, the big boat began to drift with the wind and sea.

At the helm, Hirt put the diesel in gear, pointing *Dream Girl* due east and engaging the autopilot as the big sailboat turned and headed for the deeper water of the Gulfstream. Angered over the voice mail, now he was ready to carry out his plan. From the locker beneath the helm seat, he retrieved the pneumatic spear gun and hung it from his belt, then his .45 ACP and popped out the clip. Sticky from the salt and humidity, the clip jammed as he reinserted it. Yanking it from the grip, he wiped it off on his shorts before forcing it back into the gun with a hard whack of his hand.

Next, he headed below to the starboard guest head with an offer that couldn't be refused. Concealing his anger, "Mr. McAllister," throwing open the door, "...I've decided to let you two off this tub, but first, you're going to help me launch the Zodiac."

Hungry and thirsty, and still a little out of it from two days of drug-ging, Mark stared at the gun in Hirt's hand and the spear gun hanging from his belt. He wanted to believe him, but his intuition was telling him not to trust the madman as they listened to the drone of the diesel.

"What do you want me to do?" he asked calmly.

Pointing the .45 at him, Hirt reached into his pocket and handed him the key to the handcuffs. "Uncuff one hand from the railing, then relock them around your wrists and place the key on the counter. We're going topside. You're going to operate the winch that lifts the Zodiac." Hirt cocked the hammer and put the gun to his head, watching his movements carefully.

Wary of making any sudden moves, Mark kept an eye on the .45 as he unlocked one wrist and disconnected the cuffs from the grab rail, then relocked them as instructed. He placed the key on the vanity counter, then watched him step forward and stuff it back into his front pocket. They walked aft toward the main hatch as Hirt jabbed him in the back with the .45.

"What about Stella?" he asked.

"She stays below deck until we launch the Zodiac. If you behave yourself, she gets to go with you," prodding him on with the gun.

Turning to face Hirt in the middle of the salon, "Can I at least give her a top to cover herself?"

"After we launch the Zodiac." Pointing with the .45, Hirt gestured for him to continue toward the cockpit. "Keep moving and be smart. You'll live longer."

As he thought about the FBI agent's voicemail, Hirt felt a new flush of anger and prodded him again with the muzzle. "By the way, your girl-friend at the FBI called to thank you for helping to snare my buddy Max. She wished you a happy anniversary," smirking at the irony.

Feeling the automatic in his back, Mark knew his life was on the line. Fearing that he was past the point of any reconciliation with the madman, he forced himself to think of a plausible way to express his regret.

At the bottom of the stairs leading up to the cockpit, Hirt grabbed his arm and turned him around. "Tell me something, McAllister, and don't lie to me because I'll know if you're lying. What does the FBI know about me?"

Facing his tormentor in the salon among the scattered roses, Mark was unsure if sharing the truth would save his life. "They suspect you're the mastermind behind the Vero murders, but they don't have enough evidence for a warrant. I'd like you to know Stella and I are sorry we ever got involved. We mean you no harm, Dr. Hirt."

"Uh-huh." Holding the .45 firmly, Hirt rubbed the three-day-old stubble on his chin and studied his captive with the cold lifeless eyes of a shark. "Does Foti or Beretto have a warrant out for me?"

Hoping his captor would recognize the truth, "The judge denied their last request and said they lacked enough evidence for a warrant." Hirt seemed pleased with his answer, so Mark continued. "Let us go. I'll withdraw from the case and you'll never see or hear from us again. Just promise me you won't hurt Stella."

With a skeptical look, "How do I know you'll keep your word?"

"Certainly, you can see we've had enough. Leaving a trail of two more bodies isn't going to help you escape with a new identity, which is what you're planning, right? You'd be easier to track."

Hirt considered his plea. "What about the fentanyl trafficking? What do they know?"

"You're a prime suspect, but, again, they lack enough evidence for a warrant. They seem to be caught up in this notion of deniable plausibility that you cleverly created with Croaker. So, you have a window of opportunity here."

Taking his attempt at flattery with a grain of salt, Hirt mulled the situation over. He had a feeling McAllister wasn't telling him everything. "Tell me the truth, Mr. Investigative Journalist. If you were me, what would you do?"

Knowing he was running out of time, Mark suppressed the voice of his conscience and gave him an empathetic answer. "If I were you, I would increase my odds of escape by letting us go and hiding in a country without an extradition treaty. Maybe a nice quiet city on a beach somewhere in Costa Rica."

"Uh-huh." Hirt remained implacable as he rubbed his chin and thought about the idea. "All right. After we launch the Zodiac, you two are off this boat. Any tricks...I'll shoot you both. What's two more bodies? I'm not going back to jail."

Mark nodded. "Understood." With the .45 poking him in the ribs, he stepped up the short stairway into the aft cockpit. Relishing the feel of sunshine and wind on his face for the first time in days, he felt like a convict taking his first walk outside in the prisoner exercise yard. As the boat continued to motor east, he scanned the horizon, then looked around the cockpit. No longer in charge of her electronics, or the lines, wheels and winches that gave *Dream Girl* her life and direction, he was a fish out of water.

Feeling like he'd lost his two greatest loves to the wrath of a madman, he was desperate for a plan to save them.

THIRTY-THREE

By two-thirty Sunday afternoon, the northerly drift of the current was beginning to have an effect on the yacht's direction. The wind had shifted to a twelve-knot northeasterly as they continued to motor due east at five knots in light seas. Fifteen miles off Boynton Beach, and now within the domain of the deeper waters of the Gulfstream, *Dream Girl* continued under power, guided by the autopilot.

Standing on the foredeck, the two men faced each other, one in handcuffs with his head bowed in silent prayer, the other holding a .45 with a spear gun attached to his waist. With Mark cranking the winch at gunpoint, the two had just finished launching the Zodiac, now tied off on the port rail and trailing alongside.

The close quarters and solitude of a sailboat at sea can be kind of a litmus test for relationships, forcing the passengers into either an amicable bond or devolving into mutiny and murder. As the two men tried to decipher the other's intentions, the outcome remained murky, with only one having a distinct advantage. Mark wondered if the journey would deliver the magic…or the sorcery.

As the two men stood in the cockpit, Hirt seemed to be gloating over something. There was another matter on the madman's mind, something that superseded his role at playing God. Both men realized they couldn't stay at sea forever, reasoned Mark, and one way or the other, the situation would have to be resolved, since most uninhabited islands lacked the necessary equipment for handling a medical emergency. So, returning mariners continue to tie up their boats to stay connected to their computerized lifelines, leading their lives of boisterous desperation, only to return to the sea again and try to break free.

Mark was surprised when Hirt suddenly reached around the binnacle and switched off the engine, then the autopilot. As the sailboat began to drift in silence, Hirt stood over him with the .45 and gestured at the cushioned seat.

"Sit down, Mr. McAllister." Sensing a shift in his attitude, Mark did as he was told, resting his handcuffed wrists on his knees.

Handing his prisoner the key, Hirt put the gun to his head. "Now, cuff yourself to the wheel." Feeling the .45's muzzle press against his forehead, Mark unlocked one wrist and then recuffed himself to one of the eight spokes in the stainless steel wheel as he watched Hirt deposit the key back in his front pocket.

Holding the .45 firmly, Hirt sat down. "What you were saying earlier...I want to hear more of your ideas." He continued to stare at him. "Tell me, what have you've learned from sailing?"

Mystified by Hirt's mood change like they were two friends having a fireside chat, he decided to roll with it. As their eyes met, many of the lessons Mark learned from seafaring flashed through his mind, most of them experiences related to survival. "Well, we tend to forget the most basic lessons of seamanship, or we don't recognize them when the situations apply. As sailors, that's when we get into trouble."

"Uh-huh." Hirt pursed his lips in thought, his eyes sweeping the seas around them, stopping to watch a dive boat speeding north, then coming to rest on his prisoner again. "Do you enjoy getting yourself into trouble on the high seas, Mr. McAllister?"

"Actually, sometimes I do."

Leaning forward on the seat cushion, Hirt was intrigued by his answer. "Give me an example."

"Sometimes, when I'm with my wife at night, in high winds and seas...particularly if the engine quits."

"Why is that, Mr. McAllister?"

"Well, because...sometimes you believe you're going to die."

"Like on an upside down cork-screw roller coaster you think is crashing. Or a real life horror show."

"Exactly." It was a strange comparison, but he went with the flow. Staring at the spear gun, he noticed it was loaded and ready to fire. The gun's safety was off, and the brass snap bolt holding it to his waist wasn't closed all the way. He tried to imagine a scenario that would be useful.

"Reminds me of my pre-med training at The Citadel," mused Hirt, taking pride in his military school alma mater. "So, in the situation you described, what do you do?"

"Well...if you want to live through it, maybe you put out a bit of sail to see if you can run to safety. Or, maybe you use the engine and head into the wind under power. Other times, it might be better to tie a sea anchor to your stern. In any event, you've gotta make smart choices if you want to stay alive. Anyway, a preacher I sailed with once told me that 'God sends us the seas and the winds, but how you handle the weather depends on your skills as a sailor.'"

Hirt gave him a look of skepticism. "God, huh? Not sure if God has a part in it, but if I have a particular dislike for a patient, sometimes I have to decide if I want to prescribe something that would make them overdose. It's a lot of responsibility."

Mark glanced at the gun in his hand and concealed his disgust at Hirt's murderous admission. In a way, it sounded like the twisted rant of another physician suffering from the "God complex." He recalled that Beretto had once accused the doctor of using the Hippocratic Oath as a doormat. *How right you were, Dom. Where the hell are you now, buddy?*

Avoiding any overt judgment, Mark looked away as a fish jumped a hundred yards from the boat. "I see what you mean." So there he was, sharing an almost congenial chat with one of the most treacherous criminals on the Treasure Coast just as the conversation took a hard left turn into the Twilight Zone. Still, how much common ground could he hope to build in the time he had left?

Rocking gently, the sailboat continued to drift slowly toward the north, now in deep water and the Gulfstream's grip. The skies turned grey, hiding the sun behind an opaque layer of darkening clouds. He continued to think about Stella still chained up below. Despite the confessions about Hirt's malicious medical practice, it seemed like an easy conversation he was having. If their dialogue were being recorded and played back to a jury, there might be a few yawns, but only if they weren't paying close attention. What could Mark possibly expect the psychiatrist to discuss with him? Murder and drug deals?

Certain things about Dr. Christopher Hirt were beginning to make sense to him now, including the slight South Carolina accent and the military-style precision he used in his practice that he must have learned from his years at The Citadel. What he seemed to have left behind was the code of honor and ethics touted by the school. Mark wondered how he'd wound up as Hirt's confessor. Though he still doubted if any good would come from this, he was reluctant to end the conversation.

He thought about the doctor's background at The Citadel. "So," asked Mark, "were you ever a soldier?"

"If you mean a military soldier, then no I wasn't."

"What other kinds of soldiers are there?"

Hirt firmed his grip on the gun. "We're all soldiers of a kind, Mr. McAllister, because life itself is war."

It was a twisted outlook, but again, he avoided a challenge, staring instead at the handcuffs holding him to the wheel. "I can see your point. I think of life as conflict, but I think of war as something else."

Hirt looked at the .45 in his hand, then back at Mark. "Not the way *I* handle things." A halyard clanged in the breeze, and he glanced upward before his eyes came to rest again on his hostage.

To appease him, Mark nodded in agreement. Feeling as though he'd cultivated enough common ground, it was time to ask the question; "Dr. Hirt...do you know it wasn't Stella that outed you? It was Dr. Tremelle's testimony that put you away." Discrediting the dearly departed wasn't his style, but at this point, he'd do almost anything to save her.

As if on cue, the two men could hear Stella's muffled voice coming from down below. "Somebody…anybody…get me outa here!!" she demanded, her feet pounding on the bulkhead. "Please…somebody help me!!"

Facing off, the two men looked at each other. "Look, Dr. Hirt," he pleaded, "…I've said before, we mean you no harm. I've kept my word and helped you launch the Zodiac. Now, will you keep yours and let us go?" His heart skipped a beat as he waited for an answer.

With a cryptic smile, Hirt nodded hesitantly without uttering a reply. He stood up slowly, as if he had weighty issues to resolve, and ambled down the companionway steps, presumably to bring Stella topside. Watching Hirt carefully, Mark prayed for any sign that his antagonist would keep his promise and let them go. Losing sight of him inside the boat's interior, he slid his handcuffs toward the hub of the big wheel to give him a better view down the boat's interior. Pulling hard on his cuffs, he craned his neck to see what the madman was doing below deck. What he didn't expect was to hear Hirt rummaging around in the engine room directly beneath him.

Emerging from the engine room with the .45 stuck in his back waistband, Hirt held two screwdrivers and an adjustable wrench as he made his way to one of the forward AC panels. In the relative silence of a drifting boat, Mark heard the cover panel drop to the floor, then more metal-on-metal sounds as Hirt unscrewed the double hose clamps to the seawater intake valve. Mark could faintly hear water flowing into the boat, and his stomach knotted as his worst fears were being realized. The Zodiac had been launched for his escape, not theirs.

When he got to the second panel, Hirt repeated the steps, dropping the cover to the cabin floor and unscrewing the two hose clamps. With his pockets full of stainless steel clamps, he stepped toward the bow to the forward cockpit and threw them overboard. Mark watched the hardware splash into the ocean.

The sounds of seawater gurgling into the boat became more distinct as both forward bilge pumps activated simultaneously. When the second pair of bilge pumps activated, he realized what Hirt had in mind; if the madman opened all four sea cocks, either the flood of incoming water would overwhelm the pumps or the batteries would go dead trying to pump it overboard. Once the water level reached the main batteries in the engine room, they would short out, and without power for the pumps, *Dream Girl* would go down. He figured they had twenty minutes, at best.

At the top of her lungs, Stella yelled, "MARK, I HEAR BILGE PUMPS GOING OFF!! DO YOU HEAR THAT? SOMETHINGS NOT RIGHT!! PLEASE...PLEASE DON'T LEAVE ME HERE!! I DON'T WANNA DROWN!!"

Hearing her frantic plea, with all his upper body strength, he pulled against the steering wheel spoke. The welded three-foot spoke began to bend but refused to come loose. Jerking on it like a wild man, he braced his feet on the edge of the wheel and pulled harder, the cuffs peeling the skin from his wrists. Blood ran down his hands and formed a small pool at his feet. Feeling strangely surreal, adrenaline coursed through his body as he questioned the absence of pain. Finally, the stainless steel spoke gave way and clattered to the deck. He picked it up, the only weapon at his disposal. Gripping the metal spoke tightly in his cuffed hands, Mark rushed to confront the madman but slipped on the blood and fell backward, hitting his head hard on the starboard main winch.

Unconscious, he fell to the floor of the cockpit.

Stella, I....

THIRTY-FOUR

With the FBI's BAU case load backing up, Beretto had just concluded a rare Sunday afternoon office conference in their Atlanta headquarters to get his team caught up on the five open homicide cases they were working. He managed to maneuver around the whining by reminding his agents that homicidal maniacs don't take Sundays off. Ironically, he didn't yet know the full truth of his words.

Two of the cases involved unsubs with a profile similar to that of the Max Croaker serial murder case in Florida. More at ease after Croaker's demise, Beretto had directed his team to focus on the active cases. Weighed down by his new case load, he entertained himself with a brief fantasy of joining the McAllisters on their cruise with Madani, imagining what his protégé would look like in her bikini.

Recounting McAllister's help with apprehending Emilio Rosa two years before, Beretto walked briskly toward his corner office with a satchel full of dossiers. Through the glass door to her office, he met Madani's eyes as she finished a phone conversation. As she hung up, she motioned him inside. Dressed in a flattering white blouse and short black skirt, she leaned against her desk as Beretto stood in the doorway.

"Good meeting, boss. Just got a new lead on the Gatorland Partners homicides in Gainesville. Managers are jumping off like rats from a sinking ship."

"That's interesting. Let's find out who's behind the consortium." She nodded as her boss continued. "So, what did our guy McAllister have to say when you called?"

"He didn't pick up, so I left a voicemail."

"Must be having a good time on their anniversary cruise. He call back?"

"Not yet."

Beretto looked concerned. "When was that?"

"It's been two days."

"That's not like him," giving her a grim look. "I've never known him to not answer a call from the BAU." Adjusting the shoulder strap on his satchel, "They were headed for the Abacos, weren't they?"

"As far as I know."

The news did not sit well with him, and he seemed to shift into another gear. "Okay, Gwen. Could be the lousy cell service in the Bahamas, but let's do a GPS trilateration on both their phones. Call me with the results. I'll check with Lt. Foti in Vero for anything he may know."

"Yes, sir," rounding her desk and taking a seat at her computer.

Sprawled on his back in the cockpit, Mark slowly regained consciousness, uncertain how long he was out. He could feel a new welt on the back of his pounding head as Stella continued to call out to him.

"MARK...IF YOU CAN HEAR ME, YOU'VE GOT TO STOP HIM!! HE'S GOING TO SINK US!!"

As the swirling stars in his head subsided, he wanted to answer her, but not knowing where Hirt was, he held back. Standing up, he saw they were still adrift, the boat rocking lightly as he surveyed the sea and sky to get his bearings. Glancing overboard, all four of the bilge pumps were still pumping as he picked up the steel spoke and staggered below to stop the madman from sinking them. Starting his search in the navigation cabin, he tiptoed around the pieces of the VHF radios strewn on the cabin floor. It wasn't a good sign. The sounds of sea water sloshing around in the bilge under his feet unnerved him as he crept forward with the steel spoke. *Yeah. Happy anniversary. Let's go for a sail, have a few laughs.*

Suddenly, from behind him he heard Hirt's voice. "Put that down before this really gets ugly."

Mark ducked down and spun around to whack him with the steel spoke. In the narrow space of the companionway, he swung it as hard as he could, aiming for the .45 in his hand. He missed, striking the teak bulkhead to his left, then back to his right as he swung it repeatedly.

The madman pulled the trigger. Mark expected to see a flash and hear the blast from the gun, but nothing happened. The automatic had jammed.

Mark lunged forward with another swing that landed a strong blow on his forearm. Unfazed, Hirt grabbed the automatic's slide and attempted to eject the shell, but the slide stuck. In desperation, Mark swung the metal spoke again, this time connecting with the gun. His hands still slippery with blood, the impact caused him to lose his grip on the spoke as it clanged loudly to the parquet floor along with the .45.

"I should have overdosed you when I had the chance!" yelled Hirt. Raising the spear gun, he pointed it at Mark's chest. Before he could pull the trigger, Mark reared back and kicked upward as hard as he could, his foot sending the gun flying, the butt hitting the headliner. With the safety off, the spear gun's impact on the headliner caused it to discharge, sending the twenty-eight-inch spear downward into Hirt's upper thigh and severing his femoral artery. Hirt let loose with a gruesome scream loud enough to wake the dead and fell backward on the parquet floor as blood spurted from his artery.

"MARK...ARE YOU OKAY?" yelled Stella.

Screaming intermittently from the pain, Hirt lay on his back and pressed his hands against the wound, trying to stem the gush of blood. The steel spear protruded from both sides of his upper thigh as he writhed back and forth in agony. Seeing his chance, Mark pounced on the madman and pinned him to the floor with his knees, holding him down as he dug in his pocket for the key to the handcuffs. Frantically, he unlocked his cuffs.

"STELLA, HANG IN THERE!!" yelled Mark. Visualizing her still handcuffed in the guest head, he immediately regretted his words.

Badly injured, Hirt began to weaken from rapid blood loss as he fought feebly to prevent Mark from cuffing his wrists. After restraining him with the cuffs, Mark pocketed the key and rolled him over to empty his pockets. He stuffed everything he could find into his own pockets, including Hirt's wallet, scribbled notes, screwdrivers, wrenches, and what looked like written passwords on scraps of paper. Stuffing the tools in his pockets, Mark put Hirt's wallet and all the personal stuff into a Ziploc he found on the table before returning to his antagonist and squatting over him.

Applying both hands, Hirt continued to try to stop the blood flowing from his severed artery. Knowing he only had minutes to live without a tourniquet, he was desperate. "Twenty-one million in diamonds if you help me, McAllister."

"I don't want your money, Hirt. Is that what we stopped off for in Highland Beach?" Agonizing in extreme pain, Hirt didn't answer. Unsure of what he could believe from the mortally wounded psychiatrist, he felt a moment of pity, but with sea water continuing to gush in and the bilge pumps unable to keep up, Mark had was compelled to save those he loved.

"Because of you, I've got a wife to save from drowning and a boat to save from sinking." Staring at the spear protruding through his thigh, "Get my point?" He grabbed a dish towel from the galley and handed it to the dying man. "Press this on the wound until I get back. May God forgive you for all your evil deeds."

Finding their deck shoes, he put his on and grabbed Stella's. Holding the key to her cuffs, he staggered to the guest head, threw open the door and stepped into two inches of water. The terrified look on her face turned quickly to one of joy as she focused on the key in his hand. With ligature marks on her neck and a hurt lip, she said, "Thought I was gonna drown. What took you so long?"

"I had a psychotic psychiatrist to deal with," unlocking her cuffs. She wrapped her arms around him and held him for a time before shaking her arms to get the blood flowing.

"Where's Hirt?" she asked.

"Handcuffed, with a spear through his femoral artery. He's bleeding out and may not make it," giving her a dubious look.

"I might be okay with that," she said. "He was going to drown us."

"It could've been me if his .45 hadn't jammed," he explained. "Can you walk?" A little shaky, she stood up, leaning on him for support. "Here, I brought these for you," handing her a tank top and deck shoes. "There's a lot of broken glass in the salon."

She noticed the skin peeled away and the blood dripping from his wrists. "That from the cuffs?"

"Found out I'm no Houdini."

"Let me find some bandages for you."

"That can wait. I'll live. Let's fix the leaks first. We're taking on a lot of water, and time is not our friend right now." Looking out the porthole, he could see they were still drifting, miles from shore, and in no danger of running aground.

"Then let's use what time we have wisely," she said.

"Okay. Here's what we're gonna do. I need you to take a look at the portside AC water intake and tell me what you see. I'll take the starboard," handing her a screwdriver and wrench. "Go. Now. We can't afford to drain the batteries." With her hands still numb from the handcuffs, she grasped the tools awkwardly and continued to flex her wrists.

Sloshing his way to the first AC panel, Mark could see Hirt had disconnected the intake hose from the sea cock as the water gushed into the companionway. With the missing hose clamps on the sea bottom, he shoved the hose back onto the fitting, but the force of incoming water pushed it off again.

"Stella, how many hose clamps do you have over there!?"

"None!!" She pushed hard on the hose, trying unsuccessfully to keep it connected to the fitting as sea water continued to gush in.

"Try to hold it in place until I can bring you one from spare parts!!" Mark sloshed his way aft down the companionway to where Hirt lay bleeding, still pressing the towel on the wound but losing strength. Angry over the missing clamps, Mark grabbed him by his T-shirt.

"If you want any help from us, tell me what you did with those hose clamps!"

Barely conscious, Hirt tried to articulate what he'd done. "Too late, McAllister," he whispered. "Th...threw them over...board."

There were no words to describe the anger he felt for what the madman had done. "Forget you!" Stepping over him, Mark made his way to the engine room to search the spare parts inventory. Needing eight clamps, he was lucky to find only three and grabbed a roll of duct tape, thinking it might work for the fourth fitting. Glancing at the batteries, the four bilge pumps were going full blast, but the water level was still rising, now within two inches of the main battery terminals. He figured they had about five minutes to reverse the flow of sea water before the batteries shorted out. Then it was game over, and he and Stella would have to abandon ship.

The teak companionway floor was now covered with water and getting deeper toward the bow. "Okay, this is all we have," handing Stella one of the clamps. "For now, we'll have to use one clamp per intake." Stella held the hose in place as Mark tightened the clamp as tight as he could make it, stopping the leak. "Good. One down, three to go. C'mon."

With the sailboat beginning to list to starboard, the couple worked feverishly to complete two more repairs. Out of hose clamps, the fourth repair proved more challenging, with only a roll of duct tape. Wrapping it around the hose and fitting, the temporary fix was holding but continued to leak. With the main batteries getting low, two of the bilge pumps had already ceased working. He hoped there was enough power to start the diesel so the belt-driven alternator would kick in and begin a recharge.

"I'm going topside to see if the engine will start," he said. Stepping over Hirt sprawled in the companionway, he stopped at the breaker panel to switch everything off except the starting batteries and binnacle electronics. Ready to turn the key at the pedestal, he said a prayer before engaging the starter. The diesel emitted a sickly groan, then stopped, sputtered, and came to life.

"Hah!!" he shouted, ecstatic that the Bosch 175-amp alternator was now working to recharge the main batteries. With the Zodiac still trailing alongside, he set a speed of four knots with the autopilot.

Checking the radar, the screen showed a massive group of thunderstorms approaching from the northeast that looked frightening. With so much water still in the bilge and forward cabins, Mark was beginning to doubt whether they could keep her afloat. The yacht's bow continued to plow, then roll excessively from side to side on each wave. They needed a way to evacuate the sea water faster. Remembering the two manual bilge pumps stowed away in the aft locker, he stumbled to the stern and lifted the cover to assemble them.

Below deck, Stella stepped to where Hirt lay in a pool of blood as he took what could be his last few breaths. Standing over her tormentor with a contemptuous look, she forced herself to focus on the man who had so viciously assaulted her. Squatting over him, she wrestled with her conscience, trying to decide if she would render aid to the man who had likely ended the lives of her two friends, and who tried to end her own.

Unable to move, his eyes almost closed, Hirt watched her lips begin to form the last few words he might ever hear. "Tell me the truth and I'll help you live. But I want the truth. Nod your head if you murdered my two friends Kelly Ann Granata and Katherine Tremelle. Confess to me, and before God, and I'll fix you a tourniquet for your leg." She glared at him expectantly.

Without hesitation, Hirt nodded his head and raised a blood-covered hand to touch her. "Twenty-one million in diamonds," he whispered, wanting to feel comforted by her, to feel her warmth and softness, to feel her forgiveness. Unsure of his meaning, the grief she felt for her murdered friends kept her hands at her sides.

In a trance-like state, Stella spoke what sounded like an incantation; "It would do all our hearts…a world of good…to see you in…a box of wood….but, today…today I'll show you God's mercy." From the bottom of her tank top, she tore off a section of cloth, and with the screwdriver from her back pocket, she fashioned a tourniquet. Twisting it tightly, she managed to stop the hemorrhaging but had a feeling it might be too late. For the last time, she looked him in his half-closed eyes as Mark joined her from the helm.

"As if we didn't have enough on our plate, Stella, there's a really nasty storm coming, and it's moving our way fast."

She looked at her husband. "How fitting." Together, they squatted over Hirt to decide what to do with him. There was a lot of blood everywhere, all over his clothes, the floor, and spattered on the bulkheads. The wound around the spear had coagulated, and he'd stopped breathing. Mark extended two fingers to his carotid artery to check for a pulse.

"I can't feel a pulse," he said calmly. "I think he's gone." Checking again on his wrist, he crossed himself and offered an appropriate verse.

In a soft voice he said, "Like Christ said, 'What is a man profited if he gain the whole world, and lose his own soul?'"

"Amen," added Stella, sharing a moment of silence.

Glancing fore and aft at the sea water puddling on the floor, they knew time was running out. She said, "Let's prepare for the storm. I'll get a blanket from the V-berth."

Mark nodded. "Okay. Let's get him wrapped up and take him topside. I'm gonna check the water level in the engine room first." Slogging down the companionway, he peered through the open engine room doors to see that the water level was unchanged, still hovering two inches below the batteries.

Weary as they were, they found enough energy to wrap him up and drag him topside, through the cockpit, over the winches and onto the portside deck. In the distance, to the northeast, there were several boats fleeing southwest from the massive purple-hued frontal system that barreled down on them. Unnerved at the thought of yet more water to deal with, they watched a pinkish hue forming on the teak decks as the rain slowly rinsed the blood stains away.

"Let's lay him in the dinghy," Mark suggested, climbing down into the Zodiac. Together, they laid him to rest in the deepest section and tied each limb to the inflatable's life lines.

"What about the rainwater? Will it sink?" she asked.

"It's self-bailing," he explained. Climbing back into the cockpit, he felt the first heavy barrage of ice-cold rain as it pelted the deck, then a strong wind and what felt like ice cubes hitting his face. Leaning over the rail, he checked to make sure the pumps continued to discharge a full stream of sea water. Once again, all four were operating at full capacity, but what he really needed was to lighten the load of water in the bow to keep it from submerging.

"I'm gonna head into it," adjusting their course and increasing their speed to six knots to give him more control over the helm. The seas continued to build, now with ten-foot rollers that caused the boat to plow instead of rising on each crest.

"Shall I reattach the AC panels?" she asked him, the rain pelting her face.

Shouting over the howling wind, "Let's leave them off so we can check for leaks." He spun the wheel to counter the starboard list as the bow dove under a ten-footer. "She's not handling well."

Holding on to her Dallas Gun Club cap in the wind, she glanced at the cut still bleeding through his deck shoe. "I'll clean up below. We sure don't need any more broken glass."

"That may be the least of our worries. In this kind of storm, those clamps have to hold. If they don't, we may have to abandon ship." The waves crashed over the foredeck and cascaded over the dodger each time the bow plunged. "Stella, while you're below, make sure all the hatches are watertight and see if you can find our phones in case we need to send a Mayday."

"What about the VHFs?" she asked.

"Hirt destroyed them. Looks like he put his knife through the single side band."

Frowning, she said, "So, we've got no way to send a Mayday."

"Nope."

Stella went below, and minutes later, popped her head up from the main hatch wearing her foul weather gear. Handing him his set of gear, "Found our phones," she yelled over the howling wind, "…but the batteries are dead and I can't find my charger."

"I know there's a back-up phone charger somewhere onboard," he yelled back. "I just need to remember where the hell I put it. I just reset the autopilot, so now we can get these manual pumps going." Pointing ahead at the storm, "We've got to get this water out before it sinks us!"

THIRTY-FIVE

Abaco and its cays are scattered over more than a hundred square miles of magnificent aquamarine waters. Its two major islands, Great and Little Abaco, have a myriad of smaller cays flanking the island and they were billed as a yachtsman's paradise. Beretto could see why the couple had chosen the two islands to celebrate their anniversary.

At his headquarters in Atlanta, he watched the blip on the trilateration monitor continue moving northeast as he stood next to Madani. "Something's not right," he concluded. "They're not answering their phones or attempts to hail them on VHF. Something's going on." Glancing at the storyboard, "According to Foti, Hirt's been dodging their surveillance and hasn't been seen anywhere for three days."

"That's not good news," leaning over the monitor in her black pantsuit. "Credit card records show he made reservations for today at a marina in Marsh Harbor," looking up at her boss. "The yacht is hundreds of miles from their intended destination. So, what're they doing seventeen miles east of Boynton Beach heading into the teeth of a monster storm?"

"Gwen, let's get the Coast Guard to do a flyover."

"Will they do that without a Mayday?"

"Maybe if we ask them nicely. We're the FBI, remember? Get the Palm Beach commandant on the phone."

"Yes, sir."

Dream Girl was a good boat, which in some spiritual way had become part of them over the years. She was completely undeserving of the indignity of being lost to sabotage by a murderous hijacker. Down eighteen inches by the bow, she plodded her way into the teeth of the gale, crippled by the vengeful acts of a madman. It was a harrowing night, made worse than what they expected by the added water weight as Mark and Stella struggled to keep the yacht afloat and deal with the fifty-knot winds and sixteen-foot seas.

Total darkness enveloped them as clouds thickened and the rain came down in sheets, blotting out the constellations and moonlight. Over the shrieking wind, he yelled to his first mate, "Keep your harness clipped to the lifelines. I don't want to lose you!"

The merciless wind had transformed what were choppy waters an hour ago into mountains of furious seas. With the wind slamming the rain and occasional hail into their faces, the two spent the night slipping and sliding in the rain-soaked cockpit. Completely exhausted, they took turns operating the manual pumps as they fought to reduce the water weight inside the boat.

Mark could feel a heavy weather helm and wrestled with the damaged wheel to keep her bow pointed into the fury of the storm, wishing he could figure out a way to reattach the missing spoke. The possibility of having her roll over and lose her mast required him to keep the bow from falling off more than twenty degrees. An occasional rogue wave would hit and send the boat corkscrewing and crashing down sideways. Earlier, he'd gone below to turn off all systems that weren't essential to their survival to conserve power, including the auto pilot, which he couldn't trust in such a blow. It was a hard lesson learned from Hurricane Matthew three years ago.

Sometime during the night, they noticed the furious storm had stripped away the Zodiac that carried Hirt's body. Now, only the inflatable's nose ring and lifelines dangled from the heavier line still attached to the port side cleat. In his fight to keep her afloat, Mark asked himself, "What else could possibly go wrong?" But, as he discovered, you should never ask yourself that question.

Around four-thirty in the morning, just as they were beginning to reverse the flow of water out of the boat, the hose with duct tape came loose when they were hit hard by a rogue wave. The sea water began rushing in again, swamping the companionway floor for the second time and flooding into the portside stateroom. After tying off the wheel, they managed to repair the hose with copper wire foraged from the spare parts locker, and this time, the repair was holding. Among the spare parts, Mark found a phone charger that he immediately put to use as *Dream Girl* continued to slog northward into the eye of the storm at three knots.

At about five-forty-five a.m., they noticed the wind began to die down, the seas subside, and the torrential downpour faded into light rain. The night sky began to clear, and the couple found themselves counting millions of stars. Teeth chattering from the cold rain and soaked to the bone, they felt like the tide was beginning to turn in their favor as they made a wish on a shooting star just before dawn.

Signaling the storm's end, by six-thirty the gulls were swooping and chirping their cries once again, and the skies turned slowly from purple to pink, then to amber and bright orange. Minutes later, golden streams of light broke through on the horizon, spreading in every direction, outlining the blue clouds in gilt as if the entire eastern sky had caught fire. Then the sun broke above the skyline with the brilliance of a thermonuclear detonation, proclaiming the promise of a new day ahead.

Pushing *Dream Girl* to six knots to help drain the excess sea water, they stood in awe of the spectacular sunrise for a few minutes before Mark heard his phone ring. Handing the wheel off to Stella, he smiled for the first time in a long time. "Wonder who that could be."

Listening on the phone, in the background he heard the unmistakable sounds of a turbocharged helicopter in flight as he rejoined his wife at the helm. "Who is *this*?"

A few moments of heavy static passed before he heard a response. "This is Chief Petty Officer Mike Steinberg of the U.S. Coast Guard. Is this Mr. McAllister?"

"Yes," putting his arm around her waist, "...and are we glad to hear from you."

"We've been asked by the FBI in Atlanta to do a flyover, but we couldn't get airborne until the storm subsided. Are you in need of assistance, sir?"

Filled with both sadness and jubilation, he didn't know where to start with an answer. "Not unless you have some spare two-inch hose clamps you can drop off."

Through the background noise and conversation, they waited for Steinberg's reply. "We're equipped with pumps and medical supplies, but fresh out of hose clamps. Can you make it in under your own power?"

Giving Stella a reassuring look. "We can make it in with what we've got."

"Copy."

"We had an attempted hijacking and some flooding issues," explained Mark, "...but we seem to have it under control. Where are you?"

"We are heading southwest toward your position, about four miles northeast of your vessel."

Mark pointed into the brilliantly-lit eastern sky as the sun continued to rise. "I can barely hear you over the static but we can't see you yet." There was a garbled response that was rendered unintelligible by more static before he continued.

"You should know that somewhere in this vicinity...is our inflatable carrying the body of the murderous psychiatrist who hijacked us." Stella pointed into the bright sky at the helicopter as it came into view on the horizon. "We can see you now," confirmed Mark.

There was noise and a loud background conversation, followed by CPO Steinberg; "When you say 'body', are you referring to Dr. Christopher Hirt?"

"Yes, sir," replied Mark. As the Coast Guard chopper descended and approached, he spotted two crew members in orange jumpsuits and headsets in the doorway as it began to hover at about two hundred feet.

"For the record, how did he die?" asked CPO Steinberg.

"He accidently severed his femoral artery with a spear and bled out. We weren't able to save him."

Unable to picture the optics, Steinberg simply answered, "Copy that." Over the whine of the turbine, Mark could overhear a lively conversation taking place among the crew before CPO Steinberg responded.

"Okay, then, *Dream Girl*. If you are no longer in need of assistance, we've been ordered to initiate a search to locate Hirt's body."

"Understood. Good luck," giving Stella a sympathetic look. "I know he's lurking around here someplace."

"Copy. I've relayed your status to our base in West Palm. Have a better one." They watched the chopper complete a 360-degree rotation before heading south as the man in the doorway waved.

After going below to look for leaks and check the battery voltmeters, he returned to her at the helm wearing his tan "Bora Bora" cap with the manta ray on the front. "Batteries are fully charged, and our repairs are holding."

With her hair a mess and smudged mascara adorning her cheeks, she smiled and put her arm around him. "Have you ever seen a more beautiful sunrise?"

Giving her an affectionate squeeze, "Not on this planet." Weary of hearing the diesel grinding away for the past several hours, "Help me set the main and jib?" Stella seemed to blossom at the idea, and within a few minutes, they were enjoying the sound of the wind whispering over the sails again, close hauled into a light easterly breeze and cruising at six knots.

Giving him a puppy-dog look, "There's something I've got to do," she said solemnly, handing off the wheel to him and peeling off her foul weather gear. She went below. When she returned, she held the two homicide case files, a bottle of Cordon Bleu, and two snifters in her arms. Removing the cork, she poured a generous amount into each glass.

Toasting, she said, "To new days ahead."

"New days ahead," he repeated, clinking snifters and taking a sip.

"And, to the dearly departed," as she tossed the rest of the cognac back in one gulp, wincing from its effect. Obviously, she had something more in mind. Stella climbed over the cockpit seats and sat down at the edge of the leeward rail with her back to him. In a solemn mood, she opened the file folder and gathered the photos to study them one by one.

The first photo was of Dr. Katherine Tremelle. Heartsick over her demise, she hesitated, then slowly tossed the next three photos overboard where they floated face up as they were swept out to sea. There were no words exchanged as Mark watched them pass astern, recognizing that it was her own personal way of letting go, a sort of private burial at sea. It had been more than just a rough patch for her, an ordeal with a deranged psychopath who challenged her very right to survive in an otherwise privileged life.

Reaching into the second folder, she pulled the photos of Kelly Ann Granata, her murdered fitness coach. After Stella silently said her good-byes, they shared the same fate as she tossed them overboard one at a time, passing slowly in the wake of the boat. He wanted to put an arm around her but feared it would interrupt her process of letting go. Instead, Mark poured another shot into her snifter and reached out to hand it to her. Tossing it back, the cognac went down smoothly, soothing her soul as a trail of photos found their final resting place.

There had been a time, Stella remembered, not that long ago as a young girl, when she believed in the future. Running headlong then, it was a future she couldn't wait to embrace. But now she wanted to slow the world down, the future looking more and more like someplace she wasn't sure she wanted to be. It was never her desire to witness the end of Hirt's life, but deep down inside, she knew the world was better off.

As Stella sat at the rail saying her final goodbyes to her dearly departed friends, in the bright light of a new day, Mark was organizing the contents of Hirt's pockets on the helm seat. Laid out in front of him were his Florida driver's license, credit cards, and his membership card to the American Medical Association, all of which he planned to turn over to the police upon their return to Vero Beach.

There were passwords scribbled on scraps of paper, along with one curious series of numbers written on a Post-it note that may have been some sort of code. Smeared with a light streak of blood, the handwriting was sloppy, typical of doctors, he thought. Moisture had caused the ink to smudge, and so it was hard to read. Unsure of what the scribblings meant, he stuffed it back in his pocket for further analysis. Along with his phone, he put the rest of the deceased's personal effects back into the Ziploc and continued to study the digital entries on the handheld GPS.

With a long line of photographs trailing in their wake, he sipped his cognac as he thought again about her idea of being less visible on the internet. With the fame that being an author had brought him, he had always struggled to find the right balance between his public and private lives but never imagined himself as a man seeking internet anonymity. But lately, it seemed like everyone he knew was talking about reducing their exposure to social media in their need for a real sense of privacy. Maybe it was the onset of middle age that made him feel this way, or his immediate state of mind blended with the dark events of the season. He wasn't sure.

Done with her private ceremony, Stella put the folders aside and rejoined him at the helm. Together, they watched the brilliant orange ball levitate higher in the sky as a large Hatteras heading northeast was silhouetted on the far horizon. Putting his arm around her, to invigorate her mood, he came up with some choice words. "Just as surely as every winter that has descended has ended, spring will surely follow."

She rewarded his notion with a smile. "I like that. Now you sound like the author I fell in love with."

"Here, take the wheel for a minute," he said, "...let me show you something. Maybe you can help me figure this out." Reaching into his pocket, he pulled out the Post-it note and hit a button on the GPS to bring up the display for comparison. After further scrutiny, they could see the writings on the Post-it were actually identical with the numbers displayed on the GPS;

Latitude 2623.5213 north,
Longitude 8003.9197 west

Knowing what he was thinking, she couldn't resist the urge to ask, "What would we do with twenty-one million in diamonds?"

"Well...we do need a new inflatable."

She thought that was funny. "What kind would we get?"

With a poker face, "Perhaps one without dead psychiatrists in it might be nice."

She looked at the horizon, then back at him. "I do have a few charities in mind."

"Like?"

"Like that place that cares for battered women in Vero, Safe Space. And Suncoast Health to help with drug addictions and mental health issues. Maybe the Vero Beach Lifeguard Association. I heard they need to raise some money for a new pavilion."

Mark turned the wheel five degrees to port to catch a wind shift as *Dream Girl* picked up speed. "I like where you're going with this. All three groups work to preserve life. We can't fix everything he broke, but donating a healthy sum to those causes would be a good start."

Thrilled they were on the same page, she broke it down. "So, say... half for the charities, and half for another circumnavigation? Would that be fair?"

Grinning from ear to ear, "Done."

"What would we have to do?" she asked with a smile.

"Reverse course."

She reached for the Cordon Bleu sitting on the cockpit seat and poured a generous shot into each of the snifters, handing one to Mark. Lifting her glass high in the morning sun, she offered a toast; "To our new inflatable, and our worthy partners in life." Clinking glasses and tossing the cognac back, the burn was even better than before.

She set her glass down, came to attention and saluted smartly. "What are your orders, *mon capitaine*?"

Thrusting his arm forward holding an imaginary cutlass, in a pirate's voice he shouted, "Avast me hearties! Prepare to come about!"

Made in the USA
Columbia, SC
11 January 2020

86318623R00195